BY SARAH ADAMS

The Rule Book
Practice Makes Perfect
When in Rome
The Cheat Sheet
The Temporary Roomie
The Off-Limits Rule
The Enemy
The Match

The
TEMPORARY
ROOMIE

The TEMPORARY ROOMIE

A NOVEL

SARAH ADAMS

DELL
NEW YORK

2024 Dell Trade Paperback Edition

Copyright © 2021 by Sarah Adams
Excerpt from *The Cheat Sheet* by Sarah Adams
copyright © 2021, 2022 by Sarah Adams

Published in the United States by Dell, an imprint of Random House, a division of Penguin Random House LLC, New York.

Originally self-published in the United States by the author in 2021.

DELL and the D colophon are registered trademarks of Penguin Random House LLC.

LIBRARY OF CONGRESS CATALOGING-IN-PUBLICATION DATA
Names: Adams, Sarah, 1991– author.
Title: The temporary roomie: a novel / Sarah Adams.
Description: 2024 Dell Trade paperback edition. | New York: Dell Books, 2024.
Identifiers: LCCN 2024003082 (print) | LCCN 2024003083 (ebook) |
ISBN 9780593871775 (trade paperback; acid-free paper) |
ISBN 9780593871782 (ebook)
Subjects: LCGFT: Romance fiction. | Novels.
Classification: LCC PS3601.D3947 T46 2024 (print) |
LCC PS3601.D3947 (ebook) | DDC 813/.6—dc23/eng/20240125
LC record available at https://lccn.loc.gov/2024003082
LC ebook record available at https://lccn.loc.gov/2024003083

Printed in the United States of America on acid-free paper

randomhousebooks.com

2   4   6   8   9   7   5   3   1

Title page art by Igor, Hanna Syvak © Adobe Stock Photos

Book design by Sara Bereta

To my readers who have been with me since the beginning. You know who you are, and this one is for you! Thank you for your never-ending support. I love you.

A NOTE FROM SARAH

Hello, reader! Although this book is very much a romcom and written in a way to uplift and leave you feeling nothing but happy and hopeful, it does contain heavier elements. For those who need a little extra assurance before they begin reading, I have provided a content warning below. However, please be aware that the content warning *does* include spoilers.

XO Sarah

Content warning: Please be advised that The Temporary Roomie *features a woman currently walking through an unplanned pregnancy she chose to keep. A birth without complications takes place in the story with a brief, non-graphic labor scene. However, there are no on-page details of the birth. The story also features themes of parental neglect that took place in the main character's past. There is light swearing and implied intimacy.*

The
TEMPORARY
ROOMIE

CHAPTER 1

Jessie

The line rings three times before Lucy answers. "Hey, Jes—"

"HE DIDN'T SHOW!" I immediately yell at my best friend.

Lucy chuckles. She's lucky she's not anywhere near me right now, or I'd pinch her in the tender spot under her arm for taking this so lightly. "Who didn't show? Your grandaddy or my brother?"

"Drew. Your obnoxious brother!"

"Quit yelling!" Lucy yells back.

"I can't!"

"Why not?!"

"Because I'm fired up! This is Drew's way of getting back at me for hating him so much. He agreed to help me today, *planning* to stand me up and make me look like a fool in front of my grandaddy. I bet he's walking into the sunset with a devious smile, wearing a white linen suit right now."

"M'kay, first, it's still morning. And second, you really don't know him at all."

I frown. "You don't think he'd wear a white linen suit? I'm positive he—"

"No. What I mean is I'm sure he has a good excuse, because last night when I called and asked him to help you, he didn't even hesitate before saying yes. Have you tried calling him this morning?"

"Ha! Have I tried calling him?! Only fifteen times. It went to voicemail all of those times. I'm sorry to inform you, Lucy, but your brother is a class-A jerk, and I was right not to trust him."

What I don't admit to Lucy is that this is my own fault for ever letting myself rely on a man who would love nothing more than to ruin my life. I can't really blame him, though, because the feeling is mutual. Believe me, if there was literally anyone else in the world I could ask to pose as my fake fiancé, I would. I even asked a random guy in the grocery store last night, but oddly enough, he said no. Actually, it wasn't so much *no* as it was him speed walking away from me clutching his bottle of mustard. I was forced to rely on Drew because I was out of time and options, and that's a terrifying place to be in life.

Last night, my grandaddy (the man who raised me) called to let me know he was surprising me and coming for a weekend visit in the morning (which is now). I would normally be ecstatic about a chance to see my favorite human in the world, but that is *not* the case when I'm about to be found out as a big fat pregnant liar. *Liar, liar, maternity pants on fire!*

I didn't even have a good reason to lie to my grandaddy—he's never made me feel like I needed to be someone I'm not in order to have his love. But for some reason, when I had to call and tell him I was pregnant, I panicked and said I was also getting married.

Now, in all fairness, I also thought I *would* be getting married. I was naïvely convinced my boyfriend at the time had gone on the road with his band because he needed some time to process this big development in his life, and then he'd be back. I thought he needed to throw a little (read: huge, mega, horribly mean) tantrum over this sudden change in his life plan and then he would boomerang right back to me. Breaking news: he didn't. Some boomerangs don't circle back, apparently.

My ex-boyfriend, Jonathan, bolted just like my dad did, and now, after several long months, I've finally come to terms with the fact that he's not coming back. (Jonathan, not my dad. I lost any hope of that man returning when I was still drinking out of a sippy cup.)

So, when I called my grandaddy and told him he'd soon be getting a great-grandchild, I also might have mentioned that I was getting married. Since the word *delusional* is not very pretty, we'll say it was hope that drove me to tell that lie—hope that my life wouldn't be following the same path as my mom's, since that one clearly didn't turn out well.

Surprisingly, I've maintained this lie pretty well up until now. I've gone home to Kentucky to visit my grandaddy several times since announcing my impending nuptials . . . but unfortunately, my dear, *dear* wonderful fiancé was always too busy with work to be able to come along. *The work of a prestigious lawyer waits for no man!* (And yeah, I have no idea why I also turned Jonathan into a lawyer. I think at that point, some part of me must have known he was never coming back.) Anyway, it was all fine and dandy until the surprise trip my grandaddy sprung on me last night.

Then Lucy talked me into faking a relationship with her brother, to whom I dream of feeding laxatives via a surprise coffee delivery to his office. Drew, the physical embodiment of how a person feels when they are assigned jury duty. But wait, there's more!

Drew is:

- The human version of a popcorn kernel stuck in your teeth.
- The man so boring he eats celery for dessert.
- The only person in the world with whom it would be more pleasing to run barefoot over a trail of pointy Legos than have a thirty-second conversation.

In case anyone is still confused, I absolutely can't stand Dr. Stuck-up Marshall.

I pull back the curtains again and stare out at my driveway like a peeping Tom. If Drew pulls in right now, he'll see my face pressed up against the glass, with a squished piggy nose and death-glare eyes, and he'll keel over at the sight of it. I'm forced to let the curtain fall again when a mom pushing her toddler in a stroller sees me and looks like she might call the cops.

"Jessie, I'm sure Drew has a good explanation. I know you're determined to hate him, but I promise he's one of the good ones."

"No. My grandaddy is the only good single man left in the world—and if those old grannies at bingo were smart, they'd snatch him up. So, no . . . I do not believe Drew is one of the good ones, and I'm certain he did this on purpose. He's mad at me for throwing the bag of diapers in his face, and this is his retaliation."

"What diapers? No—you know what? I don't want to know. At least tell me what happened when your grandaddy showed up and Drew wasn't there."

Crickets. I don't say a word, and I'm hoping Lucy will think the line went dead and give up and go about her day.

"Jessieeee." She drags out my name like she just found out I ate all the cookies from the cookie jar. "What happened when he showed up?"

I sigh dramatically. "He didn't, okay? He called me this

morning saying he woke up to a flat tire and had to have it towed to a mechanic. He said he'd have to take a rain check on the visit."

"Oh my gosh! Then why in the world are you so upset with Drew? You didn't even need him!"

I blink. "Because *he* didn't know that! I never told him because I wanted to see if he'd show or not. And he didn't, so HA!"

"You are unbelievable." I know Lucy is shaking her head right now. "This hate needs to stop. You both act like babies, and I can't handle it anymore. Also, you need to tell your grandaddy the truth."

"I already did," I murmur under my breath.

"What was that?" She's being so pious now.

"I said I already told him I don't have a fiancé. Well, actually, he guessed it. He asked to reschedule for next weekend, and when I told him I thought Jonathan would be out of town that weekend, and the weekend after that, and the weekend after that, he told me he already knew and had pretty much guessed since the beginning that there was no fiancé. I guess it was suspicious that Jonathan hasn't been around at the same time as my grandaddy even one time in seven months." Duly noted: I need to fabricate better lies in the future.

Actually, I feel a tad bit silly now for ever making it such a big deal in the first place. I thought he was so proud of me because I was getting married, starting a family, following the path of the typical American dream. But get this—he's just proud of me for being me. He doesn't care a bit that I don't have a husband; he's just happy he gets to see me become a mom. At that statement, my heart swelled to the size of Texas. Once again, my grandaddy has proven that no one will be able to top his goodness.

"That's amazing, Jessie! So now all that's left is forgiving Drew."

Forgiving Drew? Over my dead body. "Oh, honey, this animosity has only just begun."

"Very mature." I can hear the eye roll in her tone. "Tell you what . . . why don't you go eat some pickles like you love, and I'll try to get ahold of Drew to find out what's going on? And then maybe we can circle back around to the forgiving each other thing."

"Bleh—no to both. My cravings have moved on to Flamin' Hot Cheetos now."

"You know, it really makes me mad that you eat whatever you want all the time and barely look pregnant. I was an elephant at your stage of pregnancy."

I know, people! I'm small for a woman in her third trimester. I get it. Everyone mentions it all the time, and it makes me feel terrible. They all look at me like I'm starving myself and my poor child will never be healthy or go to the Olympics because of me! I'm just petite, okay?! My doctor even offered to write me a note to keep in my purse that states my child is measuring perfectly and my size is more than acceptable for a healthy pregnancy. Fine, maybe I had to beg and plead (and sob) for her to write it, but it doesn't matter—that slip of paper is laminated in my purse, so every humiliating tear I shed was worth it. That old lady at the grocery store had to totally eat her words when I whipped it out and flashed it in front of her smug, know-it-all face.

When I don't respond, Lucy asks, "Jessie? Are you okay?"

I'm trying to hide it, but I can't. I let out a sharp sniffle and swipe the tear from my cheek because I'm extra sensitive about my size. And basically anything and everything all the time.

"Oh no, are you crying?"

"No."

"Yes, you are."

"No, I'm not," I say through very obvious tears. "I never cry."

"Mm-hmm."

"Crying is for suckers." My voice is cracking and wobbling because of my rude pregnancy.

"Oh, hon," Lucy says, with nothing but fondness in her tone.

"What?" I ask, going to the bathroom to rip off a piece of toilet paper and blot my eyes before my mascara has a chance to run.

I don't know what comes over me these days. One minute I'm completely fine, and the next I'm watching an erectile dysfunction commercial and weeping because it's so freaking sweet that that couple holds hands while soaking in their side-by-side bathtubs! And don't even get me started on the dog food commercials full of puppies.

"Only two more months," she says, knowing how completely over pregnancy I am. She knows it because I text it to her first thing every single morning. Combine that with my hatred of her brother, and it's really a miracle she hasn't blocked me from her life yet. A terrible thought hits me: Maybe she's only my friend because I'm her boss? I'm the owner of Honeysuckle Salon, where Lucy works, but surely she's not friends with me for that reason . . . *Gah,* now I'm crying more. This is ridiculous. Drew! I need to keep thinking about Drew so I can channel all my emotions toward hatred instead of weeping.

"It still feels so far away," I say, unsuccessfully pushing away my emotions. "Two months might as well be an eternity as long as I have insomnia and this baby continues to kick me in the ribs."

"He'll be out soon enough."

"He?" I ask, like maybe Lucy performed a secret ultrasound I don't know about and determined the sex of my baby before I did.

"Or she."

"But you said *he* first. Do you think it's a boy?" I could end this guessing game by just asking my doctor, but I'm not ready to know yet.

Lucy doesn't get a chance to answer that question. "Oh, it's him! Drew is beeping in on the other line. I'll call you back with what he says."

"Don't bother."

"Do you at least want me to have him call you?"

"Nope," I say, closing the toilet seat lid and sitting down. "He wouldn't get through because I already blocked his number. Well, I blocked it after sending him a lovely little message I'm sure he enjoyed." It was cathartic, and I don't regret it no matter how disappointed in me Lucy will be.

She sighs deeply. Poor thing is weary to her bones of all this fighting. "Okay, well, I'll call you back in a few minutes and *not* tell you what he says." She'll tell me. Lucy can't keep things to herself. It's physically impossible for her.

"Okay. Hey, Luce? You're beautiful and I love you!"

"Mm-hmm," she murmurs before saying she loves me back, because Lucy is so sweet that she's incapable of not returning affection, and then she hangs up.

I let my shoulders slump and stare at the plain blue wall in front of me, anxious to not allow the feeling of loneliness to creep up on me too close. Then a loud boom followed by a hissing noise under the sink makes me jump out of my skin. I rush to the vanity and drop down to my knees, and before really thinking about it I fling open the cabinets. *Water.* Water sprays from under the sink like an open fire hydrant, soaking my face, body, and bathroom in a harsh, stinging deluge.

Wonderful. Just wonderful.

CHAPTER 2

Drew

THREE HOURS EARLIER

I'm dead.

I am a walking zombie after the night from hell. I'm not sure if there was a full moon or what, but three of my patients all went into labor around the same time yesterday. One ended in an emergency C-section around two A.M., and the other two (God bless them) labored naturally for close to twenty hours total. I have practically been living at either my clinic or the hospital for the past thirty-something hours because I didn't want to be too far away from my patient who was experiencing complications, but now that the storm is over, all I want to do is go home, shower, and pass out for maybe the rest of my life.

Even just trying to get down the main hallway of the hospital feels like I'm walking through a warped room in Willy Wonka's factory. Everything is tunneling and the lights feel strange, like I'm floating but also dragging. I've worked a lot of long hours over the last few years, but this stretch feels like the hardest yet. Normally, I can rest for at least an hour or two in one of the on-call rooms even when I'm needed at the hospital for extended stretches. But not this time. It was one freak situation after another, and I was a human bouncy ball, pinging all over the place.

When I pass a vending machine, I realize I haven't eaten in . . . well, I have no idea how long. I barely know what day it is now. My stomach grabs me by the collar of my scrubs and screams at me to feed it. I'm tempted to flatten myself against the glass and nap for one tiny minute before the protein bar drops. I don't get the chance, though.

"Hi, Dr. Marshall!" A nurse named Shannon pops up beside the vending machine, ponytail perky, fresh-faced for her shift. Since I feel like death warmed over, her exuberance for the morning makes me want to grimace. "I heard about that emergency C-section you did earlier for the twins—uh-mazing! I wish I could have been here to see it."

I lean down and shove my hand into the slot, the flap thing scraping against my knuckles as I pull the protein bar out, and I wonder why they haven't discovered a better way of making these things yet.

"Yeah. It went well. Thanks." I try to smile, but it doesn't work. My brain is no longer sending signals to my face, apparently. *Must. Get. Home.*

I sling my backpack over my shoulder and start unwrapping the protein bar while walking toward the doors. Shannon falls into step beside me, and I find it odd. We've never talked outside of dealing with a patient or exchanging pleasantries.

"Cool! So . . . have any fun plans this weekend?"

"Sleep," I say around a bite of the bar. Normally, I'd give a better effort at conversation, but not today. I can't. I'm about to give up on everything and curl into a ball on this nasty hospital floor, then sleep for a minimum of eight hours.

"Oh, yeah! I bet you're exhausted. Well . . ."

I can see the sliding double doors. I'm almost out of here.

Shannon takes two extra steps to get a little ahead so she can turn and face me, walking backward. "After your beauty sleep, if you're bored and need something to do, I'm around. Call me." She wrinkles her nose in what's supposed to be a cute smile before she hands me her number on a piece of paper and bobs off, but I don't like it. Not one bit.

First, I'm not going to call her because I have a policy of not getting involved with anyone I work with. It's just how I do things. It makes life easier and drama-free in my career. Second, I'm not going to call her because if I do manage to get any downtime this weekend, I will use it to do absolutely nothing.

My sister, Lucy, and her four-year-old son, Levi, were living with me until recently when she married my best friend, Cooper. Before she lived with me, Cooper was my roommate, and before that, I roomed with a few other guys from med school. It's been years since I've lived alone, and I'm ready to enjoy my empty house on my time off. Maybe I'll walk around in my underwear. No—naked! Yeah, that's it, I'll become a nudist when I'm home. Free to sit my naked ass anywhere I want.

I'm six feet from the exit when another nurse steps into my path. *For the love.*

"Dr. Marshall! So happy I ran into you!"

What is happening? Is this a joke? Does everyone know I'm about to die of exhaustion and they're pranking me? Because honestly, nurses don't talk to me like this. I always have a firm, unapproachable wall up.

"Hey . . ." I trail off because I *do not* know her name.

"Heather! I'm Heather. I assisted you on the Murphy family's birth last week."

"Oh, that's right. Sorry, Heather." Not right. I don't remember her.

She smiles wider. "Yeah, no problem. Anyway, just . . . wanted to see if maybe you'd be interested in getting a drink at some point? There's a really great bar on Second Avenue I've been wanting to try."

Am I in some sort of twilight zone? What. Is. Happening?

"Uh—thanks for the offer. I really appreciate it." *I really appreciate it?!* What am I, turning down a job offer? "I actually have a rule, though, that I don't date colleagues. It just keeps everything simple; you know?"

This time I do muster up a smile, although I'm afraid it looks closer to a grimace. Oh well. Everyone needs to get out of my way so I can go sleep. Heather does not get out of my way. She stays firmly *in* the way.

"Sure, and that's a great rule." Her shoulder hitches up coyly. "But surely you could make an exception just this once." Her lashes flutter, and it makes my eyes feel even drier. "I bet we could have a *really* good time together."

Subtle as a freight train, Heather.

I'm not proud of it, but I'm in survival mode now, so I pull my phone from my pocket and look at the screen, pretending to be getting a phone call at six in the morning. "Sorry, I don't think . . . oh, excuse me, I gotta take this."

She looks crestfallen for sure, but I don't stick around long enough to give her a chance to respond. I hike my backpack more firmly onto my shoulder and press my phone to my ear. I make it two steps before Siri asks loudly, "*How may I help you?*"

Nice. Smooth.

I don't look back to see if Heather heard. I walk at a frantic pace to my Jeep, hoping no one else will appear out of thin air and proposition me. *Definitely not something I've ever thought before.* I make it to my old Jeep, throw my bag in the back seat, and then slide into the passenger seat and lock the doors behind me. I'm not sure what was happening in that hospital, but clearly everyone has lost their minds.

Leaning my head back against the headrest, I debate calling an Uber because I know driving this drowsy is not safe. I pry my eyes open enough to request a ride and then sink back against the seat again, preparing to doze until it arrives.

Tap. Tap. Tap.

My eyes fly open, and I shoot up so fast I give myself whiplash. Something snaps angrily in my neck. That, however, is the least of my worries right now. No, instead, I rub the now sore spot in my neck while turning to look at Dr. Susan Landry, one of the other doctors who works in the same practice as me.

Feeling safe that it's not another nurse about to come on to me, I roll down the window.

She chuckles, eyeing the dark rings under my eyes. "You look terrible."

"Thank you for noticing. I feel terrible too."

I like Susan. She's an amazing doctor, and we've always had a great working relationship. There's no nonsense between us. We never see each other outside of work, and we keep everything professional. It's just how I like it.

"Although apparently the nurses in there didn't get the memo that I look terrible. I got asked out twice in five minutes." I rub my neck. "It was the weirdest thing. I blame it on the full moon that sent all my patients into labor."

"Really? Because I blame it on the fact that when your sister came and had lunch with you in the cafeteria last week, she went on and on about how single you are and how you need to find yourself a girlfriend and settle down."

I groan inwardly and curse my sister and her good intentions. "But how does anyone know about that?"

"Gossip travels fast within those hospital walls, and one of the nurses was sitting behind you guys. Apparently, the whole nurses' lounge knew by one o'clock."

Well, this is bad. The whole staff being alerted to my singleness is something I wanted to avoid. It's why I've always been vague about my personal life. "Well, I guess it's fine. I'll just have to be firm about my rule."

"What rule?" she asks while tightening her raven ponytail.

"I don't date colleagues."

Her eyebrows rise. "Ever?" Something about the way her voice goes up an octave alarms me.

"Yeah . . . it's just something I do to keep everything professional at work."

Her smile goes nervous, which is strange because I've never seen it do that before. "Well then, I guess I shouldn't toss my hat in the ring like I was planning to." She tries to cover up her embarrassment with a soft chuckle, but it doesn't work. I can still see how vulnerable she is, and I am absolutely too tired to deal with this gracefully. My eyeballs feel like they've been doused with pepper spray.

"Oh—you were going to . . . ask me out?" Now I'm worried my policy won't be enough. What if Susan is offended I won't bend my rule for her? Will our working relationship become awkward?

She shrugs a little, her smile quirking hopefully. "Yeah, to the fundraiser gala. I was thinking since we get along so well, and we're both single—"

"I'm not," I blurt, before I have the chance to stop myself.

Her eyebrows crinkle together. "You're not?"

"Nope. I actually already have a date to the gala." *I don't.* "My girlfriend." *Don't have one of those either.*

Susan looks understandably confused. "But you told your sister you were single . . ."

"Only because she doesn't know about it yet. It's new. I'm dating her best friend, and I know she won't like it." *Drew, stop.* "We're serious though." I can feel my brain shaking its metaphorical head at me. *You tired, tired fool.*

"Okay, but then . . . why didn't you say that at first? Why mention your rule?"

Goodness, Susan. So many questions.

"I forgot I was in a relationship. Like I said, it's new. And . . . I'm sleep-deprived." There, that last part is real at least.

"Gotcha," Susan says, like she still doesn't fully believe me. "Well, I'm looking forward to meeting her at the fundraiser." Why do her words feel like a taunt? A challenge? This is bad, but I can't worry about it now.

My Uber driver finally arrives and carries me home, where I stumble inside, feeling more drunk than I've ever been from the effects of alcohol. I throw my phone on the couch along with my backpack, then go into my room and strip down to my underwear. I normally shower when I get home from work, but not this time. Sleep. Sleep is all I need.

It's only when I'm falling asleep that I feel a nagging thought . . . almost like I'm forgetting something . . . something I was supposed to do today. But no matter how hard I try to wake up enough to remember it, sleep overpowers me, and I give in.

A few hours later, I wake up with a jolt. I sit up ramrod straight in bed as I suddenly recall what I was supposed to do today. "Jessie!" I hiss through my teeth like an expletive.

I hop out of bed and go straight into the living room, where I find my phone on the couch along with fifteen missed calls from the woman herself. *Dammit.* I'm in so much trouble. I was supposed to go over to her house at nine o'clock this morning and pretend to be her fiancé in front of her grandaddy. It was a ridiculous idea, and likely the reason my subconscious concocted the same ridiculous scheme when talking to Susan.

When my sister called late last night and asked me if I'd do it, I said yes. Probably because I was really distracted with all the humans I was in the middle of bringing into the world, and also because Jessie and I got off on the wrong foot (and every foot since). She hates me, and I saw this as a good opportunity to bury the hatchet between us and start over. I'm willing to forgive her if she's willing to forgive me—and that's saying a lot considering how she treated me the first time we met.

Our initial encounter was when I got home from a long shift at the hospital to find her pacing like a feral animal in my driveway, ready to pounce the moment I opened my door. I had been avoiding Lucy and Cooper after they decided to date even though I asked them not to. I didn't handle their new relationship well at all, basically giving them the cold shoulder for three weeks. Since I had been ignoring their phone calls and holing up at the hospital, I didn't realize my nephew had gone in for emergency surgery to have his appendix removed. Don't worry, Jessie came over and informed me. Very loudly. Very angrily. She also tossed a pack of diapers into my arms and said if I was going to act like a baby, I might as well dress like one. The forethought she had to put into that insult was astounding.

I'd never met the woman before, and she was up in my face, pregnant belly practically pressing against me as she very thoroughly explained exactly how I should get my head out of my ass, stop acting like a chauvinistic dirtbag, and go show up for my sister. So you can see how it was pretty easy for me to dislike her from the get-go, and every other interaction between us has looked pretty much the same. The last time I saw her, she was eating an entire bowlful of pickles. Like thirty pickles! As a medical professional who happens to specialize in maternal care, I advised her to be careful of her sodium intake. She showed me her favorite finger as a response.

We are mortal enemies now, and I had a chance to end that, but instead I've made it worse.

For all of thirty seconds, I feel terrible. I let Jessie down in a big way, and I wish I could fix it. But then I read the last text message she sent me, and I decide maybe I don't want to bury that damn hatchet after all.

JESSIE: I hope you know that you are scum. I would rather walk around with dog poop clinging to the bottom of my shoe than have to look at your ugly face one more time. You want a war, Andrew? You got one.

CHAPTER 3

Jessie

"I'm so sorry Levi woke you up at five again this morning." Lucy is sitting across from me at the breakfast table as we both nurse our coffees.

I moved in with Lucy last week after my pipe-bursting fiasco. I had to shut off my water, but I really thought it would be one of those situations where I'd just pile on the dry shampoo until they could repair the pipe. I thought wrong. Once the repairman went under my house, he found that not only do I have old pipes, I also have black mold due to said old pipes leaking for an extended period of time. Isn't that wonderful? *So* much fun.

Thankfully, Lucy and Cooper were sweet enough to let me move into their guest bedroom for as long as I need (which, according to Bob the Builder, will be about a month). That would have been fine—if Levi didn't take it upon himself to become my human alarm clock, specifically one that wakes me up three hours earlier than necessary every day.

"It's fine! Don't worry about it," I tell Lucy, hoping I sound genuine.

She can see right through me. "No, it's not. You're miserable."

"Well . . . only because I still have insomnia at night, so mornings are really the only time I sleep well. But that's okay!" See? I can be nice even though I feel like Ursula the sea witch under this sunny smile. Because the truth is, I love Levi to pieces. That said, if he wakes me up one more time, his favorite teddy bear might go missing.

"It's not just Levi, though. I know the hot water has run out twice now while you've been in the shower."

I wave a dismissive hand like *pssshhhh.* "Cold showers are all the rage, and it's not anyone's fault that this house has a small hot water tank."

"*And* you have to watch TV every night with me and Cooper. I know it's driving you nuts not having a place of your own."

I set my coffee mug down. "Are you trying to convince me I'm miserable here? Because I'll give it to you—you're making some headway."

She grins. "Yes. I am."

My shoulders slump. "Oh. Do you want me to leave? Lucy, I'm so sorry! I should have thought about how inconvenient it would be for you and—"

"Oh my gosh, I'm going to slap you if you keep talking! No, you're not an inconvenience! I love having you here. But I also know living with another family while you're in your last trimester is probably really annoying."

"I don't have any other options. I can't afford to rent anything on top of paying my mortgage and saving for this baby's birth." To say I'm scraping my nickels together would be an understatement. I'm not only scraping, I'm diving under couch cushions and searching grocery store parking lots with a magnifying glass, and never once have I turned up my nose at a penny.

"Actually . . . I can think of somewhere you can stay for free."

The mischievous glint in her eye makes me frown deeply, because instinctively I know who she's referring to.

"No. Never. Not his house."

"But Drew has a spare room! And he's great with roommates because he's always had one."

I stand up from my chair. "And he's evil and unbearable to be around. So no. Absolutely not. I'm done with him, and you know this." I wish she would give up trying to force Drew and me to like each other. It's not going to happen. I won't let it.

As I'm walking out of the kitchen, Lucy yells, "But Drew is hardly ever home! You probably won't even see him. You'll have the house practically all to yourself."

I want to say her words don't call to me like dark magic, but they do. Possibly because at that exact moment, I step on a little metal racecar, and there is a fifty percent chance I now need a new foot. I don't show my weakness to Lucy, though, and I'm just stubborn enough that I will set my own alarm for five A.M. every single day only to prove how happy I am here and not at all in need of a quiet place like Drew's evil lair.

CHAPTER 4

Drew

"Can you help me find a woman to take to a medical fundraiser gala in a few weeks who will be cool with pretending she's my girlfriend in front of my colleagues?" I ask Lucy as she puts two pizzas in the oven.

"Sure."

My eyebrows fly up. "Really? I thought you'd say no, or at least have to think about it for a minute."

She closes the oven door and stands back up—and now I can see her devious smile. "I don't have to think about it at all. I know the perfect person."

My own smile drops. "No."

She rolls her blue eyes, which are only a slightly lighter shade than mine. "Ugh. Why are you two always saying that word? Jessie would be perfect!"

I cross my arms and lean back against the counter. "I think you're confusing the word *perfect* with *horrible, dislikable, rude, obnoxious, irritating* . . . I could go on if you want."

Lucy does not look amused. "Jessie is none of those things."

"She hit me in the face with a pack of diapers."

Lucy pauses and scrunches her face. "Okay, yeah, admittedly that wasn't her finest moment, but she did it because you were being a childish ass toward me and Cooper. She's very sweet most of the time."

Not buying it. "I've never seen any evidence."

"Well, you not showing up to help her that day her grandaddy was coming into town definitely didn't help things."

"Exactly! So what makes you think she'd even be interested in helping me enact the same ruse? More than likely she'll wrap me up in chains and toss me off a bridge, toasting my lifeless body with champagne as it sinks to the bottom of a river."

Lucy's mouth is slightly open, and she shakes her head. "You two have disturbing perceptions of each other, and they're wildly inaccurate. By the way, would you ever wear a white linen suit?"

"Hell no."

She gives me a sassy duck lip expression and says, "See?"

My sister has lost it. She has a horrendous witch for a best friend who has singlehandedly ruined her sanity. I get it—Jessie ruins my sanity too.

"No, I don't. But even if I did ask her—which I won't—what makes you think she would do it?"

"Because you both have something the other needs, and you could very easily make a trade."

I want to ask what she's talking about, but in the next moment Cooper comes through the door that connects the garage to the kitchen and makes a beeline for Lucy.

"Hi," he says in a sappy, soft voice as he gathers her up in his arms and clasps his hands behind her lower back. "Sorry I'm late. Traffic was really bad today."

I'd be lying if I said it wasn't still a little weird for me to see my best friend and sister like this, all affectionate and married. I'm getting used to it, but some days, when the loneliness feels too heavy, I have a hard time looking at them.

"That's okay," Lucy says, taking on a dreamy look while angling her face up to him. She taps her index finger to her lips, and Cooper takes the overt hint by bending down and kissing her on the mouth.

Annnnd gross. Two seconds in and Cooper is already kissing Lucy way deeper than any brother should ever have to witness his sister getting kissed. I gouge out my eyes real quick and then turn away, too scared to look back until I'm sure they are done exchanging saliva. I thought getting married would help them both cool off in the PDA department. Nope. It's been over a month and it seems to only be getting worse.

After what feels like a hundred years, I hear the disgusting sound of lips de-suctioning from each other. I'm honestly kind of annoyed at them. Before Cooper met my sister, life was good. I didn't feel like anything was missing. I worked hard, and occasionally I played hard. I dated a sufficient amount, but nothing ever got serious, and everything felt comfortable that way. And then . . . Lucy came along and stole my best friend. But that's not why I'm mad. I'm upset because now I see them together—a family—and I want what they have. I want to love someone like Cooper loves Lucy, and I want someone to love *me* like Lucy loves Cooper.

The uncomfortable truth is, I don't get many second dates. In the past, I'd tell a woman I'm a doctor and she'd be all in. But then by the end of the date I'd break the news that I'm a gynecologist, and when I blinked, all that would be left is a trail of smoke from how quickly she ran away. Apparently it's going to take a very specific type of woman to feel comfortable having a committed relationship with a man in my profession. And I honestly get it.

I hear Lucy whisper to Cooper that I'm in the room, and he

laughs. "Dude, sorry. I didn't realize you were standing back there."

"You should be. That was horrifying to witness. As payment for seeing and hearing way too many things, you have to help me talk Lucy into setting me up with a woman for a night."

Cooper's eyebrows shoot up, and clearly his mind has gone somewhere less G-rated.

I grimace. "Let me rephrase that: I need a fake girlfriend to go with me to a fundraiser so I don't have to date my colleague."

His face clears, and he looks relieved that I'm not asking Lucy to find me a hookup. Apparently these two have really high opinions of me these days.

"Didn't you just ditch Jessie for something similar to this?"

I throw my hands up. "I didn't ditch her. I was sleep-deprived and *forgot*. There is a difference. But even if I did do it on purpose, could you really blame me? Who in their right mind would help someone so rude and abrasive?"

"Well, you're not exactly daisies and roses yourself there, *Dr. Stuck-up.*" Jessie suddenly appears from around the corner like an evil genie I accidentally summoned. My skin prickles at the sight of her sharp green eyes. They are blazing. Strangling. Smothering. One dark-blond eyebrow is cocked up, her arms crossed over the yellow T-shirt pulling tight against her chest and small baby bump. The corner of her mouth is tilted. She looks like venom wrapped up in sunshine.

"Jessica," I say, giving her a short nod like we're in a saloon in the Wild West. If I had a cowboy hat on, I'd tip it down, so it covered just one of my eyes. I need a piece of wheat.

Jessie's gaze falls down the length of my body, tripping like a rock skipping across a pond. Face. Shoulders. Biceps. Torso. Thighs. Feet. At first, I think she's checking me out, until her head tilts and she smirks. "Your fly is down."

I chuckle once. "Nice try. Did you steal that shirt from a toddler?"

"Nope. From your mom."

Somewhere in a schoolyard, a group of teenage boys all crow with laughter.

"You two aren't very nice," my sister mumbles quietly from the sideline. *Poor Luce.* She's still hoping Jessie and I will kiss and make up, and no doubt that's what she was imagining would happen if Jessie moved in with me. *Over my dead body.*

Jessie and I lock eyes, and both of our smiles fade. Blue rams into green, tension racing between us like a current. It's not the good kind, though. It's that special brand that has turned friends into foes, made business partnerships crumble, and sent countries to war. It's not a delicate string tying us together. It's quicksand, gripping our ankles and pulling us both down inch by inch until we're smothered. It's loaded and charged, and—

Lucy's loud clap zings around us. "Okayyyyy! Who's hungry? The pizza will be coming out of the oven any minute, so everyone grab a plate."

Jessie walks up and stops right in front of me. I know I'm partially blocking the cabinet that holds the plates, but I'm a mean bully now and make no attempt to move out of the way. She, of course, won't back down either. She'll drill a hole right through my body to get to the dishes if she has to. Inching up closer, she stands directly beside me, and her arm presses against mine as she reaches partially around me into the cabinet.

In the second before she pulls away, she leans close to my ear. "I'd watch your back if I were you, Dr. Stuck-up. I'm not good at forgiving and I definitely never forget, but I'm *excellent* at getting even."

I tilt my head just enough to look her right in the eyes. "Looking forward to it, Oscar."

Oscar is the nickname I christened her with the day she started calling me that awful *Dr. Stuck-up,* and she still has no idea what it means. When she's not calling me by that little gem, she calls me by my first name, *Andrew* . . . which I might hate even more. Every single thing between us is an equal back-and-forth, so if she calls me Dr. Stuck-up, I call her Oscar. She calls me Andrew; I call her Jessica. It's how things are done around here.

Her full mouth blooms into a wicked smile before she pulls back with her plate and walks away, promises of future torture hanging in the air.

That's when I look down at my jeans. "Dammit," I mumble, and then I zip up my fly.

CHAPTER 5

Jessie

Dinner was a tense affair, as it usually is when Drew and I are forced to breathe the same oxygen. I feel bad that we're both so disagreeable around Lucy, who is just a sweet little sprite, an angel-fairy sent to the world to bestow goodness and happy vibes on all of us. But it's Drew's fault. He had a chance to mend the strife between us, and instead he threw new logs on the fire. It burns before my eyes.

Drew's not in the room right now. He walked down the hall *again* to make a secretive phone call to his doctor, saying the meds still aren't working and the butt rash is getting worse. At least that's what I'm assuming the calls are about. So I'm on the floor with Lucy's little boy, Levi, and we're putting together a puzzle while Lucy and Cooper snuggle on the couch. Basically, our nightly routine.

I'm trying to focus, but this twenty-piece dinosaur puzzle just isn't holding my attention. My eyes keep sliding down the dark hallway in the direction of where Drew disappeared. I have no idea why, but I'm curious about who he's talking to back there.

It's definitely not because I wonder if he has a girlfriend or anything. I mean, he may be attractive from an objective point of view—like, classically speaking, I suppose his broad shoulders and muscled frame might be considered paintable—but his personality is garbage. How he could get any woman to date him with his macho, man-in-charge demeanor is beyond me. I don't even know how he's managed to have any patients at his practice. I would never want to see a stuck-up, know-it-all mansplainer like him.

"Uh—I'll be right back. I need to go to the bathroom." I state this out loud like I have never before done in the history of my existence. I look suspicious as I stand up and walk like a nut-cracker toward the hallway. Right leg, left arm. Left leg, right arm. Or should it be the opposite? *How do I normally walk?*

"Why are you walking like that?" Lucy asks.

So not like this, apparently.

"Trying not to pee myself," I say, because that's an excellent excuse for every abnormality when you're in your third trimester. Then I scurry down the hall. A couple of feet into the dark, I hear Drew's voice coming from a cracked door at the end of the hallway. Levi's room.

I inch forward, my back pressed against the wall like Ethan Hunt from *Mission Impossible* until I can hear him.

". . . no, no, I promise you're not bothering me at all. It's okay to be nervous—this is your first baby. It's perfectly normal and expected."

He's on a call with a patient? I guess that makes sense. He is a doctor, though I have trouble actually picturing it. Also, I know I should turn and walk away to give him privacy while he's on a medical call, but anyone who would think I'm capable of turning and walking away right now is clearly unacquainted with me. I'm getting a glimpse of Drew in the wild, and I fully intend to put on my safari hat and pull out my binoculars.

I step forward an inch more and peek through the crack. There he is, phone to his ear, profile to me. He's starting to get the slightest five-o'clock shadow, and his mussed brown hair looks as rebellious as his attitude. I'm not afforded many moments like this where he looks away, giving me enough time to examine him without repercussions, so I seize the opportunity to catalogue each of his features. His soft blue cotton T-shirt pulls, hugs, and kisses his upper body like it wants to have his babies. His facial features are symmetrical and sharp, perfection chiseled out of a rare, smooth stone, contrasted beautifully by his full, soft lips. But it's his dark-blue eyes that are the real killers. They'll pull you in and knock you out in a flash if you're not careful.

But I hate him, so it's fine, and I barely even notice his attractiveness.

"You did great just now. How was your pain during that contraction on a scale of one to ten?" There's a brief pause while he listens to whoever is on the other end of the line. "Okay. Well, I tell you what. I'm going to hang out on the phone with you until the next one starts so we can time it together, and then if—" Another pause. "No, don't apologize. It's okay to cry. You went into labor with your first child while your husband is out of town. That's a lot to deal with, and if I were in your position, I would have already gone through a whole Kleenex box." He chuckles, and for some reason I find myself smiling too. I almost don't recognize this side of Drew. He's . . . *tender.*

Suddenly, I can't stand here and listen any longer. I need to get far away from this version of him. I skip the bathroom and go right back to my place on the floor beside Levi, absentmindedly picking up a dinosaur tail and trying to shove it into the spot where its head should go. Levi notices and silently takes the puzzle piece out of my hand, then replaces it with the right one. *What a kid.* I think this is his way of apologizing for waking me up at the butt crack of dawn every day.

After a minute, Drew comes back into the living room. I peek at him from the corner of my eye and watch him stuff his phone in the back pocket of his dark jeans.

"Everything okay?" Lucy asks him.

He nods and lets out a deep breath. "Yeah. I just might have to go into the hospital later tonight depending on how one of my patients progresses over the next hour." Drew's eyes lock with mine, and I hate that I've heard how tender he can be. I suddenly blush under his attention, which is so ridiculous I want to kick myself.

Drew crosses the room and sits down in the armchair directly behind me. He does it on purpose; I know it. There are plenty of other seating options in the room, but he chose the one hovering over my shoulder so he could breathe down my neck and rattle me.

Well, no rattling here, buddy. I'm easy as Sunday morning.

"Get your knee away from my back!" I snap over my shoulder. Okay, maybe not so much Sunday morning as Monday evening, stuck in bumper-to-bumper traffic.

"Why? Is it bothering you, Jessica?" He doesn't move his knee. He presses it more firmly against my shoulder blade. Not painfully, just with the purpose of reminding me that he's *there*. And just like that, the familiar Drew is back, and I hate him all over again.

"I mean it. Stop touching me." My words are sharp little razors.

"I'm not touching you. *You're* touching *me*. I'd appreciate it if you'd remove your back from my knee."

I whip my head around to pierce him with my eyes. "I was here first!"

He shrugs. "Well, I'm here now."

"Children, please," Cooper says, interjecting with a smile and a hand gesture toward Levi. "If you want to stay with us grown-ups, you'll have to behave."

"I have no problems with that," I say, scratching the back of my head with my middle finger.

Drew leans closer, and his breath tickles my ear. "Real mature."

"Get a mint." For the record, though, he doesn't need one. I think he must have chewed gum after dinner. *Spearmint.* I bite my lip, because it's not fair. I know my breath smells like garlic-pizza-death while he's a walking Winterfresh commercial. If he smiles and exhales, I'm sure a blast of icy-cool air will rush out in a puff. I want to drag it all into my lungs, but I force myself to take shallow, barely-life-sustaining breaths instead.

"I'm going to have to separate you two, aren't I?" Lucy is giving us both the *mom eyes.* Will they teach me that look in the hospital once I deliver?

Drew sits back in his seat, and neither of us says a thing. We're both being so immature, but I don't care. Drew makes me do irrational things, and apparently I have the same effect on him.

Our war of silence (less impressively known as *quiet mouse*) begins as Cooper tells Levi it's time for bed and to give us all hugs. There's a brief reprieve in hostility as the pudgy little dumpling wraps his arms around my neck and sparks my growing motherly instinct to cherish this hug forever. He then moves toward Drew, who reaches out quick as a snake and drags Levi up into his lap to tickle his nephew into oblivion. Levi squeals with laughter and Drew's ferocious smile splinters my heart into pieces for two unbearable seconds. Then Cooper and Levi disappear down the hallway, and it's just me, Drew, and Lucy again—immersed in stone-cold silence. I swivel around so I'm sitting adjacent to Drew and he can't touch me anymore.

Lucy's tender heart can't stand this, so she groans loudly and sits forward on the couch. "Good grief. You two need to get over all this animosity. You're both adults acting like two-year-olds. Does that not bother you guys at all?"

I don't know, does it, Andrew? I blink, suck my cheeks in, and keep my laser beams focused on him. His blue eyes sparkle as he tips an eyebrow that says, *You wanna answer that, Jessica?*

So neither of us speak, and Lucy pulls out the big guns. "Fine. Then, Drew, maybe Jessie would like to know all about how you need a fake—"

"Don't!" Drew breaks first, jutting his finger out to point at his sister.

I shift my shoulders so I'm sitting up nice and tall now while aiming a delighted smile at Drew. "What is this interesting news you're keeping from me, *Andy*?" Oooh, he must really hate that name because his jaw flexes. I file that away under *IMPORTANT*.

"It's nothing." His voice is hard as granite.

Lucy shifts a little more toward the edge of her seat with a sigh. "And maybe you, Jessie, would like to tell Drew that you're miserable here and would like to stay in his—"

"LA LA LA—nothing! Jessie would like nothing," I say quickly, and Drew smirks.

Lucy throws up her hands and stands. "You two are unbearable to be around. I'm going to pour a glass of wine—don't kill each other while I'm gone."

"No promises," Drew and I both say in non-adorable unison.

Lucy disappears into the kitchen but then promptly sticks her head back around the corner and, giving her best impression of an auctioneer, says in a fantastic rush of words, "Drew told his colleague he has a girlfriend even though he doesn't, and now he needs a date to a gala!"

Drew's eyes widen, and his cheeks burn red. I want to drink that blush up through a straw and savor it for the rest of my life. I bust up in an obnoxious laugh, pointing at him like I'm the sort of person who delights in giving wedgies.

"And Jessie wants to stay in your guest bedroom because she's miserable here but is too prideful to admit it!"

I gasp and clutch my heart. The knife hurts so bad. Drew takes his turn laughing while Lucy runs away like a coward. *Yeah, you better run!*

I turn my angry gaze to Drew and let Lucy's revelation roll over me like a tidal wave of sweet, *sweet* revenge. "So . . . got yourself caught in a bit of a lie, did you, Dr. Stuck-up? Better hope whoever you choose doesn't stand you up!" I add extra emphasis on the *p* sound.

"If you hadn't blocked my number, maybe you would have heard me say I didn't stand you up." He pauses and then amends his statement. "Well, not on purpose at least. I had a—"

"Yeah, yeah, Lucy told me. You were sooooo tired that it just slipped your mind that you had agreed to come to my house mere *hours* before. Sorry, I'm not buying it." Honestly, when Lucy called me back and told me what happened with Drew, I couldn't decide which explanation made me feel worse—that he stood me up out of vengeance, or that he completely forgot about me because I'm *that* unimportant. Not true—I can decide. Being put aside and forgotten hurts the most. And yet, you'd think after having it happen to me repeatedly, it wouldn't sting so much.

Drew sneers and rolls his eyes, his large hand gripping the side of the armchair like it wronged him.

"You're impossible." Drew is looking away and out the window, but finally his eyes slowly magnetize to mine. "What is it you want to hear? An apology? Because I already tried that, and any chance of that happening again flew out the window when you called me a scumbag and then blocked me."

"I do *not* want an apology or anything from you. Not now, not ever. Hence the blocking."

"Great. Well then, I guess Lucy was wrong and you really don't need a nice, quiet, restful place to stay for the next few weeks. And I mean it's too bad really. My house is spacious, and you'd practically have it all to yourself since I'm never home." He's gloating now, a self-satisfied smile on his mouth as he leans forward to rest his forearms on his knees. "And I bet you love sleeping on that little twin bed in Lucy's spare room." *It's horrible, squeaking every time I turn over, and the room is so small it would never fit my queen bed even if I wanted to move it.* "Yeah, I don't blame you. I wouldn't want to stay at my house that has a large empty bedroom perfect for moving your own stuff into, complete with an en suite bathroom and soaker bathtub."

I dig my nails into the carpet, because dammit that does sound amazing. I want to cry at the beautiful picture he just painted. I want my privacy back. I want to sleep until eight A.M., and I *don't* want to share a wall with Lucy and Cooper anymore.

"Why are you taunting me?" I ask with narrowed eyes.

He tilts forward, getting a little closer. His eyes are such a deep blue. "Because it's fun."

I want to smack him. My fingers are all begging me to do it. I bet I could reach.

But then Drew's eyebrows pull together, and his eyes soften to something more tender and compassionate. If only for a fraction of a moment, I get a glimpse of what other people must see when they look at Drew. Reliable. Safe. A man who would move heaven and earth for someone he loves. But then his gaze clouds over, and he's once again indifferent, because I am not someone he loves, as I've taken great care to ensure.

"And I don't know . . . maybe I see some merit in Lucy's suggestion," he mutters.

"What suggestion?"

"That we help each other. You act like my girlfriend for one night, and I let you stay in my house rent-free."

I sputter a sharp laugh. "You're joking! I would never act like your girlfriend after all that's happened."

He holds his hands out in front of him. "Hey, I wasn't the one to suggest it. I know it's a bad idea, I just . . ." He's quiet for another moment, claiming control of the conversation and forcing me to wait in anticipation of his impending words. "I think it could actually work."

I don't know why, but that statement makes my stomach tumble off the edge of a cliff.

"How do you figure?"

He shrugs, and I don't notice the way his cotton tee pulls against his muscular chest. Not at all. "As long as we both know upfront what we're getting into and agree that it will be torture for us both, I think we could make it work. I'll stay out of your hair, and you stay out of mine."

My mouth is opening to tell Drew to go lick rust, but my mind clasps a hand over my mouth. *Now, now, darling, let's not be so hasty.* There's no doubting that Drew dangled a lovely carrot in front of my face with all that sexy talk about having a house all to myself. I'm already dreaming of what it would be like to lie in my own bed again.

And then it hits me.

Oh, the revenge I can get on him is too good. Too easy. Too simple. I'm almost afraid my battle plans are projecting above me because they are that *obvious*. And yet, as I stare into Drew's blue eyes, I don't think he sees it. I think he's underestimating me—and for that, he will pay.

And it will all go down at his gala, in front of everyone.

"I think you're right, Andrew. I think we could make a deal."

CHAPTER 6

Jessie

It's moving day. Last night Drew and I came to the agreement that I'd be his fake girlfriend in exchange for staying rent-free at his house until mine is finished. It feels sudden to be moving out the next day, but I don't have much of a choice. All last week they worked on fixing the pipe that burst and getting the water turned back on, but starting Monday they will begin phase two of construction, which is remediating the mold. Step three will be replacing any parts of the house where the wood has rotted away, and apparently the damage is extensive. So, this weekend was the last time I could get in this house to move my things out before the big construction begins.

I came home after dinner at Lucy's and packed up pretty much my whole house (thankfully, she still had all her boxes from moving to Cooper's house). I told Lucy I was just going to pack a few things, so she didn't need to come too, but then I ended up staying awake all night and packing the entire thing since this insomnia is apparently going to keep me from ever sleeping again.

Lucy comes over early in the morning, thinking she will help me box up my room before the guys get here to move it out, but there is nothing left for her to do. I've never seen anyone so pouty about being relieved of their packing duty before—pouty and suspicious.

"You're bringing all of this to Drew's house?" Lucy's eyes trail over the boxes littered around my bedroom. There's more—lots more—in the living room, bathroom, and kitchen too. Drew is going to flip when he sees all of this, and the joy that brings to my heart will sustain me for the rest of the year.

"Yeah. Why not?" Despite my effort, my devious smile is starting to show. I wish I were wearing a cape so I could pull the hood up and let it shadow my face.

"It's just . . . maybe a lot for two or three weeks. I thought you'd only pack a few boxes."

I shrug casually, but inside I'm cackling like a demented criminal. Playing the long game gives me life. "It just looks like a lot because all I had were the big boxes you gave me. They're not totally full."

"Oh, okay, sure." She's not convinced, because she's not ignorant. She tries to pick up one of the boxes and can't because that sucker is loaded down. She gives it one more attempt but looks like she's trying to lift Thor's hammer. It's not budging. Lucy squints at the boxes, trying to figure out my secret plan. Finally, she shakes her head slowly, a quiet grin on her lips, then looks at me. My scheme is discovered. She knows I'm going to torture Drew with my belongings. *All* my belongings.

I raise my eyebrows, daring her to call me out and refuse to aid me in my plans to provoke the emotional deterioration of her big brother. Surprisingly, she doesn't. In fact, I think she's a little excited to see how this all plays out. Her blue eyes—almost the same shade as Drew's, but his are deeper, darker, and not nearly as innocent—sparkle with a conspiratorial glint. "You packed all of your throw blankets, right? You don't want to get cold over there."

I grin. "And the matching pillows." Lucy and I both start laughing like two people who just got away with replacing all the diamonds at Tiffany's with rock candy. The doorbell rings, and my brain translates it as the first bell of a boxing match. *It's on, Drew.*

"Hello?" Cooper's voice cracks through the air first—a warning shot. "We're here."

"In here!" An angry, twirling flutter whirls around in my belly with the knowledge that Drew is in my house. He's somewhere on the other side of that wall and has no idea of the plans I have for him. I pull my metaphorical hood down a little lower. Villainy brews in my chest.

There are footsteps in the hallway now. I hear Cooper's laugh first and then turn just in time to see Drew's eyes sweep over my room. He's wearing black athletic shorts today—the color of his heart—and a light hoodie, looking like maybe he just finished a workout. His eyes sweep up and down every box tower and suitcase in sight. They skitter across my feet and roll over my stripped-down mattress. They perform a thorough investigation, and almost as if he can sense my need for him to look at me, he avoids my eyes. It's a miniature form of torture, though I don't know why. I want to stomp over to him, plant my hands on either side of his scruffy jaw, and yank his gaze down. *Me. Look here, you!*

"No" is all he says.

So polite, as always.

Now his eyes slither like a snake across my floor, creating a path through the maze of boxes and then slowly, *slowly* up my body until his gaze locks with mine. A heavy breath is expelled from my lungs. *You. I see you.*

"What do you mean 'no'?"

Cooper walks over to Lucy and wraps his arm around her waist, leaning down to kiss her temple. "Do you think there's going to be blood?"

Lucy lightly elbows him in the side. She never encourages this incivility. "Help me start carrying some of these out," she says with a worried glance between me and Drew, then she leaves the two of us alone. I want to ask if that's wise, but I guess we're going to be living together, so we might as well get used to it sooner rather than later.

Drew's arm rises, forearm flexing angrily as he points a menacing finger at a box. "No." And then points to another box. "No." And then repeats this pattern fifteen more times, like he's shooting imaginary fire bolts at all my boxes. They go up in flames. He stomps through my house, pointing at everything he can find.

I follow along, trying not to dissolve into laughter, because this is turning out exactly like I predicted. He's my pawn, and he doesn't even know it. We end in the kitchen on his final, triumphant *no*.

"You can't bring all this crap to my house."

I gasp like I am deeply wounded. "It's not crap! I need all of this around me to be comfortable." *And to torture you every day that I'm living in your house.*

Everyone knows Drew is a minimalistic neat freak. Having all my little trinkets and girly items scattered around is going to wind him up like a knotted ball of yarn.

He is stone-faced as he spins around, whips out a pocketknife like a Boy Scout, and tears into one of my boxes on the counter.

"*Hey!*" I snap, going to stand beside him as he dips his hand in and retrieves one member of my set of snowman Christmas mugs.

Drew holds Frosty up to my face, carrot nose to human nose. "Explain to me why you need this in August."

"It has deep sentimental value." Frosty winks at me.

"Mm-hmm." He's not having it.

I force myself to hold his bottomless blue gaze and arch an eyebrow. He has at least a foot on me and seems to grow taller during these matches of will. I'm not scared though—not of him physically hurting me, at least.

"Well, Andrew, do you need a fake girlfriend or not?"

I think I see a grin touch the outer corner of his mouth, but I can't be sure. "Do you need a roof over your head or not, Jessica?" *Touché.*

"It seems we're at an impasse."

"It seems we are, because this is my first weekend off in a very long time, and I don't intend to spend it running multiple trips between our houses so you can be surrounded by all of your sentimental objects. So, as far as I am concerned, Frosty is staying right where he's at."

"No one asked you to help me move, Dr. Stuck-up. By all means, go enjoy your weekend. Throw baby kittens into a lake or slash the neighborhood kids' bike tires. You know, the things you normally do with your spare time."

"You know I can't do that."

"Why not? You already have your pocketknife on you."

His gaze drops to my stomach. "You shouldn't be lifting boxes, and if I leave you'll try to pick up the slack."

Self-preservation instincts flood my system, and I flash Drew an angry smile because I *hate* feeling reliant on other people for help. "My physical well-being doesn't concern you, so leave. I'll be just fine without you." *Better,* actually.

He rolls his eyes and scoffs. "Come on. Quit being ridiculous. We both know you need help moving today." He plops his heavy hand on the top of the box, and it lands with a thud. "So, as your official unpaid mover, I say this stays. You can enjoy your sentimental mugs when you move back home in two short weeks."

I slap *my* hand on the box like I'm going to tug it toward me, silently saying it will come with me even if I have to strap it on my back. I look down and see Drew's knuckles whiten as his grip tightens more firmly around the cardboard. It's denting.

I want to growl. What does he know? Maybe I really do need this box full of cheerful holiday mugs! Maybe I'm dealing with severe anxiety and snowman mugs are the only things that bring relief! I don't need any of it, of course, but that's beside the point. *He* doesn't know I don't need it.

Our gazes lock, and I think we would both stand here all day, searing each other with angry glares, trying to intimidate the other. There's an unspoken rule in place: first person to remove their hand loses. Grandaddy has told me my greatest strength is my stubbornness and resilience. Of course, he's also told me it's my greatest weakness as well. I'm convinced that, in this moment, it's my superpower.

Drew's lashes fall and rise as he blinks slowly, and staring at him like this, I can see his pupils grow, blanketing the blue until his eyes are mostly black. His mouth slants and I squirm, but not out of intimidation. Apparently, no one has told my unborn baby that winning against Drew is my greatest high in life, because the little thing ruthlessly squashes itself right down onto my bladder. I know without a shadow of a doubt that if I don't run to the bathroom in one minute tops, things are going to get ugly.

Drew misses nothing where I'm concerned. His gaze slips to my crossed legs and notes how I'm bouncing a little. I don't want to bounce, but my body has taken matters into its own hands. It's on autopilot so I don't pee myself.

His grin tilts, indulgent as dark chocolate buttercream frosting. "Something wrong, Jessica? You need to step away for a minute?"

Never! Absolutely not. I am glued to this box. It is an extension of me now. "No, I'm wonderful. Thank you for asking, *Andy.*"

I watch suspiciously as his eyebrows crunch together, and he lightly touches the pads of his fingers to his throat. He's hiked up the sleeves of his hoodie, baring his forearms, and I don't notice the way his veins wrap around the undersides, twisting like tempting little vines up his arms. I would have to be desperate to pay attention to those things.

"I'm suddenly so thirsty," he says. "Mind if I get some water?"

I swallow, dread filling me like lead as I see the direction his mind is moving in. "N-no. Go right ahead."

What a pincushion.

Drew turns on the faucet and, slow as Christmas itself arriving, plucks the snowman mug off the counter and inches it toward the stream of water, other hand still firmly splayed out on the box. He fills the mug up with only a slow, subtle stream of water, looking over his shoulder at me with a false apologetic smile the entire time.

"Gross—I think there's some dust in this mug. Better pour it out and refill it."

I try to focus on anything besides that stream of water. The Sahara Desert. Hot, dry sand. Thanksgiving turkey. Everything that is devoid of moisture. My fingernails bite into the side of the cardboard, and I'm practicing every technique I can think of to not give in to the urge to pee. But *oh gosh,* this isn't working. I'm seriously about to wet myself in this kitchen over a Frosty the Snowman mug set.

Drew can sense my urgency and has zero sympathy for my predicament. He thrives on it. His powers grow stronger. "Bouncing an awful lot there, Oscar." I still have no idea why he calls me Oscar, but I know whatever the reason, it's deeply insulting.

I'm a human pogo stick at this point with how badly I'm bouncing, but I refuse to give in yet. I shake my head in sharp, tight movements. "Nope. Just full of excited energy for move-in day!"

"Oh good. For a second there I thought maybe you had to pee."

"Nah—I don't do that anymore."

He gives a strangled laugh, and for the slightest moment I'm mesmerized by a genuine smile playing across his mouth. His eyes glow, like when you hold a marble up to the light and the blue intensifies. I like it. I think maybe if he smiled more often—

My train of thought is cut off when that smile drops away and morphs into something devilish again—like he could sense my charitable thoughts and had to immediately remedy the situation. He picks up Frosty with a glare so full of heat I'm afraid that poor ol' snowman is going to melt.

"Cheers to new roommates." He presses it to his lips and tips it back, drinking gulp after gulp, Adam's apple bobbing up and down his throat, making me feel as if all that liquid is somehow magically teleporting into my body and adding to what I've already got in here. I have a swimming pool inside me now.

I can't take it anymore.

"GAH—YOU WIN!" I yell, letting go of the box and scrambling out of the kitchen and toward the bathroom as fast as I can. I pee for no less than two minutes straight, wash my hands, and also try to wash away my shame. It's still fully intact as I make my way back to the kitchen, dragging my feet like a child headed to eat a big bag of carrots.

I turn the corner to the kitchen and there's Drew, leaned back against my counter, James Dean raised from the dead. Because he's wearing athletic shorts, I can see that even his calves are strong. I wish I didn't know that about him. My eyes then zero in on the item hanging casually off of his hand—the empty Frosty mug. He holds it like a bandit from the Wild West would a gun, like he'll sling it around his finger and tuck it away in a holster.

"Feel better?" I don't answer, so his smile just grows, and *huh,* turns out Dr. Stuck-up has dimples. I want to rise up onto my tip-toes and stick my fingers in both of them. "While you were gone, I had a change of heart. I think I do like these mugs after all. Let's bring them."

I'm disgusted as I watch him drop Frosty back into the box, pick up the whole thing like it only contains a single feather, and then wink at me as he leaves the kitchen. I feel that wink like a sun flare across my skin.

I'm going to have to up my game with this one.

CHAPTER 7

Drew

It's taken all day to move Jessie's junk into my house. So much for having a weekend off. I had to burn my entire Saturday helping the roommate I don't even want move into my home. She doesn't need all of this stuff—I know she doesn't. She's just having us move it all to get under my skin, because she's evil and gets some sort of sick delight from watching me feel miserable. Which is why any time Cooper and I dropped off a load of her boxes to the house, I'd smile, hum, or whistle the entire time we unloaded.

We had to make three separate trips, by the way. *Three.* I think we moved every single thing she owns minus her living room set— and that was only because I drew the line there. She thinks she's being so sneaky, but I can see all of her plans to unpack this shit into my house, to integrate all of her girlie things with my masculine things and make me go berserk. Joke's on her. None of this gets to go in my living areas. She's going to have to stuff it all in her room like a life-sized vending machine. She'll need a giant claw to sort through it all.

Mark my words, Jessie's stuff will not touch my stuff. And no,

I don't mean that as an innuendo. There's no need for one where Jessie is concerned because in no way am I thinking about her stuff and my stuff touching, and . . . well, shit, now I'm thinking about it as an innuendo.

"Dude, lighten up with your grip, would you? If you squeeze the steering wheel any harder, you're going to leave permanent finger marks behind."

I force my hands to relax by clenching and unclenching them one at a time. I convinced Cooper to let me drive this last load back to the house because I felt so wound up I needed something to do other than just sit in the passenger seat and bounce my knee. Apparently, driving isn't helping either.

"Sorry. I didn't realize I was doing that."

"Yeah, obviously. You've been over there in your own world for the last ten minutes. At one point you were shaking your head, and your jaw was flexing. Super creepy."

I glance briefly at Cooper, then look back at the road. "I was not."

He scoffs and pulls out his phone, holding it up toward my face.

I squint at it. "You took a photo of me while I was driving?"

"Yeah, I did," he says, not sounding the least bit remorseful. "I sent it to Lucy so she could tell me what this moody face of yours means."

Why am I friends with him?

"And? What's her verdict?"

"Sexual frustration."

I almost crash. My hand jerks and for a split second the whole truck snaps to the left. Thank God no one was beside us. *Embarrassing* would not begin to cover how I'd feel having to admit I sideswiped someone because my sister proclaimed that I'm sexually frustrated.

"WHOA," Cooper yells, pressing his whole arm against the door to brace himself. "That's it! Pull over."

I frown and look quickly at Cooper, then shift my eyes back to the road. "What? No. There was a bunny in the road—I had to swerve to miss it."

I feel his angry eyes on the side of my face. I almost hurt his baby. He'll never forgive me. "Pull over."

Cooper isn't often serious. The last time I saw him angry was when I was chewing him out for going behind my back to date Lucy. The tone he's using now is the same as it was that day—which is why I put on my blinker and pull over into the nearest parking lot.

"It was a bunny," I murmur under my breath.

The moment I have the truck in park, Cooper flies out of the passenger seat, slamming his door before rounding the vehicle to jump in the driver's seat. We look like a married couple in a tiff. Well, fine. If he's going to slam a door, I am too. I hop up into the passenger seat, and I pull the door shut with a loud *bam*.

He scowls at me and then rubs his hand over the top of the dashboard, whispering, "It's okay, baby. I won't let that sexually frustrated man crash you."

I roll my eyes and position my elbow on the side of the door so I can lean on my fist. "Does Lucy know about this romantic affair you're having with your truck?"

"Whatever. Hers is worse. She steals the keys and takes it out for late-night rendezvous to get ice cream. The number of sprinkles I find on the seat after is obscene."

Cooper starts the truck, backs up, and we pull out onto the main road again, only a few minutes from my house now. It's insulting he didn't even trust me to make it the last few miles.

"Lucy's wrong, though. I'm not sexually frustrated," I say, but Cooper looks unimpressed by my declaration. In fact, he has the gall to laugh. "What? I'm serious. I was doing great before Jessie showed up. And for the first time in my adult life, I had my house all to myself. So if I'm frustrated, it's because I can't walk around naked anymore."

"If you were enjoying your nudist sanctuary so much, why did you offer for Jessie to move in with you?"

I look out the window. "You already know this answer. We made a trade. I need her to act like my girlfriend at the fundraiser."

He shakes his head. "The real reason."

"That is the real reason. I couldn't find anyone else to do it. I needed someone to help me, and Jessie needed somewhere to stay. Problem solved."

"I call BS."

He's serious. He really thinks this was all staged for me to get to spend more time with Jessie? Ridiculous. "Oh wow, yeah," I say, completely deadpan. "You caught me. I want Jessie soooooo bad. I love that she constantly fights with me and makes my life miserable. I love seeing her green eyes flare when she says something biting, and I am actually happy to have her moving in because I secretly hate living alone, and—" I stop myself when I realize this is sounding less and less like a joke and more like my subconscious thoughts climbing out of hiding.

My eyes cut to Cooper and I see his lips pressed firmly together, a laugh strangled in his throat.

"Just shut up," I tell him, pulling my hood up and sinking down in the seat like a teenager who hates his parents. Cooper's hands go up in mock surrender as I reach over to turn up the radio and drown out any uncomfortable realizations coalescing in my head. It might have sounded like the truth, but it wasn't. I was just kidding around. The only part of that whole statement that might have had a sliver of truth to it is when I said I don't like living alone. I actually miss having Lucy and Levi around to talk to at the end of the day or watch a movie and eat pizza with. It's sort of depressing to finish an entire large pizza on your own.

Truth is, I don't even like being naked. I tried it last night after I went home because I thought I should make at least one attempt at nudism before Jessie moves in. I spent the whole night buck naked. I was just cold. I felt weird and don't really have a desire to do it again.

But the rest, the whole part about Jessie and wanting her—yeah, that wasn't true.

Once we get to my place, I help Cooper move the last few boxes inside but then make him carry them upstairs where the ladies are by himself, because I'm in a terrible mood now. I go hide away in my own room and take a shower just so I don't have to talk to anyone—especially not Jessie. No, I take that back—especially not Cooper. He gets a big head when he thinks he's right about something and then won't let up. I don't care to see his eyebrows wag at me all night.

I take the world's longest shower and then linger in my bedroom until I'm sure the coast is clear and Cooper and Lucy have finally left for the night. Finally, I open my door, peek out (this actually looks way more manly than how you're picturing it), and see that everything in the living room is quiet and still. I've never before been so thankful that my room is on the ground floor while all the spare rooms are upstairs. If I time this right, I'll probably never have to come in contact with Jessie for the rest of her time living here.

I tiptoe toward the kitchen (again, picture a warrior trying to outsmart his enemy in combat rather than the pathetic maneuver this really is). I quickly assemble a sandwich in the dark so Jessie's not alerted by the light and then carry it back to my room, never having loathed myself more than I do in this moment. Tomorrow will be better, though. After a good night's sleep, I'll feel more in charge and ready to face her.

I wake up in the morning feeling disturbed. I lie in bed for longer than necessary, remembering my dream in way too much fantastic detail. I remember how Jessie's lips felt pillowy soft against mine, how she tasted like a vanilla cupcake, warm, fresh out of the oven. I don't want to start the day; I want to fall back asleep and back into Jessie's arms.

It's fine. I'm fine.

But I'm not fine, at least not when I go out in the living room and stop short, blinking and staring at all the cutesy accessories spread out all over my house. I know for a fact I made it clear all of this shit had to stay in her room. I specifically told her if she wanted to bring every throw blanket she owned, *fine,* but she had to find a way to contain them upstairs in her room. Not here, draped across the back of my couch. So please explain to me how I'm running my fingers across a soft pastel pink blanket, squishing a frilly, fuzzy pillow between my hands, and reading a dish towel draped over the oven handle that says "Oh, for fork's sake" and has two forks kissing.

Ah, geez, there's more. It's everywhere. Like the flu during the winter, her stuff has mutated and multiplied all over my home. My clean countertops are cluttered. Drawers are stuffed, and my world is spinning. There's a set of salt-and-pepper shakers wearing BFF T-shirts. A fluffy rug is rolled out in the living room. (What kind of messed-up person puts a rug over carpet?!) Picture frames filled with Jessie and her grandaddy sit on my entertainment center. A froufrou ottoman has replaced my mid-century coffee table. Pillows—so many damn pillows lining the couch there's nowhere to sit anymore.

I spin. *Candles.*

I twist. *Succulents.*

I bend. *A woven basket containing* more *fuzzy pastel blankets.* How many does one woman need?!

There isn't an inch of my house that hasn't been touched—*vandalized.*

Anger scorches through me because once again, she found a way to slide under my skin. She's there, chiseling away at my bones with something sharp. I thought there was no way Jessie would be able to unpack all of this around my house because it's Sunday and I don't have to go in to work. I had the whole day blocked out so I could stand like a centurion and make sure she kept all her crap contained to her little ten-by-twelve cubicle upstairs. Once again—and for the last time—I underestimated this woman. From the looks of it, Jessie was up all night.

My hands are braced on the kitchen counter, shoulders bunched up to my ears, jaw working when I hear the soft padding of feet approaching behind me. *Jessie.*

"Morning, roomie." Her voice runs up my spine and knocks against every vertebra.

I release my palms from the counter and turn to face her—my opponent. My eyes collide with baby-blue sleep shorts and a matching tank top. With curves and tanned skin. With sleepy eyes and wild hair. With the most deadly of opponents: a gorgeous woman.

I'm not worried, though. It's just a little physical attraction. Just a man and a woman and all that. Nothing too serious to be concerned about. It would be one thing if I secretly enjoyed her feistiness or her constant need to push my buttons. But I don't. *Don't, don't, don't.*

"Looks like you were busy last night." I sound like a monster guarding his cave, even to my own ears.

She smirks at my obvious agitation, and now I'm even grumpier that I've let her see how well her plan worked. I should have wrapped myself in that pastel blanket. Worn her fuzzy house slippers. Poured coffee into her hot-pink "Boss Babe" mug and smiled as I sipped from it.

"I have terrible pregnancy insomnia these days. I can never sleep."

I resist the urge to go into doctor mode and list off several ways I could help her remedy that insomnia. Instead, I focus on the situation at hand. "Pretty sure I made it clear that all your stuff needed to stay in your room." I fold my arms. These are business arms.

Her eyes sparkle and gleam in false innocence. "Oh no! Do you not like my stuff being in your space? Oh dear, I'm so sorry. I'd be happy to go move it all, but . . ." She moves her hand to her small belly bump and rubs it affectionately. "I'm a little worn out from all my hard work last night. I think I better put my feet up and rest for a while because I'm starting to get some sharp pains." Her eyes widen into big doe eyes, and she blinks her long dark lashes slowly. "Unless . . . you want me to spend the day moving it allllllll the way back upstairs." Now she rubs her lower back like it's giving her great pain, like she's the size of a bus rather than looking like she swallowed a pebble.

I sink my teeth into my lower lip and bite until I nearly taste blood, because once again she has found a way to best me. *This woman.* She's going to be the death of me in so many ways.

"Don't worry about it." I turn around so I can say the next words without letting Jessie see how truly annoyed I am. "Go put your feet up." It's important to note that I only added that last part in case she's not faking those pains. The obstetrician in me cannot allow her to hurt herself in the name of a stupid prank war.

Besides, I've already figured out a way to get even, and the first step is to find that snowman mug for my morning coffee.

CHAPTER 8

Jessie

My phone is balanced between my ear and my shoulder, laundry basket perched against my hip. My eyes are glued to the TV, and I absolutely cannot believe Grandaddy is going to win this bet. *Again.*

"I told you he was going to send Brandy home this week." He's so smug when he's right. No humility with this one.

I blink at the screen, not willing to give up hope just yet. "No way! There's absolutely no way. They went to the beach of devotion together last week! And he showed her the childhood photo that sparked all the bullying he endured! No way would he send her home after that."

Grandaddy scoffs, and I know he's sitting in his brown-and-yellow-plaid recliner, feet up, decaf coffee in hand. This is our Sunday-night tradition: *Love Experiment,* laundry, and coffee. We make a bet at the beginning of the week on who will be sent home the following Sunday, and the loser has to buy the winner a pack of Oreo cookies. So far, I owe him three packs when I next see him.

"I have more chemistry with my mailman than Tray has with

Brandy. You should have seen the sparkle in old Bill's eyes when I gave him a poundcake at Christmas. Brandy should have made Tray a poundcake."

The producers are really dragging out this elimination. After this week, there are only two left until Tray will have to choose the love of his life—aka the woman he'll break up with a week after the show, but I don't care. No one does. We're here for the drama and the kissing.

A shadow swoops by in my peripheral. It's Drew carrying a laundry basket full of clothes toward the laundry room. Wait! No! I need to do laundry. I have work tomorrow and not a single pair of clean underwear. I'm not even exaggerating. I wear everything I own before I dare darken the doorway of the laundry room.

"HALT, YOU!" I yell, and Grandaddy acts dramatic about the decibel level of my voice.

Drew freezes in his black sweatpants and hoodie and turns to me. Our laundry baskets stick their tongues out at each other. Mine is a bright yellow. His, a drab gray. "What?"

"Are you going to do laundry right now?"

"No, I just like to carry my laundry around because it's fun," he says with a serious face.

I *will not* crack a smile. *Will not!*

"They're about to call it!" Grandaddy says in my ear. "It's about to rain Oreos."

"Shut it."

Drew lifts an obnoxious brow. "You're the one who asked."

"No, not you!" I peel my eyes from Drew because Grandaddy is chanting *Bye-bye, Brandy* and I need to see it for myself.

When I turn away, Drew disappears down the hallway. Ah, no! He's getting away. I need that washer! "Andrew, wait! I need the washing machine!"

"Ow. Quit yelling in my ear," Grandaddy harrumphs.

Drew calls out, "You snooze, you lose, Oscar."

I growl and bounce impatiently, mumbling under my breath how much I hate Drew.

"So, living together is going well?" Grandaddy asks, and I can see a knowing smile on his mouth through the phone.

"It's torture. I want to pinch him every second of the day."

"Now, see, that's exactly why Tray will send Brandy home. Neither one of them wants to pinch the other."

This again? He's determined to think there's something between me and Drew. And he's right, there is something: animosity.

"I don't think that's the way love works."

"Oh yes it is. If your granny was still alive, she'd tell you. If a partner doesn't make you want to blow steam out your nostrils, you better start kicking up a storm of something, or your passion is gonna shrivel up faster than a pickle on a sidewalk in summer."

I roll my eyes. *Senile old man. Doesn't know anything.* Drew and I don't have chemistry. I don't even think he's hot anymore. I made it official this morning with a cleaning ritual. I was going to light sage and wave it around the room, but I don't have any and don't even pretend to know where to get those little wands people use, so I just spritzed a liberal amount of my body spray around instead. Boom, cleansed.

The sound of water rushing in the laundry room pulls my attention away from the TV. That jerk is stealing the washer right out from underneath me, and this episode is taking ages to finish. One of the contestants started crying before Tray could even announce the woman that has to go home, so now he's having a sidebar with Blondie, trying to console her. It's so embarrassing. I love it.

And now I'm angry at Drew for making me miss it.

"*Ugh!* Grandaddy, text me who wins. I have an annoying roommate to murder."

I hang up quickly and throw my phone onto the couch. In the laundry room, I find Drew wearing a quiet smirk and dropping a scoop of detergent into the drum of the washer. "*Stop! I need that washer!*"

"Tough. I do too."

I set down my basket and cross my arms. "What's so important that you need washed?"

"None of your business."

I give a patronizing smile. "Aw, pooped your pants again? Don't worry, you'll grow out of it one of these days."

His dark-blue eyes slice over to me, and he squints a fake smile. "Run on back to your ice castle, Jessica. You can do laundry tomorrow."

"Oh, really? Tell that to my butt that's gonna have to go commando in the morning if you don't let me do laundry tonight!" I immediately regret saying that.

Drew's eyes drop to my lower half, and he smirks before turning back toward the machine. Now he's really not going to let me do laundry.

"Should have thought about that sooner. Last night while you were up redecorating my home would have been a perfect time."

I can't hide my grin. It *did* bother him. This is my punishment—forced commando. It was worth it. I knew Drew was particular about things, and mixing all my stuff in with his has upset his well-being. All day I've watched him walk from room to room and cringe. His color scheme before was gray, white, and black. Now it's an array of rainbow pastels, fuzzy materials, and a messy pile of shoes he has reorganized more than once already. I go behind him and scatter them out a little just to make his hair stand on end. Literally. I've learned that when Drew is stressed he rakes his hands straight back through his hair, making it all stick up at crazy angles. He forgets to smooth it back down half the time, but I refuse to find it adorable.

"That washer is huge—just let me put my clothes in with yours." I try to hip-check him out of the way, but he won't budge. He's a tree trunk with deep roots. I try to lift my laundry basket to dump it inside, but he outstretches his arm so it's anchoring my basket down. The top of his biceps presses against my chest, and my shoulder digs into his armpit. He smells good.

"No."

"Why?" I'm struggling.

"Because that's just not how it works. I wash my scrubs separate from everything else. All those bright pinks you have will bleed onto them." It doesn't surprise me at all that Drew is particular about his laundry.

We're body against body. I'd like to think we're both working hard to stand our ground against the other, but I know if I were to check the replay cameras, I would see myself red-faced with puffed-up cheeks trying to maneuver him out of the way, and he would be leisurely eating a sandwich or something.

"Not if we wash them on cold." My voice is a grunt, and it makes him chuckle deep in his chest.

His face angles down to me, lips tilting. "Are you even trying right now?"

I want to reach up and pluck every one of those beautiful eyelashes out of his lids. He doesn't deserve them. "No, because I don't want to injure you with my super strength."

"I'll live. Give me your best shot. Really put your back into it."

"I hate you."

"I have no idea how I'll sleep tonight." He uses one arm to keep me away from the washer and bends down to retrieve his scrubs, then tosses them inside. In the middle of that movement, the hem of his hoodie rises up three inches, revealing a sliver of taut, smooth, tanned skin, along with the waistband of his black Calvin Klein underwear. I don't realize until he shuts the lid to the washer that I've stopped fighting and am a useless pile of bones. My mouth is slightly open, and I think my tongue was hanging out. If just that tiny peek at what's living under Drew's clothes made me short-circuit so completely, I can't imagine what seeing the whole thing would do to me.

Wait. What? No. There will be no seeing Drew's body. *None. Don't even want to!* Bleh.

Thoroughly freaked out by that train of thought, I clear my throat and spin away, storming toward my room. Or the freezer, so I can dunk my head into the ice tray. Drew's chuckling lingers in the air behind me, and I decide to let him think he's won. Victory is always sweeter when your opponent underestimates you.

Ten minutes later, I hear the door to Drew's bedroom shut. Feeling confident that the ogre has retreated into his cave for the night, I walk on tiptoes all the way back down the stairs, yellow laundry basket in tow. I'm a dirty little sneak all the way into the laundry room, and when I open the lid of the washing machine, I smile down into the murky water, then dump all my undies inside to mingle with Drew's scrubs. I will not go commando tomorrow, and Drew will not win this match tonight.

Unfortunately, though, when I read my text message from my grandfather, I'm informed that *he* did win.

GRANDADDY: Four packages of Oreos. I win. Tray needs a
    pincher.

In the morning, I wait until I see Drew drive off in his car before I walk downstairs. I personally moved the laundry over from the washer to the dryer before bed because I didn't trust Drew to not let my undies sit and mildew. But when I open the dryer, it's empty. Drew's clothes are missing, and so are mine. Misplaced hope pushes into my heart and I think maybe he folded my laundry for me, or at least put them in the living room.

One thorough sweep of the house later, I realize I might never see those panties again. That freak hid my underwear! All of them! Is this life's way of punishing me for wearing every scrap of my clothing before washing them? Wonderful. Looks like I get to go underwear-less today.

Just before I leave the house for work, I get a text.

Sᴇxʏ Dʀᴇw: Be careful outside today, Commander. It's a little breezy.

Apparently, that asshole also stole my phone, unblocked his number, and gave himself a new contact name.

CHAPTER 9

Jessie

I'm a stewing, angry little panty-less troll all morning. My thoughts are nowhere but on all the ways I plan to exact revenge on Drew (in addition to the gem I already have planned for the fundraiser, of course). Over brunch, Lucy finally notices my intensity.

"What is it with you today?" She has a big bite of blueberry muffin in her mouth. "You look like you're constipated."

I am. I'm constipated with revenge. *Ew.* Yeah, that was a little gross. "Sorry."

"You're not going to tell me? Is something wrong?"

Other than the fact that these jeans are chafing my butt? No. For some odd reason, I don't want to tell Lucy what happened with Drew. It's irrational to want to keep it to myself. It was a rude prank he pulled; I should be overflowing with joy to slander that man further. Instead, it feels like it's a little secret between me and Drew. I'm holding on to it like a captured lightning bug in a jar. In the dark I'll watch it flicker, and I'll smile.

I should tell Lucy . . .

"Just tired. Still not sleeping well." I avoid looking at her because I'm afraid she'll see that I'm still holding back half the truth.

The bell over the door chimes at the coffee shop—our favorite place to go for a midmorning coffee break when our schedules magically align, and we both have an hour off at the same time. Lucy looks over my shoulder. A smile lights her face, and in my opinion it doesn't match the words that come out of her mouth.

"Look, Drew just walked in!"

My heart kicks into overdrive. "*What!*" Irrationally, I drop my sunglasses from my head to my nose, grab for a dinky paper menu, and hold it up to my face. "Do you have a floppy hat?!"

"You know I don't."

"But you're a mom."

"You say that like it's an explanation for why I'd have a floppy hat hidden on my person."

I peek wide eyes at her over the menu. "Why do you carry around an enormous purse if not to be prepared for everything? Never mind. Has he seen us? Don't draw attention."

She waves her hand over her head. An astronaut in space sees her because her movements are so exaggerated and waves back. "Drew! Over here!"

"You're not getting anything for Christmas this year."

She sticks her tongue out at me playfully. I make a distorted ugly expression. When I feel a big shadow loom over me, I haul the menu back up to my face and unfold it like a newspaper until my nose practically touches the ink. I feel Drew's voice rather than hear it.

"Hey, Luce. Who's your mysterious friend?" He says it with a hint of amusement. He knows it's me. I should just put down the menu, but I don't. I want to hide from him, and I'm not entirely sure why.

Actually, I am. It's that damn sliver of skin I saw. It did something to my brain—altered me like a computer virus. This morning I noticed that Drew built a little shelf above his bedroom door and placed my Frosty the Snowman mug on it like a trophy. Who does something like that?! *Me. I would, and frankly, I'm annoyed I don't get to.* Point is, he's still the same old annoying, gloating, selfish Drew he's always been . . . but I don't know. Before, I could think of him as a robot. A spawn of the devil. Now I know for a *fact* he has flesh. Gorgeous man flesh.

"I don't know. Who am I at lunch with?" Lucy asks, knowing better than to invent a story on her own.

"Nobody. No one is here, go about your day."

Below the menu, I can see Drew plant his hand on the top of the table. Above me, his shadow grows. And then his finger peeks over the edge of the menu and he pulls it down, revealing his stoic face and jet-black scrubs. No smiles for miles. Good. I don't want to see his hideous dimples.

When the menu is down, he sees my sunglasses and lifts an eyebrow. He wants to smile but holds back. The feeling is mutual. His hand rises again and peels the sunglasses off my face. I wish more than anything I could be a sunglasses nesting doll. How great would it have been if there were a smaller pair of sunglasses under these, and then a pair of goggles under those, and then tiny little 1800s spectacles under all of them?

Without the protection of my eyewear, I'm left vulnerable to attack from Drew's deep, dark, angry blue eyes. What does he have to be angry about?

"I have lavender scrubs at home now." His voice is so low, anyone around me might think he's talking sexy to me. I know otherwise.

I press my lips together and try to stifle a laugh. "Good for you—not conforming to gender color stereotypes."

Lucy is completely lost, her eyes bouncing back and forth between Drew and me. "I don't get it."

He smirks and keeps his eyes on me. "When someone mixes hot pink with light blue, the result is lavender."

I hold Drew's gaze and have to suck my cheeks in to keep from laughing. There's no way his scrubs are as bad as he says. I've washed those undies a dozen times already—the color wouldn't have run so potently. He's being dramatic as always.

Lucy's phone rings, and she answers it hesitantly, like she's afraid to leave Drew and me unchaperoned for any length of time for fear that we'll murder each other in cold blood right in the middle of this coffee shop. His eyes get darker, and I think maybe we will.

"Hi, Mom . . ." we hear Lucy say as she trails off toward the door.

Drew's eyes squint a little. I squint back a little more dramatically. The edge of his mouth twitches. Suddenly, it's getting warmer in here, and I realize it's because Drew is still hovering over me, soaking up all the refreshing breeze I would normally be able to feel.

I lean back in my chair a smidge and wave my hand in a sharp, annoyed movement. "Okay, back up. Enough with the looming. Are your scrubs really lavender?"

He rises to his full height, and now I feel like an ant down here. He nods an affirmative to my question.

"How? When you wash colors on cold—"

"I wash my scrubs on hot."

Oh. Well, that would do it.

"Guys, I'm so sorry, that was Mom, and apparently Levi just started throwing up with some sort of stomach bug!" Lucy reappears at the table and starts shoveling her keys, sunglasses, and wallet into her purse. "I think Molly had a cancelation today, so I'm going to call her and see if she can cover for me with my two-o'clock appointment." She wraps up her muffin and shoves it into her purse too. "I'm so sorry to cut our brunch short, Jessie, but I've got to get to Levi and relieve my mom." She rushes around the table and is almost to the door when she realizes something important. "*Oh shoot!* I drove you here, and the salon is in the opposite direction of my mom's house."

"It's okay, you go ahead. I'll call an Uber to take me back."

Lucy gives me a guilty look.

"Go! Levi is waiting on you. Tell him Aunt Jessie is going to drop off a present for him later to make him feel better."

Lucy still doesn't move. She jingles the keys in her hands and shifts on her feet, debating whether she should really leave me or not.

"I'll take you." Drew's words pierce through me, and my eyes collide with his.

Me? Ride in a car with Drew? No. I don't even fully know why I'm so opposed, but . . . just no.

Lucy looks so relieved, and not at all as if she's going to hurl like I am. "Thank you! You're the best, as always!" She rushes up and kisses his cheek, then mine. "See you guys later." *Wonderful, now we both get stomach bugs too.*

The door chimes with Lucy's exit, and Drew smirks for reasons that scare me a little. Maybe he plans on taking me to the lake and dumping me in. "I'm going to order a coffee," he says, his back already turned to me.

"And drink it somewhere else!" I say. "By the way, I'm not riding with you! You're dreaming if you think I'd ever put my life in your hands behind the wheel of a car!" The whole coffee shop turns to look at me. The barista's eyes say, *I will kick you out of here, lady.* Drew's backside gloats.

I get in Drew's Jeep—which is surprisingly old and not flashy—and he locks the doors. Most vehicles do that automatically when you put them in drive, so I don't know why he needed to do it as soon as I got inside, other than to freak me out. Which it doesn't.

What freaks me out is how much this Jeep smells like him. It's a 1990s Wrangler with a soft top and years of memories packed inside. His scent is so ingrained in the upholstery I feel like he's wrapping his arms around me. On the dashboard, someone carved *Val hearts Drew,* and I want to run my fingers across it. How long has he had this? How many girlfriends has he driven around in it? So many questions are buzzing around my head, but I can't ask any of them because we don't have that type of relationship. If only rideshares weren't so expensive, I could be sitting happily in the back seat of a stranger's car, not wondering who Val is or how long ago she loved Drew.

He puts the Jeep in drive and away we go. It's silent. No music. I can, however, hear my heart beating.

"So . . ." His big hands close around the steering wheel.

"Nope." I look sharply out the window. "Not talking."

"Your maturity never ceases to amaze me."

I roll my eyes at my reflection. Man, it does look immature.

"Are you having a good morning?" The sincerity in his tone shocks me enough to turn and look at him. Drew and I have never, not once, had a normal, non-fighting conversation. And when I look at him, I see a smirk grow and his eyes bounce down to my lower half and back up, telling me that wasn't a sincere question at all. "Anything of interest happen so far today?"

"Well, some freak stole all my underwear and is hoarding it in private like a dirty little weirdo . . . so yeah, I guess that was interesting."

He smiles, gaze fixed on the road. "Dirty little weirdo indeed. What a strange thing to do."

I glare at his mouth. "Where are they?"

He shrugs. "How should I know?"

I poke him in the ribs to teach him a lesson and immediately wish I hadn't, because 1) I've now not only seen evidence that he is warm flesh and blood, I've felt it, and 2) we've had a strict *no intentional touching* rule, and for some reason I just broke it. My action shoots like a flare gun into the air, announcing this new breach of contract.

"Give them back. You don't want to wage war with me, *Dr. Stuck-up.*"

He immediately takes advantage of the broken rule and presses his finger under my armpit. It's so annoying being forced to laugh when you want to scowl. "I thought our war was already being waged?"

"You've seen nothing yet," I say, my voice dripping with warning like a woman who has a dagger strapped to her thigh. I'm dangerous, and he should be terrified to mess with me.

"You have a coffee spill on the front of your shirt."

I gasp and look down. "Nuh-uh. I don't see one."

"It's on the underside of your belly."

Oh great! Just great. My cheeks flame red as I try to crane my neck over to see the part of my belly I know I'll never catch a glimpse of without a mirror. I feel like a clumsy toddler. "Just . . . keep your eyes on the road from now on!" *Super comeback.*

Drew chuckles, but I sit back angrily and cross my arms. There's a minute of painful silence before he speaks. "Why do you hate me so much?"

My heart skips, but I try to keep my face impassive so he doesn't notice. "Umm, I don't know, maybe it has something to do with you standing me up when my grandaddy came to visit."

He shakes his head, his brown locks a little more unruly today than normal. "*Before* the day I accidentally overslept." I don't answer right away, so he glances at me and then looks back at the road, his hand tightening around the wheel, making his forearm flex. "You hated me before that."

My mouth starts drying up. This isn't a conversation I want to have with him. He's tiptoeing toward the truth that I don't want to acknowledge—not to myself and definitely not to him. I did hate him before I met him. I hated him before I knew a single thing about him. "Lucy. You were a jerk to her, remember?"

He makes an unimpressed humming sound and cocks his head to the side, eyes squinting in thought. "Even that first time you showed up at my house, you acted like you'd hated me for a hundred years before that, and we'd never met. So what was it?"

That is the million-dollar question.

"What can I say? You're just hate-able right from the start." My words were meant to be cutting, but they came out oddly weak. Drew doesn't look wounded like I hoped. He looks . . . intrigued. Curious. He's not buying my insta-hate story. He's a journalist who just got a lead on his next scoop. The look in his eyes when his gaze flashes to me is terrifying, so I hurry to change the subject before he can push any further toward the truth. "Aren't you supposed to be doctoring people right now?"

"I was at the clinic, but I have to go into the hospital for a little while today. Just stopped for a coffee—and apparently a hostile pregnant woman—on the way." He shows the first signs of a smile, so I look away. I need to get out of this Drew-infused vehicle. It's making my brain mushy.

We pull up in front of my salon and park. Drew then swivels his big torso so his back leans in the corner between the door and the seat. He surveys me, eyes scanning like lasers, trying to comb through my thoughts.

Needing something to do other than let Drew see me sweat, I flip down the visor and open the flap, revealing the cosmetic mirror, and look for the stain on my T-shirt. There's another little love note to Drew scribbled in Sharpie. *Beth & Drew forever.* I frown. "How long have you had this Jeep?"

"Since I was sixteen."

"I would think since you're a big-time doctor now you'd be excited to get a sports car or something, trade up like the rest of them do."

He shrugs. "I can't bring myself to get rid of it. Too many good memories, I guess."

Oh no. Drew is sentimental? That's exactly the sort of thing I didn't want to know about him. I would like to take that information and bury it at the bottom of the ocean where I can never find it again. Drew is a monster with a cold heart—not a man who chooses a ratty old Jeep full of memories over a hot new sports car.

Staring at him now in this tight space surrounded by his scent and adolescent memories leaves me feeling sort of breathless. The stain—*right*! Focus on finding the stain, Jessie. I still can't quite see anything in the mirror, though, unless I lift my butt off the seat and angle my belly toward the mirror, which I will literally die before doing in front of Drew. I give up with a grunt and slap the visor mirror closed again.

"Want me to show you where it is?"

"No," I snap. "I don't need your help, thank you very much."

"It's not a big deal. It's just a tiny stain right—"

I slap his hand away from where it was inching toward my belly bump. "I said no! Stick to your own side and stop trying to feel me up."

He scoffs, annoyed, and shakes his head. "Right. You wish."

"Never! Not even in my dreams." Why did I have to mention that last part? It's almost like I'm admitting I dreamed about him last night. It was not a polite dream either. I saw more than just that tantalizing sliver of his skin, and I think that's why I'm so riled up by him today. I'm not supposed to be dreaming about Drew! Or anyone. I'm on my own, and that's just how I want it for now. No more men until I complete at least ten years of therapy to undo the damage left by the others.

"You sure about that? You're telling me you've never even had one tiny dr—"

"Well, Dr. Andy," I say, firmly cutting him off. "It's been torture as always. Thanks for the ride I didn't want." Wow, I'm so mean I can barely even tolerate it myself. I reach for the door handle, but Drew grabs my wrist.

We both look down at where his hand circles it, and he lets go.

"Hang on." He opens up the glove box, pulls out a Tide to Go pen, and tosses it into my lap. "The coffee stain is about three inches below your navel."

"Don't talk about my navel," I say, then I glare down at the pen like it's a grenade. "I can't believe you just had this on hand."

"Never hurts to be prepared."

"Of course." For some reason, it does not surprise me in the least that Drew has a stain-remover pen in his Jeep. He's probably got a change of clothes in that glove box too, and a protein bar in case of emergencies.

I hate that I have to accept his offering, but I will because I don't want to face a whole salon of women today with a coffee stain down the front of my shirt. I tuck the pen into my purse, then unlock the door and start scooting out. I look like an Oompa Loompa rising from a candy binge.

When I'm out, Drew rolls down the window and calls out to me. "By the way, you shouldn't be drinking too much coffee. Caffeine isn't good for the baby." He's smiling like the devil as he backs out of the space and starts driving off. He just *had* to get in one last hit before he left.

I fist my hands at my sides and yell, "I WANT MY UNDER-

WEAR BACK, YOU PERV!" A woman in the parking lot tosses me an angry glance, then finishes escorting her elderly mother into their car. *Oops.*

When I get home that night after work, Drew is locked away inside his room (coward), but there's a pile of my panties in front of my bedroom door with a note on the top that reads, *Some dirty weirdo dropped these off earlier. He said not to invade his laundry loads with your underwear anymore.*

CHAPTER 10

Jessie

It's a slow Tuesday morning, and it's only Lucy and me in the salon. Levi's tummy troubles yesterday ended up just being a case of too much sugar at Grammy's house, so Lucy is back at work today. I'm not due to have another client for twenty minutes, which gives me a chance to pull my planner out of my purse and hunker down behind the reception desk. I don't know why I feel the need to hide when I do this, but I do. I have a planner I bought solely for this purpose, and every day I pull it out and place a solid X through the calendar box with my aqua-colored gel pen, telling me I've made it one day closer to my due date. Leaning my elbow against the counter, I prop my hand under my chin and smile as I trace my finger along the freshly inked square.

One day closer.

"Whatcha got there?" Lucy materializes out of nowhere to peer over my shoulder like a snoopy mom trying to catch me getting up to no good.

I screech and slap my planner closed. "Nothing!" Anger is the first emotion I rush to when I'm embarrassed, which would explain why my eyes are blazing and my tone is clipped.

Lucy blinks and backs up, hands raised. "Wow, okay. So sorry. I didn't realize I would be stepping into something, but clearly I am." Trying to be angry at Lucy is like being angry at a bunny for having too fluffy of a tail. It's impossible. I just want to feed her carrots and make her happy.

I sigh and my shoulders drop, and I remove my hand from its protective clutch around the planner. I extend it to Lucy because I'm really trying to get better at trusting someone other than only my grandaddy. "No, I'm sorry. I snapped because I'm embarrassed."

"About what?" She carefully takes the planner from my fingers and thumbs through it. "What am I looking at here? It's just a planner. I thought you were peeking at something dirty."

I laugh. "It's my due date countdown, weirdo."

Lucy's eyebrows scrunch together. "Why would you be embarrassed about that? I have your due date set up as a countdown on my phone. It's going to shoot off virtual confetti on the big day."

"You do?" I ask with an incredulous smile. Why would she do that? Why would she care that much?

Lucy smiles, and the last of my embarrassment slips away. She's seriously the most disarming person I've ever met. They should find a way to clone her for military de-escalation purposes.

"Of course! You're my best friend. My sister from another mister. My *ma'am*." (Which I know is the highest of compliments since it's her and her mom's nickname for each other.) She pats my belly, knowing she's one of the few in the world who can without getting her arm whacked off. "I can't wait until this little dumpling gets here. So why in the world are you embarrassed of this?" She holds up the offending sparkly planner.

It's silly, I know. It's my child. I *should* be excited that he or she will be entering the world soon. But because of the way this all came about—because I can remember the way my ex's face looked when I broke the news to him—I also feel immense guilt. I feel like I have no right to be excited about the baby because he blamed me so harshly for "tricking him" into becoming a dad. And then I think of the emotional train wreck that is the life I will be bringing my child into, and I can't help but feel this baby deserves so much better than what I have to offer.

I feel like I'm doing something wrong by anticipating my baby's birth.

Of course, I don't tell Lucy any of this, because just the thought of it makes me break out in vulnerability hives. Instead, I point to the planner. "All the glitter. It's an embarrassing planner is all. Not very grown-up."

She laughs and shakes her head, easily buying the lie. "Hardly something to be embarrassed of. I like the glitter!" She playfully bops me on the head with it before tossing it back on the desk in front of me. "Own your happy pleasures. And now that I know yours is glitter, prepare for everything I buy you from now on to be glitterized."

Oh good. I know she's serious too. Is this how everyone's weird collections begin? One tiny lie, and before you know it your whole house is decked out in baby elephant decor. Looks like I get to be *glitter girl.*

The door chimes, and Lucy and I both look up to see the delivery man enter with his dolly and my monthly order of hair product inventory stacked high on it. I gladly show him to the storage room, seizing the chance to escape Lucy and our unwanted conversation.

The rest of the day moves pretty slowly yet peacefully. A happy little snail day. Lucy and I have a handful of clients and a few walk-ins but nothing too strenuous. I'm happy and comfortable in the salon, and it's only when the clock starts to near that five o'clock mark that anxiety kicks in again. Because today I won't be heading home to my house; I'll be going back to Drew's house—aka the torture house. And yes, I realize that would make a fantastic haunted house name.

I'm sitting in my empty salon chair, leaned back, legs crossed, watching Lucy finish up the perm she's been placing in her client's hair, but I'm not *seeing* any of it. Instead, I'm picturing that sliver of Drew's skin again. Always. Like when you stare at the sun too long and it burns an image in your eyes. All I see is tan. No, golden. No—*bronze.*

"Has Drew always been so persnickety?" I ask Lucy.

She glances over at me, amused by my sudden blurt-out. "Yes. But in his defense, it works for him."

"How do you figure?"

She shrugs slightly and continues rolling rods in her client's hair. "Drew is one of a kind. He's focused, he knows what he wants at all times, and that's why he's always been the reliable one . . . the guy you turn to when everything falls apart, and somehow he can hold it all together. It's his decisiveness, his attention to detail, his drive . . . all of those aspects are what have gotten him to where he is today in his life and career. It works for him."

"Well, it just annoys me." Lucy and her client both sputter a laugh. "I'm serious. It's that decisiveness that makes him think he rules the world. He needs to be knocked down a few pegs."

Lucy *mm-hmms,* unconvinced. "It's only a matter of time before you drink the Kool-Aid with the rest of us. Drew might be overbearing at times—trying to fix things when he should be quiet and making sure everything is sitting at a ninety-degree angle on any given surface—but . . . he's also got the most golden heart in the world. He's lovable."

Suddenly, Lucy's client pops her head around to look at us with bright eyes. "You've sold me. Any chance he's into old ladies?"

I push myself up out of the chair, rolling my eyes dramatically as I pass by Lucy's station, headed for the front desk. "Believe me, you don't want him, Mrs. Ellis. He's the most obnoxious man in the world. Smug. Bossy. Opinionated. Likes to gloat. And . . ." His dimpled smile flashes in my mind, quickly followed by that sliver of skin. Why is it bothering me so much that I can't quite accurately describe the color?

My grandaddy would probably say it's like the top side of a biscuit, brushed with butter and fresh out of the oven, but never mind. I need to stop thinking about Drew because it's getting me too heated—and not the good kind of heated. The angry, want to cut off the hot water while he's in the shower, blast the AC, and then run off with his towel and clothes kind. And just for the record, I'm not thinking of him in the shower in a good way either. Like I wouldn't open the curtain or anything before I stole the towel. I would just snatch it and run off. But then again . . . what if he has one of those fancy showers that is all open and doesn't have a door? Then I'd definitely see him naked.

Shoot, what was my point again?

"Wow, are you okay? You just sort of trailed off in the middle of talking and zoned out. Now your face is super flushed." Lucy is the most concerned person in the world right now as she tells Mrs. Ellis she'll be right back, then crosses over to my station so she can feel my cheeks and head. "Do you have a fever? I think you do."

I swat her hands away. "No, I do not have a fever! I feel fine. Quit being such a mom." *I was just thinking about your brother naked in the shower.*

Lucy does not look convinced, and now Mrs. Ellis is concerned too. "I don't know, sweetie. I think Lucy might be right. Your face looks like my first-place-winning tomatoes from the fair last year."

I feel like she's more interested in plugging her winning vegetation than my health.

And of course now that they're bringing attention to my face, it's heating up even more. I'm a furnace. Combustible. "I'm fine, ladies. Really."

Lucy is peering at me like I might suddenly keel over. "You're headed home now, right?"

"Yeah, as soon as I finish cleaning up my station."

Lucy rips my purse from the hanger next to me and drapes it over my shoulder before pushing me toward the door. "Don't worry about it. I'll clean it and lock everything up when I'm done with Mrs. Ellis. Your face looks alarmingly flushed. I'm going to text Drew and have him check your blood pressure when you get home." She looks over her shoulder and naturally has to fill in her new BFF. "My brother is an ob-gyn and also Jessie's roommate."

I mash the brakes. "*No!* Oh my gosh, Lucy, I'm fine. Don't you dare text Drew!" I can barely manage to stay five feet away from him without coming unglued. Imagine if he were right next to me . . . checking my heart rate with his fingers on my neck or wrist . . . *nope.* Just nope.

Her eyes go round. "Geez, look at those cheeks. I could fry bacon on them. Mrs. Ellis, do they look like they're getting worse to you?"

"Oh, honey, yes. Go home and let that doctor check you out." *Not the most ideal choice of words, Mrs. Ellis.*

"Okay, that's it, I'm leaving because you two hens are fussing over me way too much. And Lucy"—I look over my shoulder as I head out the door—"do not text Drew or you will be dead to me."

Traffic was exceptionally brutal today, which is only adding to my agitation. As I step out of my car and storm my way into the house,

I do start to worry about my blood pressure a little. I don't know why I'm so worked up. It was one tiny little glimpse of Drew's abdomen a few days ago, and suddenly I can't get it—or him—out of my head. He's so obnoxious. And prickly. And unthoughtful. *Yeah, that's good, Jessie. Focus on all of that.*

Bottom line, I enter that house looking for a fight. I'm feeling strongly attracted to Drew, and I need to squash that desire. At least it's just physical. All I need is one good argument with the man to remember each of the reasons I want to handcuff him and send him off on a boat to the Bermuda Triangle.

I storm inside the house, throw my purse on the couch all willy-nilly, not even worrying that half the contents have fallen out (extra points because that will annoy the snot out of Drew), and then I stop dead in my tracks. Everything looks clean. Gray, white, and black. Where's all the color? *Where is all my stuff?*

I'm going to kill him.

"Andy? Are you here?" I peek my head around corners like I'm afraid he's going to jump out with a boogeyman mask on. Actually, I file that idea away for a rainy day. "WHAT DID YOU DO WITH ALL MY STUFF?" I yell out. When he doesn't respond, I'm convinced he's not here. My fight will have to wait—but I swear, if he packed up all my things and gave them away, I'm going to ruin him.

I stomp my way up the stairs, taking out all my aggression on the carpet and really letting my feet drive my frustration home. When I make it to the top of the steps, I'm out of breath and exhausted. I just need a little predinner nap and then I'll be ready to—

What the hell? Why won't my bedroom door open? It's unlocked and I'm able to turn the handle, but it's like there's something on the other side pushing against the door.

I lean my shoulder into it, and finally it gives way . . .

. . . to my bedroom, stuffed to the brim with all my boxes.

My jaw drops and my blood boils to the surface of my skin and out through my pores as I take in the room, packed completely full of boxes I can only assume contain all the stuff I unpacked over the weekend. They are stacked one on top of the other and lined all around my room, covering my bed and any usable surface. I don't even bother going inside because Drew has made sure to stack them in such a way that I can't even walk around if I want to. Definitely can't get to my bed. Definitely going to wrap my hands around his neck and squeeze.

What was he thinking! I know I sort of started this little prank war, but seriously, Drew?! I'm pregnant! I'm like really, *really* pregnant! I need a place to lie down and rest. Growing a human here, no big deal.

The sound of a door slamming downstairs makes my head tic toward the stairs like an angry killer robot—target set and ready for brutal combat. With newfound energy, I stomp my way down the steps just like I did on the way up, except now I'm rewarded with knowing Drew gets to hear it. I sound like a herd of elephants.

"ANDREW MARSHALL!" I yell down the stairs as I descend to battle.

"Jessica, get down here!" he bellows back.

Just as I make it to the bottom of the stairs, he steps into view (wearing lavender scrubs that I have to try very hard not to laugh at). His face is cut into stern lines and his pupils are two punctuation marks at the end of a sentence that reads, *Not even if you were the last woman alive.* The way he looks only fuels my volcanic anger. I'm certain I look nothing like his suave, stoic tyranny. My cheeks feel like I could lay them onto a shirt and iron out all the wrinkles. My eyes are bugging out. I'm a rabid dog you really don't want to get stuck in an alley with.

"Come sit down."

"*No.* You moved all my—" He takes my arm and pulls me along with him to the living room. "*Ow!* Let go—you're hurting me!"

"I've held newborn babies tighter than I'm holding you." It's true. His touch is gentle as a breeze, but I refuse to dwell on it.

"It's your scales—they chafe my angelic skin." I can only see the back of his head, and I'm frustrated by it. I want to see if my quip earned a grin or not.

He doesn't let go until we make it to the living room, where he plops me down in an armchair.

"You can't put me in timeout. I'm too old for it. I'll just get up."

Drew drops down to one knee beside me, the square lines of his jaw still cut into sharp, serious angles like he's completely ignoring me. He's a member of the Queen's Guard, and he won't pay attention to me even if I snap my fingers in front of his face. Even if I stick my tongue out and dance around shaking my butt. He's focused on my face, my neck, my fingers . . . why is he holding up my fingers? Why is he pressing on them like that? Why are his calloused hands so pleasant to be touched by? I figured Drew's hands would feel soft and buttery from how often he has to wear gloves, but they're not. Maybe he gets these calluses from the gym? I know he goes every morning before work, because that's what he's done the last two mornings.

I'm mesmerized now. I don't know what he's doing, but whatever it is, he's so intense about it. I don't think my face has ever been this close to Drew's before. Our moment in the kitchen when we were fighting over Frosty the Snowman was the closest, but this is so much closer. I can see where each of his eyelashes connects with his lid, where his smile lines would appear, and the flecks of black floating in his deep blue irises.

I'm completely silent as Drew takes my arm, his hands tenderly moving across my skin as he adjusts my arm to lay it across the side of the chair. I'm convinced Drew could have a full beard if he wanted, because every day around this time he looks like he could use a shave. Like if I ran my hand over his jaw right now it would scratch me.

Now Drew is dipping into a bag beside the chair and pulling something out. Wait, not just something . . . a blood pressure cuff!

Lucy and I are so over.

I blink several times to resist the hypnotic trance he's lulled me into. "You have got to be kidding me. I don't need my damn blood pressure taken." I try to fight it by pulling my arm back, but Drew's warm hand lies firmly over my arm. *Don't move.* His jaw tics, and he looks almost angry. What does he have to be angry about?

"Stop squirming. Lucy told me about how flushed and disoriented you were at the salon. She's worried about you." His eyes scan over me again, and he touches the back of his hand to my cheek. "And she's not wrong. Your face is abnormally flushed."

Oh good gracious. This is not happening. Every look, every touch, every scan of his dark eyes is making my problem worse. I need to get away from him. Now.

I slap his hand away. "Yeah, of course my face is flushed. My awful roommate packed up all my stuff and piled it in my room. I can't even lie down on my bed! Don't you think that's a good enough reason to get worked up?" He grimaces slightly, like maybe he's a little embarrassed. *Good.* "When did you even have time to do that?! I thought you were at work all day."

"I might have . . . come home during my lunch hour and packed your stuff."

"And moved all those boxes in such a short amount of time?" I narrow my eyes. I want him to have to say it out loud.

He scrunches his nose a little. "And hired a moving company to come in and move them upstairs when I went back to work." I stare at him, wishing on every star that when I blink, he will go *poof* and disappear. I blink three times and he is, unfortunately, still there each time.

"Just where was that generosity on Saturday when you were busy complaining about the precious time you were sacrificing to help me move?"

"In hindsight, it was childish to have all your stuff moved back to your room. I'm sorry, I was just trying to get back at you. But right now I'm a doctor, not a roommate, and I'd really like for you to let me check your blood pressure because"—this next part looks like it pains him deeply to say—"I'm genuinely concerned about you."

I fold my arms, ripping the cord and squishy ball of the blood pressure cuff out of his hand. "No chance. You're not *my* doctor, and I'm not concerned enough to go get it checked out, because I know the real reason I'm flushed."

I realize my mistake as soon as Drew's brow rises. "What is the real reason, then? Lucy said it started right before you left the salon, so I know it wasn't the boxes."

I squint. "Well, aren't you just Nancy Drew. Do you get paid extra for these mystery-solving skills or is it included in your fee?"

Drew's eyes shut tight and he tilts his head up toward heaven, pressing the heels of his hands to his eyes. He can't handle me. I'm too much. I think he'd like to yell right now, but he's holding it in because of my possible high blood pressure. Now he's scraping his hands back through his hair, making it all stand on end but not fixing it. It's actually a really sexy sight, especially the way his biceps flex against the sleeves of his scrubs. All I want to do is lean forward and run my fingers through those unruly dark locks and put them back in place.

And the flush is getting worse. Super.

"Jessie. I swear . . ." He trails off, and I'd really like him to finish that sentence, but he doesn't. It's left as a warning. "Let me check your blood pressure. It's important."

It's now clear that the only way I'm going to get off the hook and avoid an assessment is to tell Drew the truth. *You're so freaking hot sometimes I can't stand it.* I'll die before I admit that to him, so instead I growl and extend my arm.

"Fine. Take my blood pressure. But when you see that it's perfectly normal, you owe me a cookies n' cream milkshake."

He releases a sigh, then gets to work squishing the little ball thing. I stare at him as the cuff on my arm tightens, but instead I feel it in my chest. It constricts with every methodical blink of his dark lashes.

"Close your eyes and take deep breaths." His voice rumbles in a way that makes my insides tingle. But I can't close my eyes, because I know what I'll see: *Tan. Golden. Bronze.*

"Nurses never tell me to close my eyes. I think I'll keep them open."

His eyes shift from the cuff and peek up at me. "Because you like staring at me?"

"Because I'm afraid you'll run off with my purse."

He drops his eyes again, but there's a tug at the side of his mouth. I try to regulate my breathing and find some sort of Zen when the cuff is at its tightest because my blood pressure *has* to be normal or else Drew will never let me live it down. I shut my eyes only to make sure I win. A small tickle at the base of my wrist triggers my senses, and I peek one eye open. Drew's thumb moves two centimeters back and forth against my skin like he doesn't realize he's doing it.

I frown, and the cuff releases. The harsh sound of Velcro ripping splits the silence. "Well, doctor, will I live?"

Some of the rigidity of his features softens, and his lashes rise so his gaze meets mine. He drops the blood pressure cuff into the bag, then leans forward so his forearm rests on his knee. He grins lightly. "Your blood pressure is good, but I'm concerned about your ego overdose."

The self-control I harness to keep myself from sticking my tongue out at him is beyond impressive. He knows though; he can see my thoughts. He holds that grin and shakes his head a little.

"Excuse me for worrying about you."

Wait, huh?

"You were *not* genuinely worried about me."

"I wasn't?"

"No." That absolutely can't be it. I won't allow it. "You were only worried that Lucy would kill you if something happened to me under your watch."

He shrugs and fiddles with the zipper of his medical bag. "Hmm, I don't think that's it."

"Yes, it is," I say, my tone almost coaxing. Like I'm swinging a pocket watch on a chain in front of his eyes. *You will believe me.* "We're mortal enemies."

He looks up at me with an unreadable expression painted across his sharp features. His mouth opens like he's going to say something, but then he closes it and stands instead. He stares down at me, narrowing his blue eyes a fraction before turning around and heading for the front door.

"Where are you going?" I say to his back.

"To get your milkshake. Rest on the couch while I'm gone. I'll move your boxes out of your room when I get back." And with that, he shuts the front door behind him and leaves.

I blink several times, feeling that flush creep back up again.

CHAPTER 11

Drew

Jessie is passed out asleep on the couch when I get back with her milkshake. I cross the room and quietly set the ice cream down on the coffee table in front of her, then sink into the armchair. I let my head fall back against the cushion and slide my hands down my face, finally letting myself unwind for the first time today.

Work was exhausting. It is every day, but today was particularly hard. I had to break awful news to one of my patients, and she wept in my office. I let her have as much time as she needed in there because it's really hard not being able to console my patients. Being a male in this profession, I don't offer physical comfort in any way. Not sure if it's the norm or not, but it's a protective boundary I've drawn for myself and my patients. I offer comforting words, maybe squeeze their hand, but then I step out and let one of my nurses do the real consoling.

And because of what happened at work today, my heart is tender and a little broken. When Lucy texted me worried about Jessie, I lost it. I floored it home. All I could think about was worst-case scenarios. She's in her third trimester, so a sudden spike in blood pressure could mean preeclampsia, and although facial flushing is not normally a sign of high blood pressure, it can be. For some reason, I wasn't willing to risk that uncertainty. I needed to know for sure that it wasn't a spike, and the way I felt when I confirmed that her blood pressure was normal can only be described as immense relief.

But here's the thing that's tripping me up: I never lose my cool under pressure. In the office, if a nurse suspects preeclampsia or any other life-threatening disease, I never show it on my face. I follow the procedures in my head that get me from point A to point B until we figure out what's going on. *But, damn* . . . The way I felt when I thought Jessie was in trouble—it was ridiculous. Absurd. Embarrassing. Definitely not professional. It was something I felt deep in my gut, or chest, or . . . I don't know. I'm not really willing to dive into where the emotion came from yet. I'm just relieved she's okay.

I hear Jessie take in a deep breath like she's stirring from sleep. I sit up and find her green eyes squinting at me. She has a pillow mark slashed across her cheek that makes me smile.

"I must have fallen asleep," she says, pushing up on her elbow, then swinging her legs around so she can sit up. I watch—a little too closely—as she removes the messy bun from the top of her head and lets her hair fall to her shoulders. It's kind of crinkly and wavy and wild, and I really like it like this. She stretches her back before gathering her hair again to retie it up into a neater bun. I have to bite my tongue against asking her to leave it down.

Her eyes fall to the Styrofoam cup and she looks up at me with something like gratitude. "You really did get a milkshake for me?" She says it like I'm a freaking hero. Like I just lifted a house off of her trapped body.

"Yeah. I told you I was going to."

She picks it up and takes a tentative sip. "Yes, but I didn't think you actually would. I expected you to come back with a bag of broccoli or something."

Man, I should have done that.

"Not tonight."

We fall into silence for a few moments while Jessie drinks her milkshake. Finally, she looks up, giving me a quizzical smile. "This is kind of weird."

"What is?"

"You." She nods toward me. "You're being nice to me, and I feel like it's a trap."

I chuckle, realizing how ridiculous our relationship is that she has reason to believe I'd be up to something by being kind to her. "I could say the same. For once, you're not aiming your flaming arrows at me. What's that all about?" Is it just my imagination or did her flush creep back up? *Don't get out your blood pressure cuff.*

She clears her throat lightly. "Too tired, I think. I'll go back to making your life miserable tomorrow. Do you want to . . . watch some TV?"

Watch TV? With Jessie? That seems awfully friend-like to me, something we have definitely never been. Could it really be this easy? Can one health scare tip us over whatever it is that's made us constantly fight and finally have a friendship? Do I want that? *Yes.*

Cooper's annoying voice echoes in my mind, telling me I've got it bad for Jessie, and I mentally push him down a flight of stairs.

"Uh—sure. Yeah. Let me just grab a shower real quick. You go ahead and put something on."

"Okay. Is there anything in particular you want to watch?"

"Whatever you want is good."

"Okay." She gives me a soft, uncertain smile, and *damn, she's right. This is so weird.*

What are we doing right now? How am I supposed to feel about a roommate who hates me, and annoys me, and is pregnant with some other dude's baby, and is living under my roof in exchange for acting like my fake girlfriend, and whose expression when she smiles I sort of love?! It's too messy, and I don't like messy. I like nice clean squares, neatly stacked in a row and color-coordinated. It's why I couldn't handle it when Cooper started dating Lucy. Suddenly he jumped into her square and it messed everything up. It takes some time for me to get used to a new organizational system.

I text Cooper because I'm a masochist who loves pain and suffering.

> ME: Jessie and I are going to watch TV together . . .
> COOPER: Naked?
> ME: What? No. Why would you ask that?
> COOPER: Just trying to figure out why you'd text me you're watching TV together if it's not because you're naked.
> ME: Because we're going to WATCH TV TOGETHER.
> COOPER: I don't get it.

I should have texted Lucy. She'll understand right away. In fact, my point is proven when another text immediately comes through.

> LUCY: OMG!! Cooper just told me you're going to watch TV with Jessie!!!!! This is BIG! What does it mean?! Are you friends now?? More than friends? Do you love her? She's so amazing; please love her!

Okay, so maybe a text from Lucy wasn't any better. Now I'm overthinking watching TV, wondering if maybe I should bail and just go to bed. Have I ever just watched a show with a woman before? It feels intimate for some reason. I give myself a mental shake. I'm being ridiculous.

While I'm in the shower, I think of my relationship with Jessie so far and try to give it a place in my mind. It's been clear-cut up until this point. She's rude to me, I'm rude to her in return. She hates me, I hate her back. She pranks me, I retaliate. She gives me the cold shoulder, fine, I couldn't care less. Those boxes all stacked neatly—nice and tidy. But then a new round shape enters the mix, and it looks like Jessie smiling at me. It looks like me rushing home to check on her health. It looks like watching TV together on a weeknight.

Those shapes don't stack up, so I don't know what to do with them.

As much as I despise it, it looks like my only option is to see what happens. Going with the flow has never been my specialty, but I think where Jessie is concerned, I have no choice.

CHAPTER 12

Jessie

Drew comes back into the living room, and I try (I really do) not to notice how good his hair looks damp. The swirl of masculine scents wrapping around him. How cute and down-to-earth he looks in a hoodie and sweatpants. And his feet are bare. What am I supposed to do with that? Now that I've noticed, I feel like he might as well be naked.

Geez, Drew. Must you be so scandalous while we watch TV with your oh-so-naked feet?

Oh goodness, those feet get propped up on the coffee table. Am I supposed to be attracted to the sight of bare feet? No. Absolutely not. This pregnancy and all these hormones raging through my body have turned me into an insane foot fetish person. I need to get in with a therapist ASAP because the sight of Drew's feet is making my heart pump like a racehorse at the Kentucky Derby.

"What are we—"

"*Nothing!*" I blurt quickly, nearly throwing my freshly popped bowl of popcorn across the room.

Drew blinks at me, uncertain what to do with that sudden outburst. "You okay over there?"

"Who me? Definitely. I was just afraid you caught me drooling over Zac Efron, that's all." *Yeah, that's good, Jessie. Put him off your scent.* "Yeah, his bare abs were on just a minute ago and I couldn't take my eyes off them. I mean, talk about one hot male specimen. Delicious." *Delicious?*

His head cocks to the side a little, and he takes in a tentative breath like he's going to say something but changes his mind. Instead, he grins slightly and turns his eyes to the TV . . . the TV that's not even on, because I was in the kitchen popping popcorn while he was in the shower. So, instead of pointing out the obvious—that I'm lying through my teeth—he just stares with a quizzical smile at the blank screen and then turns back to me.

I blink at him, daring him to call my bluff and make me admit I'm flustered because of him. I don't think either of us wants to go there, so he just chuckles and reaches for the remote.

"Got it. Zac Efron gets your engine going."

I make a gagging face. "Never mention my *engine* again."

He smiles, eyes crinkling in the corners like I've never seen them do before, and starts mindlessly scrolling through Netflix. "What? You don't want to admit you have an *engine*? You know, it's not something you have to be embarrassed—"

"*Oh my gosh, Dr. Stuck-up,* please stop! No one likes it when you turn into a gynecologist in the living room." I chuck a pillow at his head, feeling a new weightlessness between us. It's making me high.

He only laughs harder, still not meeting my eyes as he continues on. "No need to be squeamish, Oscar. If you'd like, I've got some pamphlets at the office that shed invaluable light on this particular topic."

I'm pelting him with popcorn one by one. They are tiny buttery cannonballs. Drew pulls his hood up to protect his face and scrunches his body into a ball. His laugh is incredible. I'm submerged like I've jumped into warm lake water in the summer. I float on my back and smile up at the blue sky.

"Okay, okay, I'll stop. It's just too easy. My friends are always so weirded out by my profession."

I force myself to swallow a piece of popcorn and then choke out a laugh. "Yeah, well, that's because it's sort of weird that you're a young, h—" The word *hot* dies on the tip of my tongue. Drew definitely heard where that was going, though, because his eyebrows rise in conceited question. "Hhhhhappenin' kind of guy."

He frowns and meets my gaze, the lightheartedness from a moment ago dimming. "So because I'm young and *happenin'* I'm not allowed to care about women's health? Like I went through all those years of undergrad, medical school, and residency all so I could look at women's bodies whenever I want?"

Well, I guess when he puts it like that . . .

He doesn't give me a chance to respond before blowing out a breath and shaking his head. "Sorry. Didn't mean to jump down your throat about that. I guess sometimes I just get sick of the stigma, the idea that I'm a creep for going into gynecology—but it's fair. I get it that it's uncomfortable for some people." Why do I get the feeling there's so much more going on under the surface of this conversation?

I shift in my seat, pulling my legs up under me just to have something to do. "So, why *did* you choose this career then?"

Drew's eyes snag on mine, and his eyebrows pull low. Not in an angry way, just skeptical. Like he can't believe I actually care. "When I was doing my rotations early on in medical school, the labor and delivery unit was where I felt the most joy. Honestly, so much of the medical field is doom and gloom, death and dying,

prescribing and fixing. But women's health deals mostly in pre-
ventative measures, and it revolves so much around life and family. From the first birth I attended, I've thought it was the most
incredible experience to get to be a part of, and for me, it's the
greatest honor to work alongside women to bring their babies
into the world." He pauses and shrugs. "This is the only field of
medicine I've ever felt so much hope in."

Hearing the conviction in his voice, the sincerity and gentle-
ness, I completely believe him. More than that, I feel like I know
him in a new way. I can see the vulnerability behind his eyes, and it
tugs at me.

"Okay," I say simply, with a quiet smile. "You've won me over. I
mean, you'll never be *my* ob-gyn because that would just be a very
odd boundary to cross for roommates, but you've made me feel
more comfortable with your occupation."

"Really?" It's cute the way his brow crinkles.

"Yeah." And I mean it. His reasons hit home with me, and I
think it was probably unfair and ignorant of me to assume he had
any other motives. "Is that why you're single? I mean, other than
your severe and chronic obnoxiousness? Are women not comfortable dating you because you're an ob-gyn?"

I give a taunting grin and he mimics it, shifting so he sinks a
little farther into the armchair. He looks oddly relaxed. We've
never let our guards down this much around each other before,
and I have to admit, I like seeing him like this. I like knowing he
wears *this* black hoodie any time he can. It's so worn out the white
logo on the front is peeling and cracking.

"It's definitely been an issue."

"How much of an issue?"

"Like I rarely get a second date kind of issue." His finger runs
along the seam of the armchair, and his eyes track its journey.
"Over my last dinner date, I finally told the woman I was a

gynecologist, and she did a spit take with her water. It was dramatic, but I also sort of understand the reaction."

"I'm sorry. That must really suck to devote your life to women's healthcare and then not have a relationship because of it."

He shrugs. "Eh, not a big deal. I'm always busy, so I don't have much time to sit and care about it. I figure my career won't bother the right woman. She'll trust me."

Something pokes me in the chest saying *I'm* not really bothered by his career, but I choose not to give it attention. Instead I decide to steer the conversation in a different direction. "Wow, would you look at that? We've gone ten minutes without fighting. I think that's a record." My voice sounds too much like I belong on *The Truman Show* and am trying to act natural.

"And your flush has finally worn off." *He just had to go and mention that.*

I touch my fingers to my cheeks, begging them to behave. "Yep. Told you—nothing to worry about."

He's silent a minute. Staring. His eyes softly blink, and his mouth is resting in a neutral line. He looks like he'd be comfortable to stay like this forever. I need him to look away.

"I'm sorry about overreacting earlier," he tells me. "I—uh—had a tough day at work, so I guess worst-case scenarios were fresh in my mind."

This moment is so tender, and quiet. I'm scared to speak too loudly. It'll pop whatever this is, and the vulnerability I see in Drew will be gone.

"It's okay. I imagine it's difficult knowing you're responsible for so many people."

His eyes are still connected with mine, zeroed in, ignoring any sign of life around us. He nods slowly. "Oddly though, I've always felt that way. Even before becoming a doctor, my family, friends, Lucy . . . they all look to me for assistance, or guidance, or protection. It's just been my role in life." He says it and I hear what he's not saying: *Sometimes I wish it wasn't.* I feel for him. I've never been the one who seems to have it all together, so I can only imagine how hard it would be to carry the responsibility of being *dependable.* "Everyone except you, that is."

"Except me?" My heart rate increases. My palms sweat. I'm afraid he can see right through me.

"From the moment we met, you've been adamant that you don't need me. Not even for friendship. I haven't decided how I feel about that yet."

"Well . . ." Any sort of witty comeback shrivels up in my mind, and I'm left with nothing. A giant blank. His dark eyes pull me in, and I'm terrified I'm going to blurt out the truth I've kept gagged and chained in the back dark corner of my heart. *Say something!* Anything but the truth: *I'm scared to need you.*

"So, you thought I had preeclampsia?"

He looks disappointed by my shift in conversation. "It's always something to be aware of in your third trimester." He pauses a second, and I can see the moment he shifts fully into the role of medical provider. "That condition doesn't run in your family, does it? Like your mom never had it, did she?"

Everything freezes.

No. No, no, no.

This question triggers me every single time I'm asked it, because the truth is, I know very little about my family, let alone their health records. All I have are the small bits my grandaddy can offer me, but that's it. And just like that, I feel all the walls in my heart begin to shoot back up. Self-preservation is an instinct I can't shake, and it's kicking in in the form of fight or flight right now.

"Not sure," I say, pointing toward the TV and trying to signal Drew to pick something already. "How about that one?"

"You've never talked to her about it?"

"Nope. Hey, how about a *Seinfeld* rerun? That could be fun."

"It's important. You should ask her sometime."

I clench my hands around the popcorn bowl, feeling that familiar anger snap inside me. "Hmm, well, do you have a good way of summoning the dead that I don't know about?" I let my eyes slide to Drew and see the moment his lips part. He looks floored.

"Damn. I'm sorry, Jessie. I didn't know."

"It's fine." Aka *It's not fine, now shut up please.*

I nod toward the TV again, but he doesn't choose anything yet.

"How long ago did she—"

"Okay, listen." I whip my head in his direction. "We're not talking about my family. Not now, not ever. Got it?"

Now Drew sits up straighter. Both of our spines are slowly growing stiff as boards. "Why are you getting so pissed off right now? I'm sorry I asked about your mom, but I truly didn't know—"

"But see, that's the problem with you! You stick your nose where it doesn't belong and continually try to fix people or make decisions for them when they never asked for you to. You act like this is your role in life, but it's a self-appointed role. Some people don't want or need to be fixed. I'm not your patient."

He expels a heavy breath and runs his hand through his hair, and it sticks up on the right side. I want to curse him for making himself look even sexier while I'm angry at him.

"Is this how it's always going to be? You biting my head off about everything? I mean, geez, Jessie. I was trying to have one freaking conversation with you, get to know you the smallest amount, and you can't even handle that."

I can feel my expression harden, because he's right. We were almost friends. I was on the verge of letting him in, and I absolutely don't want to let that happen. "Yeah, this whole thing was a bad idea. We're not friends, and I don't like you, so let's just quit pretending."

His midnight-blue eyes pierce me, and for a moment he looks shaken. "I wasn't pretending. I was trying to give us a shot at being civil to each other."

I stand up from the couch—slowly, because my belly makes power exits difficult, but I eventually manage it. "Well, you can give that dream up right now. I don't need any more friends. I'm full up, thanks. Let's get through your stupid fundraiser, and once my house is fixed I'll go back home, and we can each forget the other ever existed."

"You sure know how to make a guy feel good," he calls over his shoulder as I storm toward the stairs. "You forgot your popcorn, Oscar."

"Tell you what, just go ahead and shove it up your ass, Dr. Stuck-up."

"You need a new insult. That one is worn out."

I make it all the way upstairs before I let myself cry. I hate crying. It makes me feel weak and broken. I've felt that way too many times in my life, and I'm sick of it.

But when I wipe my tears away and fling open the door to my bedroom, I'm instantly reminded of my obnoxious, nosy, prying roommate. "ANDREW!" I yell and then jump when his voice sounds right behind me, hands gripping my biceps to gently move me out of the way. Unwanted chills fly over my skin. His body brushes against mine as he passes me in the doorway, and honestly, I'm a little shocked. Part of me expected him to storm out of the house for the night since I was so rude to him, but he was already on his way up here without me having to ask.

"Yeah, yeah, I'm moving them out. Don't get your panties in a wad."

I grin mockingly up at him. "Why not, when you make it look so appealing?"

We stare for two long seconds, mimicking each other's frightening, lunatic smiles, until Drew's eyes lower to my mouth. My stomach drops down to my feet, and I take a retreating step back.

Haven't I scared him off yet?

CHAPTER 13

Drew

I didn't sleep at all last night. I'm a dead man walking, and I feel that metaphor in so many ways. All night my thoughts circled around Jessie, looking at our conversation from every angle and wondering what I should have done differently. I spooked her, jumped too many steps ahead at once. I felt a tinge of friendship and got greedy. I wanted it all—to know everything. I would have stayed up all night downloading as much information from her as she'd have allowed.

My own desire to know her sort of shocked me. I didn't realize until the moment I was given a morsel of kindness how much I've been repressing my hope of . . . friendship . . . a relationship . . . a civil acquaintance with Jessie? I don't know what to call it. Some mix of all of those.

Now I'm in the kitchen making breakfast, and Jessie hasn't come out of her room yet for the day. I heard her come down around one A.M. and watch TV, still struggling with insomnia. I listened to that entire episode of *Seinfeld,* trying to get up the courage to go out and talk to her again or sit down beside her and finally watch together like we had planned.

If I had to guess, I'd say she'll hide away all day. She'll punish me for trying to push the line. *Get back over there in the "I hate you" zone.* I don't want to be in that zone anymore. I don't want to fight so much. Those few minutes of real conversation were not enough, and it only scratched the surface of what I want from her. Now I feel like digging, uncovering everything I can about Jessie. I'm an archaeologist, and all I need is someone to get me a shovel and one of those little dust brushes.

I crack four eggs, whisk them, and pour them into the pan. They sizzle and pop, and their aroma fills the air. I scramble them around in the pan, and just as I'm dumping them out onto a plate, I hear footsteps behind me. It's Jessie. My heart hammers, and for reasons I don't fully understand yet, I feel like smiling at the sight of her here in the kitchen. She's not punishing me.

She's wearing a pair of jeans and a simple tight gray T-shirt, her bump sticking out like a little basketball. I look at her, and she looks at me. She blinks, I blink. Since she doesn't make an attempt to say anything, I don't dare speak either. I don't know what I would say, honestly. *I'm sorry?* I'm not. I do want to know about Jessie's mom, and her dad, and her family, and what her favorite color is, and if she had to have braces in high school, and if she stays all the way to the end of the movie credits or gets up and rushes out before the line builds up.

I watch Jessie's eyes drop to the eggs on the plate I'm holding, and I see the desire in them. I grab another plate out of the cabinet and slide half of my portion onto it. She watches closely with a hesitant brow. Trying not to make any sudden movements, I set the plate down and slide it across the counter toward Jessie. Her lips press together as she surveys the scrambled eggs, like if she accepts them, she's accepting more than just breakfast. She's right. It's a peace treaty in the form of squishy, delicious, yellow proteins.

Never has my kitchen felt so quiet and yet so loud at the same time. I can hear her breathing. I can hear my own heart beating in my ears. Something is different between us today, and every cell in my body is hyperaware of it. Neither of us is saying anything, but I don't feel like we have to. This is our truce. We do nothing but bicker and fight, and this is us saying, *Let's not ruin anything with words today.*

Jessie delicately picks up the plate and then lifts a bite of eggs to her full, soft pink lips. She grins around the fork, and I'm mesmerized as I allow myself to watch her with new eyes. I've always had a filter around Jessie, a yeah-she's-cute-but-her-heart-is-cold-as-ice lens I viewed every encounter with her through. Now I'm seeing her without it, and there's vulnerability, and fear, and a painful childhood. There's humor and strength, and playfulness. Now that I've taken off that filter, I'm not sure I'll ever be able to put it back on. Jessie is starting to make sense to me, and she's only becoming more beautiful as she comes into focus.

We both finish our breakfast in silence, practically staring at each other the entire time, and it's oddly the most comfortable I've been in forever. She has to get closer to me to put her plate in the sink after she finishes her eggs. My back is leaning against the portion of counter just beside it, and I'm not going to move. Jessie comes forward slowly, one foot in front of the other like she can sense this thing humming between us and is scared to get too close. I watch her every step of the way, and she watches me. Without words to distract us, we're each highly aware of each other.

The hairs on my arms stand on end when she sets her plate in the sink and her arm brushes against mine. She pauses beside me, both of us facing different directions, and slowly her eyes rise to mine. I hold my breath. *What now?* her gaze asks.

I shrug lightly and smile.

She smiles too, and it's the prettiest thing I've ever seen. It's light filtering into a desolate, damp cave. It's the first taste of watermelon in summer. It's a monarch butterfly landing on your finger.

And just like those things, it's fleeting.

I'm staring at her mouth when her smile fades. She backs up, nods briefly, grabs her keys off the counter, and leaves the house. All I can do is frown at the front door and spend the rest of the day obsessing over this silent interaction. I'll replay it a hundred and two times in my head, trying to decipher if it meant something, but the truth is, it was probably nothing. Maybe I'll wake up later and realize it was an odd dream. Either way, I know I won't be able to look at Jessie the same way after this.

CHAPTER 14

Jessie

This day has gone on forever. Forever and a half actually. Normally my clients are all pretty easygoing and I'm able to understand exactly what they want and achieve their desired look. Something was in the water today, however. Maybe it's because I've hit the exhausted part of pregnancy where no matter what I've done I feel as if I just swam up Niagara Falls carrying an elephant on my back; or maybe everyone else woke up crabby. Either way, no one looked happy after the first big reveal of their hair, and I had to do second passes on everyone's style.

Basically, I'm walking through the door feeling like a huge failure and really hoping that my nemesis isn't inside waiting to make my day even worse. We didn't say a word to each other this morning over breakfast, and it was the strangest truce of my life. It was even . . . dare I say, sexy? Can eating breakfast even be sensual? Part of me thinks I'm losing all sense in this house and maybe he is too. It's like a vortex that's sucked us both in and is spitting us out slightly warped.

The problem is, I'm not sure which version of Drew I'll get

when I go inside, and even more concerning, which version of him I want. Best to prepare for battle.

I turn the door handle and step inside. It's quiet, and at first I think that maybe I'm alone, until I hear a sound from the kitchen.

Wait . . . was that a . . . moan?

I hesitate a second at the door, but then I hear it a second time and now I can confirm that it was *definitely* a moan, and it was *definitely* coming from Drew, and I'm *definitely* feeling a lot of conflicting emotions that I don't know how to process. Is he . . . entertaining someone in there?

Oh god.

Oh no, no, no.

This is the day of nightmares, and it won't stop.

I turn as quickly as I can and dart for the front door, trying not to make a sound so he and his person in there don't hear me. Except, of course, my purse, which is hanging off my shoulder, becomes the victim of centrifugal force and arcs off my body and into the wall beside the door like it's trying to knock down the whole damn thing. The sound is horrific. There's no missing it.

"Jessie?" Drew's alarmed voice suddenly calls out from the kitchen.

Oh, this couldn't get any worse.

"Oh god. I'm so sorry. Don't mind me, I'm leaving!" I say loudly while moving out the door.

"Wait." His voice is getting closer. "Where are you going?"

He's right behind me now, and I throw my hand over my eyes to turn around and face him. "Leaving! I didn't mean to walk in on you."

There's a small, confused pause. "What the hell are you talking about. Jessie, look at me."

I hesitantly drop my hand away and find Drew standing there in his black sweatpants and a white T-shirt.

"You're clothed," I say, like it's the most startling revelation in all of humanity.

"Yeah . . . what did you expect?"

"Your penis." My face flames at my own admission.

Drew's eyes are saucers as he chokes on a surprised laugh. "Wh—why would you expect my penis?" He takes an awkward step away from me suddenly, like I might reach out and peek down his pants anyway.

"I came in and heard your . . ." I really struggle over this next word. "Moan."

"My . . . m—" he cuts off, eyebrows pinched together, then a wry grin twists his mouth. His whole demeanor suddenly relaxes. "Wait. What exactly did you think I was doing in that kitchen?"

"I hardly think I need to spell it out for you."

"Oh, I think you do."

I narrow my eyes. "I thought you were . . ."

"Having sex?"

"That's the one."

He crosses his arms with a grin. "I'm surprised you'd give me that much credit with how often you remind me of my *horrible personality*."

I shrug. "Maybe she asked you to not talk. I'm not one to judge the particulars of intimacy or how someone musters through it with you."

He rolls his eyes, and this is the first time I notice how dark the circles are under them. There is so much tension living in his features today. "I haven't heard any complaints so far. But no—I wasn't having sex in the kitchen. The sound you heard was one of pain."

His hand dashes up through his hair, and I tell myself that I really don't care what is wrong with him or why he was in pain. It doesn't matter. I'm exhausted and it's been a long day and I'm just relieved I didn't have to walk in on my roommate doing things I'd rather not see him doing with anyone.

Except, something about him really looks off.

"Come back in the house, Jessie. You're safe from the affronting sight of my penis."

I ease back into the house and close the door behind me, eyeing closely my roommate that I hate more than pumpernickel bread. Normally his muscled frame is ramrod straight, ready for anything. But right now, it's drooping. *Odd.*

He goes into the kitchen and begins unloading the clean dishes from the dishwasher, and even though I tell myself I really don't care about whatever is happening to him, I can't make myself stop watching him. I hover on the threshold of the kitchen, assessing him. Tracking every single one of his movements and replaying them against how he was moving this morning.

I decide to perform an experiment.

I step fully into the kitchen and wait until he puts a bowl away in the cabinet. I deliberately scoot that same bowl over two inches like he did it wrong the first time. He doesn't even notice. Not a sigh. Not a grunt. Not an eye roll. In fact, he's not commenting on my presence in here at all, and that might be the most startling aspect of this encounter yet.

With arms folded, I lean back against the counter and throw a large piece of bait into the water, knowing the real Andrew won't be able to resist. "If you make love like you put dishes away, I'm willing to bet that your predicament of never getting a second date has nothing to do with your profession."

I'm not proud of that comment—and if I'm being honest, I know it wasn't even my sharpest poke. But listen, I'm exhausted and it's all I can muster right now.

I nearly fall to the ground in shock when the only response I get from Drew is a quiet and uninterested *hm.*

"Okay." I push away from the counter. "What's wrong?"

He looks at me. "Nothing." But his eyes are squinted into little slits. His jaw is flexing.

"You said your moan earlier was from pain. What did you hurt?"

"It's nothing."

"Clearly it's something, Andrew, so tell me or I'll be forced to turn all of your scrubs lavender."

He doesn't laugh or flip me the bird. He attempts a smile, but it never fully hits his mouth. "It's no big deal. I have . . . a small migraine."

I imagine I'll look back on this moment later in life and find it startling how quickly I push away from the counter and slingshot across the kitchen to Drew's side. I'm sure I'll want to scold myself for the all-encompassing need to comfort him I have now. But in this moment, all I can think about is that Drew is in so much pain he can't even bring himself to slice me with a cutting comeback for any insults.

"What the—Jessica, what the hell are you doing?" he says as I press my hand to his forehead, then his cheeks. Back and forth. I do this three times before I feel I have a good grasp on his body temperature.

"Checking for a fever."

This makes him gently swat my hand away. "I don't have a fever. I get these sometimes."

"Migraines?"

"Small migraines."

"No such thing. I've had a migraine before—only once, but it was brutal and I can attest that when you feel the need to use the word *migraine,* it's no small thing."

He turns back to the dishwasher and bends to retrieve the silverware basket. I immediately take it from his hands and place it back on the rack. This earns me a mild glare. "Jessie, I'm in no mood to . . ."

"Exactly. You're in so much pain that you can't even fight with me." I wrap my hand around his wrist—firmly—and tug until he follows.

"Where are we going?"

"To your bedroom."

And *see* . . . the man doesn't even so much as toss a dirty remark back at me. The Drew I know (and hate) would have said something wonderfully mean about how only in my dreams would I get to hear him moan with pleasure. But no. He's silent.

After I've fairly dragged his butt into his room, I turn him and push against his shoulders so he's forced to sit on his mattress. He sighs as he relents, and I can't tell what it's directed at because his face is so contorted with pain it's hard to interpret.

"Lie down."

"I've got stuff to do."

"I've had a long day and I don't have the energy to fight with you more on this. Lie down, Andrew."

He searches my eyes for a few seconds, and whatever he sees in them convinces me I'm not to be messed with right now. Slowly, and accompanied by several grimaces of pain, he gently lays his head on the pillow. I pull his blankets up over him and he frowns at me the entire time.

"You don't need to do this," he says, but I don't acknowledge the comment.

After making sure he's not going to try to dash out of bed, I go to his curtains and close them.

"Jessie . . . stop. I don't need help."

"Yes, you do," I say, frowning at how light the room still is. He doesn't have blackout curtains, and that's not at all acceptable when your head feels like there's a jackhammer chiseling away at your brain. So after grabbing a blanket from the living room, I toss it up over the curtain rod, darkening the room two shades.

Next I go fill up a sandwich baggie with ice and bring it to him. He is looking at me as if I'm an alien when I take the homemade icepack and put it on his head. "Have you taken headache medicine already?" I ask.

"Yes." Those squinting dark-blue eyes continue their frantic search of my face.

"Do you feel nauseous?"

"Yes."

"I'll go get you some Sprite."

As I turn, he catches my wrist gently and pulls me back, tugging me down until I sit on the edge of the mattress beside him. "What is happening right now?"

I look everywhere besides his face. "I'm making you rest and take care of yourself because clearly you're one of those doctors who saves lives but is incapable of basic self-care."

"I don't . . . that's not what I'm doing."

"You can barely keep your eyes open because of the pain, Andrew, and you were unloading the dishwasher."

His jaw flexes and he shuts his eyes tight for a second because of what I'm sure is a flash of severe pain. "Why help me though? Especially after last night?"

I choose my words very carefully. Both for his sake and my own. "It's purely selfish. It doesn't feel right picking on someone when they're hurting. I'd rather nurse you back to health quickly so I can return to pissing you off as soon as possible."

He hums lightly and I realize he hasn't let go of my wrist yet. In fact, his hold has sunk a little lower to where it's almost as if he's holding my hand. "Who knew you were so noble?"

"Do you always get migraines?"

"No. Only occasionally when my sleep and stress line up in just the right unbalanced proportion." He sounds defeated by this. Like he's offended by his own body for being human.

"And instead of lying down at the first sign of it and reducing your pain, you decide to tick some household chores off your to-do list?"

He puts his fingers to his temples and rubs. "I don't like feeling helpless. Or relying on anyone to take care of me. The dishwasher needed unloading, so I was unloading it."

My brain is telling me to get up and leave him be. But my heart, for some reason, has me glued in place. "Have you ever considered that maybe some people like to feel helpful, though? And by pretending you've got it all together you're depriving them of the joy of helping you?"

He cracks an eye open. "Is that how you feel?"

"Oh no, not me. Remember, I'm only helping so I can return you to the battlefield."

When a few seconds go by without his response, I shift my weight so I can stand, but this time Drew's hand darts out and lies across the top of my thigh like a seatbelt. "Stay a minute."

The rush of sparks that hits my stomach at the feel of his hand against my thigh is so intense I'm afraid he can see them. *What am I doing? Why am I here? And why do I care if he's hurting or uncomfortable?*

Drew's eyes remain shut, but his hand never leaves my thigh as he asks, "Why was your day long?"

"You should sleep."

"I get bored easily. If you don't distract me, I'll be tempted to get up and vacuum the living room. Or superglue the doors to your car shut."

I'm glad his eyes are closed so he doesn't see me smile. "I couldn't make anyone happy today. Everything that could go wrong did."

He hums quietly. "Some days are just like that. I'm . . . sorry it was a rough day."

I'm watching in silent awe, wondering what this thing is that's sparking between us, when Drew hisses through his teeth and presses the heel of his hand to his forehead. I tip forward and move the icepack from the back of his head to the front, and then, because I'm apparently out of my mind, I trail my hand from his forehead to his temple, down the side of his face to the tense muscles in the back of his neck. I knead my fingers there, hoping to bring him some relief. But the longer I touch him, feeling the heat of his skin and watching the way his body relaxes under my touch ever so slightly, the more aware I become of my breath picking up. Of desire gathering in a corner of my body that I should not be gathering for this man!

And that's why I abruptly pull my hand back and stand.

Drew's eyes fly open, and I don't see pain in them—I see the same shocking desire I just felt reflected back at me. Maybe that's why he doesn't try to stop me again as I make my way to his door. He does, however, say something that's going to have me tossing and turning in my bed all night long.

"Jessie. Thank you for helping me. Also, there's a milkshake in the fridge for you."

I glance sharply at him over my shoulder and blink.

"I got one earlier . . . and . . . they were having a buy-one-get-one-free sale," he says awkwardly.

Andrew Marshall, as it turns out, is a horrible liar.

Inexplicably, I smile the rest of the night.

CHAPTER 15

Jessie

"Shhhh, I think I hear the garage door opening!" I tell Lucy, my not-so-willing partner in crime. You would think a friend would help another friend prank Drew out of the goodness of her heart, but no. I had to barter with a night of babysitting. Joke's on her though, because I would have watched Levi regardless.

We both stop talking, registering the sound of a car pulling in, and we jump into position.

"This is not a drill! I repeat—not a drill!"

"Who are you yelling at like that? It's only me!"

"I'm sorry! I'm just nervous. I really want to pull this off."

Today, I'm trading my babysitting services for Lucy to play along and pretend to be my midwife. Here's the trick: she's not going to be a regular midwife. Oh no. She's going to be my "birth guru." Aka something we completely made up and intend to freak Drew out with.

Drew and I haven't spoken much to each other since his migraine. We have seen each other, though, and it's been super unnerving. Unnerving in that we haven't fought once.

Two days ago, one of Drew's patients went into labor, so he didn't get home until one in the morning. I wasn't waiting up for him or anything, I just couldn't sleep because of this annoying pregnancy insomnia. But when he got home, he took one look at me on the couch, his eyes swept to the empty cushion beside me, and his eyebrows rose in question. I nodded, and he sat down. We never touched, never spoke, only watched TV side by side until we both fell asleep watching *Seinfeld* reruns.

In the morning, he wasn't there when I woke up, but there was a steaming cup of hot coffee on the coffee table and a note that said, *It's half-caf, go crazy.* We had one more brief silent stare-down last night after work while we both did laundry. I carried my hamper into the laundry room, but Drew was already in there and had just thrown his clothes in. He saw me, then he hitched his head toward the washer, telling me to put mine in with his. It was honestly the most erotic experience of my life doing laundry together. Geez, the close quarters! The mixing of colors when I know it gets under his skin! That moment when he leaned behind me to shut the lid on the washer and his chest brushed against my back—*come on*!! I'm dying over here.

And did I mention Drew unpacked all my stuff again? The BFF salt-and-pepper shakers are back on the kitchen countertop. My fuzzy throw blankets are draped across his charcoal couch. My stuff kisses Drew's stuff everywhere I look, and it's his doing. This is a metaphor for something bigger—I can feel it in my bones.

So now, it's two weeks until the fundraiser I have to attend with him, and I'm determined to yank the rug out from under whatever this delicious tension is between us. I can't let any friendly feelings toward Drew get in the way of the revenge I have planned for the night of the event. I must stay focused. Drew is not going to be a permanent part of my life, so it's time to put our relationship back in the zone I'm most comfortable with: the war zone.

Lucy gets in position behind me on the floor, and I lean back against her. She hovers her hands above my head, wiggling her fingers in a musical fashion. She immediately starts giggling.

"Don't! You can't laugh, Lucy. You'll give us away!"

"This is why I didn't want to do this with you. I can't lie. I'm going to burst out laughing immediately."

I look up at her. "Okay, I read an article about improv the other day, and it said if you feel like laughing on stage, think of a solid color and nothing else. Apparently, it helps."

Lucy nods once. "Got it. Wait, this isn't working. Yellow is making me want to laugh more."

"Okay, think of red."

A weird laugh gurgles in her throat. "So much worse! Gosh, red is a hilarious color."

She's right. Red is so freaking funny. Probably because we are draped in the color in the most hilarious fashion possible. We're going to blow it. I can feel it. I've never been good at keeping a straight face, and everyone knows Lucy isn't good at it either, so we're doomed. Drew is going to walk in, and I'm going to blurt, *This is all a joke! Ha—gotcha!*

Except we hear the rattle of the door in the kitchen, and suddenly I don't feel like laughing. I want to throw up. To be honest, I'm not sure what I'm trying to accomplish with this prank. All the others were to get under his skin, to annoy him. This one feels different. It feels . . . no, never mind. Not letting myself go there. I'm pranking Drew so when he overreacts and loses it, I will be reminded of why I don't like him. Yeah, that's it. I'm doing this to put him back in the *obnoxious* category of my brain.

We hear the door open. Drew steps inside the kitchen and tosses his keys down. Every sound feels sharp and jarring. I know he hasn't seen us yet because we are facing the opening that leads from the living room to the kitchen and we haven't seen Drew's face. Lucy nudges me in the side and begins making a loud *ommmm* meditating sound. *Showtime.*

As expected, Drew's head pops around the corner, eyebrows quirked up and an incredulous look on his face as he takes in Lucy and me. "What the hell did I just walk in on?" he asks, the sound of his voice startling me after three days of near silence. He fully steps into the room, looking much too sexy in his black scrubs and dark two-day-old stubble lining his jaw. Forget about Zac Efron—Drew is the one who looks delicious.

Miraculously, I don't bust up laughing when I imagine what Lucy and I look like from his point of view. Her fingers are still hovering over my head, looking like she's sprinkling me with pixie dust, and she and I are both dressed in these super creepy, all red cotton gown-drape things I found on Amazon. They completely swallow us whole and make us look like we belong in an even scarier version of *The Handmaid's Tale.*

Lucy continues to *ommmm* like we rehearsed as I deliver my line. "Not that I owe you any explanations, but Lucy got certified earlier this week to be my birth guru. We are centering ourselves in preparation for the birth."

"Exactly," Lucy says, using a snooty voice I've never heard from her before. "Now scram, Drew. I need Jessie to concentrate. According to my training, it's important that the spiritual waves we are producing between Jessie and the baby not get interrupted by outside forces."

Green. Black. Orange. Burgundy—oh gosh, it's not working. I'm thinking of all the colors and it's taking everything in me not to look in Drew's horrified eyes and lose it laughing.

"I'm sorry—just one second." He holds up his finger. "Did you say . . . birth guru?"

"Mm-hmm." That's all I can manage. If I open my mouth, an eruption of laughter will spill out.

Luckily, Lucy can sense my distress and takes over in a surprisingly heroic way. "Yes, you heard correctly. Thanks to gurusofbirth.net, I am now certified to perform Jessie's spiritual birth."

Drew smells something fishy and crosses his arms, squinting his eyes. "What is it you're doing there with your hands?"

"Oh, this," Lucy says in her Zen voice as she continues to sprinkle me. "This is goddess birth energy. Only the birth guru can fully harness its powers, but I am choosing to bestow it on Jessie."

"Uh-huh. And what does it do?"

Lucy lifts her nose higher in the air. "By sprinkling it on the top of Jessie's head, it flows through her entire being and connects with the unborn child, signaling to it that the end of gestation is near."

Oh, she's good. That was all completely ad-libbed. *Bravo, Lucy. You missed your calling.*

Drew's lips are parted, but he's looking like he has no idea where to begin. Finally, he takes his hand and runs it over his face. I can't tell if he's believing this performance or not.

"And what's with the red getups? Why are you both wearing those?"

Feeling like I have a good handle on my amusement, I brave a response, putting on my most annoyed expression. "I knew we should have done this while you were gone! Lucy, I told you your brother would be nothing but judgmental." I sit up, and Lucy assists me. "These are the ritual garments, *Andrew.* They are meant to strip away anxiety and clothe me in honesty and trust in my body. They will protect me from feeling any pain during labor."

You know those cartoon characters that, when angry, their heads pop off and spin in a circle with smoke spewing out of their ears? Yeah, that's not Drew. He looks more Zen than Lucy and I are. In fact, his super calm is sort of freaking me out.

"Protect you from . . ." He breaks off, his expression mystified. His eyes move to Lucy. "And you are now a certified . . ."

"Birth guru," she finishes for him. "And, yes, I am. I was skeptical when Jessie first told me about it, but after I watched all the YouTube videos, I was sold."

"The YouTube videos?" he echoes in an incredulous tone, clearly still trying to decide if we're messing with him or not. But when he glances over and sees the printed-out "birth guru" certificate with Lucy's name on it, something snaps inside him. I can see it in his eyes.

"Of course you wouldn't be supportive." I muster up a few fake tears, trying to push him over the top, and now Drew looks floored.

"Now, now . . ." Lucy rubs my back. "Don't let him ruin your mental sedation with his negativity."

"MENTAL SEDATION?!" His voice nearly shakes the walls. "What did you give her?"

Lucy remains the ever-proper guru despite his heightened state. "The most powerful birthing prescription in the world—vibes of joyousness administered through thoughtful eye contact." Vibes of joyousness?! Okay, that really did sound like she just pulled it out of her butt.

I'm worried Lucy might have taken it too far and Drew will finally realize we are just pranking him, but no, he looks downright livid. We are getting closer to cartoonlike anger. The ends of his hair are about to catch on fire and turn him into the next Marvel character that fights off birth gurus all over the world. Which . . . was not supposed to happen. He was supposed to call our bluff after vibes of joyousness. I feel a tinge of concern.

"Jessica, may I have a word? *In the kitchen.*" He points behind him like I'm a naughty puppy that needs to be put in her crate until she can stop shredding all the pillows and eating crayons.

I rise from the ground with Lucy's help and then level him with an indignant scowl. "Whatever you want to say to me, you can say in front of Luc—" Drew swiftly turns me and starts pushing me along with him into the kitchen. "Hey, watch it! Pregnant lady here. You can't just toss me around like a rag do—"

Drew spins me to face him, and in one swift motion lifts me up and plants me on the counter. Apparently, he *can* move me around like a rag doll. How did he make that look so easy and graceful? He literally just lifted two humans! Maybe he's experiencing one of those adrenaline-induced super-strength episodes.

He plants a hand on either side of me and narrows his navy eyes. My skin erupts, and I'm sure my face is turning the same color as my guru garment. Oooh, he smells incredible leaning in close to me like this. I wonder what kind of cologne he wears, and if he'd notice if it suddenly went missing. Can I trail my finger along his jaw? Would it be prickly? His eyes pinch together and his jaw tics. Now would probably be a good time to laugh and tell him the truth, but I want to see how far I can go before he realizes it's a prank. Also, I can't seem to form words with him this close.

Without meaning to, my eyes drop to his lips. If he asks, I'll say I'm just checking to make sure they're still there. *Yep! There they are!* Heat ripples between us, and goosebumps blanket my skin. I can hear my inner bad girl telling me to lean forward and take those sexy lips for my own. I want to wrap my arms around his neck and hang on to him like a little monkey. He's sturdy. He could handle me.

But the rational thinking portion of my brain reminds me that I am pregnant and vulnerable, and Drew is just the sort of man I don't need to get mixed up with. He's the guy you lose your heart to on the first date. He's the one you tumble head over heels and do irrational things for, like get a tattoo on your butt cheek just because nothing else feels like an adequate symbol of your love.

I've known this about Drew since the day Lucy first told me about her brother and showed me his picture. It was weeks before he ever did anything frustrating, but I decided then and there to hate him—because I knew if I didn't force myself to see all of his bad qualities, I'd like him way too much. As a woman freshly hurt by yet another man, I wasn't about to let that happen. I'll never let myself feel reckless romance with a man again. No, somewhere later down the line, I want a reasonable man to marry, someone who makes me smile but never evokes strong feelings. I want someone to share life with, but I never want to have to worry about feeling devastated if I lose him.

And when I look back up into Drew's indigo-blue-jean eyes, I know he would be devastating.

"I cannot believe you would have my highly unqualified sister deliver your baby." Drew's voice is low thunder in the distance. It's shaking me.

"Y-yes. I am having her be my birth guru. I've thought it through, and—"

Drew pushes off the counter and turns his back to me, raising a single arm to grip the back of his hair in frustration. He whirls around to me again, looking madder than a hornet. "You know, Jessie, this is a new low, even for you. Stooping to putting your child in danger just out of spite for me!" This is the part where I should yell *HA-HA* and dance around him obnoxiously, but I don't feel like doing that, because now I'm pissed. How could he say that to me? "And thinking those damn garments are going to keep you from feeling pain! Come on. Joyful vibes? I thought you were smarter than that. You need a doctor or a midwife to assist you, not a self-made gu—"

"Okay, stop. I've heard enough. And you know what? I can't believe you!"

"Me?!" he asks with raised eyebrows. Drew stalks back to me, planting those big hands beside my hips again and leveling me with his stormy gaze. "What could you possibly be angry with me about?"

"So many things!" I say, my voice rising so high it squeaks. "But I'm mostly upset that you would ever think me capable of truly making a decision like this! You weren't supposed to believe me! Not for a second. You were supposed to laugh and shake your head and see right away that it was a—" My voice loses steam when I see Drew's lips begin to curl in a devious smile. My anger rushes out of me and is replaced by despondency.

"A what, Jessie?" he whispers, his mouth only two inches from mine.

I take in a long breath through my nose and then, on a rush of air, admit, "A prank."

A full smile replaces his ferocious scowl, and my stomach sinks. He *did* know it was a prank. This whole time he knew, and he was getting me back.

It doesn't seem possible, but Drew leans even closer without our lips touching. "Never try to prank the master."

My eyes shut tight for a moment before I open them again. Unfortunately, when I do, they drift down to their new favorite resting place: his mouth. His fine, smiling mouth.

"When did you realize it was a prank?"

"From the word *guru*." Why is he still whispering like that? I need him to talk at a normal volume so my skin will stop prickling like this. So my heart will stop racing. So my mind will stop pretending this is the beginning of something. "I only said all that to get you to admit it. I would never believe you'd let my sister deliver your child after watching a few YouTube videos."

My hands are pressing into the counter beside my thighs, and Drew's thumb lightly brushes against my pinky. Intentionally? Yes. Look, he just did it again! My womanly organs all cheer like their home team just scored the winning goal.

I swallow. "Oh, okay." I sound drunk.

And then Lucy's voice cuts through the moment from the living room, and Drew dashes away from me like we're doing something wrong before Lucy rounds the corner. *Interesting.*

"Hey, umm, guys? Can I leave yet? Is the prank over? Oh shoot! Was I not supposed to say *prank*? I don't think I was."

Drew and I both chuckle, and he leans back against the sink, folding his arms. "It's all right, Luce. The joke's over now."

"Oh good!" She looks relieved, but then her eyes zero in on his shirt. "But wait . . . you don't look—"

"YOU DID GREAT, LUCY!" I say, a touch too loudly. I get ready to jump off the counter, but Drew catches me before I make the leap, grabbing my hips to help me down easily. I feel his hands like I'm not wearing anything at all. His touch is dangerous, and I want to shake him off like a wet dog. I brush by him without making eye contact and put my arm around Lucy's shoulders, guiding her toward the front door. "Really. You did amazing. Thanks for your help." I'm trying to send her telepathic vibes not to mention the prank anymore.

Mercifully, she understands and leaves with only a quiet smirk and a last glance at Drew. Once she's gone, Drew and I stand in the living room. He has a gloating smile on his face, just like I imagined he would.

"Yes, fine, you're the supreme prankster. I bow to you, great sir."

"Thank you. That's all I want to hear . . . every day from now on please."

I narrow my eyes. "Not likely."

Drew's gaze is glittering. He's so proud of himself. "I'm going to go change out of these scrubs and then I'll make us some dinner. I think it's the least I can do for thwarting your plans so epically."

He's backing toward his bedroom, which is situated just off the living room. I need to hold his attention for approximately ten steps. "Wow, how noble of you. And just what sort of dinner do you make for losers?"

"Comfort food. Maybe chicken soup?" *One more step.* "I'll even throw in some crackers and a warm blanket to drape over your lap, because I'm nice like that."

Drew barely gets his last word out before pushing open his cracked bedroom door, causing a bucket of water to rain down on his beautiful head. His whole body goes instantly rigid, shoulders bunched, wet eyelashes blinking like windshield wipers, mouth open. I am doubled over laughing, completely unrepentant.

"You!" Snort. "Fell." Another laughing snort. "Right into." I have to wipe my laughing tears away. "My trap!"

Drew still hasn't moved. He's soaked to the bone, and his scrubs cling to his muscled body in a way that almost makes it feel like the joke is on me. His head begins to shake side to side in slow, deliberate motions. "*This* was the real prank, wasn't it?"

I'm still laughing so hard I can't speak, so I settle for a nod.

"The guru bit was just a decoy?"

I nod again. Drew is clever and observant, so I knew he'd spot the bucket-of-water-above-the-cracked-door trick a mile away if he wasn't distracted. I needed to get him high enough on his own success to dull the rest of his senses, disarm him before the main event. I'm brilliant, and I tell him so in his own words.

Pointing a theatrical finger in his direction, I declare, as if I'm in a Machiavellian play, "Never try to prank the master!"

And then, to my complete dismay, Drew smiles a megawatt

smile that stuns me for the rest of eternity. His teeth sparkle and his eyes crinkle in the corners with pure, unadulterated happiness. His soaked shoulders shake and water drips from locks of his wavy hair down his square jaw, and I want to weep at how handsome he is. Drew is looking at me, and he looks completely happy. He does not overreact; he does not say mean things—he laughs. Unfortunately, he does *not* fall back into the obnoxious category.

"Well done, Oscar. But you better watch your back now, because I'm coming for you."

CHAPTER 16

Drew

"I need a good prank idea," I tell Cooper and Lucy the minute the music dies down enough to talk.

They dragged me out with them for drinks, and there just so happens to be karaoke at this bar (Cooper loves karaoke but is trying to play it off so cool like he had no idea it was karaoke night). Jessie was invited too, but she couldn't make it because apparently her client was taking longer than expected. She told Lucy to go on without her, but I'm not disappointed she's not here. I haven't been sitting here all night obsessively worrying about her and whether she's overworking herself. Not a bit. I'm so chill. *Vanilla Ice, baby.*

"A prank?" Lucy asks, looking awfully judgmental for a woman who just participated in one for the opposite team.

"Don't make that face. Jessie started this prank war. I'm just trying to keep up."

"Mm-hmm," Cooper mumbles against his beer with a knowing look that I want to punch off his face. "Why don't you just pull her pigtails? Or write her a check-yes-or-no note?"

"Shut up."

Lucy sits forward, face forming an uncomfortable expression. "What sort of prank? Nothing too mean, right? I just don't like the idea of you picking on Jessie."

"Believe me, she can handle it."

Lucy takes a sip of her watermelon margarita. "I don't know. Just be careful, Drew. She's been through a lot, and not in the way that most people have 'been through a lot' but then you learn really someone just ran over their dog when they were a kid and that's the only tragic thing that's ever happened to them. Jessie has already been through more heartache than most people experience in a lifetime."

My mind races back to the night she blew up at me over mentioning her mom. "What sort of heartache?" Am I even allowed to ask that? Jessie would probably murder me if she knew I was prying into her life without permission.

Cooper gives Lucy a private look. It's annoying.

"I know, but I have to tell him!" she says with wide eyes. "Jessie *never* will, and I'm afraid if he doesn't know, he'll go too far." She turns back toward me just as someone hops up to the mic and blows into it. Music starts up, forcing her to practically yell over "Baby One More Time." "Jessie's mom died in a car crash when she was little."

In no way do those words match the pop song being screeched over the speaker. It almost feels irreverent.

"But that's not all," Lucy continues. "Her dad was a deadbeat and split while Jessie was just a baby. Even after her mom died, he never came back." No wonder Jessie doesn't want to talk about her family.

"So her grandparents raised her?"

Lucy nods. "Until her grandma died while Jessie was still really little. Her grandpa raised her alone after that. He's amazing. She's literally lost everyone in her family besides her grandaddy. And though most of it happened when she was too young to remember, I know it hurts her still, especially now that she's pregnant and having to answer so many questions about her medical history."

I sink five inches down in my seat, wishing I could slide all the way to the floor. I'm an idiot, the biggest idiot to ever walk the face of the earth.

The woman's pitchy voice bellowing through the speakers drowns out our chances at conversation for the next two minutes, and I'm left alone with my thoughts. Once she trips off the stage, I lean forward and ask the question I've been dying to get an answer to. The last piece of the Jessie puzzle.

"What about her child's father? Is he in her life at all?" I haven't noticed any dudes hanging around or her talking on her phone too much, so I doubt it. But still, I need to know for sure. Not sure exactly why I feel the need to know, but I do.

Lucy shakes her head. "That's the one thing I still don't know about. I'm sure you've noticed, but Jessie is extremely closed off to any kind of personal talk."

"I've noticed."

"Yeah, so all I know is that he left. Not sure why, but it's definitely been hard on her."

This news is pulling some very strong and unexpected feelings from me. Because I'm her friend? Because I'm a doctor and hate having to see women birth their babies alone? Because no one deserves the sort of life she's had so far? I think it's a mix of those reasons and also another one that I'm not willing to admit yet.

My sister sighs. "It breaks my heart that she's been so mistreated . . . especially when she's literally the sweetest."

I scoff. "Unless she's around me—then she's the feistiest, least agreeable woman on the planet." *And completely adorable.*

Cooper is eyeballing that stage like it holds all his unrealized dreams, but Lucy leans forward, eyes narrowed on me. "I know! Which has always been odd to me. You seem to trigger her in ways no one else does. Literally, no one. Jessie loves everyone—but not you. She's strongly opposed to—"

I hold up my hand. "Yeah, yeah, I get the point."

"Just hide in her closet and jump out and scare her," says Cooper, still staring at the stage and clearly only halfway tuned into this conversation.

"Huh?" Lucy and I both say at the same time.

Cooper begrudgingly drags his eyes back to our table and shrugs while taking a sip of his beer. "Oldest prank in the book. Hide, then jump out and scare her. Simple. Easy. Effective. No preparation needed."

I stare at him. "That's a terrible idea."

"Is it? She'll scream, you both will laugh, she'll fake punch you or something, you'll pull her up close, and then *boom*—making out before you know it."

Because I'm excellent at keeping my emotions concealed, Cooper has no way of knowing that his idea has my heart hammering against my chest with excitement when I say, "I'm trying to get back at her for all of her pranks—not make out with her."

Both Lucy and Cooper laugh in a way I don't appreciate.

"Okay, suuuuure." Lucy leans into Cooper's side so he can drape his arm around her.

Cooper smiles. "We all know all this fighting and pranking between you two is nothing but foreplay. You like her; she likes you—"

"But you guys are too stubborn to admit it, so you have to revert back to adolescent ways to test the waters."

I bounce my finger between the two of them snuggled up in

the booth. "I really hate when you two do this. Your united front is obnoxious."

Cooper slides out of the seat and sets down his beer before grabbing Lucy's hand. "All right, enough chitchat. Come on. I know you've been dying to sing all night, Luce. Personally, I hate karaoke, but I'm not one to stand in the way of my wife's desires, so let's go sing some Shania Twain."

Lucy gives a flat, unamused smile before letting him pull her out of the booth. "Oh yes, my passionate love for karaoke— I totally forgot."

She stands up, and he kisses the top of her head. "I know you better than you know yourself." He holds out his phone toward me. "Film this, would ya? For the grandkids one day."

"Just admit you're going to post this on Instagram later with an eye roll emoji and a caption that says, *Lucy made me do it.*"

He smirks. "Admit you've got it bad for your roommate."

"Touché. Give me your phone."

I'm in Jessie's closet. In her freaking closet. I'm a grown man— a doctor!—who is looked up to, respected, and trusted to keep people alive and bring humans into the world, and I'm standing in a woman's closet for a dumb prank. I rushed up here the second I got home from work.

The longer I stand in here, the worse this idea becomes. Why did I let Cooper talk me into this? He just *had* to plant ideas of making out with Jessie in my head—which would also be a bad idea! I can't just make out with her on a whim because I feel like it. She's been through serious trauma. She's had a man leave her with a child, a child who will be entering this world very soon.

And yet . . . if she wants to make out with me, I sure as hell am not going to stop her.

That woman makes me completely crazy—but lately it's turned into the good kind of crazy. I go to sleep thinking about her, wondering what kind of stupid prank she's going to pull on me tomorrow. I stare at the ceiling, seeing only her smiles and the way her nose crinkles when she wants to stick her tongue out at me but also wants to act like an adult. I love knowing she paints her nails when she can't sleep. Every morning I make it a point to look at her toes and note what color she chose the night before.

I can't deny it anymore: I'm attracted to her. Actually, I'm not sure I ever denied that. What I have to come to terms with is that I think I'm starting to have *feelings* for her. I find myself wanting to know as much about her as I can. We've lived together for over a week now, which means we only have another week or two left before she moves back to her house, and I'm already dreading it.

Anyway, this is a terrible idea to hide in her closet. I'm getting out before she comes in and—

Oh shoot. Is that her? Yep. She just walked into her room and closed the door behind her.

I'm stuck in here with my bad decision. This is terrible, and my pulse in my neck is telling me I'm a freaking idiot and going to pay for this in a big way. Grown men shouldn't hide in women's closets—ask any stalker locked away behind bars. Annnnnd now I've officially waited way too long to jump out, and I'm going to look extra pervy if she finds me. I need to just commit and jump out before it gets to be too long, but I'm way too embarrassed. I do not want her to know I ever even considered this choice.

Maybe I can just hide in here all night?

I hear Jessie humming to herself and moseying around her room, and this only adds to my anxiety.

I pull out my phone and shoot Lucy and Cooper a group text.

ME: I hate you both. I'm in Jessie's freaking closet.

LUCY: Bahahahahahaha

COOPER: *kissy face emoji*

ME: No. I've been standing in here too long, afraid to jump out. I'm going to look like a major perv now and she's really going to hate me.

LUCY: How long have you been in there while she's in her room?

ME: Like three minutes

COOPER: Dude . . .

ME: I KNOW! What do I do?

LUCY: She's pregnant—she's bound to go to the bathroom soon. When she does, sneak out.

ME: Okay yeah, that's good.

COOPER: Just jump out and get your kissing on.

LUCY: DON'T listen to Cooper. Believe me, you will not end up making out.

I peek through the crack in the closet door, trying to see if Jessie is still out there, just in time to see her grab the bottom hem of her shirt like she's going to take it off. NO! Oh god, please, no. This is awful now. I've waited in this damn closet way too long, and if she finds me after changing her clothes, she's really going to think I'm some sort of pervert.

I immediately turn around so my back is to the closet door. No way will I have "peeping Tom" weighing on my conscience as well as "closet stalker." *Please, please, please go into the bathroom.*

She doesn't. Her feet are drawing near the closet. *What do I do?!* There's nowhere to go in here, nowhere to hide. My heart is pounding so hard I feel like I'm going to pass out, then suddenly the doors to the closet open, and it fills with light.

The next sequence of events all happen within a one-second span and go something like this:

Jessie screams.

I turn around.

Her eyes go wide.

I notice she's wearing nothing but a towel.

Her fist collides with my face.

Everything goes black.

"Drew, I am so, so sorry!" Jessie says, hovering beside me in the bathroom as I press a wad of tissue to my bleeding nose. She's still only wearing a towel with her hair up in an adorable messy bun, and I find it all highly distracting.

Focus on the gushing blood and pain radiating through my right cheekbone.

"It's all right, really," I mumble through the toilet paper, still slightly out of it.

"I didn't realize it was you! I was just freaked out when I opened my closet and found a man in there, and when you turned around, I reacted before I could think." *She smells like coconut.* "I would have never punched you if I knew it was you."

"Are you sure about that?" I say with a grin I instantly regret as pain shoots through my cheek.

She gives me a pitiful, remorseful look. "I'm serious! You annoy me, but I've never meant to cause you bodily harm!" I've never seen her like this—genuinely worried and upset.

I can't help it. I reach out an arm and pull her up to me, giving her a consoling hug. But when my hand wraps around her bare, warm shoulder, I remember she's wearing absolutely nothing but a towel, and I quickly release her. "It's my fault anyway."

This seems to wake her up. Her sage eyes ignite, and she whacks my biceps. "Oh yeah! Why am I the one over here apologizing? You were the pervert lurking in my closet!"

I hold up a defensive finger. "Okay, first, not a pervert."

"Says the man who stole my underwear once."

Yeah, those incidences look bad when lined up side by side. "Only because it made sense in relation to *your* prank. And second, the moment I realized you were going to change clothes, I turned around! Third, it's all Cooper's fault. It was his idea to hide in your closet." And I will never listen to him again.

I think that towel must be working its way loose, because Jessie reaches up to clasp the ends closed.

"But *why* did Cooper tell you to hide in my closet?"

I groan because it sounds so ridiculous. I don't even know why I thought it would be a good idea in the first place. *You wanted her to kiss you.* And that desire still stands. In fact, it's growing stronger. That seed has taken root, and now it's a vine wrapping around every thought, overtaking all of my rationality.

"I asked him for prank ideas, and he said popping out of a closet and scaring someone is the oldest in the book. I thought it was a funny idea until I was standing in there and realizing how creepy it was. And then, just as I was about to abort, you walked into the room. I couldn't bring myself to scare you, and then I realized I had been in there too long to just stroll out without looking like the weirdest man ever, so I was going to wait it out until you went into the bathroom and then sneak back out."

Jessie's pink lips press together, and her shoulders are shaking. She's laughing through her nose.

"Just let it out." My voice sounds stupid with this toilet paper wad pressed to my nose.

And she does. Jessie laughs and laughs. At least she doesn't want to punch me again. "You both are clowns. Are you kidding me? You thought hiding in a pregnant woman's closet was a smart idea?! What if you scared the baby right out of me?"

"Not physically possible. But now that I know you're a freaking MMA fighter, you better believe I'll never cross you again. Where did you learn to punch like that, anyway?"

Her bottom lip juts out and I realize she's experiencing sympathy for me. *Sympathy.* Jessie, the woman who has claimed to hate me, has now taken care of me when I had a migraine and showed tenderness toward me after being punched in the face. It's weird, but I'll take it.

"My grandaddy made me take self-defense classes all through high school so I could always take care of myself. You're just lucky I didn't kick you in the groin." Her eyes sparkle as her lips pull into a sweet smile, and I'm momentarily breathless.

For a split second, noticing her smooth tan skin, light freckles dusting her chest, pronounced collarbones, and delicate mouth makes me feel guilty. Wishing I could run my finger across the slope of her shoulder all the way down to her fingers and see if she sighs makes me feel like I'm doing something wrong. I'd wrap my hand around hers and pull her up close to me until I could feel her heart beating against mine. I'd smell her hair. I'd taste her lips, her neck, her shoulder—and wanting to do those things makes me feel downright dirty, no doubt because of my career and learning to not see women in my practice as anything besides patients. I mentally shake myself, because I'm not in the office, Jessie isn't my patient, and I'm allowed to be just a man right now.

Except . . . maybe my eyes are telling Jessie a little too much of what I'm thinking, because suddenly her smile dims a little and she takes a step away. Her eyelashes fall, and I see the moment she realizes she's still wearing a towel.

"Okay, well, if you're all right, then . . . I think I'll just . . ." She hitches her thumb over her shoulder. "I better go. Call me if you can't get the bleeding to stop and need me to drive you to the hospital." It's pretty cute how she's fumbling around, bumping into the wall as she turns, and then nervously chuckles over her shoulder. "There's a wall there."

I smile and lean back against the counter, still holding the toilet paper to my nose.

Her cheeks have bloomed into roses, and I get the feeling she doesn't hate the attention I'm showing her but isn't sure how to handle it either.

Jessie backs her way out of the bathroom, then gives me a short wave. "Bye."

I don't say anything, just hold my smile as she slips away.

I cross my ankles as I lean back against the counter fully and silently count how long it takes before she comes back. *Two, three, four . . .*

Jessie pops back in, face fully aflame now and an embarrassed smile curling her lips. "Yeah, so I forgot this is my bathroom . . . can you just . . ."

I'm already pushing myself off the counter and walking toward the door, unable to wipe the stupid grin off my face for the rest of the day.

CHAPTER 17

Drew

SUNDAY

I shut the fridge. "We're out of creamer."

Jessie is standing beside me, holding a cup of black coffee, looking like I just told her she has to pee in that mug and drink it.

"*No,*" she whispers dramatically.

"Not a fan of black coffee, I take it?" I already know she won't drink it without cream, but I ask anyway so she won't know I've been tracking her every movement since she moved in.

"Drew"—I'm still not totally used to hearing my name fall so casually from her lips—"creamer is one of the few magnificent little wonders in this world. I refuse to go without it, and no, I'm not being dramatic." When she smiles like that, I don't stand a chance. I will bend to her every desire every time.

"All right then." I scoop up my keys.

She sets down her mug and hurries after me. "Wait, where are you going?"

"To the store to get you creamer."

She's bobbing behind me, trying to grab the keys. "No! I didn't mean you had to go. I'll go. It's for me anyway."

I hold the keys up high so she can't take them. They jingle playfully. "I need a few other things too."

"Then make a list, and I'll get them while I'm there. I better go ahead and buy Grandaddy more Oreos anyway."

I grin down at her attempts to hop in the air for the keys and her inability to do so because of how uncomfortable it is with her swollen belly. I'm so mean, hanging them like a bone on a string over her head. "Nope, I'm going."

Determination settles in her stubborn green eyes. "Fine. Then we're both going."

"Great."

"Wonderful." Her chin angles up. "I'll drive separate."

"You'll ride with me."

Her eyes narrow and she waits three beats before responding. "Only to help preserve the planet."

"Such a hero."

CHAPTER 18

Jessie

MONDAY

There's a knock on my bedroom door, and because it's only us here, I know who it is. My stomach flips as I turn the handle and find Drew standing there with a hesitant smile. He leans his shoulder against the frame, does a slow perusal of me in my shorts and tank top, and then meets my eyes.

"I accidentally made too much dinner. Come eat with me."

"Is it poisoned?"

"No, my vial was empty."

I twist my lips to the side, trying to look like I'm contemplating it and didn't make up my mind the second he asked. Because truth is, I'm spending all my free time with Drew these days. He knows it. I know it. But neither of us will admit it out loud, because it's too scary.

CHAPTER 19

Jessie

Everything took too long today. So many highlights, so many women wanting to reinvent their look. At five o'clock, I wanted to throw my bowl of lightening cream against the wall and yell, "Yeah, yeah, you look fine! Go home and love yourself as you are!" But I stood there like a good little hairstylist and finished taking a woman's hair from a level four brunette to an ambitious level seven warm blond until eight o'clock. Because in the hair world, you don't get to clock out at five. You stay until the job is done.

I floor it all the way home. *Home.* Drew's home, I mean. His Jeep is in the driveway, and I feel an eagerness to get inside.

I open the door too exuberantly, and it slams back against the wall. He's sitting on the couch with a bowl of ice cream and nearly throws it over his head. He's wearing his trademark at-home look: Hoodie. Sweatpants. Bare feet.

Except, thanks to me, he also has a swollen black eye.

He's adorable, and I have to admit it to myself, or I'll burst.

"Is a killer chasing you or something?" he asks, wide eyes looking to where I flung the door open.

Oh, right. He can't know I rushed in here like a maniac so I could see him. I look over my shoulder. "Yeah. Gosh, you should have seen him. Big. Burly. Scary knife." I shiver and shut the door, smiling when my back is to him.

"In that case, lock it." He grins, and my heart flutters.

My legs are crying out for me to go to the couch and sit down beside Drew, but I'm still not sure if I'd be welcome there or not, if I *should* go there or not. I think it would be a bad idea.

There, woman, you've seen him like you wanted, now go to your room and behave.

Drew leans forward and rests his elbow on his knees, bowl of ice cream in hand, and takes a casual, unhurried bite, staring at me the whole time. "Are you going to stay over there all night?"

"Maybe."

"Okay." He takes another bite with the spoon upside down in his mouth and slowly pulls it back out. So yeah, I can't stand here watching him eat ice cream all night like a freak. *I can't, right?* No. I can't.

He licks his lips and sets the bowl down, stands, and then nods toward the couch. "Sit."

Drew disappears into the kitchen, and I shuffle over with weak legs. I sit down. Cross my legs. That feels weird, so I uncross them. I lean back and then feel like Santa with my jolly round belly, so I sit back up. How did I sit before Drew came along?!

"Here." He's in front of me now, holding out a bowl of ice cream. *Cookies n' cream, mmm.* I laugh, though, when I see a single floret of broccoli perched on the side of a scoop. His grin is tilted and making my world spin. "Balance, you know?"

"Balance," I say with a solemn expression.

And that's that. He sits beside me on the couch, and we eat our ice cream while watching the most boring documentary in the world. *It's so good.*

CHAPTER 20

Jessie

WEDNESDAY

D rew doesn't come home after work, so I can only assume he's at the hospital for a delivery. Or he's on a date. I don't know, and it kills me all night. I try to watch a romance movie, but I can't focus. In my head, every scene is Drew with another woman, Drew kissing a different woman. It's absolute torture. I could have just texted him and asked what he's up to, but . . . that feels like too much. Too close. Too friend-like, or worse, relationship-like.

So instead I wait up—I mean watch TV!—on the couch for no reason other than I have insomnia like always. I don't know at what time I fall asleep, but somewhere in the middle of the night I wake up when I feel something warm drape over me.

I squint my eyes open and see Drew standing beside the couch, turning off the TV with the remote. The room goes black and I can't see him anymore, but I can still feel and smell him near me. In my sleepy state, I nearly ask him to lie down with me.

"Were you on a date?" I don't mean to ask this, but it's better than throwing a snuggle invitation at him.

He leans closer. "You should go get in bed. You look cold."

"I'm okay right here."

He grunts, and then I feel a second blanket wrapping around me. He tucks me in like a burrito and quietly says, "I was at the hospital. Get some sleep."

I do, and I dream of Drew the whole night.

CHAPTER 21

Jessie

THURSDAY

DREW: Was this really necessary?

DREW: *large framed photo of cat wearing an adorable beanie mounted on the wall*

ME: It was absolutely necessary.

DREW: I'm failing to see how.

ME: It boosts morale. You don't want to live in a house low on morale, do you?

DREW: Ever since you moved in, my house seems to be bursting with it.

ME: Do you actually want me to take it down?

DREW: . . . No.

CHAPTER 22

Jessie

FRIDAY

DREW: Where is it???

ME: I don't know to what you are referring.

DREW: The mug. My mug. What did you do with it?

ME: Andrew, we have so many mugs. How could I possibly know which mug you're talking about?

DREW: You know . . . white . . . looks like a snowman . . . has a carrot nose? Was on a shelf above my bedroom door and now it's gone?

ME: Ohhhhhhhhhh.

ME: You mean this one?

ME: *picture of me drinking out of the mug at the salon with a devious smirk*

DREW: Put it back . . . or else . . .

DREW: *picture of Drew holding a Sharpie with the cap off up to beanie-cat picture*

ME: You wouldn't!!

DREW: You have until midnight to return my mug.

DREW: P.S. I called in takeout from the burger place you like with the nasty fries. Can you stop on the way home and grab it?

ME: Only if we can rent that new movie.

DREW: I already got it.

CHAPTER 23

Jessie

W ell, I'm here. At Drew's fancy-schmancy fundraiser thing *without him*. One of his patients went into labor this morning, so he's been bouncing back and forth between his practice and the hospital all day. I thought maybe we were going to have to bail on the event (and my epic revenge plan), but he texted me about two hours ago saying he would meet me here and to grab my ticket off the kitchen counter.

Needless to say, I was not too thrilled about the idea of showing up by myself.

So that's why I'm hiding in the uncomfortably cold bathroom like a loser. I texted Drew incessantly as I was getting ready to ensure this very thing didn't happen. *Are you going to be on time?* I texted at least five different times as the hour to leave the house grew closer. *Yep!* he'd say. *Still on time?* I asked before I ever stepped foot in my car. *Yep! I'll see you there,* he said.

And then, as I was walking into the glowing ballroom of the fanciest event I've ever been to outside of prom a hundred thousand years ago, Drew texted me: *Traffic. Gonna be late. So sorry.* I wanted to hit the ground and army-crawl my way out of there, but it was too late. I'd been spotted by too many of the high-profile doctors and power couples.

I rushed to the bathroom, and that's where I'm still lingering, pretending to obsess about my hair, wash my hands, and reapply lipstick every time someone new walks in here. My hands are going to be shriveled-up prunes by the time Drew finally arrives.

A woman comes into the bathroom for the second time and eyes me warily, and I realize it's time to leave my post as bathroom attendant. I swallow and look at myself in the mirror one more time, really wishing I had bought the more modest dress the online store tried to sell me instead of this one. It's like it knew. Snooty sales attendants could somehow see me through my computer and were silently sticking up their noses, trying to thrust their gray, lifeless maternity dress into my cart. But nooooooo. I had been watching *Dancing with the Stars* and was feeling frisky. So I bought the slinky jet-black number with the high knee slit that appeared right next to the one a woman at my stage of gestation *should* purchase.

I hiss when I spin to look at myself over my shoulder. *When did my butt get so big?* Seriously. It's so bubbly. Like the peach emoji got implants and some dimples. The woman comes out of the stall and follows my gaze to my rear end as she washes her hands.

"Tell me straight—is my butt too big in this?"

If you're imagining we have a moment of sisterhood, you're dreaming. This woman looks as if I have wholly offended her *genteel* sensibilities and is planning an epic snub. She rips off a length of paper towels and blots her hands before saying, "It's definitely not a dress I would have chosen for you."

Oh great. I'm going to cry now as Miss Demure leaves the bathroom in her ravishing gold dress, hip bones protruding from beneath the fabric, tiny firm booty twitching up and down with

every step. She wasn't offended that my dress was too provocative; she was offended that I stuffed my maternal body inside this
provocative dress.

The moment I'm alone again, I pull my phone out of my clutch
and FaceTime Lucy. "Come on, come on, come on," I whisper
impatiently as it continues to ring. I know I don't have long until
someone else walks in.

Finally, Lucy answers, and I say, "Thank God. Luce, do I look
like a wanton strumpet?"

She's sitting on her couch, snacking on popcorn and wearing
her glasses. I'm so jealous. "Have you been watching a lot of BBC
period dramas again?"

"Beside the point. Do I?" I spin around and give her a nice butt
shot.

She whistles. "Look at that booty! You look killer! If you're a
strumpet, I want to be one too!"

"You're lying. If I look so incredible, why do I feel like crying
and hiding all my overly accentuated parts?"

"Because you have hormones raging through your body at all
times. But I swear to you, Jessie, you look lovely. Has Drew seen
you yet?" There's a mischievous glint in her eye.

"No. He's running late, which isn't helping my nerves at all. I
may look tough, but I don't think I'll be able to take it if he tells
me I look hideous and he's too embarrassed to be seen with me."

A slow grin spreads on Lucy's face. "I have a feeling he's going
to make you feel nothing but beautiful when he gets there."

I squint at the screen. "Why do you look like that?"

"Like what?"

"Like a canary feather should be hanging out of your mouth?"

I take one last look in the mirror and try to stuff my overflowing cleavage back down inside my dress, but that somehow makes
it worse.

"No, stop, you're making them angry. They're trying to revolt by swelling up more." *Super.* "Just relax, Jessie. You're gorgeous."

At least I look classy from the neck up. My blond hair is curled into soft 1920s-style finger waves that frame my face with one side pinned back. My eye makeup is dark and smoky, and even I can admit I look runway ready. Then my eyes drop to my black velvet dress and swollen stomach.

"Nope. I'm coming over to your place. Pop some extra popcorn."

"Wait! Jess—"

I end the call before Lucy has any time to protest and toss my phone into my little clutch. I swing my peach booty all the way out of the bathroom, ready to leave a trail of smoking tracks in my wake. Drew can kick me out of his house for all I care, and this prank I have planned tonight isn't even worth it anymore. To be honest, I've been rethinking it all week. It's settled—I'd rather be woken up every single morning by Levi than let Drew see me in this dress.

I open the bathroom door and leave the sterile fluorescent lighting to step into the warm opulence of wealth. *Oh my gosh, I'm the pregnant version of* Pretty Woman *right now.* I feel my mortification rising as eyes land on me when I attempt to gracefully glide my way to the front doors. I feel exposed and embarrassed as I try to avoid eye contact with everyone I pass. Why are they staring? Seriously, it feels like everyone is staring. I want to cry. No, I am *going* to cry.

And then, I see him.

Across the room, an entire ballroom length away, I spot Drew standing just inside the entrance. *Holy handsome, Batman.* Do they have stylists on call at the hospital, just waiting to turn doctors into red carpet celebrities at the drop of a hat? Of course the first thing I notice is Drew's hair. It's styled with a satin sheen pomade and waving away from his face in a wonderfully tousled look that somehow perfectly matches my own retro vibe. At first, I think he's Cary Grant to my Doris Day. But then my eyes trail the length of his muscular body encapsulated in a tight, well-cut navy— almost black—suit that looks so fabulously out of place among all these other stuffy suits, and I realize we are the rebels at this event. He's the James Dean to my Marilyn Monroe.

Drew looks tall, lean, and powerful while casually talking with someone who stopped him near the door. I don't think this man even knows the meaning of insecurity, because he's never needed to feel it. He's everything everyone wants—everything *I* want.

It's official. I'm out of here.

I look around, frantically trying to find a menu or something I can hold in front of my face, but there's nothing. *Nada.* What's a girl got to do to find a tall fern or ficus to stand behind? How about a heavy drape? Damn those BBC shows filling my head with improbable nonsense. They always have a plethora of ferns to conceal themselves with.

When I look up again, Drew is already staring at me. *Caught.* Even from all the way over here, I can tell he is completely ignoring the man jabbering his ear off. Drew's gaze zeroes in on me and runs from my hair to my toes—so intense I feel his eyes as if they were his hands.

Goosebumps trickle down my bare arms when his eyes meet mine again, and a slow smile spreads across his mouth. His head tics side to side as if to say, *You would.* He breaks eye contact with me long enough to disengage himself from the man beside him, and then his gaze is back, locked on me as he walks across the ballroom.

My heart pounds in my chest, and I'm thankful I'm in a room full of doctors so they can resuscitate me when Drew Marshall's sexy stare makes me pass out.

As he gets closer, I feel myself teetering forward, wanting to run over, wrap my arms around his neck, and trail kisses down his clean-shaven jaw. *Easy, Jessie. You're on a mission tonight.* Poor Drew, he's completely oblivious to the trap he's unknowingly walking right into, the trap I set the moment he presented this idea of me posing as his girlfriend. Tonight is my chance to even the score after he left me high and dry in front of my grandaddy (yes, I know said grandaddy didn't show—details, details), and I'll squash my growing feelings. Just because he's sexy as sin tonight and I may or may not be developing feelings for him doesn't mean I'm going to abandon my plans. It means I need to double down on them.

Drew stops right in front of me, and I try not to let my knees buckle. I have never been more nervous in my life.

"You're late," I say, in a voice I hope doesn't betray the way I'm trembling.

Drew shocks every nerve ending in my body when his mouth forms a half smile and his hand rises to lightly slide the tips of his fingers along the waves of my hair, brushing my temple and cheek and then falling all the way down the length of my arm. His hand stops to lock with mine, and instinctively my fingers close around his in a possessive, primal grip that I'm not proud of. They say the first rule in retail is to convince a customer to hold the object they are interested in, because their brain will subconsciously claim it as theirs. Apparently, the principle also applies to humans. Drew feels like mine now.

He leans forward, his smooth jaw brushing against my face as he whispers, "You are absolutely beautiful."

His raspy, quiet, meant-only-for-me voice tears its way through my fragile emotions and wrecks me in the process. Drew pulls back but hovers closer to my face than we've ever been. I could bump his nose with mine. I smell his masculine cologne, see the black flecks in his navy eyes, feel a string pulling tight between our mouths. I could tip forward just the slightest bit and our lips would touch. *They need to touch.*

I thank my lucky stars when a voice calls out from beside us and slices our moment in half. "Dr. Marshall!"

Drew and I pull apart, but he doesn't let me remove my hand from his. He introduces me to his female colleague who interrupted us. Dr. Susan Landry is her name, and I think I'm supposed to know who she is, but my mind just says, *Blah, blah, blah, Drew's hand feels so good in my hand. What a manly hand he has.* I want to hold it up to my face and stare at it. It's a big hand, which every woman knows only adds to the allure of a man.

Wow, how long have I been thinking about Drew's hands? A while, I suspect, because now both Drew and Dr. Landry are looking at me and I'm not sure what to say. I blink at the woman. "So sorry. Pregnancy brain. I missed what you said."

She laughs, and her kind smile is disarming. I relax a little. "I was just saying I'm so happy to meet Drew's girlfriend! He's talked so much about you this past week."

Yeah, that's jarring to hear. Surprisingly, it's not unpleasant, but definitely jarring. I look up at Drew and see the slightest widening of his eyes. Apparently, I speak Drew's eye language now, because I understand that this is the one we are meant to be in a fake relationship for.

Keeping my hand locked with Drew's, I take the other and wrap it around his biceps, leaning into him and hugging his arm. And *Geez, Drew.* He has a ridiculous muscle under here. I'm definitely distracted by how my body is reacting to Drew's body right now, but I press on with a polite smile and begin to set my trap.

"Only this past week, baby? Well, I guess you would have more to talk about since we finally moved in together."

Dr. Landry's eyebrows rise. "Oh wow. That's serious. Congratulations, you two. But I guess you have even more to be congratulated on besides a housewarming." Her eyes fall to my stomach, and for some reason Drew and I never discussed how to handle this part of the ruse. My instinct says he would want me to make sure everyone knows it's not his child, but guess what, bud? You stood me up, and it's time to pay.

I rub my belly and stare up at him like my entire universe dangles off his pinky. "Thank you. I hope the baby has Drew's eyes. I've never seen a blue so deep."

Drew's face goes a little pale and his arm stiffens beneath my touch. *Oops! Did your lie just get a little more complicated, Drewsky-Woosky?*

He smiles tensely. "Not sure how that will be possible," he says with a slight chuckle, clearly trying to let our dear Susan know he's not about to become a biological father.

I also know from the time I've spent around Drew since Lucy and Cooper have become an item that he despises PDA. Every time they kiss or snuggle, Drew grimaces.

Which is why I sidle up even closer and nuzzle his earlobe with the tip of my nose (and for the record, I have zero problems with PDA, but this is even making me nauseated). "Stop trying to keep your hopes down. Babies end up with their daddy's eyes all the time."

"Aw—well, you guys are just too . . ." I can see Dr. Landry struggle with the word. "Sweet. Congrats to you both, and I'll see you at the table for dinner."

"See you over there," Drew says in a calm, polite voice. When she's far enough away, he looks sharply down at me, his voice nothing even close to calm or polite. "What the hell was that?"

"What?" I blink up at him innocently. *I'm just a little lamb out to pasture.*

Drew looks around and must realize there are too many people still within earshot, so he extracts his arm from my grip and puts his hand on my lower back, steering us toward the bathrooms, though not the ones where I was previously hiding. No, he somehow manages to find us a private single stall bathroom.

Once we're in, he locks the door behind us, and now I'm stuck in this tiny cell with the most attractive man alive. But I won't kiss him. I *won't*. The name of the game tonight is to put Drew Marshall back in his rightful place, somewhere far, far away from my mind and heart.

"What was all that back there?" His voice is low and rumbly, and his dress shoes click against the floor as he advances closer to me.

I take a retreating step, and my back hits the wall. "Nothing. I thought you wanted me to be your girlfriend."

"You almost sucked on my earlobe. That's taking it a little far, don't you think?"

I shrug, not wanting to tip him off too early. "Okay, so you don't like your dates to be affectionate—got it. I won't give you a hickey at the table."

His eyes narrow. "I like affection, for the record. Just not quite so much in the middle of a conversation with a colleague."

"It's okay to not like affection. Some people aren't good at it, and that's fine." Why am I goading him like this?

His eyes flare and he steps so close the tips of his shoes touch the tips of mine. Also, my belly is grazing the front of his suit jacket, and somehow that feels incredibly intimate. "I'm perfectly good at showing affection. No—actually I'm *great* at it. If I wanted to"—his eyes drop to my mouth—"I could show you the best damn affection of your life."

Show me!

No . . . don't show me.

SHOW ME.

"I don't know. You seem awfully defensive to me."

He looks down at me and smiles—a wolf dressed in a designer suit. "You're taunting me right now. Why is that, Jessica?" His hand rises to land on the wall behind me, pinning me in place. I sink my teeth into my bottom lip and tell myself, *Do not give in, woman.* "Almost seems like you're playing a game with me right now. What's the outcome you're hoping for?"

I angle my chin up like a dagger even though all I want is to melt against him. "I don't know . . . what do you think it should be?"

He's quiet for three breaths, and because he's so close, I can feel all three of them against my lips. The tension between us is tangible and humming through every inch of me. I want to grab the front of Drew's shirt and pull his face down that last inch, but instead I keep my hands splayed out against the bathroom wall, willing them to stay put.

"Why did you let Susan think this is my child?"

The question shakes me momentarily, and I hope he doesn't see it on my face. "I—I thought that was what you wanted. Really sells the devoted girlfriend story."

"Is that the real reason?"

No. The real reason is because I want to tangle him in a lie so tight that when he finally has to get out of it, he will be humiliated. That's the real reason. It's step one.

. . . isn't it?

"Mm-hmm," I hum, still not fully able to keep myself from glancing up at his mouth, unwilling to stop myself from imagining what a kiss from him would be like. Firm? Sweet? Tender? Harsh?

No. Bad, Jessie.

Drew's lips curve upward because I've been staring and he knows why. One of his hands lowers to my hip, and I feel his fingers press into my side. I can't let this happen. It would ruin everything I'm trying to achieve, and yet . . .

Maybe one kiss won't hurt anything.

Unfortunately, a knock on the bathroom door startles both of us. Drew bites his lips against a smile as he holds my eyes for one more second before shaking his head and shrugging back down the cuffs of his suit jacket. *Good. Perfect. No kisses tonight. Staying right on track.*

But as he raises a single eyebrow and holds out his arm for me to take, I waver in my plan of retaliation. I planned it before I came to really know Drew, before we became friends . . . now, I wonder if it's worth it. I wonder if maybe I could let myself enjoy this night as his pretend girlfriend . . . if I could let myself fall for Drew.

No.

I don't want to.

Drew Marshall is about to be pranked harder than he's ever been pranked in his life.

CHAPTER 24

Drew

We are seated at the table, waiting for dinner to be served, and Jessie is fondling my ear. Not in a sensual way—although it probably looks like it's intended to be; it feels more like an annoying gnat pestering my face. My hands itch to swat hers away. Everyone at the table is staring at us like they are deeply disturbed, and honestly, I don't blame them.

I realize this is my fault though. Jessie thinks I don't like PDA because of all the gagging I do around Lucy and Cooper, so naturally she's going to climb all over me in public because of this unspoken tit-for-tat game we have going on between us. It's like a human version of Battleship.

I smile tightly and twitch my shoulder, trying to push Jessie's hand away without the whole table realizing what I'm doing. But it's a big round table, and they are all staring. Now I'm just shoulder-hugging her hand, which makes me look even more lovesick and disgusting. I take a more direct approach and cover her pesky little hand with mine, then lower it down to her lap, holding it tightly there.

She squeezes my hand under the table. It says, *Let go.* I squeeze back. *Not a chance.*

We both flash each other a soft, smitten smile so the table believes our once-in-a-lifetime romance, but under the table our hands are warring. Goodness, she makes me want to laugh. And kiss her.

When I first spotted Jessie across the room tonight, my stomach dove into a free fall. She looked so classic and feminine and *curvy,* and my heart was beating out of my chest for her. It hasn't stopped since. I would have kissed her in the bathroom if that knock on the door hadn't interrupted us. I wanted to more than I've ever wanted anything. Even now, I look over into Jessie's forest-green eyes as they sparkle from the warm lighting, and I feel like groaning. I can hardly take it. I want to scoop her and her mischievous smile up and take her home.

The table continues to buzz with medical talk like it has been ever since we sat down, and I'm hoping once our dinner arrives everyone will give the constant jargon a rest. That's the major flaw of doctors all grouped together for social events: we can't talk about anything besides medicine. It's how we're hardwired. So many years devoted to nothing but studying and learning and memorizing as much as possible will do that to a person. Back in school, when everyone else was partying and socializing, our noses were deep in a textbook. The most social contact we had was a study group, which is basically what this is now. An ultra-elegant study group.

I know Jessie has to be bored to death. Maybe if the conversation were more interesting, she'd be less determined to pinch her way out of my hand. Her fingers are like a little crab scurrying across the sand.

"Dr. Marshall, I've been meaning to ask you—what happened to your eye?" Susan asks from across the table. Of course Susan would notice it. It's more of a slight greenish shadowy bruise now than it was a week and a half ago when Jessie gave it to me. For some reason, I've loved this black eye. I love that Jessie gave it to me. I love that when I look in the mirror, I remember the sheen of terror in her green eyes when she thought she'd really hurt me. It was the first time she had ever looked at me without a mask of indifference or hatred.

Jessie lights up at this question. She gives an overindulgent smile, flashes her eyes wide in excitement, and props her elbow on the table with her fist under her chin like someone's just told her I'm about to jump on the table and give everyone a striptease.

Too bad for Jessie, if she plans to take me down, I'm dragging her with me.

I lean forward, a conspiratorial grin in place, and tilt my head toward her. "I try not to kiss and tell, but truth is, this one got a little overeager in the—" My sentence is cut off when Jessie's foot collides with my shin and she shoots me a dark look.

"Kitchen," she finishes for me, not breaking eye contact. "I opened a cabinet right into his face by accident." Something in her gaze promises her statement will come to fruition if I continue, but it won't be by accident.

Everyone hums their understanding, but it's clear they don't believe her. My seed was planted, and her face is turning into boiling lava. I feel triumphant. Smiling, I lean toward Jessie to . . . to what? I don't know exactly. All I'm conscious of is my need to get closer to her. To run my finger over her blushing cheek. To kiss her. To hold her. Her narrowed eyes soften and her lips part slightly. We're trapped in this moment together, and everything I'm feeling she's feeling too. If I could just lean a little—

A hand claps against my back. *Of course.* "Drew? Ah—I thought that might be you!"

I'm ready to murder whoever just interrupted this moment

between us when I look up into the eyes of my old mentor of sorts from med school. Despite him being a teaching physician at the time, Richard was one of my first friends in the medical world, and he's likely the only person who can escape my murderous intentions in this circumstance. Once I had decided to focus on obstetrics and gynecology, he was the one I went to with my concerns about being a young male in the profession, afraid I'd never get any patients. He laughed and told me he would only let me soak his shoulder with tears once I tried being a gay black man in the medical field, or a woman in the same profession having to work twice as hard to prove herself just as capable as a man. I liked him immediately. Dr. Green taught me the best thing I could ever do as a male ob-gyn was shut my mouth and listen to the women around me. I'm good at applying this principle in my practice, though not always so much in my personal life.

"Dr. Green, it's good to see you," I say, standing to shake his and Mr. Green's hands. "And Henry," I say, addressing Richard's husband. "How are you? I don't think I've seen you two since Dr. Green's retirement party." It's when I look down at our clasped hands that I realize how red mine is thanks to my little pincher crab. I slide my gaze over to Jessie and see her sitting demurely, hands resting in her lap like a patient angel, but I know she's seen the pinch marks because her lips are pressed together, holding back a fierce laugh.

If Henry notices the odd red splotches, he ignores them with grace. "I don't feel like we see *anyone* since Richard retired." He tosses him a reprimanding look. "I've been begging him to come out of retirement just so we can go places again. He compromised by letting us come tonight."

Richard laughs and guides Henry around the table to take the two available seats closest to me and Jessie. He pulls a chair out for Henry, making me wonder belatedly if I did that for Jessie.

Richard looks at Henry with narrowed eyes after they've taken their seats.

"And force you to miss me again during all of those long work days? Never."

Henry looks to Jessie and me with extra-wide eyes and a mocking smile. "So considerate of him."

We all laugh, and then, trying to be discreet, I cut my eyes to Jessie, hoping she won't look bored. Because for some reason, I want her to enjoy being here with me—meeting my colleagues and the people who were so integral in the early years of my career. When my eyes land on her, my heart jolts. Her head is tilted softly to the side, and her green eyes are sparkling with a genuine smile. She looks *happy*.

I don't realize I have fully turned my face to openly stare at Jessie for goodness knows how long until Henry's voice shocks me into reality.

"Drew, who is this beautiful young woman you're so fondly gazing at?" he asks, a note of mischief in his eye, like he was excited to call me out in front of everyone.

Without a second thought, I raise my arm to lay it over the back of Jessie's chair and run my thumb against the side of her shoulder. I notice her look down to where I'm tracing a lazy pattern against her skin, and I could swear her skin flushes. *See, I can do affection.*

Jessie looks up at me quickly, and her eyes search my face like she wants to see for herself the look Henry was referring to. Except, she doesn't look happy about it at all. Am I imagining it, or does she tuck her shoulder in so I can't brush my fingers against it anymore?

"This is . . . my girlfriend, Jessica Barnes. Jessie, this is Dr. Richard Green and his husband, Henry. Dr. Green was my mentor in medical school."

Jessie's gorgeous, full lips tip into a soft smile, and that's that. She welcomes them into her friend group with an ease she never gave me, and I have to try very hard not to be jealous. But I am. I'm jealous and wondering what I needed to do from the beginning to get the same sweet treatment as Richard and Henry. Maybe if that day when she showed up ready to fight me on Lucy's behalf I had just kissed her then and there, we could have avoided all this unpleasant dueling.

But even as I think of all that "unpleasant dueling," I'm smiling, because truthfully, I needed it. I haven't realized until this moment how weary I had become of my constant need to remain professional and put together. Even in my family, I'm the one who solves problems, the responsible one, the guy who's always ready to help when they need me. And don't get me wrong, I love being that guy. It suits me well, but sometimes I just need a break from it. There's never been any other force in my life to show me there's a different way or what I'm missing . . . until Jessie. After living, fighting, and playing with her, I realize just how deprived I've been of pointless joy. Laughter for the hell of it. Smiling just because I feel like it. It's been good, and I don't want it to end.

As fast friends, Richard, Henry, and Jessie all make a pact to call each other by their first names, and Henry wastes no time scooting his chair a little closer to Jessie and diving into a long series of get-to-know-you questions. Richard and I head over to the open bar to bring drinks back to the table and spend the next twenty minutes catching up. I try to stay focused on the conversation, but Henry keeps laughing at things Jessie says and I can't help but glance over frequently. Jessie's dimpled smile kicks me in the stomach each time I see it, and I wish I could lean over and kiss it. I realize how much more enjoyable these events would be if she always came with me. Jessie even manages to get the rest of the table to ditch their professional medical talk as she animatedly tells a story about when she accidentally cut off the tip of someone's ear in hair school and then convinced one of the EMTs and the poor guy missing part of his body to let her come into the ambulance and help bandage it up. She walked away from the incident with *both* of those guys' numbers. Only Jessie could manage something like that.

When I hear Henry ask Jessie if she knows the sex of her baby yet, I find myself leaning in a little closer. I've never heard her mention a pronoun when referring to the baby—in fact, she doesn't mention the baby much at all. The whole thing feels very mysterious, but I've been too much of a coward to ask her about it.

"I don't. I'm going to let it be a surprise."

Henry *awww*s and says it's the last true surprise you can have in life, and I doubt he even picks up on the tension in Jessie's shoulders. I do, though. I've started picking up on Jessie's little cues, and I can spot them from across the room now. I also know she has five different smiles: 1) polite, 2) go jump off a bridge, 3) genuine, 4) sultry, and 5) uncomfortable.

The one she gave Henry was definitely number five, and I want to know why. I want to know everything about her.

Conversation breaks up when servers begin to bring plates of food to the table. I notice something in Jessie's demeanor change. The spark that was present earlier in the night has dissipated. Maybe she's tired? Nauseous? I don't know, and it's killing me. Jessie is only my fake girlfriend tonight, but I still feel responsible for her. I want to take care of her.

I use the opportunity to lean a little closer to Jessie. My thigh brushes against hers, and she peeks up at me. "Everything okay?" I ask quietly.

"Mm-hmm," she says, with a smile that doesn't reach her eyes.

She picks up her water, her hand trembling slightly, and takes a deep swallow. *Something is definitely off.* And then, like a switch was flipped, Jessie's eyes pop up and she makes me add a new smile to my list: *wicked*. I watch curiously as she digs somewhat mindlessly in her clutch, looks at me over her shoulder, raises a taunting eyebrow, and drops her eyes to my mouth. Her soft pink lips dare me to lean forward and take them.

My pulse quickens, and I'm so distracted by her lips and whatever it is she's silently trying to tell me that I barely notice something tumble out of her purse. "Oops. Can you grab that for me, *Andrew*?" Something in my mind tries to alert me that she used my full name—the one we only use for each other during battle—but the more powerful part of my brain is too busy fantasizing about Jessie to pay attention to it.

Is she giving me some serious bedroom eyes or what? She looks like she wants me *right now*. It's the same look she was giving me in the bathroom, but a more intense version. I can't take my eyes off of her. I'm hypnotized, and she looks like a bronzed goddess in her black velvet dress, green eyes blazing, soft skin begging for me to glide my hands all over it.

Before I even realize it, I'm sliding off my chair a little to grab whatever it is she dropped, eyes never leaving her. My eyes should *never, ever* leave her again. If they do, it will break the spell, and I'm ready to admit this is not a spell I want to break.

I aimlessly feel along the ground for the item, and I have to stretch so far my knee practically touches the ground, but I finally grab hold of the little box and hold it up for Jessie to take. It's then that she bites down on her bottom smiling lip and gasps so loudly I nearly jolt. Her hand flies to her chest and pushes against her cleavage like a dramatic heroine in an old black-and-white film. The word *yes* tumbles loudly from her lips.

I blink, spell broken, and realize the trap instantly. I don't need to look down to see what's in my hand, but I do anyway. *Yep*. It's a ring box.

"Yes! Of course I'll marry you! I thought you'd never ask!" She's bubbling over with all the excitement of a woman deep in the throes of love.

I'm shocked—and then mortified as the entire ballroom suddenly erupts in applause.

"Show us the ring!" Henry calls above the clapping that's ringing in my ears like a fire alarm.

I'm still resting on my knee, box poised in front of me, stunned into stone-cold silence. Jessie reacts for me, leaning forward slightly to open the box and reveal a tiny (fake, I'm sure) diamond ring. It's so small it should come with a magnifying glass. *Great.* A brilliant addition to the prank, Jessica. Well done. I'll be a laughingstock.

A fresh round of gasps is released around the table, and I finally look up into Jessie's eyes. Hers are locked on mine, and she looks as if she's trying not to die of laughter. I consider telling her to go right ahead, and I'll get to work on her grave.

"You are a dead woman," I mumble through my fake smile.

She sinks her teeth into her bottom lip again and slips the ring from the box right onto her finger. She throws the icing on the cake when she pronounces, "You outdid yourself, Drew! You remembered I love grand gestures. You never forget anything, do you?" Her eyes slide from the pathetic excuse for a ring down to me, and I see nothing but bitter revenge boiling in her irises. It's then I realize she's been planning this since the beginning. She bends over slightly to whisper in my ear, "What's worse, Dr. Stuck-up? Being stood up? Forgotten? Or getting tangled in a lie in front of five hundred colleagues with an itsy-bitsy, teeny-tiny ring?"

Anger, mortification, and betrayal all war and sizzle beneath my skin. I thought . . . I thought we were friends now. Apparently I was wrong.

"Bless him, he's blushing!" someone at the table whispers, and

I want to die. No one will forget this, and I'll either have to keep up a fake engagement for the rest of my life, tell the truth and humiliate myself, or tell everyone I broke things off with the mother of what they believe is my child and look like a complete jerk. Either way, I'm not coming out of this in a favorable light.

I manage to peel myself off the ground and retake my seat, suddenly feeling the need to loosen the tie around my neck. The room is swirling, and everywhere I look smiles are beaming at me and offering congratulations.

"Drew, give her a kiss—don't leave the poor girl hanging," says Richard from somewhere within the hazy rush of anxiety I'm feeling.

I slowly turn to Jessie and can see her chest and shoulders shaking with restrained laughter. This only ignites my fury more. I'm angry—no, I'm *pissed* at Jessie, but I'm also not so far gone that I'm going to waste this moment.

She angles her self-satisfied smirk toward me and presents her cheek, still enjoying her moment of control.

If she's going to ruin me tonight, I'm going to ruin kissing for her from now on. I'll make sure that, in comparison, any first kiss after this one tastes as dry as burnt toast.

I curve my hand firmly around the back of Jessie's neck and lean forward. She gasps at the pressure of my fingers against her skin, and everything around us melts away. My eyes drink up the features of her face, her pink mouth, the curve of her long dark lashes, her delicate collarbones extending out under taut, golden skin. I can't wait any longer. I need her kiss like I need air.

My mouth covers hers in a sweet, fragile press that she wasn't expecting. No doubt my eyes look hungry, and the pressure of my hand prepared her for a firm collision—but I'm not some anxious frat boy cornering her at a party. I've got nothing but time and patience as I tilt her face so our lips can meet over and over again in luxurious coaxing presses. My heart pounds, and the rhythm of her mouth's movement accelerates. She smells like coconut and tastes like heaven, and the sudden gentle grip of Jessie's hand on my knee spurs me to lightly brush my tongue against her lips, coaxing them to part so we can deepen the kiss. Jessie nearly falls off her chair trying to slide closer to me. I can't help but smile against her needy search of my mouth, but then, sensing my amusement, Jessie pulls her lips away and her eyes flutter open. She looks shocked and startled and drugged. I want to gloat, but instead I can't resist dragging my thumb across her lower lip one more time.

We stare at each other, both frowning in disapproval as the room erupts in applause, catcalls, and whistles. Suddenly, I'm angrier than I've ever been in my life. Not because of the prank—although I'm going to have a hell of a time unraveling it—but because of her obvious hatred behind it. I feel like an idiot for seeing the last few weeks as anything other than what they were: a setup. She let me think we were becoming friends so when she squashed me in the big reveal, it would make her victory twice as sweet. Just like the bucket of water above my door.

But I don't know . . . somehow those thoughts don't feel right either. There's more to this, more lurking under the surface, but I don't see it yet.

Finally, I grin (read: sneer) and take her hand in mine, holding it up in the air like I'm the one who actually won this match.

CHAPTER 25

Jessie

'm a mess, and I just want to go home. Drew wasn't supposed to kiss me. He wasn't supposed to . . .

No, I can't even let myself go there. It was too good, and even though I won this round tonight, I still feel like I lost somehow. Is this how people feel when they go on a game show and pass on the hundred thousand dollars to see what's in the box instead? *Don't open the box, people!* There's nothing in that stupid box but unwanted feelings.

After my supreme prank and Drew's very un-supreme kiss (just let me have this one), we had to endure an entire dinner as well as a silent auction together, both stewing in our own versions of anger but keeping smiles plastered across our faces. Between Susan and the Greens, I felt as if we were on a celebrity talk show. No one has ever been more interested in a relationship than those three. Drew and I were pulling fake dating stories out of thin air, smiling and chuckling when it was warranted, but all evening I could feel the silent pressure of his hand against my shoulder, reminding me that he hadn't forgotten, that we have the mother of all fights on the horizon.

My retaliation completely worked, so why does the thought of Drew angry make me want to run out and buy an entire frozen section of ice cream just to make him smile at me again?

Finally, someone comes over a speaker and announces that the dance floor is open. *Oh great, now we have to do the electric slide with these bad attitudes?* I can't spend any more time next to Drew and his handsome face, and dark blue eyes, and telepathic anger. Oh, but wait! I drove here! I can save myself!

Discreetly, I gather my purse and rise out of my chair, hoping to slip past Drew while he's talking to Richard without him noticing. But of course he does notice, because he notices every movement I make, and as soon as I stand, his hand catches mine. The smirk he tosses up at me turns my stomach inside out.

"Not leaving without me, are you, buttercup?"

Now we're two parents in the middle of an ugly fight but not wanting to upset the kids. "I didn't want to interrupt you two, honey bear," I say, turning my smile to Richard and then back to Drew. "You stay and enjoy yourself! I'll just see you at home, okay?" I flash him my pearly whites. *Cheese! Everything is fine, random onlookers!*

The corners of Drew's eyes crinkle. "I'm not going to let my pregnant fiancée walk to her car all alone after dark. Come on, gumdrop, I'll walk with you." Drew is acting so over the top. His sugary-sweet demeanor is prickling all over my skin like I rolled in a pile of sandburs.

Drew stands up, and I wish I didn't find him even more attractive, but after that incredible kiss, I do. He looks stronger somehow. More capable. And knowing how his lips feel . . . *No! Don't think about the kiss.*

"Oh, wait, you two!" says Henry, drawing our attention back

with a little wave of his hand. "Before you go, we wanted to run something by you guys." He and Richard share a private look that seriously worries me. "We were wondering if you would like to join us next weekend at our house up on Barren River Lake—like a little engagement celebration weekend! It's such a beautiful place right on the edge of Kentucky and only just over an hour away. Enjoy a little restful weekend before your sweet baby arrives."

Ugh. They are so nice. Under any other circumstance, I'd be all over a relaxing weekend away with a sexy man like Drew and sweet new friends. But as everything stands, a weekend away with him would only lengthen this nightmare. *No, thank you.* It's time to move on from Drew.

"That is such a sweet offer, and normally we would love to, but—"

"But nothing. We'd love to go," Drew interjects with a smile that borders on insanity, and his hand drops to my low *low* back in a wayyyyy-too-familiar touch. I think this is the moment in his villain story when he first turns bad. Chills chase that thought all over my skin.

I take a step closer to Drew and pat his chest, talking through my smiling teeth like a ventriloquist. "Honey, I think you've forgotten—you're on call this weekend."

He chuckles, and I feel it in my palm. "Actually, it's the weekend after that I'm on call. I'm free as a bird this weekend." He bops the tip of my nose.

I'm going to wring his gorgeous neck. I don't want to go to their stupid lake house and pretend to be congenial all weekend. What I need to do is get away from Drew forever. *Nothing* is going as I planned.

"Well then . . ." I swallow. "Looks like we're coming to your lake house!"

Maybe I can eat something spicy and send myself into early labor before next weekend . . .

Faster, Jessie, faster!

I whip my car into the driveway and cut the engine. I took the opportunity to sneak out of the fundraiser while Drew was caught talking with a blabbermouth at the door, but as I was pulling out of the parking lot, I saw him exiting the venue. We locked eyes through the window of my car, and he picked up his pace into nearly a full jog toward his Jeep.

Because I love taking the high road, I stuck my tongue out, then peeled out of the parking lot. Now I'm home, Drew is only a minute behind me at most, and I'm going to accidentally break my water as I leap out of the car and race my way up the stairs. I'm out of breath and exhausted when I make it into my bedroom, shutting and locking the door behind me.

I sag against it and drag in as much air as I can, feeling grateful no one is here to witness me fighting for my life after that mild exercise.

BANG, BANG, BANG.

"AH!" I screech and then cover my mouth. How did he get up here so fast? I don't even hear any panting on the other side of the door. *Showoff.*

"I know you're hiding in there. Get out here."

My, my, someone's throwing a temper tantrum.

Feeling empowered by the locked door, I lean against it and angle my lips toward the crack. "You know, someone once told me that manners are important, and I think you're missing a special word there, mister. I'll give you a hint. It starts with a *p* and ends with—"

"Jessie," Drew barks from the other side. The fact that he used my shortened name makes me want to run for the hills. This is serious. "Come out here and face me, woman."

I'm a tiny little mouse safe inside my mousehole, and he's the big mean cat trying to swipe his paw inside. "No thanks. I'm good in here." My stomach growls. I should have brought some cheese with me into this mousehole.

"You can't stay in there forever."

"Not forever. I just have to wait long enough for one of your patients to go into labor, and *then* I'll sneak out. I'm not without a plan."

"I'll quit my job."

"You wouldn't."

"My full-time career is now sitting here and waiting you out. Don't think I won't." He growls, and it stirs the pit of my stomach. "I can't believe you did that to me tonight."

"Can't you? We've been pranking each other continuously since I moved in. You should have seen it coming. I don't understand why you're so mad." I do understand, though. It was a cheap shot tonight. It felt wrong from the beginning, and it feels wrong now.

He scoffs mildly. "You don't see why I'm mad?" His voice is doing that thing where it sounds light and airy, which is honestly scarier than if he were yelling. Not scary because I feel that I'm in any danger around Drew—I know he's not like that—but scary because it feels like we are on the precipice of something. His emotions are loose and wild, and everyone knows in the heat of the moment is when the real truth spills out. It's when words are said that no one can take back.

"Well, let's see. Tonight, my fake girlfriend tricked me into getting down on my knee and proposing to her at a *medical fundraiser* with the world's dinkiest, most insulting ring in front of five hundred important doctors, scientists, and a few celebrities, all of whom came up to offer their sincere congratulations for a union that's not really going to happen and then poorly contained their horrified shock at the fake diamond ring on your finger that's literally the size of a punctuation mark." Okay, yeah, that sounds pretty bad when he lines it all up like that. "But I'll tell you what makes me the most upset."

"Do you have to?"

I can practically feel his white-hot anger searing through the door, and I want to hide under my covers. "I'm most upset that this wasn't like all the other pranks." His words are sharp needles resting on my heart. "Was it, Jessie?"

I swallow and flick a piece of chipped paint off the door. "I don't know what you're talking about."

"Yes, you do." It sounds like his forehead is resting against the door too. "This one was malicious. It was meant to humiliate me, and"—he sighs, and I imagine him running his hand through his hair—"you've been planning this since the day you moved in, haven't you? Everything was just building up to this prank. You still think I stood you up on purpose and haven't forgiven me."

I stay quiet, afraid to say anything. But apparently my silence is telling enough.

"Thought so. Damn, I'm an idiot." He laughs, but it's humorless. "Here I thought this last week we were . . ."

"Were what?" I lean against the wall and stare at the crack between the door and the doorframe, almost wishing I hadn't asked that question.

"Flirting," he says, so matter-of-factly. "Weren't we? All those other little wars just felt like messing around, having fun . . . like they were leading to something else between us. Was I wrong?"

Again my silence speaks volumes, but I know it's telling the wrong story.

He's not wrong, and I'm quiet because tears are leaking down my cheeks, and I don't want him to know it. I don't want him to know I'm crazy about him and every day I spend with him I like him more. He has a horrible singing voice but still belts out a song every morning while he cooks breakfast, and he always makes double for me, pretending he accidentally added too many eggs. I still have terrible insomnia, so every night I go out and fall asleep on the couch watching reruns of *Seinfeld* or a BBC show. The past few times, I've woken up in the morning with my pillow from my bed under my head and an extra blanket draped over me. One time I woke up with socks on my feet. I've never thanked Drew for it, because I'm scared to admit how much it means to me.

And now, I absolutely will not tell him I have feelings for him, because I never want a man to have power over my heart again. It feels easier just to let him think I hate him, let him believe I like being on my own.

It sounds like Drew's forehead gently lands on the other side of the door, and I imagine us face-to-face, separated by only two inches. "I'm not afraid to admit it to you, Jessie. I have been flirting with you. I *like* you. Yeah, you made me furious at first and still do sometimes, but it's good. I really . . . I thought you felt the same way." He sounds tired all of a sudden.

I clear my throat lightly so he won't hear the wobble from my tears and then force myself to kick him away *Old Yeller* style. "I'm sorry, Drew. You're not my type. I'm just . . . not attracted to you in that way." I'm tempted to duck and cover due to the lightning that will definitely strike me down any second. As extra penance, a magical inscription will appear on my gravestone that reads, *Jessie Barnes was never as attracted to anyone else as she was to Drew Marshall.*

I hear another humorless laugh followed by a small thump on

the wall like he hit it lightly with his fist. I flinch. "Fine. Okay, Jessie. Glad to know I'm not your type. I'll get out of your hair now."

I put my hand flat against the door. "Drew, wait!"

His footsteps stop. "What?"

"The lake house weekend with the Greens . . ." I wince at the fact that I'm bringing this up at a time like this, but I have to.

His voice sounds dark and clipped when he says, "Don't worry about it. I'll find a way out of it."

I pinch my eyes shut, knowing I have no right to ask this but wanting to anyway. I'm too scared to have Drew in the way I want him, but I'm also not ready to give him up completely either. "Actually, it's near my grandaddy's house. I was thinking maybe we could . . . make another deal. I'll go with you to the lake house for a night if you drive up with me to visit my grandaddy after? It doesn't have to be more than a night. I just want to check on him. He knows the truth now too, so you don't have to pretend to be my fiancé." Drew doesn't answer, so I keep talking. "And I miss him but don't feel comfortable driving that far alone at this stage in my pregnancy." Some of that is true. Not the last part, but I know Drew won't argue.

"Geez, Jessie. We're friends—or at least I'm yours. Not everything has to be exactly even between us at all times. Just ask me to go with you and I will."

No. Then I would feel beholden to him, and I don't want that. I want to remain as emotionally untethered from Drew as possible. "Please, Drew. This is the only way I feel comfortable. Just say we have a deal."

He's quiet. So quiet I think he walked away. He *should* walk away. There's no reason for him to continue to be kind to me, and maybe on another level I'm trying to force his hand, force him to show me he's just as terrible as my dad and Jonathan and he will put his own needs over mine forever and always.

Of course Drew doesn't work that way though.

"Fine. We have a deal. But I'm done after this one. No more deals."

Drew walks away, and I sit on the edge of my bed for a full twenty minutes just staring at the wall. I put my hand on my belly and feel the baby kick. I think he or she is telling me I made a mistake, but I can't be certain. *The little traitor.* But honestly, I don't blame him or her. I would take Drew's side too.

I finally get myself up, change into my PJs, and leave my room, on tiptoe all the way down the stairs. I like to eat when I'm upset, and right now I plan to scoop up the entire contents of the pantry and carry it upstairs like I'm a chipmunk preparing for winter.

At the bottom of the steps, I pause. Drew is in his room with the door shut, but I can still hear his voice. Maybe it's just in my head because I know the conversation we just had, but he sounds like a sad man trying to convince someone he's happy.

"Hey, Mia. This is Drew Marshall. You wrote your number on my coffee cup the other day at the coffee shop." Wrote her name on his cup?! Who does that! "Yeah, sorry it took me so long to give you a call. I had kind of a busy week."

I'm not spying. I'm not. My ear is only pressed to his door because I thought I heard an evil spirit in the wall and I might need to call someone about purging it.

Drew chuckles at something she said. "Cool. Yeah, so I was wondering if you're free sometime this week for dinner? I'd love to take you out." *Oh, would you, Drew? Would you just* love *to?*

I bet this is all a ruse. A sham. He knows I'm eavesdropping and is making this all up just to make me regret turning him down. *Well tough, buddy.* I've never felt better. Lying to Drew about not flirting with him was the best decision I ever made. I'm happy to not have to worry about fighting him off anymore. He can go out with Coffee Shop Woman and have a fabulous time for all I care!

Good riddance!

Drew's voice is a mumble after that, too quiet and far away to hear what he's saying, and I wonder if I can go get a glass to help me listen through the door before he hangs up. Nope, too late.

The door opens and Drew stands there without a smile, expressionless. "Eavesdropping?"

"Yes. Planning a date twenty minutes after getting rejected by me?"

"Yes." Not even a hint of shame from this one. "Is there a set amount of time I'm supposed to wait after being rejected?"

"Not at all."

"Great." He steps slightly closer. "Because I'm going out with a woman later this week." I try not to flinch at his words. He must notice something, though, because his demeanor softens a little. "Jessie . . . I'll ask you one more time if there's something between us. If you say yes, I will gladly cancel with her. But if you say no—"

"No," I say quickly, ripping the Band-Aid off. It's going to leave an ugly red mark on my skin, but it's what I had to do.

Drew gives a final nod. That's that. We're done here. Show's over, folks.

CHAPTER 26

Jessie

"Oh, hey, girl!" I greet Lucy when she hops into the passenger seat of my car. "You look adorable in your sparkly little cocktail dress!"

Her bright-blue eyes beam over at me. "Thanks! Oh my gosh, I'm so excited you want to go out tonight. I have needed a girls night for *so* long."

"Yeah, you have! And you deserve it." I sound like a valley girl in an old nineties movie, but I'm not sorry.

She clicks her seatbelt in the latch and swivels to look at me as I put the car in drive. "So where are we going? Dinner? Dancing?" She shimmies her shoulders, and knowing what I do about Lucy, I bet she regrets it instantly. But then she really takes in my outfit for the first time and hesitation is in her expression.

"Oh my gosh, better!" I say, wagging my eyebrows.

Her eyes narrow. "Where?"

"Get this: we are going to enjoy a nice relaxing evening of finishing off a fabulous bag of Twizzlers while sitting outside Bask."

Her head tilts in suspicion. She's on to me. "Isn't that the place Drew is taking his date tonight?"

I morph my face into innocent shock. "*What?* Is it? I had no clue." But really, I had no clue Drew would tell Lucy about his plans. It's inconvenient they are so close.

I glance at Lucy in time to see her shoulders drop and arms cross. "We're going to spy on my brother, aren't we?"

"Noooo," I say, like that thought never crossed my mind and I love sitting outside restaurants while I eat stale candy just for fun.

"We are." She flops back against the seat and pouts. It's all drama with this one. "I can't believe you let me get all dolled up and made me believe we were doing something fun tonight, when really I have to stare at my ugly brother through a restaurant window!"

I scoff. "Okay, well, you're totally wrong. He's not ugly." I glance sideways and find her burning a hole through my face.

"Last I heard, you *weren't attracted to him in that way.*"

"What a little loose-lipped pouty-pouterson! Can he not keep anything to himself?" I say, deeply put out by him divulging our conversation to Lucy. How much of it did he tell her? Did he mention that all the pranks were really just him flirting? Or that he *likes* me? I still can't wrap my mind around it. Drew. *Drew Marshall likes me.* At least, he did before I kicked him in the metaphorical groin and ran away. What can I say, though? He's not in the plan. Drew was never supposed to happen. He was supposed to hate me, and I'd hate him in return. No grand feelings, no recklessness. And definitely *no* new relationships with a baby coming shortly.

"Okay, that's it—turn around and take me home. I didn't sign up for this." I hit the child locks and gun it. She gasps in outrage. "Are you seriously holding me hostage right now?!"

"I'm really doing this for you."

"How do you figure?"

All right, she's got me there. This has absolutely no positive outcomes for her. "Fiiinnne. I just don't want to go alone, okay? Please go with me." Lucy can't say no to me (or really anyone). It's her biggest failing in life, and I'm milking it now.

"Oooh, here's an idea: you don't have to go alone because YOU DON'T HAVE TO GO AT ALL."

"OW!" I wiggle my knuckle against my ear. "I think you burst my eardrum."

She rolls her eyes, not looking regretful at all that I'll have to wear a hearing aid from now on. "Why do you care anyway? It's not as if you like Drew." She pauses and whips her head around, auburn locks flying dramatically around her. "Or do you?!"

I grimace and pretend to gag like *Ew, Drew? Hate him, grossest human I've ever met.* "Absolutely not. I just think he's lying and not really on a date tonight. I want to catch him." Because who could find a date that fast anyway? And do women really write their names on the sides of to-go coffee cups outside of the movies? *I think not, your honor.*

I have had plenty of time to think about it the last two days since I overheard Drew setting up this little "date," and I'm almost positive it's a sham. He got his pride hurt so he wanted to rub his ability to pick up women in my face. A little salt-in-the-wound trick. Well, ha!—*I'm on to you, Drew. And I'm about to catch you in the saddest solo dinner date ever.* Maybe he won't even be there. Maybe he's sitting on a bench by the lake, throwing bread to ducks while melancholy music plays in his earbuds. *One can only hope.*

Lucy gripes and complains at me all the way to the restaurant, but I mostly tune her out because I'm on a mission and won't be deterred. Once we pull up at the restaurant, a valet comes to my door and opens it, revealing the plush taco-print robe I didn't bother changing out of. "Oh, no! Sorry! We're not valet parking. We're just waiting here for a friend."

He's judgy as he takes in my outfit. "This is a valet-only zone, ma'am. You can't park here."

"So sorry. I'll move!" I shut the door and drive the car forward about four and a half feet.

Pesky valet knocks on my window, shaking his head. "Not here either. You're going to have to pull around to the parking lot."

The parking lot?! But that's at the back of the building. I'll never be able to see in the windows that way. How am I supposed to stalk someone without being able to see through a window?

Lucy's bottom lip juts out. "*Oh poo,* I guess your plan is foiled and we have to go home." She mock snaps like it's bumming her out.

I point a stern finger at Lucy. "That's enough sass from you."

Doing as I'm told, I pull around to the parking lot and get out of the car. Lucy follows suit, her heels clicking on the pavement, a panicked expression on her face. "Wait, wait, wait—where are you going? Uh, Jessie, where are you going dressed like a human taco?!"

"*We* are going to get a better look in that restaurant." I can feel the giant wobbly topknot bouncing enthusiastically on the top of my head with each step.

"Oh no we are not," Lucy says, scurrying up behind me in her flashy dress. Good for her. She never wears flashy dresses. I'm surprised Cooper shared her with me tonight. "Are you serious? I just noticed your matching burrito slippers! No one can see you like this! Take it from someone who has been caught in all manner of embarrassing situations . . . *you don't want this,*" she says, gesturing wildly up and down my body.

"That's the difference between us—you get caught. I do not."

Her eyes bug out. "Rhyming, Jessie? *Rhyming!* This isn't the time!"

"It's always time for a good rhyme."

"Jessie, stop." Lucy tugs on my hand, pulling me to a halt. "Why are you doing this?"

"I told you, I want to catch him in the lie." Someone is not paying close attention when someone else is talking. Not to point fingers, but . . . it's Lucy.

She's exasperated. "The real reason, please."

I sigh and shift on my burritos. I can't tell her the truth—she'll tell Drew. Not because she means to divulge my feelings to him, but because she's Lucy and can't lie or keep a secret to save her life. Letting my eyes speak louder than my words is the only hint I'm willing to give her. So I hold her gaze and shrug in a look of resigned defeat, the pathetic look of a person not wanting to admit the truth but who is also helpless to hold it inside much longer. I'm a prisoner to my own fear, and that's how it has to be right now.

"I just need to, okay? It's important to me."

Lucy's eyebrows crunch together, and her lips pull to the side. She assesses my face, thinking it over for a few seconds. Finally, she groans . . . loudly and with an open mouth. "Okay. Let's do this. But please, for the love, don't let him see us. I'm too old to be spying on my brother."

I scoff, offended that she would even feel the need to say that. I'm wearing a taco robe and plush burritos on my feet—believe me, if there were an option where I didn't have to be here tonight spying on Drew, I'd take it. I tried to sit at home like an uninvested bystander, and it didn't work. TV couldn't distract me. I matched each of my socks in a flash. I ordered a luggage set off the Home Shopping Network that I'll never use. In the end, I had to come and see Drew on this date for myself, because apparently I love torture.

Lucy and I sneak around the building, opting to hover on the opposite side from the judgy valet and peek through the glass. The restaurant has nearly floor-to-ceiling windows except for a three-foot-tall brick edging, so we have a mostly unobstructed view of the warmly lit, expansive dining area. There's a shiny black concrete floor and so many Edison bulb light fixtures I'll have a filament spot burned into my eyes for the rest of the week. The tables are made of a dark oak wood, and the chairs are black tufted leather. It's trendy, and moody, and exactly the sort of place I'd love to go on a date. Instead, I'm standing outside with my nose pressed to the glass, dressed like a taco shop mascot escaped from duty.

Lucy bounces beside me. "Do you see him? Can we go yet?"

No . . . I don't. *I don't!* My eyes scan around the restaurant with jubilant glee as I take note of every single patron and not a single sign of Drew in sight. "*I knew it!*" I fist-pump the air. My heart is exploding. This was all a ploy to make me jealous! He said he wouldn't sit around and pine after me, but he can't help it. He's definitely on a bench somewhere, Sufjan Stevens playing in his ears. And now I get to gloat, dropping cryptic little comments over our bowls of cereal in the morning, making a big show of wanting to know every detail of his date. Am I mean and horrible? Yup, but fighting with Drew is the only outlet I have for the desire that builds inside me every time he's around. It's the only way I can let it out.

It's going to be—wait. *No.*

Lucy gasps. "There he is! Walking toward that table across the room! He must have been in the bathroom . . ."

My heart sinks all the way down to the lettuce in my burritos as I watch him smile at the woman now sitting in front of him. She's beautiful. A down-to-earth, curvy, I-rolled-right-out-of-bed-this-pretty-and-radiant sort of woman. She looks *sweet.* Sort of like the way Lucy looks with those wide, innocent doe eyes. I would never have pegged this woman to have scribbled her number on Drew's coffee cup. I bet it was the only daring thing she's ever done. Good for her. *Good. For. Her.*

Lucy puts her hand on my arm. "Looks like he really is on a date."

Thank you, Captain Obvious! I'm glad I didn't say that out loud. Lucy doesn't deserve my wrath. It's my own fault for not telling Drew the truth. I made my bed, and it's time to lie in it. Alone. And cold. And manless.

"Yeah, it's fine."

"Fine? Your jaw is clenching so hard I'm worried for your teeth."

I relax my face and give her a pacifying smile. "Better?"

"No. Now you look like a serial killer."

"You're full of compliments tonight. Let's go, I need some Twizzlers now."

Before we turn away, I see the woman put her hand on top of Drew's, and I'm filled with the urge to go rip that arm from its socket. Just as the woman's hand touches his skin, it looks like Drew gets hit with a bolt of awareness and his eyes shift like magnets to where Lucy and I are standing. We both gasp. Lucy does what she does best and drops to the ground, out of sight. I do a spin roll until my back meets the brick siding. I wish I could drop to the ground too, but I'm eight months pregnant now, so the only thing that's dropping these days is this baby.

"Do you think he saw us?!" Lucy asks.

"Nah—we're good." He totally saw us. "C'mon, we better get out of here. NO, DON'T STAND UP! Army crawl, woman!"

"Oh my gosh, if I get knee scrapes from this, I'm never forgiving you."

We hightail it out of there, and when we pull up outside her house, I give Lucy the whole bag of Twizzlers to take inside as an apology for the one-and-a-half-centimeter scrape she complained about all the way home.

When I'm alone on the couch again, I rub my hand over my belly and tell the baby what an idiot he or she has for a mother. I can't decide what's worse, letting myself develop feelings for an incredible man like Drew when I'm eight months pregnant or pushing him away when he showed the slightest bit of interest.

My lengthy inner monologue gets interrupted when the front door opens and Drew steps inside. I hunker down into the couch cushions and pull my blanket up to my chin like I've been here all night. *Niiice and cozy.* Would it be over the top if I snored? I'm just about to try it when I accidentally make eye contact with Drew. Ugh. I want to groan at how fantastic he looks tonight in his dark jeans and heather-gray Henley shirt pulling against his chest.

His blue eyes flare and his mouth forms a mocking smile. "Comfy?"

I make a show of snuggling in, knowing full well he saw me at the restaurant. I'll die before I admit it though. "Sooooo comfy. Date go well?"

He toes out of his shoes. "I don't know. Why don't you tell me? Looked like you had a nice front-row seat."

"I have no idea what you're talking about."

Drew crosses the room to where I'm lying on the couch. He plants one hand on the armrest above my head and the other on the back of the couch—trapping me. His blue eyes almost look black right now. "I saw you."

I gulp.

"How is that possible when I've been here on this couch all night?" Thank God couches can't talk.

Drew smiles slowly. "Cute taco robe by the way." I'm covered up to my eyeballs with a blanket, so this is his way of calling the cards in my hand before I've even laid them on the table. His finger rises near my shoulder and leisurely flicks the blanket down an inch, revealing the collar of my adorable leisurewear. He doesn't even drop his eyes to it, just holds my gaze with that lazy, confident smile. It makes me want to *disrobe* him.

"Seems odd to spy on a man you have zero interest in. You sure there's no previous statements you'd like to amend, Oscar?"

"Nope," I say, willing myself not to look at his beautiful mouth. Two out of three buttons are undone on his Henley tee, making a small V-shaped patch of chest visible. My fingers itch to undo that last button. Ladies all across the world chant for me to do it. "Still can't stand you," I whisper, sounding weak and like a woman staring at a fresh stream after weeks of dehydration.

"Great." Drew rises back up to his full impressive height and walks toward the kitchen. "Then you'll have no problem with me taking Mia to lunch on Friday."

"None. I hope you have a great time." *I hate Mia and hope she chokes on an olive.* I hate that he went out with her! I hate that he looked like he was having a good time! I hate that I feel so broken I can't let myself love a man again. I want to be like normal women and allow myself to tumble into infatuation naturally, with no restraints, not thinking eighteen steps in advance. But life has taught me to look ahead for the potholes, to identify each and every potential arrow to my heart—and most important, Jonathan taught me that I'm easy to leave.

Drew comes back into the living room, drinking water out of the Frosty the Snowman mug. It's all he uses now, and when he's done with it, he rinses it and puts it back up on that shelf above his door. He plops down on the end of the couch near my feet, and I pretend to be deeply offended at the prospect of sitting close to him. I scrunch my legs up as far as my belly will allow, like I can't afford to catch his cooties.

He smirks at me, dimple popping, and reaches over to snatch the remote from my hand. "Hey! I was watching that!"

Casually, he changes the channel. "No, you weren't." *No, I wasn't.* He flips it over to some boring documentary he knows I'll hate just to spite me. I'd try for the remote, but it's hopeless. He'll just hold it above his head like he always does, and I have zero agility with my belly sticking out a mile in front of me. So I just lie over here and sulk, though I'm secretly smiling to myself that Drew didn't go back to Mia's place after their date. In fact, I'd say it ended pretty early for a successful date. Which means it probably *wasn't* a successful date.

"Why are you smiling like the Grinch over there?"

I clamp down on my lips and shake my head in a *No reason* look.

He hums his suspicion and reaches over to pull my blanket down an inch to cover the portion of my toes that was hanging out and cold.

CHAPTER 27

Jessie

It's lake house day. *Super!* I'm so glad I made this happen. *Not.* If there wasn't a promise of seeing my grandaddy on the other side of it, I'd be canceling so fast. What I don't understand is, why hasn't Drew canceled? There's absolutely nothing in this for him except to reconnect with his old mentor—but I'm not even sure that's important to him.

Currently, Drew and I are standing opposite each other in the kitchen, angrily wolfing down bowls of Raisin Bran Crunch (he insists on healthy cereal but doesn't realize I secretly mixed Cinnamon Toast Crunch into mine). We're staring at each other like we're in some sort of warped cereal-eating competition. I almost choke twice.

We both take the last bite at the same time and then go shoulder to shoulder at the sink and drop our bowls in. We're synchronized swimmers as we turn opposite ways and flow out of the kitchen. I grab my heavy suitcase, Drew rips it out of my hand and glares at me, then picks up his own. We *stomp stomp stomp* out of the house, lock the door, and go to the Jeep. This is how we've been operating for the past week, ever since our fight after the fundraiser.

He's mad at me for humiliating him and turning him down outside my door, and I'm mad at him for breathing. Also—I don't love that he went out with Mia again. It was just a lunch date, but Lucy told me Drew said they had a *nice* time. Well sure, Drew, if you like nice times, then why don't you just go ahead and buy an Instant Pot and dorky matching polos and marry her already. You two will have a very *nice* life with adorable Christmas cards, I'm sure.

Gag me.

Drew doesn't want nice. He wants spicy. He wants some grit. He wants a good fighter. *He wants me.*

Do I want him?

BAM. Drew slams our luggage into the back of the Jeep, so I slam my passenger door shut just so we're even. And then we're off. Locked inside a steel cage together as we barrel silently down the interstate toward a weekend of fake bliss and love. There's so much tension between us that I can't even imagine a happy outcome for this trip. How are we going to act lovey-dovey when clearly we both feel like throwing on some boxing gloves and stepping into a ring?

After forty-five minutes of silence, I break. "Have you thought about how you're going to explain me away after this weekend?"

I look over at Drew, letting my eyes land squarely on him for the first time today. His brown hair is tousled and styled, and his hunter-green T-shirt makes his blue eyes look startlingly sharp. His outstretched arm resting on the top of the steering wheel tenses. Veins roll.

"No."

Okay, got it. One-syllable answer means *Shut it, Jessie.*

I bite the inside corner of my cheek and look out the window.

"You probably should." My words feel radioactive. Instinctively, I know I don't need to be pushing this . . . but I can't help it. I have to. I feel the need to push every single one of Drew's buttons. I can handle fighting with Drew—I can't handle silence from him anymore.

I glance out of the corner of my eye and see his hand wrap tighter around the wheel. We are quiet for five minutes, and just as I'm thinking he's closed the conversation for good and we will spend the rest of our days as silent monks, Drew's voice jumps out at me.

"I've got it!"

I squeal and drop the package of peanut M&Ms I was holding. They scatter everywhere, and it looks like a candy factory vomited all over his Jeep. "Drew!" I whack him on the arm.

He's not remorseful in the least. One of the M&Ms landed in his lap, so he picks it up and pops it in his mouth with a self-satisfied grin. "Sorry. I've got my story ready."

"What story?" I ask, sitting back to fold my arms and pout in my seat.

"The story I'm going to tell everyone to explain what happened to you."

I don't quite like the grin on his face right now. "That's why you've been silent over there?"

"I needed some time to come up with something good." He clears his throat like he's preparing an important monologue. "It started so well. Our love was strong, and we had a whirlwind romance. Jessie, in particular, couldn't keep her hands off me. I mean, seriously, her desire for me was just insatiable. Every single night she would beg me, 'Drew, please—'"

"Okay, I think you've made your point, Casanova. Move on."

He grins at the road before letting it morph into an expression of pure agony. "And then one morning on a weekend trip to

Dr. Green's lake house, I walk in on Jessie FaceTiming a man in the nude!" He gasps and covers his mouth like one of the Golden Girls. "As it turns out, Jessie had been having a secret fling on the side, and the baby is not mine, but *his*. Even worse, Jessie knew it all along but just wanted a doctor's salary to support her." Drew shakes his head lightly, like his imaginary grief is too much to bear. "It was a heartbreaking tale. But luckily, the Greens were there to comfort me while I sent Jessie packing in an Uber."

Drew says all of this in a way that lets me think he's truly planning on this. I can see it now, a cunning smile spreading across his face before he runs out of our room into the kitchen and relays an entire fake story to the Greens at my expense. My humiliation is on the horizon, and I'll never be able to see another doctor in Nashville again because there will be a bounty out for my head after word spreads. My face will be printed at the top of their doctor newsletter (I can only assume they have one) with a giant red target over my face. I'll never receive good healthcare again.

"You wouldn't dare!" I say with decisive emphasis on each word.

He chuckles like a maniac. "Oh, I would. In fact, I will."

I have limited options for attack, stuffed in the car like this, so I lick my finger and stick it in his ear.

Drew jolts toward his door with a disgusted groan and uses his shoulder to wipe his ear. "You did not just give me a wet willy?!"

"I DID! And when we park, I'll give you a purple nurple too! You can't say those horrible things about me! It makes me sound so heartless. Imagine if I pass any of the doctors in the grocery store after word spreads? They'll open up their egg cartons and start pelting me."

"Ah yes—doctors are known for public egg floggings."

"Make up a different story."

Drew's eyebrow rises. "Make me."

Smoke billows out of my ears as I narrow my eyes into dangerous slits. "I know things about you now, Dr. Stuck-up. I can blackmail you *all day*."

He barks out a laugh. "Oh yeah? What dirt do you have on me?"

"When you fall asleep on the couch, you fart. Like, a lot. Real stinky stuff."

"I do not." *He doesn't.*

I hum and tap my chin in a quick obnoxious movement. "I don't know. Who are people going to believe—the sleeping man, or the woman there to witness the rapid-fire flatulence? I bet Mia would be interested in hearing what she's signing up for."

Drew's eyebrows crunch together. "What does Mia have to do with any of this?"

Doesn't he see it? Mia has everything to do with it. My mood has never been more sour than after witnessing Drew on a date with another woman. My insides started aching that day, and they haven't stopped.

"Just thought she'd like to know her man has bad gas before she decides to crawl into bed with him."

Drew glances sideways at me—no smile anymore—and then looks back at the road. "Mia won't be getting in my bed, so don't waste your breath on trying to blackmail me regarding her. It was just a date."

I have to bite my cheeks to keep from smiling. That doesn't work, so I suck them in, making me look like a fish. I turn my face toward the window, because Drew absolutely cannot see how much of an effect that news is having on me. I feel like a balloon, freshly filled with helium and ready to drift off into outer space. "That's a shame."

He grunts a laugh. "Yeah, clearly you look heartbroken for me. I can see your reflection in the window."

I wipe my smile off and paste on an over-the-top frown. Paint my face and I'd be a sad clown. "Better?"

Drew quickly glances at me and rolls his eyes, but I can see the hint of a smile in the corner of his fine mouth . . . his fine mouth that I've had the privilege of kissing and would really like to kiss again.

"You're ridiculous."

"You're ridiculous."

"*You are,*" he says, reaching over to slide my hairband down—wrecking my perfect ponytail!

I reach over to pinch under his arm, but he grabs my hand and locks it in his. I try to tear it away, but he just intertwines our fingers, his grip tight and possessive, and rests our hands on the armrest between us. "You can have this back when you learn to behave."

I huff and puff and put on a big show of hating his hand against mine, but inwardly I'm dying. Have two hands ever fit together so perfectly? Has the feel of another's skin against mine ever set me on fire before?

Drew keeps my hand captive—aka we hold hands—the whole drive, neither of us letting go of our pride. We've got shields in front of our faces in the form of glares and scowls, and we use our words like swords. I know his pressure points, and he knows mine. When Drew's thumb tenderly runs up and down mine, we both throw extra insults at each other just to disguise the intimacy neither of us is willing to admit lives between us. Never have two more prideful, stubborn people existed.

It's a tightrope we walk, and I'm feeling less and less confident in my ability to make it safely across.

My phone rings as we pull up to the lake house, and Drew finally releases my hand so I can answer it. It's my contractor on the line, and he has bad news. Drew puts the Jeep in park and watches with an expression of concern as I receive the update.

"It's worse than we thought. Most of your subflooring is rotted too. We've been trying to replace boards on a need-to-fix basis only, but the more we tear out, the more problems we find."

"So what does this mean?" I'm afraid he's going to say they had to bulldoze the house and start over, that I'm suddenly out four hundred thousand dollars and they are taking me to prison because I can't pay it.

"It means an increase in your bottom line and also a few more weeks added to the completion date."

Tears are stinging my eyes, and I will not let myself let them out. I don't think I'm doing a great job of hiding them, though, because Drew's hand finds mine again and he squeezes. I spend the next five minutes trying to talk my contractor into putting all of his manpower into finishing this project on time, because I have a baby coming and I would really like to have a home to bring said baby home to. He tells me *No can do* in a thick northern accent that feels abrasive to me in my fragile state. So now my house is due to be finished around the same time as my due date. Wonderful. Perfect. *Splendid!*

I hang up and stare blankly out the front windshield, letting my thoughts fall into their final slots like the Plinko game.

"Talk to me," Drew urges, leaning forward and trying to catch my eye.

"Everything is fine," I say in a high-pitched screechy tone. "It's only that my life is over, and my baby is going to be homeless, but it's fine."

"What are you talking about? What did the contractor say?"

I take a deep breath, gathering all my strength so I don't release a sob all over Drew. "They ran into complications—more things to be fixed—and they don't think the house will be done until the same week as my due date."

"Oh." Drew's shoulders relax like I didn't just tell him my whole world is falling apart. His nonchalant attitude pisses me off.

"What do you mean *Oh?* This is bad, Drew. Do you understand what this means for me? I might not have my *home* to bring my baby *home* from the hospital to. I won't have a place to set up its crib, or the rocking chair—not that I even have any of those things because when Lucy offered to throw me a baby shower I turned her down like a lunatic, because I was too scared of becoming a mom." My voice is hysterical now and I'm sure I'll be embarrassed about this later, but for now it's all gushing out like I just hit an emotional artery. "I added a few things to a baby registry online but haven't even bought a single thing off of it yet because I didn't want to have to pile more boxes at your house and make you mad. But no, that's a lie—I'm blaming it on you when it's really my fault. I didn't order anything for the same reason I haven't found out the sex of the baby. If I order things, if I have things, it makes it real, and I haven't been ready to face that yet."

I finally take a shuddering breath. Once the words are out, I don't even want to look at Drew. I just spewed my emotions all over him, and if there's anything I've learned about men, it's that they don't like dealing with women's drama. Except for Grandaddy. He'll listen to my blabbering all day, and I wish I could go to him right now. He's the only person I've ever been able to trust to make things better for me.

Drew doesn't rush out of the car and leave me behind. He squeezes my hand. "Jessie, look at me." His words are not tender. Not sweet. They are rough and they say *I mean it.* I square my shoulders and look in his navy eyes. "Neither you nor your baby will be homeless. You live with me, and my house is your house as long as you need it. Order your stuff. Ship it to my place. It's time to stop avoiding, to face what's coming—you're about to become a mother, and you can do it. You're strong enough."

I want to be angry at Drew as he lets go of my hand and hops out of the Jeep, but I can't. He's right. And he's probably the only person in the world who can actually give me the kick in the pants I need. My baby is coming soon. It's time to pull up my big girl panties and get ready. I'm going to be a mom—*I can do this*. And thanks to Drew, I don't have to be homeless.

CHAPTER 28

Jessie

D rew is infuriating. I already knew this, but now he's doubly infuriating. Ever since we walked through the doors of this lake house, he's been touchy-feely. He uses every opportunity to touch my hand, my hip, my neck, the side of my thigh. I get we're in a fake relationship, but *goodness*. I thought he hated PDA! Something is different with Drew. Something changed after our drive. I don't know what it is yet, but it's making me want to become a turtle and pull my head back into my shell.

Right now we're all standing on the porch admiring the view of the expansive lake and listening to Henry explain all the renovations they've done since buying the property after Richard retired, but I can't even focus because Drew is pressed up behind me, arms wrapping me up in what some people might call a hug. It's not, though. Drew and I are sworn enemies. I've angered him, humiliated him, and poked his ego more times than I'm proud of, so this absolutely cannot be a real hug. Except, I can feel his heart beating against my shoulders. He feels like a solid brick wall with a pulse, and it's making the world around me feel fuzzy. Henry might as well be a parent in *Charlie Brown* right now because all I hear is *wah wah wah wah*.

My eyes drop from the lake view to the Drew view, aka his tan forearms draping heavily over my chest. I can smell his deodorant and natural skin scent. The two mix and swirl through my senses like a tornado of masculinity wrecking everything in its path. Drew destroys me. I want to drop my chin and brush my lips across the warm skin and let the light hair on his forearms tickle my nose.

"Does that sound good to you, Jessie?" Henry asks, wrongly thinking I've been paying attention to anything he's been going on about.

I must stiffen, alerting Drew to my distress, because the evil man drops his mouth beside the shell of my ear and whispers, "What do you think? Does that sound good to you?"

The hairs on my arms stand at attention, ready to intercept every sensation Drew wants to toss their way. In my fantasy, I lay my head back against Drew's chest and close my eyes. No . . . I spin around, hook my arms around his neck, and try to re-create the kiss from the fundraiser. Also in my fantasy, I'm not pregnant, and Drew and I don't have such a complicated relationship. And maybe he's naked.

Instead, I put the heel of my tennis shoe on top of his toes and push down. Drew's hold on me tightens like he's bracing himself through the pain, but he doesn't release me.

"Sure, sounds perfect!" I pretend I know what they are talking about, because lying is the polite thing to do.

"Oh good!" Henry claps his hands together once and then pats Richard on the arm. "You can go get the lobster out of the freezer so it'll be thawed by the time we need to throw it on the grill."

Wait, what! Lobster?! That's what I agreed to? *Bleh.* I despise all things seafood, and while pregnant I can barely even stand the smell of it. Drew knows this, because one night when I first moved in he brought home lobster takeout, and I immediately threw up in the kitchen trash can.

Richard scurries off to do his husband's bidding as Henry stands there staring at us like we are a priceless French painting he wants to hang above his fireplace. Little does he know this is all a sham. We're not a priceless French painting; we're a replica, laser-printed and sold for $9.99 at a bargain-hunting store.

"You two are just adorable together. I'm so happy you could come this weekend," says Henry, making me feel terrible for lying to him.

Drew takes a giant liberty and leans down close to kiss my cheek. His scruff feels like sandpaper, and I begrudgingly love it. "We are too."

I beam at Henry, trying out my best impression of a blushing bride, and raise my hand to squeeze Drew's forearm affection-ately. At least, it looks affectionate. He'll sense the warning in it when my nails sink into flesh. "So happy."

Henry remembers another item he needs to pull from the freezer (probably something equally disgusting, like pig toes or frog legs) and darts into the house after Richard. I waste no time flinging Drew's arm off me and using my shoulder to wipe the imaginary leftover kiss from my cheek. My expression says, *Bleh, you're gross. I hate kisses.*

"Knock it off, will you? Why are you touching me so much today?"

He smiles curiously. "Because I like touching you."

"No, you don't."

"That's not the way it works. Unfortunately for you, you don't get to decide if I like touching you or not."

I cross my arms defiantly—protectively. "Stop saying *touching you.*"

He tilts his head, a smile on his mouth. "Why?"

"Because it's weird."

"For me to touch you?"

I let my head fall back and groan. He's the only person in the world who can talk circles around me. "Drew. I don't know what game you're playing right now, but I'm telling you to *quit it.*"

"I'm not playing a game."

"It feels like one. All week you've been pissed at me, barely saying two words, and this morning you looked like you wanted to fight me in the kitchen. And rightfully so! I humiliated you, remember? Tangled you in a lie you'll never be able to get out of? And I'm so mean to you all the time! You have more than enough reasons to not like me." *Please, don't like me! Go back to hating me!*

"You misread me all week. Fighting is not what I want to do with you, Jessie."

My eyebrows fly up and my heart rate is a rapid-fire machine gun. Drew looks different today. His eyes are smoldering. He's definitive. He's made up his mind, and now he's going to be the controlling Drew I used to despise until he gets his way.

I swallow and take a step away from him. He looks amused, and he closes the gap between us again. He backs me up against the porch railing and pins me in with his hands on either side. My mouth is the Sahara Desert. All my words are dried up—not an ounce of verbiage in sight.

In the most tender touch I've ever received, Drew brushes my hair from my temple to behind my ear. "I don't think I've ever really apologized to you for what happened that morning when I overslept. I'm sorry, Jessie. I truly didn't mean to, and I was actually looking forward to helping you that day. I was hoping it would mend the strife between us. And then . . . I made it worse by forgetting."

I shake my head. I almost want to pin my hand across his

mouth so he can't continue apologizing. He's ruining everything. He can't do this to me now.

"I'm sorry. I wish so badly that I could go back in time and bring my cellphone with me into my room, set fifteen alarms. I wish I could have been there for you."

"I don't. Everything happened exactly as it should have. And you don't need to say any of this—I'm not interested in you, remember? It doesn't matter if I forgive you or not."

He should be deterred. I made my words extra saucy and defiant, and he's not even the least bit shaken.

His lips are grinning. "I believed that after the fundraiser. But then you spied on me on my date," he whispers like a villain, his lips teasingly close. "And if you're not interested in me, why do you get so flustered when I'm close to you?" Those blue eyes drop to my neck, where he then takes his knuckle and runs it up the side. "Your skin flushes every single time I touch you. Like right now." His hand has brushed all the way up the length of my neck to just below my ear. His movement stops, and he extends his fingers over my pulse point. *Crap.*

His head tilts, and his eyes stare at that one point of contact. After several seconds, he finds the answer he was looking for. His smile slants, his eyes lock with mine, and his eyebrows rise. *Want to know the answer, Jessica?*

I'm nothing if not stubborn, though, so I hold his gaze. "Don't flatter yourself so much, Andrew. My body is reacting to the coffee I had on the way here—not you."

"You didn't have any coffee."

"I didn't?" I'm staring at his lips.

He shakes his head slowly, smiling.

Where is this sudden self-assured persistence coming from? Have I not made myself perfectly clear to him? Have I not kicked him enough to spook him into running off? *Go on, man! Get out of here. Be gone!* I've been trying to get Drew to leave me alone since the day I met him. It was working . . . and now . . . it doesn't seem to be anymore.

"Want to know what I think?"

"Literally never."

He grins deeper and uses his index finger to trace the outline of my lips. "I think you like me too, but you're too scared to admit it."

"Careful," I warn, but it sounds weak. If this were a movie, I'd be holding a gun to him, but my hand would be trembling so bad he'd know I was too in love with him to ever pull the trigger. "I can march inside right now and end this whole charade, humiliating you again if I want to."

"But you don't want to. You don't want this to end just as much as I don't. You like the excuse to flirt and touch and . . . kiss just as much as I do."

My eyes widen to their maximum diameter. "We are *not* going to kiss on this trip."

His eyes say, *Oh?* He steps forward and my stomach presses into his. Our hips would meet if I wasn't eight months pregnant, and I've never wanted to be rid of this belly as much as I do right now.

Without hesitation, his hand loops behind my neck and he drops his lips to mine. It's a gentle kiss, sort of like the kiss at the fundraiser—but even more patient and aching. It's calculated in a way that says, *I know exactly who you are, and I still absolutely want you.* I feel like melting onto the floor. His lips are hot as he gently presses into mine, pulls away, tilts his head a different way, and then presses in again. He lavishes sweet kisses over my mouth again and again, gloating that I'm not trying to stop him. I couldn't even if I wanted to.

I don't know what to think or do. All I know is I'm not moving.

I'm accepting every single one of these kisses while still trying to hold up a mental guard against this man. It's the most difficult game I've ever played. With one hand braced on the back of my neck and the other firmly anchored on my lower hip, he kisses the corner of my mouth. A tease. Another hint of what could be. Slowly those dangerous lips move to the center of my mouth and hover, barely touching. I feel his smile rather than see it before he lightly tastes my bottom lip. I can't breathe—if I do, it will come out like a moan. Drew brushes his lips to the opposite corner and lavishes it with attention too. He's so thorough. There's not a single centimeter of my mouth that gets left out, but all I do is stand here receiving. And then, when my lips are fully attended to, he leaves them to drag his way down the side of my jaw. He lands with a warm, open-mouthed kiss on that same pulse point he gloated over earlier.

I want to scrape my hands down his abs, feel the taut muscles of his back, pull his hips flush with mine. But my bones are pudding. My eyes are shut. A thousand different sensations are swirling through my body, making me feel like a frayed and sparking live wire. Drew moves his way around my neck, and jaw, and mouth, taking as many kisses as he wants from exactly where he wants, because I'm not doing a single thing to stop him. I'm not participating, but he doesn't seem to mind. No, in fact, he's treating me like I'm the most delicious dessert he's ever had, and he will savor every taste.

Finally, after two and a half years, he pulls away with a soft smile, takes my shoulders gently in his hands, and peels me away from the railing I practically draped myself over when I lost all feeling in my legs.

"See. I felt nothing." I sound like a zombie.

He cups my face, looking like he could laugh at any moment. *Why does nothing make him angry at me?* His thumb sweeps over my lips like he needed to touch them one last time, and he shakes his head. "This morning, I decided I'm done avoiding my feelings for you. And whether you like it or not, you have feelings for me too. I know it. So let me know when you're done fighting it. I'll be here waiting."

Ugh! The arrogance of this man! He may be able to get his way with everyone else in life, but not me! *Not me.* Nope . . . not . . . *me.*

He turns and walks into the house. Like a ding-dong, I wait until he's almost disappeared into the house to yell, "Yeah, right! Don't hold your breath, Andrew! You'll be waiting forever!"

Forever gets cut off when he shuts the door behind him. I clasp my arms tightly around my middle and spin to look out over the water, suddenly feeling dizzy and sick and uncertain. What am I going to do? It's like Drew has X-ray glasses and can see right through me at all times. And by him telling the truth, he's completely stripped away all my power. I can't deflect. I can't sabotage. *Dammit, Drew, I'm supposed to be rubber and you're the glue! Whatever you say bounces off of me and sticks to you!* Turns out I'm working with a whole other substance. *I'm a magnet and so are you. Whatever I say doesn't matter because all I want to do is jump you and never ever come up for air.* Not quite as poetic, but oh well.

He's right. I'm just scared he's going to hurt me—and this isn't some big revelation. I've known it since the beginning. It's why I decided to hate him right away. He's not mediocre. He's not easily replaceable. I don't know if I'll ever be able to let myself love recklessly again.

Drew makes me want to try, though.

I take a deep breath and look down, running my hands over the swell of my stomach. I need more time.

CHAPTER 29

Jessie

Moment of truth. It's dinnertime.

I successfully made it through an entire day of faking it as Drew's fiancée. He hasn't tried to kiss me again and hasn't been quite as touchy-feely as he was this morning. I'm given the occasional hand brush or knee bump, but other than that, he's behaved himself pretty well. Unfortunately, even those tiny touches have set me off like a rocket.

Even so, Richard and Henry are the best. I want them to adopt me. They are both easygoing lovebirds, and the way Richard dotes on Henry even after being together for twenty years is incredible. Henry has such a tender heart, and talking with him is like sitting down in a plush chair by the fire with a warm cup of tea.

The expansive lakeside view is giving me the breath of fresh air I didn't know I needed. Just getting out of the city and stepping away from the salon with my phone off has been a dream. I have a hard time relinquishing control to other people, but being forced to let Lucy take over managing the salon for a few days is good for me and will probably help me relax more when I have to take time off after the baby comes. Honestly, though, what I've enjoyed the most is listening to Drew and Richard talk.

Drew usually tones down his medical talk around me, but here with Richard he's been nerding out. The two of them have discussed medical journals and the latest science in women's health-care, swapped hilarious birth stories, and reminisced about old times when Drew was in medical school and learning under Richard's supervision. I have loved seeing Drew in his element, and as crazy as it sounds, listening to them discuss obstetrics and gyne-cology with such reverence makes me feel special to be a woman.

The ugly truth is, I've had a fantastic day. Richard and Henry took us to a little local farmers market for lunch and then out for a leisurely cruise in their pontoon boat. Drew did wrap his arm around my shoulder during that boat ride, and I tried very hard not to lay my head in the crook of his shoulder and stare up at him like a lovesick nincompoop. I don't want to think too much about it, but something about this trip has felt too real. I keep forgetting we're supposed to be faking it, and I'm not having to force my smiles around Drew, or the way my body naturally gravi-tates toward his when we're in the same room. There's a close-ness between us that can't be manufactured, and that's truly terrifying.

But the day's fun times are coming to an end now because I'm seated at the table, waiting for Richard to bring out our plates of lobster. I probably could have admitted that I despise eating any-thing that comes with claws and antennae still attached, but that would have required admitting to not hearing Henry when he asked because I was too busy imagining Drew and me in a dark room somewhere. So now it's time to pay my penance.

"Everyone ready!" Richard shouts from the kitchen way too enthusiastically. All day they've been talking up the lobster. It's ridiculous. Never has anyone been looking forward to a dish more in their life than these people. They're a millisecond away from starting a cult that allows you to eat only lobsters. It will be the most sparsely joined entity in all of history.

"Yes, we're starving for some lobster—get out here!" Henry bellows back with a wink at me.

Are we starving for lobster, though, Henry? Are we really?

My only objective tonight is to politely choke down this horrific food and then make it into the bathroom before it comes back up. And there's no doubt in my mind that it *will* come back up. I preemptively stuffed a grocery bag I found under the kitchen sink into my pocket in case the bathroom proves too far away. Henry saw me do it. I just shrugged like *I collect grocery bags, what about it?*

Richard comes out of the kitchen, and there it is, my nightmare on a plate. He presents his husband with a freaking big grilled lobster on a bed of steamed vegetables that look almost as terrible as the seafood. I rub my hand over my belly and promise my unborn child I will sneak out of here and hunt down a Taco Bell after everyone goes to bed.

Richard sets an identical plate of red sea creature in front of Drew. Henry and Drew both *ooh* and *aah* over their spoils, the lobster winks at me, and I mentally dry heave. My gaze trickles over my inevitable future, and I gulp a little too loudly. Drew hears it and leans back in his seat, taking his beer from the table and raising it to his grinning lips. The glass bottle makes contact with his mouth, and I watch closely—intently—as he tips it back and swallows. I stare, all too happy to forget about this dinner of doom and watch his Adam's apple bob up and down. Something about this is so sexy I want to cry. This scene should be sculpted and displayed in a museum with a description card underneath that reads, *Sensual man at dinner.* With greedy intentions, my mind wanders back to the feel of his lips on mine, the way my nerves sizzled when he lingered against my mouth like we had all of time stretched out in front of us and nowhere to go.

I'm reliving my memories in delicious detail when I notice the curve of Drew's lips widen past the rim of his bottle, so much so that both of his dimples peek out. My eyes pop up to his and he's staring at me, eyebrows raised. *Whatcha thinking about over there, Jessie?*

I clear my throat, and my gaze darts away just in time to see Richard exit the kitchen and make his way toward me, holding out a plate like this is the most exquisite fine-dining restaurant in all the land. If he had a silver plate topper, he would have used it, and I would have been able to see my horrified expression reflected back at me.

"And for you, Jessie, something extra special."

Oh goody. Did they save the daddy lobster for me or something? Is it still alive and I'll have to kill it before I can eat it?

I set my voice up an octave higher than it needs to be in order to overcompensate for my inward glum attitude. "Oh yummmm, I'm so excited to eat some delicious"—Richard sets the plate down in front of me, and I frown—"steak?"

I almost can't believe my good luck. Do I harness magical powers and the strength of my mind allowed me to change that lobster into a delicious, garlicky, buttery steak? Briefly, I look at Drew, wondering if I can make his clothes disappear with my new magic. His white pocket tee stays in place, sadly, but the smile on his mouth is full of amusement.

I look down, now skeptically pushing the steak around my plate, wondering if it's just a lobster painted brown. I glance at Drew, but he betrays nothing as his eyes watch me closely. Then these three stooges start laughing like someone delivered a punch line and I missed it. I look blankly around the table, and then I see Henry wipe a tear from his eye.

"Look at your face! I'm sorry, hon. It was mean to play a prank on you, but Drew talked us into it." He's still chuckling, but it's clear he feels terrible. His heart is too wholesome to enjoy pranks performed on vulnerable pregnant women. "Every time we mentioned this lobster today, you looked like you wanted to run for the hills."

Richard nods. "While you were still outside this morning, Drew came in and told us you can't stomach seafood. He snuck out while you and Henry were sitting out on the dock and picked you up a steak."

Henry gives me an amused yet apologetic look, like he wants to laugh but is also afraid I'm going to cut up our friendship bracelet. "But he made us promise to keep it a secret all day and to really talk up the lobster. Are you upset?"

Am I upset? *Am I upset?* YES, I'M UPSET!

But not at all for the reasons everyone at this table thinks. I'm upset because Drew has my preferences memorized. He went out to the freaking grocery store and bought me a steak because he knew I wouldn't be able to handle seafood. He knows so many tiny things about me because he's been paying attention. It also occurs to me that my glass of water is the only one at the table with ice in it. No doubt Drew's doing as well, because he's noticed ice water is the only way I've been able to drink it through this pregnancy. Like a rolodex fanning out in front of me, I now see all the thoughtful little things Drew has done for me lately.

And the icing on the breakdown cake? I love pranks. Adore them, even. And he somehow managed to wrap all of this up in a nice little humorous bow. *Wonderful.* Now I'm going to cry.

I muster a smile. It's so fake, but I don't have another option. My face says, *Here are all my teeth!* I avoid Drew's gaze. "Great prank. Will you guys excuse me? I'll be right back."

I feel Drew's eyes on my back with every step I take away from the table. I turn the corner, and as soon as I'm out of sight, I bolt to the bathroom and whip out my phone.

I dial Lucy, and the second the call connects, I whisper-yell, "*I drank the Kool-Aid!*" I know I have exactly two and a half minutes to stay in here before everyone comes to the conclusion that I'm struggling with bowel issues. There will be no meeting anyone's eyes after that, so I have to hurry.

"I KNEW IT!" she yells back, not even needing me to remind her of the conversation we had in the salon, because we're always quick to get on each other's level.

I must be on speakerphone, because I hear Cooper's voice crystal clear. "What Kool-Aid?"

"Drew's Kool-Aid," Lucy tells him.

"Is that a euphemism?"

"*Ewww,* no! It's a metaphor."

"For something dirty?"

I'm too short on time to listen to their back-and-forth banter. "GO AWAY, COOPER! I'M HAVING A MELTDOWN AND I NEED TO TELL LUCY I THINK I LO—" I get interrupted when the bathroom door opens. I gasp and gape as Drew just lets himself right into the bathroom. "What are you doing in here? Get out! I could have been in here pooping!" *Shoot.* Why did I say that? I could have just left it at *going to the bathroom*!

Drew shrugs and stares at me with those blue eyes like I'm the one who's acting silly even though he's the person who barged in on a woman in the bathroom. "But you're not. You're on the phone."

"Doesn't matter. I could have been pooping *while* talking on the phone."

Lucy whispers in my ear. "You're saying the word *poop* a lot. Just thought you'd like to know. Also, do you need me here for this?"

I turn my attention to Lucy. "Yes! You stay." I point to Drew. "You leave!"

"No, I need to talk to you." I hate the way his eyes are sparkling. Like bubbling champagne, they glimmer and promise nothing but fun, good times.

"Tough. Because I need to talk to Lucy."

Cooper's voice comes back on the line. "Is that Drew? Can I talk to him real quick?"

Drew hears Cooper's voice, so he steps forward and pulls the phone out of my hand. I roll my eyes and sigh as he grins down at me. "Hey, man, what's up?" Cool, cool, cool. We're all just one happy friend group chatting it up in the bathroom.

I lean closer to hear, *not* to smell Drew. Getting a good whiff of him is purely coincidental.

"Did you get invited to the bachelor party camping weekend for Tod next month? I'm not going if you're not. Man, I hate camping. Please tell me you're not going so I don't have to go either."

"Yep. I'm going because he asked me to be in the wedding, so I'm definitely dragging you with me."

Okay, now this is too much. Can they seriously not chat about their social calendar on their own time? I poke Drew in the stomach. Unsurprisingly, it's rock hard. "Talk to your boyfriend later. Give me my phone back, *please*." I say the word with crazy googly eyes.

Drew's deep chuckle tickles me right in the heart, and he looks down at me like I'm the most adorable creature in the world as he addresses Cooper. "Sorry, I've gotta run. I'll text you about it later."

And then he *hangs up* and pockets *my* cellphone in his jeans. What kind of weird hostage lake house weekend is this?!

Drew smiles at me in this tiny bathroom, and I feel stripped naked. Not only has he stolen my sanity, he stole my freak-out zone, *and* my freak-out friend. This is like a complete Drew immersion where I'm not allowed to do anything but confront all my feelings for him. It's not good.

I glance at the door, and I think he can tell I'm going to try to make a run for it because his eyes cut to the door handle and then he shifts his body in front of it.

"Oh, real nice. Are you going to hold me hostage in here?"

"Maybe."

"Well, are you at least going to give me my phone back?"

"No."

"Why not?"

"I want to know if you're mad at me."

I shift on my feet, wondering if I'll feel safer if I wrap a towel around myself. "Why does it matter if I am or not?"

His long lashes blink a few times. He's debating his answer. "Because . . . it does. I . . ." He swallows. "I bought you the steak to be nice, and I thought you'd think us tricking you about the lobster was funny. I'm sorry if I missed the mark . . . I never would have done it if I thought you were going to be upset."

You didn't miss the mark. It was a perfect bull's eye.

I fold my arms tightly in front of me. "Only a week ago you did things to make me upset on purpose."

"Yeah . . . but not anymore. I just want to make sure you know that." He pauses, and his smile turns almost tortured . . . sad. Some of his bad boy arrogance from earlier is wearing thin, and now he just looks vulnerable. Not a side Drew shows often—if ever. He shakes his head with an embarrassed chuckle like he can't stand the way he feels right now, and I can perfectly relate. "I'm sorry. I shouldn't have come in here."

He takes my phone out of his pocket and hands it back.

"I just . . ." He's fumbling with his hands. *Drew Marshall* is fumbling. Would it be rude to use my phone to record him right now? Not to be mean, just to document how freaking cute he looks when he's unsure of himself.

He picks up a hand towel from the counter, making two perfect lengthwise folds and one in the middle before rehanging it on the rack. He taps a finger on the counter, then smooths his hand over the spot, his eyes staring intently at everything he does. Drew turns on the faucet and turns it off again. There's a boyishness about him that's making my heart skip. Is he getting up the nerve to ask me to prom? *Yes, Drew, I'll go with you!*

Finally, when my heart can't melt any more, I step forward and wrap my arms around his waist. I don't know what I'm doing. It's an awkward hug. My belly makes it so that my butt has to kind of stick out like a duck's feathers in the back, and I really smash my face against his chest—but it doesn't matter because this isn't supposed to be an intimate moment. This is me declaring friendship.

Drew is stiff for only a moment before his big hand rises and gently smooths down the back of my hair. He wraps his other arm around me and holds me tight, like he's never letting go. "We're okay?" he murmurs into my hair.

"Yeah . . ." I honestly don't know what Drew and I are, but I do know this. "We're great."

We hug another minute, and I don't tell him how thankful I am for the steak, or how funny I think the little lobster prank was, because I'm scared enough to have his arms around me—I don't need to throw emotions into the mix too.

CHAPTER 30

Jessie

After dinner, I help Henry clear the table and load up the dish-washer. He told me I didn't need to help him, but I insisted, because I'm a big coward and didn't want to face Drew again. Every time I looked over at him during the meal, our eyes locked. I felt like we were having a private conversation that I didn't mean to be having, like he could read my thoughts whether I wanted them read or not.

So I found a way to get myself a little space while he disappeared after dinner. But now the dishes have been cleared, cleaned, dried, and put away. I've also reorganized Henry and Richard's silverware drawer, wiped out the microwave, and swept the floor. I'm just about to clear the cobwebs from the tops of the cabinets when Henry stops me.

"Jessie! I didn't bring you out here to be Cinderella," he says with a chuckle as he attempts to peel the broom from my hands. I grip the stick tighter, and his sweet smile falters a little before he gives one final yank and tugs it free. "The weather's nice right now.

Why don't you go find Drew and take a romantic nighttime stroll by the lake?"

Under no circumstances can that happen. I will accidentally propose to Drew.

"You know, actually, I'm feeling pretty tired all of a sudden. I think I'll turn in early!" We both look at the clock and see that it's only eight P.M. Apparently I'm going to be turning in *super* early. I rub my belly bump like that's a suitable answer for why I'm acting so odd. "If you see Drew, will you tell him I went to bed?"

This is a good decision—going to bed early. Even though I know there's not a chance I'll fall asleep before two A.M., I can at least pretend I'm fast asleep when Drew comes in so I don't have to face him. Inside the room we are (unfortunately) sharing, I busy myself with making a little pallet on the floor. I decide to write a sign to prop up beside it with an arrow that reads, *This is where you sleep,* just to make sure he doesn't miss it.

I stand back, hands on my hips, and nod affirmatively at the luxury pallet. *Good. This is going to work.* And then I turn around, open the door to the bathroom, step inside, and scream.

"OH MY GOSH! I'm so sorry! I thought you were outside somewhere!" I say to a nearly naked Drew standing in front of the sink. He's wearing nothing besides tight black boxer briefs and has a toothbrush sticking out of his mouth. His hair is damp like he just got out of the shower. The steam swirling around him confirms it.

I need to look away. *Must look away.* But I can't.

My eyes have gone completely rogue and are scanning . . . as slowly as possible . . . down Drew's tan, muscular body like I'm needy and he's got everything I'm lacking. Strong thighs, abs on abs on abs, arm muscles and shoulder muscles and *wait one freaking second, is that a tattoo*?!

"Jessie?" Drew says, making me suck in a breath and shoot my eyes up to his. He's grinning mid-teeth-brushing, mostly naked and completely comfortable in his own skin. Speaking of his skin, I like it. I want to run my fingers across the top of those shoulder boulders he's got. I want to trace the indentations around each of his abs. Who knew this masterpiece is what he's been creating every morning at the gym? I mean, ever since I saw that tiny sliver of his golden abdomen, I knew his body would be magnificent. But this . . . this is more than I could have hoped for.

"Do you mind?" he says, amusement thick in his tone.

Oh, right! Drew probably doesn't want me to stand here all night ogling him.

I'm vaguely aware of shouting something like *put more clothes on!* while slamming the door behind me. Now Henry and Richard probably assume we're fighting. Drew chuckles on the other side of the bathroom door, and I want to chuck something at his head. But since that would require opening that bathroom door and seeing his glorious nakedness again, I refrain. I'm not sure my heart can handle any more excitement tonight. It might just give out completely.

While Drew is in the bathroom, I hurry to shimmy into my pink-and-white-striped maternity PJ set and scurry under the covers so quickly I probably broke a world record. Just as I'm pulling the sheets up to my chin, the bathroom door opens. My heart hammers painfully against my chest as Drew walks out in slow motion, steam billowing through the doorway like he's so hot his body just naturally produces it.

He's put on a pair of black sleep pants, but that's all, and my eyes still see every single inch of his smooth, muscular chest and tapered waist and—

"Tattoo . . ." I say, forgetting how to make complete sentences.

Drew's eyebrows go up, clearly enjoying this mental numbness he's creating in me. "Yeah, what about it?"

"You have one."

He takes another step into the room, using his towel to dry his hair. His muscles do *very* interesting things in the process. "I do."

It's beautiful is what I don't say. There are three large watercolor flowers surrounded by greenery, inked in soft tones on his upper right chest, curving over his shoulder to spill onto his back and biceps a little. I had no idea he even had a tattoo because of how it's positioned. You wouldn't be able to see it even in a short-sleeved shirt. It's like a sexy secret. *One that I now know.*

"I had no idea."

"Yeah, well, you've never seen me with my shirt off before."

I'm now deeply regretting not coming out on his boat a few weeks ago when Lucy invited me.

I'm trying to drag my eyes away, I really am, but it's just not happening. Don't judge me—I'm super pregnant, and Drew is basically an underwear model. "Are you going to get more?"

"Nah—or if I do, they'll be easily concealed like this one." He runs his hand over the tattoo, and I honest to goodness shiver a little.

"Why?" *Let the world see it, Drew!*

"Because. It's just best if I do." Now that is an intriguing answer.

I finally make eye contact with him again and see a slight pink-ness to his cheeks. Is he . . . blushing? "Why is it best?"

He sighs and shakes his head. "You're gonna make me say it? Fine. Apparently, women generally find me attractive, so . . . in my occupation . . . it's easier if I . . ."

I take pity and finish his thought for him. "If you tone down your hotness?"

He gives me an uncomfortable smile and nod. "Yeah, basically. Tattoos don't exactly scream professionalism . . . and I make sure when I'm in my practice, everything is completely professional at all times."

It's impossible not to realize he's letting me see him in his unprofessional state, though. He wants me to see him without his shirt on or else he would have fully dressed before coming out here.

I look down at my stripes and eight-months-preggo belly. Our contrast right now is laughable and serves as a slap in my face. A bucket of cold water. A much-needed dose of reality. I'm in no position in life to be contemplating a new relationship. I shouldn't even be thinking sexy thoughts about him. I should be locking him in this room and running far, far away.

Instead, he's currently stepping over the handy sign and pallet I made for him and heading straight for me and this itty-bitty teeny-tiny minuscule queen-sized bed. If he sits down, I'll topple over like Humpty-Dumpty and roll into him.

"*Hey! Whoa there.* I think you're missing your stop!" I say, shooting my hand out and waving a finger at the spiffy pallet I made for him. "Did you not see the sign?"

He lifts an adorable eyebrow, and his mouth hitches up on one side. "I saw it."

He pulls back the covers on his side—correction, *my* side, because all the sides are mine because he's not sleeping in here with me—of the bed. I lean over and snatch the blanket, pasting it back down on the mattress. *You shall not enter.*

"I thought doctors knew how to read. It says that is your spot right down there. On the floor. Wayyyy over there. By yourself."

"You can't be serious."

"Oh, I am."

He shakes his head. "Jessie, that is a hardwood floor. I'll fracture a bone sleeping on it."

"Well, it's a handy thing you're a doctor then and can fix your-self right up!"

"Move over."

"NO!" I lie flat on the bed and starfish myself out so he can't lie down. When I don't hear any movement, I cut my gaze to him out of the corner of my eye.

He's trying not to bust up laughing. Apparently, I'm succeed-ing in being a great threat to him. "What are you worried is going to happen if I get in there with you? It shouldn't be a problem, because *you're not attracted to me in that way,* remember?" His voice is *oh so* mocking. He's completely called my bluff.

I narrow my eyes at him (checking him out one last time) and then scoot over dramatically. "Fine. But stick to your own side, or else!"

The mattress sags when Drew gets in, and suddenly the air is filled with his scent. It's like heaven and an alpine forest mixed together, and I stay completely still. I swallow, feeling his gaze on my face without even looking. This is torture. If I move even a centimeter, the sides of our bodies will touch, and then I'll burst into flames and die. What a way to go.

I roll my eyes slowly in his direction until they collide with his. "Stop staring at me."

"It's only eight o'clock. I'm not going to be able to sleep."

"Perfect, then you should get out and go do something!" My voice is shrill.

He grins and reaches over to push some of my hair out of my face. I slap his hand away. "I don't have anything to go do. Let's get your phone out and do some shopping."

My eyebrows crunch together. Did he just say *shopping*? Because it sounded a lot like *shopping,* but his eyes say, *Let me kiss you from head to toe.* "Actually, shopping sounds great!"

I roll away from him to grab my phone from the bedside table, taking the opportunity to blow out a full breath of air. When I roll back, he's still looking at me with an expression that makes me want to lean forward and kiss him. I know he'd let me too, which makes it all the more torturous. Instead, I hoist myself up on my elbows, then scoot so my back rests against the headboard. Drew does the same, and now our shoulders and arms are smushed together. His skin is still hot from the shower, and it's transferring to me. I want to fan myself, but that might be a tad bit too obvious.

"Why are your hands shaking?" he says, leaning even closer to pull my phone out of my trembling fingers.

"No reason." *That sounded guilty.* "I mean, they're cold. What are we shopping for?"

"Baby stuff," he says casually, eyes focusing on the phone screen.

My heart stops.

"Baby stuff? Why?"

He grins slightly, and my stomach barrel rolls. "Because you need baby stuff," Drew says with a relaxed laugh that doesn't match how I feel inside. I want to squirm away. Hide from reality. Build a fort around my mind that separates me from what's coming in life—but I've done that long enough. I can't keep locking myself away from scary things.

Drew takes my hand and squeezes it. "Where do you want to start?"

"Umm, car seats?" I ask, my tone making it evident that I have no idea where to begin. Not a single clue.

Luckily, Drew is one of those people who knows everything about everything, and he starts adding items to a registry so I can buy them later. He angles the phone toward me occasionally and asks my favorite color. At some point, my head lolls to the side and lands on his bare shoulder. "How do you know so much about baby gear? Do they teach you about all this in medical school?"

He chuckles. "No. I learned it all through experience with Lucy. She lived with me while she was pregnant and after she had Levi. She needed me a lot during those years, so I got pretty familiar with bottles, car seats, and all the baby stuff."

I quietly process his words for a minute. "Drew?" I say in a soft tone that makes him look down at me. "Do you ever get tired of having it together all the time? Being the guy who takes care of everyone?"

He lowers the phone to his lap and contemplates my question. "Sometimes. It gets to feel pretty heavy when I stop and think about how many lives I'm responsible for, how many people count on me in my professional and personal life. But it wasn't until recently that I realized I even needed a break from it."

"What happened recently?"

He smirks down at me. "You."

"Me?"

He nods. "You steamrolled your way into my life and reminded me how good it feels to let go a little . . . to fight, to play, to laugh. I don't think I'd really done any of that since I started med school. My life became very objective-based, and then I met you and . . ."

"And I taught you the meaning of life?"

"You snuck your underwear into my laundry just to make me mad. And you eat a million milligrams of sodium every day. And you wanted the Frosty mug just as much as I did."

A laugh spills from my mouth. "None of that sounds like a lesson you've learned."

"Exactly. You don't teach me lessons—you help me rest."

I am speechless, because I've never been anyone's rest before. A burden, yes. Expendable, yes. And even though I know without a doubt that my grandaddy loves me and always has, I still can't say I've ever been restful to him. He didn't choose me; he was given me. He certainly made the most of it and I've never felt anything but adored by him, but still, there's something about hearing Drew say I help him rest that stirs my heart. I feel warm and bubbly and like he just wrapped a big comforter around my heart.

Drew's eyes skate down the front of my body to land on my belly.

"What?" I ask through a sudden lump in my throat. "Is something wrong?" Does he have some sort of ob-gyn sixth sense and can feel in his bones that something is wrong with the baby?!

His jaw clenches before he looks back up at me with an uncertain smile. "No—I just . . . can I feel the baby?"

Oh sweet heavens, how does he do this to me? Drew makes me feel like I just swallowed sunshine. Like I'm hot and glowing and rays are going to burst through my skin.

I can't help but smile as I take his hand and lay it across my stomach. It's not lost on me that a man completely skilled in all things pregnancy-related looks tentative and uncertain as his palm rests against me. I study his deep blue eyes as he studies my stomach. The sides of his mouth slowly rise as he gains confidence and presses in lightly, using the skills he's trained in. Drew kneads his fingers slowly across the top of my belly through my PJ top. I know what he's doing because it's what my doctor did at my last exam when she was determining the baby's position. I could go ahead and tell him, but I know he'll have more fun figuring it out for himself.

He smiles. "She's flipped, head down and back facing out. That's great," he tells me, and then we both laugh when the baby kicks him in the hand. He spreads his fingers out completely, and his eyes are full of warmth and emotions I can't name—and am almost afraid to.

"You said *she*. Do you think I'm having a girl? Lucy always says *he*."

"I don't know. That's just the pronoun that slipped out. What are you hoping to have?"

"A squishy baby."

He chuckles, and slowly Drew's hand slides behind my shoulders before he angles me back against his bare chest. I can feel the warmth of his skin through my shirt, and my eyes go wide with shock. Before I have any chance to freak out that he's trying to get frisky, he does something even better. Drew's thumbs press into the tops of my shoulders—firm and yet gentle—and he spends the next ten minutes massaging my shoulders, back, and even hips, somehow knowing every single place that has given me horrible pain over the last few months.

Eventually, he guides me to lie back, and I want to laugh at the ridiculousness of this situation. Normally, a man would be laying me down for a whole other reason. Drew, however, does it so he can pick up my feet and massage my arches and calves. His strong fingers move over me with expert care and tenderness, never crossing any lines that would make me feel uncomfortable. He basically gives me a complete prenatal massage without ever trying to take anything for himself, not expecting anything in return—and *that* is what makes me completely fall for Drew.

My eyes are closed, and I'm halfway to sleep when he kisses my temple, then pulls the covers over me, cutting off the light. He doesn't make a move to snuggle me, which I appreciate, because I'm not ready for that—but he does lay his hand over mine and rub his thumb over my knuckles. Before I fall asleep, I hear myself whispering a question I've been wondering about.

"Drew, what does *Oscar* stand for?"

He chuckles lightly and squeezes my hand. "Oscar the Grouch."

I smile into the night, not offended by the nickname but rather oddly happy.

"Do you want me to stop calling you that?"

I contemplate it, knowing that would mean asking him to stop playing with me. Stop teasing. Stop flirting. "No way."

CHAPTER 31

Drew

Jessie's head is in the crook of my shoulder, palm heavy against my chest, leg slung over mine. I'm not sure when this happened and I'm one hundred percent sure it is unintentional on her part, but I'm soaking it up. I woke up about ten minutes ago to her in this position, and I have barely breathed since. I'm afraid I'll wake her up if I do, and then she'll shoot out of bed and curse me for tricking her somehow. *No tricks, Jessie. You just like me.*

Last week was torture. She thought I was angry and moody because of the fundraiser prank. And yeah, I was pissed about that for all of one night. Then I went on a date (unashamedly to gauge her reaction) and Jessie showed up outside the window in her pajamas. That's when I knew she was full of it.

She does like me. She's just scared to death of me.

So the rest of the week I kept my distance while trying to figure out what my next step should be. Deciding to go after Jessie is like deciding to go into war—you can't take it lightly, and you must formulate a plan. Turns out, I'm moody while drawing up battle plans. Do you know what it's like to live with a woman you're crazy about but have to hide every thought, every desire, every hope from her on a daily basis? She'd come out of her room in her little athletic shorts and I'd growl. *Don't come out here in those.* She'd sit down next to me on the couch and I'd grumble. *Scoot over unless you want me to kiss your neck.*

But now it's time Jessie knows I'm here for the taking if she wants me, and I've got loads of time, so I'll wait as long as she needs. Well, until it starts to get pathetic, or she gets a restraining order. I do have some dignity. But in the end, if she decides I'm not the one for her . . . okay, that would suck, and I'm not actually ready to prepare for that yet. It might be stupid, but I'm choosing to remain eternally optimistic until she tells me to get lost.

I'm staring down at Jessie's soft face when I feel a swift kick to my ribs. It wasn't Jessie; it was the baby. I'm smiling from ear to ear, realizing how incredible it is that Jessie is pressed up against me so close that her baby is able to kick me. I know Jessie is apprehensive about starting a relationship with a newborn. I know she's scared we'll get close while she's pregnant and then I'll take a hike after the baby arrives. What she doesn't know is that part of me feels made for this—prepared. I love babies. I even loved helping my sister raise Levi. I know I can do this if she'll give me a chance.

Again, I feel a little foot nudge me. This time it wakes Jessie up, and she stirs with a sharp inhale. I know better than to be awake when she realizes she ditched her pillow to snuggle me all night, so I swiftly clamp my eyelids shut and wipe the smile off my face. I feel Jessie's head tilt slowly up to me, and it's so freaking hard not to smile. Somehow, I manage it, and she believes I'm the heaviest sleeper in the world. Ever so gently, she extracts herself from my body and rolls over to her side. It jostles me a bit, and eventually the mattress springs let me know she got out of bed. I'm cold now. I miss her already. I'm pitiful, and greedy, and I want to pull her back down beside me. *Stay.*

I peek an eye open ever so slightly to see Jessie walking on tip-toes to the bathroom. She hisses when she bumps a shoe and it clunks loudly across the floor. My ability to maintain a straight face is beyond impressive. Jessie shuts the door to the bathroom, and I hear the water turn on. She's taking a shower. Yeah, that's fine. I'm fine out here not thinking about her in there. Tohhhh-tally fine.

Nope. I get out of bed and quickly throw on a pair of jeans, a T-shirt, and a hat. I need to brush my teeth and put on more deodorant, but that'll have to wait, because right now I need to do everything I can to distract myself from the woman softly humming a song in the shower.

I grab my laptop and catch up on patient emails. I have forty-five new messages from worried women afraid their periods are too heavy, their period is too late, they might be in labor, is it normal to throw up so much in early pregnancy, is it okay to take headache medicine while pregnant? I work my way through the inbox, reassuring where needed, instructing when I think she should make an appointment, and answering frantic questions, all while listening to Jessie hum. I could get used to this.

Once I'm done, I can't distract myself any longer. I need to get out of here, because I've never been more attracted to anyone than I am to the woman in that shower. I grab my boots and try to hop into them on my way to the door. My hand is on the knob when Jessie's scream rips through the air. I'm already halfway to the bathroom when she starts yelling, "DREW, DREW!!!!!"

My mind is everywhere. It's gone to horrible worst-case scenarios, and my body is propelling itself toward her. I'm prepared to find Jessie dropped down and giving birth. I'm *not* prepared to fling open the bathroom door and find a long snake stretched out across the ledge of the shower. Jessie is definitely naked (although I'm not looking at her . . . more than once) and backed into the far corner of the shower stall.

"DREW, A SNAKE! Get the snake! AH—DON'T LOOK AT ME THOUGH!"

I should not be laughing at a time like this, but I am. Jessie is screeching at the top of her lungs, but she can't decide if she's more upset that a snake has invaded her shower or that she's standing naked in front of me.

"Oh my gosh, you butthead! I'm about to die of a snake bite in here and you're doubled over laughing!! I SAID DON'T LOOK!!!"

"Chill out. I'm not looking!"

"I know you can see me naked right now."

"Only in my peripherals. I won't look at you, okay? I have to get closer, though, to get to the snake. Want me to throw you a towel?"

"NO!!! You might startle it, and it will lunge at me! Oh my gosh, it's going to bite me while I'm exposed and naked. This is going to traumatize me, and I'll never be able to be naked again!" That would be a tragedy. I can't let that happen.

"Everything okay in there?" Richard calls from outside the open bathroom door.

"We heard screaming," says Henry in a worried tone.

"Oh, *super*. The gang's all here," Jessie says, sounding like she's close to hysterics. "Does the rest of the neighborhood want to come in and see me naked too?"

"No one but me is going to see you naked." *Ever again.* "I'll make sure they don't come in." I hold a hand out toward Jessie. "Don't go anywhere."

"WHERE WOULD I GO?!"

I turn around and peek my head out at Richard. "Uh—so, we've got a snake problem in here."

"AHHHHH! IT'S GETTING CLOSER. DREWWWW."

"Oh heavens!" Henry says, sounding like a 1950s housewife who's never heard a swear word. His hands are balled up under his chin and his face is contorted into full panic.

I give him a reassuring head shake, because I'm slightly worried for his blood pressure. "It's just a garter snake, but I'm going to need a pillowcase, please."

Henry runs to the bed and tears one off before throwing it at me. I nod my thanks and go back into the bathroom. Richard asks if I need his help, but then Jessie screeches again that no one but me is allowed to come in there, so he just smiles and nods like I'm going into war. Luckily, when I was a kid I loved catching garter snakes, so this will not be a first for me.

Back inside the bathroom, I keep my eyes on the snake—but let's be real, I can tell Jessie is still in the corner using her hands to cover everything she deems unseeable. It's adorable, and I'm crazy about her.

"Don't look—I mean it!" she warns for the hundredth time.

"Are you talking to me or the snake?"

"Ha-ha, you're so funny!" She does not think I'm funny. "Please, just hurry! That creepy tongue of his keeps sticking out like I'm lunch."

I cup my hand over the side of my face, cutting Jessie out of my peripheral vision, and slowly approach the shower.

"Ohmygoshohmygoshohmygosh," Jessie chants in a high-pitched voice with every step I take. I don't want to move too quickly and startle the snake for fear that it would then startle Jessie and make her slip and fall.

So, I move in slowly and whisper, "Will you be quiet?"

"Don't tell me what to do! I'm the one being held hostage by a snake. You're not peeking, are you?"

"If you don't zip your lips, I'm going to turn and look fully at you."

"You wouldn't!"

"I would. So hush until I have this snake in the bag."

I hear her gulp, but she doesn't say a thing as I approach.

Moving nice and slow, I set the pillowcase down and open a few inches in front of the snake. It starts hissing, and Jessie whimpers. Finally, using her curling wand that I found on the counter, I wave it toward the back of the snake, getting it to startle and slither into the bag. As soon as it's inside, I pick up the pillowcase and cinch the top closed with my fist. The snake throws a fit inside the bag and Jessie immediately lurches forward, grabs the shower curtain, and pastes it to her body like a scandalous dress.

I finally make eye contact with her and smile. Her cheeks are bright red, whether from the hot shower, the embarrassment, or the snake, I don't know. Either way, she's beautiful.

"Thank you," she says in a snooty, wobbly voice, then points toward the door. "Now get out."

I shut the bathroom door behind me, and Henry apologizes profusely like he had something to do with a snake somehow making it into his house. Richard thanks me for removing it. I laugh the whole way down to the dock, where I let it go near the lake.

Once the snake is taken care of, I sit down on the edge of the dock, still laughing over the sight of Jessie squealing with a snake hissing at her, and I wait. I know she will come find me, and I'm right. I hear her feet shuffling over the dock, and I look over my shoulder to see her wearing jean shorts and a lavender top. Her hair is wet, and her arms are crossed tightly over her chest, shoulders bunched up to her ears.

"Are you seriously still laughing at me?"

"Yes," I say, not bothering to hide my amusement.

"You're a jerk."

"A jerk who saved you from a naked snakebite."

She stops a few feet away from me and groans into her hands. "Oh my gosh, please don't say that word!"

I hop up and go to stand in front of her. "Snake?"

She drops her hands, a humiliated, pleading look on her face. "Naked!"

I chuckle and put my hands on the sides of her arms. "It's really not a big deal."

Her eyes widen. "*Not a big deal?!* Drew! I'm eight months pregnant, and you . . . you saw me . . ." She shakes her head. She can't bring herself to say the word *naked* again. This is ridiculous. I can't believe she's even giving this a second thought.

"Jessie, you know what I do for a living, right? I have seen one or two naked pregnant ladies in my day."

Her face is serious as a heart attack. "First of all, that doesn't help even a bit. And second, this is different, and you know it."

It is different, but I'm just trying to make her feel better. I'm honestly not sure what to say here. It feels sort of dangerous, like my only options are to say too much or too little.

I try to duck down and catch her eyes, but she's not having it. "Jessie, what can I say that will make you feel better?"

"I want you to say you didn't see anything and you will completely forget this ever happened!"

I'm a good liar—but I'm not that good. "I saw everything." She drops her head and makes sounds of lamenting. I smile and lift her chin up so her pretty green gaze is forced to look into mine and see the truth for herself. Her watery eyes blink at me. "I saw everything—and I loved everything I saw. You are *gorgeous.* Every inch. And I have seriously never seen a more beautiful woman in all my life."

The corners of her mouth turn down in a sort of sad smile, and her eyebrows knit together. "Really?" she asks in an insecure voice that's brimming with hope. *Don't lie to me,* her tone says.

"Really." I wrap my arms around her and let Jessie bury her face in my chest.

"Thank you," she says, the words muffled by the fabric of my shirt, and I'm not sure I've ever been so thankful for the existence of snakes as I am right now. "But I think you have to go skinny-dipping now so I can see you naked and even the score."

"I would, but I think Henry is watching us from the window, and I don't want to set the bar too high for Richard."

CHAPTER 32

Jessie

"You know," says Henry, coming back to the table to set a cup of hot tea in front of me after the snake fiasco. Drew is outside loading up the car before we head to my grandaddy's house, and given the look on Henry's face right now, I hope Drew comes back any second because it seems like I have a feelings speech on the horizon. I've seen this look before in the salon when my clients want to share with me their tricks to catch a man, or how they've kept a happy husband for thirty-plus years. (It's actually not as dirty as you might think—all you have to do is feed him a pot roast and mashed potatoes, apparently.)

"I couldn't help but hear you yelling for Drew not to look at you while you were . . . uh . . . in the shower this morning."

Oh shoot. Of course he heard me and thought that was strange. Before I can open my mouth with an excuse, Henry leans over and squeezes my hand.

"No need to get embarrassed. I completely understand. Although I've never been in exactly your situation, I have been the listening ear to many, *many* of my pregnant friends over the years, and I know it must be hard to let your man see you in the nude when your body has changed so much."

My worried expression clears. He's not suspicious that Drew and I have been faking our relationship and today was literally the first time he's ever seen me without my clothes—he just thinks I'm shy about my baby body. Okay, I can work with this. Also, I choose not to wonder why I care so much if Henry knows Drew and I are not really together. It's not like anything bad would come of it or he'd out Drew to all his colleagues. Drew is going to have to tell everyone eventually anyway—that was the whole point of this prank, to force Drew into a humiliating situation. And yet . . . I want to protect him.

"It *is* hard," I say, mustering up pretend emotion to really sell it. "I don't even feel like myself anymore." And that part isn't even a lie. It's hard to look in the mirror with this belly and these hips and boobs and find the woman I once was. I'm sure she'll be back one day, but for now I feel totally different.

My mind wanders back to Drew telling me he saw *everything* and thought I was the most beautiful woman he'd ever seen. My cheeks heat just thinking of it. I won't lie, that was a concern for me—Drew and me developing feelings for each other and taking things to the next level. How do you even begin to date someone at this phase of life? I'm about to have a child. Drew has never known me not pregnant. And then I can only imagine what things will be like down south after the baby comes out. It would be so weird to start dating *now*. Wouldn't it? But then again . . . he saw me naked and thought I was beautiful as is, and with his profession, it's not like anything would be a shock to him. He knows what he would be getting into. So how am I supposed to feel about that?

"I know you don't, but believe me, you'll bounce right back after the baby comes, so you've got nothing to worry about. And letting your fiancé see you like this is one of the greatest joys you can give your man." I can feel my face turning into lava. This feels like a very personal conversation to be having with my fake boyfriend's mentor's husband. "The way Drew looks at you . . . it's like you hung the moon. And I'm sure he loves nothing more than seeing the woman carrying his baby in all her glory."

Henry is beaming, but I am slowly deflating. His words have kicked me in the stomach.

This isn't Drew's baby. No, this child belongs to a man who had no interest in seeing me *in all my glory*.

Henry misinterprets my sudden emotions. "Oh, sweet thing, don't cry. Drew loves you just as you are." Henry chuckles happily, but I can't handle it anymore. I pull my hand from his and wipe my tears with the back of my hand.

At that same moment, Drew comes back in the front door. "You ready to roll, Jessie? The car is all—" He stops talking when I quickly push the chair out and stand.

"Sorry! I have something in my eye. I think it's a bug! Don't worry about me! I'll be fine. I just need to . . ." My voice cracks on a sob. "Get the bug out!" I move as fast as my feet will carry me back to the bedroom.

CHAPTER 33

Drew

I blink at the empty hallway Jessie just raced down, then turn my eyes to Henry. He looks just as stunned as I feel. "I'm guessing it wasn't a bug?"

Henry shakes his head. "I have no idea. We were having a little heart-to-heart, and the next thing I know she's crying and running off. Oh, Drew, I'm so sorry. I don't know . . ."

I hold up my hand and shake my head. "Don't worry about it. I'm sure it wasn't you, but I better go check on her."

"Yes, please do. And let me know if she needs anything."

I smile and nod before heading down the hallway. Even before I reach out and touch the doorknob, I can feel Jessie's mood. It's intense and blazing through the door. I gingerly crack the door open, and it abruptly slams back in my face. Whoa. This is serious.

"Don't come in here—I'm mad at you!"

Mad at me? I was gone for two minutes. What could have possibly happened in that time?

I look down the hallway and find Richard and Henry peeking around the corner. I smile and give them a thumbs-up, even though I'm sure Jessie and I look insane. I turn the handle again and feel the resistance of her pushing against the door (thankfully, it doesn't have a lock), and with a happy-go-lucky-everything-is-fine smile on my face for the Greens, I shove my way through. Jessie finally relents and moves away from the door to go pace by the window.

"I said I didn't want you to come in." Her voice sounds wobbly, and I'm almost one hundred percent sure this is why she doesn't want me in here. Jessie is not one to cry in front of anyone.

"Why are you mad at me?" I ask in a tender voice that seems to only ignite her fury deeper.

Jessie whips around, and I see tearstains on her cheeks. She takes a soft pillow off the bed and chucks it at my head, making a face like she's pitching in the World Series. I look down at the pillow by my feet.

"What was that for?"

She does it again with another pillow. The determination in her eyes is sharp and focused. Her blond ponytail swings like a sassy pendulum as she finds anything soft within her reach and chucks it at me. "For being you!"

Okay, I'm lost. I can't even begin to know what's happening right now. "Will you stop throwing things at—" WHAM. A circular throw pillow hits my face. "Okay, enough." I lean down and pick up a pillow, chucking it at her this time.

She gasps and her jaw drops. "You just hit a pregnant woman!"

"Yeah, and I'll do it again." I toss one of the big pillows she threw at me right into her face. It springs off dramatically, and her eyes slant dangerously.

She picks it up and throws it at me harder. I throw another one even harder. Before I know it, she's lunging at me with a king-sized pillow, I'm coming at her with a softer version, and we collide somewhere in the middle, pillows whamming into each other at epic speeds. (Don't worry, I keep my projectiles aimed at her head and butt. Baby is safe.)

"Jessie. Tell me why you're mad at me," I say while taking a blow to my back.

"I'm always mad at you!!" she says, with a hit so powerful the pillow splits open and feathers go flying.

"Why?!" Our voices are raised, and I'm sure Henry and Richard can hear all of this.

"Because, Drew! I didn't want to get swept up again! I wanted to find someone tolerable. A partner. Someone to eat the other half of my dinner so I don't have too much left over the next day. And then *you* showed up and ruined everything!" She's still hitting me with a pillow, but she's also crying. Feathers are sticking to her eyelashes.

I stop fighting and my hands fall down to my sides. "Are you swept up in me?"

She half laughs, half cries. She looks like she's in physical pain. "Of course I am! You're an expert-level sweeper! Look at you . . . and your dimples"—she pokes one—"and your biceps"—she pokes those too—"and your abs"—poke. "But *dammit* if it's not what's underneath all that that really kills me. Your heart is like gold, Drew—pure gold. And you're funny, and thoughtful, and I want to talk to you all the time, and you *terrify* me!"

I raise and lower my hands with a sad smile. "You terrify me too, Jessie." I step toward her, and she steps away, not ready to play nice yet.

"No, it's different. Because I'm the one having a child, and at the end of the day, you're a man who can walk away from all of it if you don't want to deal with it. Believe me, I know, because someone already *has* walked away from me. Twice." She hits me with another pillow like *I'm* the one who left her. "And what if I let you in, what if I take a chance and we do this, and then you get tired of me and the baby and leave too?"

Feathers hover in the air all around along with her words. I yank the pillow from her hand and toss it onto the bed. "But what if I don't?"

I step forward now, determined.

She blinks and eyes the space disappearing between us like it's lava climbing up to swallow her whole. "I'm not sure that's an option. No, don't come any closer!" She holds out her hand toward my chest, and I press into it easily until her back finds the bathroom door and she has nowhere else to go. She's trapped, and finally I'm going to make sure she hears me.

"Listen to me, Jessica Barnes. I'm crazy about you. I still don't know what happened with your ex, but I know you can't hide yourself away forever." I move my hands up to cup both sides of her jaw. "You don't just want a plain dinner partner, Jessie. You want fire and passion. You want pillow fights and prank wars. You want to be challenged, and fought with, and deeply *wanted*." I pause, making sure there's no room for miscommunication when I say, "And believe me, Jessie, I *want you* deeply."

She shuts her eyes tight. Her breath trembles when she releases it and opens her eyes again. Tenderness tears through my heart. "I want you too. *Please* be good to me."

I bend down and softly kiss her mouth. "I will."

Jessie and I got on the road after spending thirty minutes cleaning up feathers. They were everywhere, and one look at Henry and Richard as they eyed our mess told me they suspect we are into some kinky stuff. Actually, I would have been very happy to lay Jessie down on that bed of feathers and consummate our new relationship, but it wasn't the right time. Not only were Henry and Richard hovering outside our room, but . . . well, to be honest, I don't know when the right time will be.

There's really no sense in worrying about it, though. It'll happen when it happens, and I'm in no rush. Nothing about our relationship is normal or follows a usual plan, so we're going to have to wing it as best we can. I'm feeling more comfortable with that prospect than I used to.

Once we got in the car and were down the road a few miles, Jessie uncapped a Sharpie and gave me a questioning look. I smiled and nodded, and she wrote *Jessie + Drew* on the glove box and drew a heart around it. She then reached over and laced her fingers with mine. Her smile was tentative, and I knew everything she'd just done was a massive display of her vulnerability. I raised her hand to my mouth and kissed it. After that, she opened up to me about everything. I mean *everything*. She started with her ex, Jonathan, and told me about how they had been dating for three months when she found out she was pregnant. She had been excited, thinking he would be too. He wasn't. Instead, he was pretty cruel to her, accusing her of lying about being on birth control only to trap him in the relationship. Apparently, he is in a band that's trying to make it big, and he thought she purposely got pregnant to keep him home and off the road. Jessie cried when she told me this story, and it tore my heart in half.

The jerk packed his bags and left, telling Jessie if she wanted to have her baby that was on her, but she'd do it alone and he wanted nothing to do with either of them. *A real winner, that guy.* She also told me about her dad and how he left shortly after she was born. She hasn't heard from him since and wouldn't even know where to begin to look for him. Other than her grandaddy, Jessie has never had a loving, loyal male in her life. Part of me wants to go find Jonathan and beat him into dust, but the other part of me is thankful he moved out of the way so I could be here with Jessie, so I could take over caring for her like she deserves.

"Lucy," I say to my sister when she answers her phone. "I don't have long. Jessie just ran into the gas station to grab a snack, but I need a favor from you."

"No, I will not change all the locks on your house while you're gone so you can keep Jessie out."

I anxiously tap the steering wheel while tracking Jessie moving around inside. "First of all, you're like eighteen steps behind, but I don't have time to catch you up right now."

Lucy laughs. "Let me guess, you realized how incredible my best friend is, and now you're going to date her."

"Well . . . basically, yeah."

"What I should do is take this opportunity to go berserk on you like you did on me and Cooper and warn you to stay away from her forever. But because I'm a remarkable human being, I'll tell you I'm happy for you, and I think you and Jessie are perfect for each other."

"Your saint of the year trophy is already in the mail. Now, please grab a pen and paper. I'm going to tell you my credit card number."

Cooper barks out a laugh, because apparently he and Lucy are like an old married couple now and he's always lurking on the line without you knowing. "You don't want to do that. She'll buy enough stuff to furnish your whole freaking house in the time it takes you to cook dinner."

"YOU TOLD ME TO," Lucy yells, making me cringe.

"Luce, focus."

"Yeah, okay, sorry. Got a pen." I rattle off the number quickly and she repeats it back to me. "So why do I need this?"

"Because I'm pretty sure I'm in love with Jessie."

The line goes silent for a second and then Lucy replies, "What does this have to do with your credit card?"

CHAPTER 34

Jessie

D rew opens my passenger side door and looks down at me and the four packages of Oreos in my lap.

"You know, on second thought, you should probably be heading home. I bet your patients are really missing you today—like they are going to walk into their appointments and expect to find their favorite Dr. Marshall and then spot whichever crusty old doctor is covering for you—"

"Susan."

"—and then they are going to be so peeved at you for taking a little vacation instead of caring about the healthy birth of their child and—"

Drew leans inside to unbuckle my seatbelt. "Come on." He grabs my hand and pulls me out, nearly making my Oreos spill to the ground before I manage to gather them up in my arms like a bundle of little Oreo babies. A caveman, this one.

"Do you always get your way?" I ask, looking up at him with a saucy expression.

"Nearly always, yes."

I growl. "It's the jaw. It's hard to say no to. Hey, have you ever thought about acting? I bet you'd be so good playing Superman in a movie. Come on, let's hop in the car and take a quick trip to L.A. to get you signed up for some action flicks."

Drew is dragging me toward the front door of my grandaddy's house. "Sure thing, let's just make a quick stop inside first."

Why are my footbrakes not working?!

"Wait! Drew, Drew, Drew, Drew," I say, trying to pull my hand from his so I can sprint back toward the car and somehow take him with me.

He chuckles and turns around. "What is wrong with you?"

"You're about to go inside my childhood house."

"So?" He's so cute when he's exasperated with me.

"So . . . this is my house. All my secrets are in there . . . all my memories. I don't know if you know this or not, but I'm not great at being vulnerable."

He gives a mocking gasp. "*No.*"

I smack his arm. "I kind of feel like I've already met my vulnerability quota for the day by telling you about Jonathan and my parents."

The teasing leaves Drew's eyes, and he steps closer to cradle my face in his hands and kiss my lips. It ends too quickly and I'm teetering forward for more when he says, "I get it, Jessie. So what do you want me to do?"

"Maybe you could just go get a hotel, and then Grandaddy and I could meet you for dinner?"

"Okay."

"Really?" I say, a little skeptical that he gave in so easily. I expected at least a little bit of a fight.

He grins and kisses me again before dropping his hands to his sides. "Yeah, sounds good. I'll find a hotel and—hey." His eyebrows pinch together, and he looks over my shoulder. "Is that guy break-ing into that house?"

"What?!" I spin around and peer through the neighborhood, but I don't see anything. "Where? I don't see anyone."

I turn back to find Drew pressing the doorbell with a mischie-vous slanted smile and lifted eyebrow. "I'm not going to a hotel. I'm staying here. With you. Get over it." I want to be angry, but when he holds out his hand for me to take, my body moves to him like a magnet and I grip his hand in mine.

It occurs to me that the same reasons I hated Drew in the beginning are the reasons I've fallen for him now. He's heavy-handed. He's bossy. He won't back down from me—and he's exactly what I need and want.

Drew holds me tight, wrapping his hand around my waist like even if I tried to dart away, he wouldn't let me. We stand united like those annoying June bugs in Florida as the front door opens and I see my grandaddy's smiling face.

I put my hand on Drew's chest. "Grandaddy, meet my boy-friend, Drew."

I walk back into the living room and hand Grandaddy a fresh cup of coffee I brewed for him. He smiles up at me and pats the back of my hand, sending me spiraling through thousands of memories.

Everything about this house is familiar and exactly the same as the day I left at eighteen. The carpet is still an odd shade of brownish-taupe. There's a small screened-in porch with bright green faux turf carpet and white metal lawn chairs. The walls are wood-paneled and lined with photos of me from birth all the way up to a photo of me standing with a goofy smile and my arms spread wide outside my salon on opening day. I gave Grandaddy the inaugural haircut. There are photos of Grandma sprinkled around too, but since she died when I was little, they are mainly photos of her in her younger days.

The pillows are still navy, and the couch is still that odd brown-and-yellow plaid with big wooden armrests. There's not a single updated or trendy thing about this place, and I adore it.

Actually, that's not true. There is one update: *Drew*. He's sitting on the couch, aiming an intense smile up at me.

"So," Grandaddy says, breaking through my thoughts. "Drew, how do you feel about being pinched?"

"Grandaddy . . ." I say in a warning tone.

Drew's brow furrows. "What am I missing?"

"Nothing, just an inside joke." I look down at my mischievous grandaddy. He winks up at me from under one bushy eyebrow.

"Has Jessie told you to pinch me or something for standing her up that day? Because, sir, I swear to you, I did not stand her up on purpose. I had an all-night shift and overslept, but I wish more than anything I had brought my phone in to wake—"

"Psh." Grandaddy interrupts Drew's adorably nervous explanation and waves him off. "Never would have worked anyway. I've known her secret since almost the beginning. Jessie never has been able to pull a fast one over on me. And besides, everything happened the way it needed to. No sense looking back while you're still moving forward."

I chuckle and look to Drew. "He's full of catchphrases. I swear he moonlights writing for fortune cookies."

Grandaddy wags his finger up at me. "I don't, but you *should* be writing all this down. I am very wise."

When I look to Drew, I see him smiling softly, gaze heavy on my face. He hitches his head, telling me to come sit with him. It's so weird, having him here with me, having him look at me like that. My heart tells me to sink in and stay awhile, but the guards I've fashioned around it say, *Not so fast.*

I do go sit by Drew, though. I try to put a little space between us, but he won't have it. He tugs on my hand repeatedly until I finally give in and scoot closer. He kisses my temple and wraps his arm around me. I lay my head on his shoulder and breathe him in.

Grandaddy's short chuckle has me looking up at him. He's shaking his head of white hair and wearing a smile that can only be described as overjoyed. His eyes tell me, *This is good, Jessie girl. You deserve this.*

"If you kids will excuse me, I have a phone call I need to make."

No, he doesn't. For as much as I can't pull a fast one over on him, he can't pull any on me either. He's trying to give us a moment alone, and honestly, I'm grateful for it.

Once my grandaddy disappears down the hall, I look up at Drew. "Hey. So. Do you remember that day you took me back to the salon when Lucy had to go help Levi?"

He hums and lifts my hand to kiss my wrist.

"Well, you were right when you guessed that there was more to my original hatred for you than I was letting on."

He tenses a bit, setting our intertwined fingers down and turning those sharp eyes to me. "I'm listening."

"Truth is, I hated you before I ever met you."

He frowns. "This day is taking a turn I'm not sure I like."

"Oh, you will, believe me. And I hesitate to tell you because your head is going to grow eighteen sizes."

"I'm confused."

I suck in a deep breath, then let it out in a whoosh. This is it for me. This is the last straw of secrecy, my last line of defense against Drew, and I'm letting it go. Laying it all on the line. This is me saying, *I'm all in.*

I clear my throat and force myself to look into his eyes. "Drew, a month before I ever met you, Lucy showed me a picture of you with Levi, and I swear I thought you were the sexiest man I'd ever seen. She told me all about you and what you do for a living. She mentioned you almost every single time we were together and painted the most incredible picture of a man with her words—a man I was immediately attracted to, a man I knew I would fall for at the drop of a hat, and I wanted to avoid that happening at all cost. I knew before I ever met you that you were exactly my type—my dream man in a lot of ways. And so . . . I decided to hate you, to find anything unappealing about you and grab hold of it so I couldn't let myself get close to you. By being so horrible to you, I knew I was ensuring you wouldn't want to get close to me either." I shrug, feeling my words between us like tangible objects. "I calculated my hatred for you and multiplied it so I could keep you away from me."

Drew is quiet. So quiet I can hear the clock on the wall ticking. My palms sweat, and those vulnerability hives are starting to prickle my skin. Finally, he shakes his head and then threads his fingers through the back of my hair.

"You failed miserably from the start, Oscar. Every sharp quip, every rude jab, every sassy lift of your eyebrow and display of backbone—it all drove me wild. See, when I found out I was going to have a free ticket to act like your fiancé, I had *plans.*" The way he says *plans* has my skin erupting in shivers. He dips his head and slowly kisses my mouth, and then he pulls away to whisper, "You were strong and determined, and also *exactly* my type. I've wanted you from day one. I tried telling myself I didn't—it didn't work, and I almost crashed Cooper's truck because I was sexually frustrated by you."

"What?" I ask on a laugh.

"Shh, don't worry about it. Point is, your grandaddy is right. No sense in looking back when we are clearly meant to be together from here on out."

"I'm still terrified."

"That's okay. Me too. We just have to take it one day at a time."

And this is how we spend the rest of the day, in a weird, gloriously happy bubble. Also, I was dead wrong about Drew not liking PDA. The man is obsessed with it. He never lets go of me. If I go in the kitchen, he only releases my hand at the very last second, so our arms are stretched out dramatically between us like we're in a slow-motion movie scene.

I show Drew the rest of the house but keep him firmly away from my old room. He playfully pretends to grab the handle, but I give him the look of death, making sure he knows he's not allowed in there. And he's not. If he goes in, he will never look at me the same way again.

After lunch, Grandaddy pulls out the old photo album and delightedly shows Drew every embarrassing photo he can find. And there are a lot: the classic naked baby photo, prom when I wore my hair piled up so high on my head I'm surprised it didn't interfere with air traffic. He tells Drew what I was like as a kid—a firecracker, no surprise there—and describes the time I broke my arm trying to sneak out my window so I could go to a movie I wasn't allowed to see.

Drew sits at the old dining room table Grandaddy and I shared nearly every breakfast and dinner, just the two of us—and now Drew's there too. I try to hover on the edge, allowing myself to see it without feeling it or holding on too tight, but Drew grabs me and pulls me onto his lap to look at the rest of the photographs. I barely fit, my belly brushing up against the table, and Drew wraps his hand around me so it's splayed out against my baby bump. He rubs it tenderly and kisses the side of my shoulder. How did I get here? How did this happen? And is it all going to go away when we return to reality?

CHAPTER 35

Drew

It's been a day. A good one. A great one, actually. I feel Jessie's walls coming down more with every passing minute. She's slowly trusting me, and I don't take it for granted.

Except now I'm standing in her childhood room, staring at a wall completely dedicated to NSYNC, and I'm thinking there's a lot about Jessie I still don't know, a lot I'm scared to know based on this shrine dedicated to the young boy-band members in white tanks with spiky bleached hair in every pose possible. There's one in front of a graffiti wall. In tuxes at an award show. A few behind-the-scenes photos scattered in of them recording in the studio with dramatic faces and headphones over only one ear. It's a hodgepodge of images printed off the internet, pages ripped from magazines, and premium posters all pasted together to look like one elaborate sheet of wallpaper. Now I see why Jessie wouldn't let me in here. I tried to open the door earlier today, but she just got in front of me and gave me her scary-eyes death glare—so I was forced to sneak in while she's putting away the leftovers from dinner.

"Oh no," Jessie says from behind me in the doorway. She races to throw her body in front of the wall, arms and legs sprawled out like that will keep me from seeing this freak show. "Don't look at it!"

"Too late," I say, shaking my head slowly, unable to peel my eyes from her teen fantasy creation.

"You weren't supposed to come in here without me! I was going to prepare you! Now you're in shock. Do you need one of those shiny thermal blankets? Should I call 911?" I don't reply. Just keep staring. Jessie leaves the wall to come put her hands on my face. "Drew, look at me. It's going to be okay, you just need to look away from the wall." She starts gently turning my shoulders away, but I crane my neck, unable to escape its hypnotic spell, until finally I'm forced to snap my gaze forward.

I blink several times at Jessie. "So many pictures." At least two hundred. I'm not kidding.

"It was a different time, Drew. My teen years were confusing. Everyone was doing it . . . I couldn't resist the temptation. I'm so sorry." The seriousness in Jessie's eyes is what finally makes me crack. My smile spreads wide and slow, and before I know it we're both laughing.

"You crazy woman," I say, taking one final look at the shrine.

She grins up at me, wrapping her arms around my waist. "Don't act like you didn't have photos of swimsuit models pasted above your bed."

I shake my head firmly. "No, ma'am. Obviously you don't know my mom and dad. They would have whipped me if I had put up a degrading photo like that." Jessie narrows her eyes until I wag my eyebrows. "That's why I kept it under my mattress." I know she's going to try to pinch me, so I catch her hand preemptively. "Come here," I say, pulling her up close to me. "I haven't kissed you enough."

It's a rare thing to see Jessie blush, but she does now, and that's the first place I aim my lips. She laughs as I kiss the apples of both her cheeks. "I don't think that counts as kissing."

"Quiet. I'm just getting warmed up."

I lower my head, preparing to drop a soft, sweet kiss on her mouth, but Jessie meets me halfway, her lips crashing into mine. It's a jolt straight to my nervous system that I wasn't expecting. I'm a pretty controlled guy. I can keep my cool in high-pressure situations, and rarely do I ever feel out of my head. Right now, though, I'm nowhere near conscious thought, because Jessie has taken control of me and decided my fate without asking my opinion. *Thank goodness.* One of her hands hits my chest and backs me up against the NSYNC wall as the other slides up under my shirt to feel my abs. I cradle her jaw and grab her hip. The push and pull of our mouths is not soft. Not tender. It's mad—teeth clanking, out of breath, full of desire and passion. I'll be honest, it's not something I thought would be in the cards until well after this baby comes, but I am *here for it.*

Everything is breath, and heat, and skin, and lips, and taste. She kisses my neck, and when her tongue touches my skin, I lose my mind. I'm done for. Toast. Suddenly, Jessie has my shirt above my head and helps me whip it off. Cool air rushes across my chest and her eyes rake over me before they snag on my tattoo. She runs a finger reverently across the ink, and heat burns through me. She kisses her way up my tattoo and then my neck. Once she finds my mouth again, I decide it's my turn to be in charge.

I put my hands on Jessie's hips and slowly devour her full mouth as I guide us away from the wall. I've never, *ever* needed a woman like I need Jessie. The moment gets away from me, and the next thing I know, I've backed Jessie up to her bed. She sits on the edge, and then her head falls back against the mattress. Her smile is not nervous but rather excited as I plant my hands on either side of her face and hover over her. I brush her hair away from her neck and then trace the line of her collarbone with my finger. Her eyes greedily take in every inch of my available skin. I can't bring myself to care that we're in her childhood room right now or that this dinky bed might not be able to support the weight of both of us. My mind is lost in a haze of *want,* and all I can think about is how unfair it is that she has on more clothes than me. *Time to level the playing field.*

I reach for the bottom edge of her shirt, then suddenly her door flies open and Jessie's grandaddy, Harold, steps inside. Jessie squeals, and I jump off her, feeling like a dirty teenager who will be grounded for the rest of his life. I mostly blame the teenage-nostalgia scenery.

"Grandaddy! Knock first!" Jessie screeches and tosses a small pillow at the door, also looking and sounding like a guilty teen. *We're so dead. Definitely not going to junior prom without a chaperone now.*

"I'm so sorry, sugar!" Harold says with a hand over his eyes as he backs out of the room. I would give anything for a black hole I could jump into right now. *Anything.*

"Oh my goodness, you don't have to cover your eyes like that, Grandaddy! That makes it so much more embarrassing," she says with her hands on her cheeks to cool the flames.

I would say something right now, but nothing in particular worth saying comes to mind. I'm torn between wanting to shrink into a ball and climbing out the window to drive one hundred miles per hour until I'm home and far away from this humiliation. Instead, I laugh, because this is hilarious. *Poor Harold.* His cheeks are the color of raspberries, and he bumps into the wall while backing up with his eyes closed.

"I'd rather keep 'em covered, thanks." His outstretched arm is flailing around, trying to find the threshold of the door, but he's just getting farther away. I take pity and put my hands on his shoulders to guide him out. One glance at Jessie tells me she will never recover from this. I give her an apologetic smile as I run my hand through my hair, and she gives me the stink eye in return.

"Drew," Harold says once he's out of the room and facing the opposite wall in the hallway. "I was actually coming to see if I could talk with you a minute."

That sounds ominous. My eyes fly wide open, and I look to Jessie. Our expressions facilitate a silent communication that goes like this:

ME: Do I have to?!
JESSIE: Yes.
ME: Are you sure?
JESSIE: Quit being a baby.
ME: You'll pay for that insult later. *eyebrow wag*
JESSIE: I hope so.

And that's the moment I realize our relationship will be combustible—which I mean in the best sense.

I angle my face a little toward Harold, keeping my eyes on Jessie. "Of course. I'll be out in a minute." It's a good thing he has his eyes closed so he can't see the sexy eyes his granddaughter keeps giving me.

Harold shuts the door, and I let out something between a puff of air and a laugh before I sink down onto the bed beside her. "Well, that was eventful."

Jessie whips her head to me. "It's all your fault."

"Not true. You're the one who took off my shirt." I stare up at her with grave seriousness. "I can't believe you were about to steal my innocence. What a harlot."

She bites her cheeks against a smile and greedily takes in the sight of me lying on her bed without a shirt. Heat kindles in my chest under her scrutiny, and it takes everything in me to change the subject and not pick back up where we left off.

"Do you think I'm in trouble? Is he going to ground me or something?" I run my hand slowly down her arm and wrap my index finger and thumb around her wrist just because I can.

She watches my weird display of affection with an amused smile. "He'll probably make you go pick a switch off the tree out front so he can swat you with it."

"Did he do that to you?"

"No. He was a big softy with me. I was punished by getting one less scoop of ice cream after dinner than normal."

I pick up her hand next and trace each of her fingers until two of my own land on the pulse point below her thumb. I set my watch, and a fifteen-second countdown begins.

"Why are you always checking—"

"Shh," I reprimand softly and continue counting. She watches me with a gentle tug on the corner of her mouth and waits until I'm done checking her resting heart rate. I'll check it every day for the rest of her life, because I can already feel myself becoming obsessive. Although some women might find it annoying, I think Jessie needs someone to obsess over her a little.

"Healthy?" she asks with a taunting raised eyebrow.

I smirk up at her. "I wish I had my stethoscope. We could listen to the baby's heartbeat."

She stares down at me with a look of disbelief. She can't believe that I care about her baby—about her. It's something she's going to have to get used to, because my adoration is only going to grow from here.

After I lightly yank on Jessie's arm a few times, she concedes and lies down beside me, letting me run my hand affectionately over her stomach. I brush my fingertips across her collarbone and mentally map every freckle, every scar, every bend and dip of her skin. I lean in and kiss the base of her neck slowly, brushing my lips up and down the gentle curve between her shoulder and jaw. She sighs and shuts her eyes, a contented smile on her lips. I nuzzle her skin with my nose, breathing her in and finally letting myself believe she's . . .

"Mine." I finish my thought as a whisper against her skin before giving her a soft love bite on the top of her shoulder.

I prop myself up and stare down at this beautiful woman, amazed at how fortunate I am that the universe apparently took enough pity on me to drop her into my life when I never deserved her and never will. She gives me a warm, loving smile, her hair fanned out around her and face tilted to look at me.

"I really hope Grandaddy doesn't kill you."

Right.

Much-needed mood killer.

Let's get this over with.

I don't know what I'm so nervous about. I've spent all day with Harold, and he's been nothing but sweet and kind. Also, I'm a grown man—a doctor. Surely I can handle talking to Jessie's grandfather. He probably just wants to get to know me a little more and tell me he's happy Jessie and I found each other. I encourage myself with these thoughts all the way down the hallway toward the little dining room off the kitchen.

I felt weird about him seeing me shirtless—hovering over his granddaughter—so not only did I put my shirt back on, I also added a sweatshirt even though it's about seventy-five degrees in here. I was tempted to also wrap myself in a blanket, but Jessie said that was excessive.

Ten minutes later, I'm sitting in the dining room with sweat dripping down my forehead, wishing I had left the sweatshirt behind and cursing myself for ever underestimating Harold Barnes. Yeah, that's right—this man is no longer sweet little Grandaddy to me. He's freaking Colonel Barnes, decorated World War II hero. Want to know how I know this? Because the first thing he did when I entered the dining room was point to a chair and tell me to sit. And then he told me all of this while leaning across the table, knuckles pressing into the wooden tabletop, leveling me with a terrifying gaze. After that, the old man strapped me up to a polygraph test. I'm not even joking. A real lie detector. Where did he even get this thing? Probably the war . . .

He sat down in front of me, crossed his legs, and lifted an eyebrow. Gone was the sweet, meek old southern grandaddy gleefully showing me photo albums. This man has scars from war marking his soul. He tells me he's not old—he's *experienced.*

"How old are you?" He's been lobbing some softballs at me so far, but I'm expecting a curve at any moment.

"Thirty-three."

"What's your favorite color?"

"Blue."

The lie detector flies off the charts.

"Try again," he says with a hard stare.

I sigh. "Pink."

It goes on and on like this, and just when I think maybe he's going to keep this test pretty benign, he kicks it up a notch.

"Are you a virgin?"

"No."

"Were you in love with any of your previous girlfriends?"

"No."

"Have you ever stolen anything?"

"No—wait, yes. A pack of gum in the ninth grade."

"Are you a trustworthy person?"

"Yes."

"Are you taking advantage of Jessie?"

"No."

"Do you love my granddaughter?"

"Yes."

He takes in a deep breath after that last question and sits back in his chair, resting his hands on his stomach. He holds my gaze, and now I'm sure sweat is running down my face. Finally, after a painful amount of time, he nods.

"Okay."

He stands up from his chair and starts detaching the wires from me.

"Okay?" I say with a slightly wobbly voice that's definitely embarrassing. "That's it?"

"That's it," he says.

I let out a breath and shake my shoulders out, wiping the sweat from my brow. "So what now? Did I pass? Do I get to live?"

He chuckles lightly, but I don't know what's funny about what I just said. This whole thing has some serious hostage vibes. I mean, I respect it, but I'll definitely never forget it.

Finally, after binding up all the cords and setting the polygraph back on the shelf (like he's planning to use it again next week or something), he comes and sits down beside me. His face is back to sweet old man, but I won't let myself be fooled again just yet. He rests his elbows on the table and sets his chin on his fist, staring across the room.

"Drew, that girl in there is my whole world." He pauses, and I don't say anything. "I don't know what all she's told you, but her life didn't start out like a fairy tale. And then everything that happened with that Jonathan fellow, well . . . it tears me up inside."

I know the feeling.

He swivels his aged, knowing eyes to me, and I see nothing but tenderness now. "She deserves the world. Jessie is prickly some-times because she has a lot of hurt, but underneath all that she has the kindest, warmest, most giving heart on the planet, and all I want is for her to be safe and taken care of."

"I want that for her too."

He smiles at me for the first time since the bedroom incident. "I can see that. I trust you, Drew, and I can see that Jessie does too. I think you'll be good for each other. Just, please, I'm asking you to make sure to put her and that sweet baby first. Because if you hurt her, I might have to kill you."

I nod and hold his eye contact. "Understandable. I promise to be good to her—to both of them."

He clasps his hand firmly on my shoulder, squeezes, and then stands and walks out of the room. He didn't say it, but I know I have his blessing, and I've never felt more honored in my life.

CHAPTER 36

Jessie

"So you called me your boyfriend earlier," Drew says, stroking my hair as I cuddle against his chest. We're not supposed to be in bed together. The look in my grandaddy's eyes when he told us he put an extra blanket in the guest bedroom for Drew said, *Don't even think about it, missy.* But I've always been a rulebreaker, so ten minutes after lights out, I texted Drew.

> ME: Brrrrrr. It's cold in here. Are you cold?
> DREW: No. Go to sleep.
> ME: I can't. So cold. Limbs are freezing off.
> DREW: I know what you're trying to do.
> ME: Is it working?
> DREW: Nope. You saw the look in that man's eyes before bed. I'm afraid of what he'll do to me if he catches me in your room again. Did you know he has a lie detector?!
> ME: OH NO! Did he use that old thing on you?
> DREW: Yes. And now he knows way more about me than anyone ever should.

ME: I'm so sorry. Did it change your mind about me? Do you
       want to bail now? Is it too much?

In the next minute, Drew was sliding under the sheets of my
full-sized bed and pulling me into his chest. "Not a chance," he
said, kissing my head.

And now here we are and he's trying to trap me into a DTR.

"Ohhhhh. You thought I said *boyfriend*? Nah, I said it like . . .
this is Drew . . . he's a boy . . . and my friend. But I can see how you
were confused."

Drew leisurely runs his fingers through my hair and hums, telling me he doesn't believe my tricks for a second. "Yeah, right. You
meant it, and now I get to claim you as my girlfriend whenever I
want."

"You sound like a twelve-year-old."

"And you love it. In fact, I think you love me . . ." His fingers
never stop their ministrations, but my heart *does* stop for a fraction of a second.

I gasp and tilt my chin up to show Drew how stupid I think
that idea is. "I do not! Not even close. Like miles and miles and
miles away from love. Tolerance is what you're thinking of."

"Is that why you stare at me when you think I'm not looking?
Why you smelled my shirt earlier after I changed?" *He saw that?!*
"You just tolerate me?"

I feel like I'm on a sinking ship. Half of it is already underwater
and the captain has told everyone to abort and jump into a dinghy,
but I've climbed to the top of the stern and am holding on for dear
life. "Drew, we've only been dating for less than forty-eight hours.
How could I possibly love you already?" *How?!*

"Time has nothing to do with it, and we've been living together
for a month. Face it, Jessie, you've been in love with me since your
eyes first landed on all this sexiness." Thank God he's cracking

jokes, because honestly, he's not wrong. I'm not ready to face that truth out loud yet.

I jab my fingers into his ribs and tickle like I'm a merciless tyrant. He struggles to get away, trying to strangle a laugh in his throat so my grandaddy doesn't hear us, and he almost falls off the bed. Finally, when he can't take any more, he grabs both my wrists and pins them on either side of my head. His face hovers over mine, and I can see a dangerous mix of emotions swirling in his deep ocean eyes.

"I don't know how to put a label on what we are, but I want one. Everything about our relationship is unique, and I realize you're on the brink of a completely different life. I know going out on dates and physical affection will be limited and maybe even nonexistent for a while. I'm completely fine with all of that, and you will find I can be the most patient man in the world. But I want something, even if it's just a word that tells me you've officially let me in, that says we are together and gives me the right to adore you like I want to."

I bite the corner of my mouth and roll my eyes toward the ceiling so I don't cry. It's no use though; a tear escapes. "I'm so sick of crying over everything," I say, making Drew laugh.

He dips down to kiss the spot below my ear, and I sigh with pleasure. He rotates back so his head is on the pillow, pulling me up on his chest again. "Only a little longer . . . until you have the baby and cry even more than this."

I groan. "Terrible." Nuzzling my face against his bare skin, I breathe in the scent of bodywash and deodorant and *Drew*. "Okay, *Andrew*, you win. I'll be your girlfriend."

Drew doesn't say anything, just lets out a full, deep breath and pulls me in tighter to him. The baby must be squished because it kicks Drew right in the side, making us both laugh. He moves his hand to rest on my belly like he's already helping soothe my fussy child. I want to stay awake. I want to make out with Drew and maybe even give some of that other physical affection he was talking about a chance. We were well on our way earlier, and I loved it. Drew's mouth is so intoxicating. If he were an alcohol, he'd be aged bourbon. His kisses are sweet aromatics, his touch is a spice that burns, and his proof is so high I won't be able to walk a straight line. I want to be under the influence of his lips and hands all night, but the eight-months-pregnant side of me says *Sleeeep* in an alluring siren call. *Must. Answer. Its. Call.*

"Good night, Jessie," Drew says as his lips press against my forehead.

"Hmm? No!" I say, my protests sounding as if I've had somewhere around eighteen beers. "I'm awake. I brought you in here to mess around. Totally game. Let's get busy." But my words all slur together.

I feel Drew's deep chuckle. "Go to sleep, crazy."

And I do. It takes me all of three seconds to completely pass out, which is incredible considering I haven't been able to sleep in months. With my head rising and falling on Drew's chest, I sleep like a rock for the second night in a row. I feel safe with him, more than just physically. It's like my mind exhales and fully quiets with him.

In the morning, the bed is empty when I wake up. There's a little note on my pillow that says Drew went for a run, but I know he only did it because he's a wuss and didn't want Grandaddy to catch us together. I smile at his horrible doctor handwriting scrawled on the paper and then force myself out of bed to get ready to head back to Nashville today.

Over coffee and Oreos, I stare at my grandaddy and his white hair and lined skin. My heart aches. I don't want to leave him behind anymore. "You know . . ." I say, trying to tread lightly because I know he's just as stubborn and independent as me and will easily spook. "Your great-grandchild will be here soon."

"Is that what that round thing is in your stomach?" He grins and sips his coffee.

"So sarcastic." I run my finger over the rim of my mug.

"What is it you're wantin' to say, sugar. Just spit it out."

"I want you to consider moving to Nashville." I pop my eyes up to his and see the breath physically frozen in his lungs.

He doesn't say anything right away. Instead, his eyes travel around the house he's lived in for so long. His memories with my granny are here, and letting go will feel like letting her go for good. I'm sensitive to that, but I also know there's a new little person about to enter this world and I would love more than anything for him or her to get to know the man who raised me. I want him to be a daily part of my child's life, not just a weekend visitor. It would be one thing if I truly thought he was happy here, but I hear the loneliness in his voice during our phone calls.

"Someone once told me there's no sense in looking back while you're still moving forward," I say tenderly. "I know you think you're too old for change, but you're just getting started. Come to Nashville. Bring all these pictures with you and hang them on new walls. Granny came with me when I went, and she'll come with you too."

He narrows his eyes on me, and a light smile touches his mouth. "I'll think about it."

"Good."

After a small pause, he adds, "Thanks for wanting me around, sugar."

"Always." We each pop an Oreo in our mouth to keep from spilling any more emotions.

A few hours and a goodbye-where-I-blubber-like-an-uncontrollable-fool-to-Grandaddy later, Drew and I pull into his driveway. No sooner does he put the car in park than I lean across the console and grab the front of his shirt, pulling me to him. I slept great last night, and I've had a whole two-hour ride home to let my hormones' imagination run wild with desire for Drew. I was too tired last night, but I'm not now.

Drew's eyebrows shoot up as my lips press into his, possessive and wanting.

I intertwine my fingers in the back of his hair and try to turn the heat level up to a thousand. Drew takes in a sharp breath as I coax his lips to part and deepen the kiss. Something he said last night really got to me. There is a very real chance my body is going to be destroyed after this baby comes, and although I don't particularly relish the idea of being intimate with this huge belly, I also know it's going to be months after the birth before I'm physically able to. It's now or practically never. And no, I'm not being at all dramatic.

Except, Drew pulls away with an awkward smile. "Whoa." He chuckles, and I move to kiss his cheek and then his neck. "What's happening right now?"

I answer him by trying to take his shirt off. "What's it look like?" I kiss his strong jawline.

Drew grabs my hand and stops me, though, pulling away with a slightly panicked look in his eyes. "Jessie . . . slow down. Let's . . . go inside and talk about it first."

What?

He just put the brakes on. Turned me down. Oh my gosh, Drew doesn't want to make love to me! Of course he doesn't—I'm massive! He's had time to think about it and finally realized making love to an elephant doesn't sound appealing. What was I thinking?!

Mortification slaps me, and I feel my face burning hot as I lunge for the handle and jump out of the Jeep. Except I can't, because I'm so freaking pregnant that I can't get out quickly. Great. Now my face looks sunburned from the angry blush creeping over my skin, and I have to scoot to the side of the seat and put my hands under my butt to hoist myself up like a sumo wrestler coming home after a match.

"Jessie, wait!" Drew jumps out of his side like a spry leprechaun, and his agility makes me irrationally angry. He rushes around to where I'm climbing the front steps of the house.

"No. It's fine," I say, my voice breaking because *yep* I'm crying again. "I'm a whale. I get it. You don't want to have sex with me like this. I don't blame you—I wouldn't either."

I shove my key into the lock, intending to race up to my room and barricade myself inside for the rest of my life. Sure, I'll have to deliver my baby up there, but it'll be fine.

"No, no, no. Wait, don't go inside yet. Let me explain!"

"Save it!" I'm on a dramatic daytime television show now, and if I had a vase of water nearby, I'd throw it in his face. I finally get the key turned in the lock and fling the front door open.

I'm immediately greeted with the sight of at least twenty wide-eyed faces. The room is silent, and I immediately take in the giant banner that reads *Oh, Baby, Baby,* glittery streamers, a table full of cake and treats, a giant pile of presents, all my friends, a few ladies who work at the salon, Drew's parents, and Lucy and Cooper standing in front of everyone with matching nervous smiles.

"*Surprise,*" Lucy says quietly. "Happy baby shower."

I'm shocked. Stunned. Can't even form a coherent thought. Slowly, when the gears in my brain start shifting again, I realize Drew knew about this. *This* is why he didn't want to start up the sexy train in the driveway. And *oh my gosh, they heard me*! They all heard me crying about how Drew doesn't want me because I'm a whale.

Now tears are flooding down my face, and I have no idea if

they are from joy or embarrassment or relief. I just know they won't stop. Lucy sees my expression and takes a step toward me, but I surprise her when I quickly turn to Drew. He's standing at the door, a crooked, apologetic smile on his beautiful face. He raises unenthusiastic jazz hands.

"Surprise," he says flatly.

I blink a few times, and then my smile blooms, and all I want is to be in Drew's arms. I nearly tackle him when I wrap my arms around his waist. I feel his chuckle and then his breath on my ear.

"No part of me thinks you're a whale. And believe me, I'd take you back to my room right now if there was not an entire roomful of people watching us."

Heat and desire swirl in my chest, and for a split second I consider kicking everyone out. *Be gone! All of you!*

"We can still hear you! Do your dirty talk later," Cooper says, breaking the ice and making the whole room laugh. "I'm ready for cake."

CHAPTER 37

Drew

"Well, you pulled it off, man," Cooper says, clapping me on the back.

We're standing off to the side of the room, and I can't take my eyes off Jessie. She's by the door, wearing the "Baby Mama" sash Lucy made for her and thanking guests on their way out. I haven't been able to stop watching her and her beaming smile all day. I'm addicted to it now, already planning hundreds of ways I can keep it on her face for the rest of her life.

When I don't respond to Cooper, he says in a mocking tone, "No, Cooper, it was you and Lucy who did the heavy lifting! I couldn't have pulled it off without you two!"

I begrudgingly pull my gaze from Jessie. "Sorry. I was distracted."

Cooper's eyebrows rise, saying he already knew that. "Yeah, I gathered as much." He grunts a laugh. "You've got it bad. I've never seen such a pathetic shmuck."

"Really? I have—about two months ago, when you were marrying my sister after like two days of dating."

"It was a month, thank you very much, and I looked hot while smoldering at Lucy. You look dumb." He makes the most ridiculous puppy eyes, hanging his tongue out and panting.

I shake my head. "I do not look like that."

Lucy pops up beside me and laughs way too hard for my liking. "Are we impersonating Drew?! Here, let me try!" I can't even describe the idiotic face she makes. It's twisted and upsetting, and I just hope to God I don't actually look like that.

"All right, get out. Both of you. Out of my house." I point toward the front door, prepared to pick them both up and deposit them on the sidewalk if I have to.

Lucy props her hands on her hips. "Yeah, right! Jessie hasn't even seen the main surprise yet, and since I was the one who stayed up until midnight last night making it happen, I deserve to see the big reveal."

Oh geez, I forgot about that. Now my heart is beating so hard I can feel it in my fingers, because knowing Jessie, she could either really love what I'm about to show her or really hate it. I'm prepared for her to take one look and bust a hole through the wall in her need to leave as quickly as possible.

"Hey, preggo!" my sister yells after Jessie closes the door behind the last guest. "Drew has one final present to show you." Lucy singsongs the words and then shoves me into the middle of the room near Jessie like she's offering me up to a lion. I flash her a look of warning over my shoulder.

Jessie's eyes sparkle with amusement as she slowly moves closer to me. "Is it just me, or did she make that sound really dirty?"

"It's going to sound worse when I tell you to follow me upstairs."

"Oooh." She grins and lifts her eyebrows. "Lead the way."

"Ewww. Is this how it's going to be from now on? I don't know that I like it," says Lucy, following behind us up the stairs. "I haven't had enough time to adjust. One minute you hate Drew, and the next you're trying to get him to do unspeakable things with you at your baby shower."

"I didn't know there was a baby shower inside, okay?! Leave me alone. Besides, you and Cooper are way worse," says Jessie.

"I agree," I say as we reach the top of the steps. "I don't think I've even seen you guys sit in your own chairs yet. It's really gross."

Jessie makes an over-the-top gagging face. "Maybe we all need some PDA rules in place."

"I'll never agree to the terms," says Cooper, hooking a finger through one of Lucy's belt loops so she can't race past and beat us to the reveal like she's intending. Lucy pouts and Cooper gives me a *Go ahead* nod.

And now my palms are sweating worse than they did before my first kiss. (Melissa, I still feel bad about that awful kiss. I'm sorry.) I try to get rid of the sheen on my palms by wiping them on my jeans, but Jessie notices and gives me a wry smile.

"You okay over there?"

"Yeah." My voice box is a squeaky toy. *Nice.*

Jessie's eyes widen because now she knows something serious is about to go down. I'm seconds from changing my mind and finding a potted plant to hand her instead. What if she sees this and thinks I'm insane? What if she hates it? What if . . .

"Drew?" Jessie asks, sounding a little concerned as she takes my hand. "Seriously, are you feeling all right? You're white as a sheet all of a sudden."

I clear my throat and nod, putting my hand on the small of her back to push her down the hall a bit. We stop outside the closed second guest bedroom door, and before I have the chance to chicken out, I push it open. Jessie is still smiling at me curiously until her gaze slowly moves to the room and the smile falls from her face.

Oh no.

I knew it.

This is too much too soon.

It was a stupid idea.

She's going to break up with me.

"Jessie . . . say something . . ." I ask, afraid she's stopped breathing. I'm going to have to resuscitate her.

She's motionless, staring at the room, and I'm just about to pull her back out and slam the door with a hundred apologies when I stop short. Her jaw tics and eyes flutter several times like she does when she's trying not to cry, which is honestly about fifty times a day lately—but are these good tears or bad tears?

"You . . ." She sucks in a breath, then presses her lips together with a shake of her head like she's not ready to talk yet because she knows a sob will spill out. After another few seconds, she finally looks up at me, her green eyes full of unshed tears, and when a small smile pulls at her mouth I know these are happy emotions. "You made me a nursery?" Her voice cracks and shakes, her joy sitting so fragilely on the surface of her skin that it makes me want to cry too.

I nod just as Jessie's arms fly around my neck. I wrap her up, trying to pull her as close to me as her belly will allow. "I know there's a very real chance your house won't be done in time for the birth . . . and . . . I just wanted you to have a place to bring the baby home to and not feel displaced."

"Why would you do all of this for me?" she says into my neck.

I pull away enough to look down into her eyes. "Isn't it obvious? I love you, Jessie. I lo—"

My words are cut off when her mouth crashes into mine. She

wraps her arms around my neck again and nearly pulls me over. I spin Jessie around to lean her against the wall.

She smiles up at me in between kisses and whispers, "I love you too."

I look back and forth between both of her eyes and then dive back down to take her lips, but Lucy interrupts before I get the chance.

"Mm-hmm . . . and we're the gross ones. Come on, Jessie! Peel that pucker away from my brother and look at this nursery already!"

Jessie laughs and rests her forehead against my chest before sliding out from under my arm to walk around the room with Lucy and admire everything. She cries again when she realizes I bought her the things off of her secret registry we made together, the one she thought only existed so she could go back and buy it all when she got home. The moment she fell asleep that night, I purchased it all and had it overnighted. What's the point of having an incredible salary if you can't spoil someone with it?

"Thank you," Jessie says, looking at me with equal parts awe and terror. I know her—I know it scares her to receive a gift like this from a man, but I plan to show her over the coming days, weeks, months, and years that she can trust me to love her well. To give her gifts not because I need anything from her, not because I'm apologizing for something terrible I did. Just because I love her.

"Yeah, yeah, Drew mashed his finger on the Buy Now button— big whoop! Cooper and I are the real MVPs here," Lucy states with zero delicacy, making me and Jessie both laugh.

Cooper runs his hand down the gray velvet curtains like he's modeling them on QVC. "And how about these bad boys? Just take a look at how level that curtain rod is."

"Did you hang the curtains, Cooper?" Jessie asks, her smile so big and wide I'm sure her cheeks will hurt tomorrow. *Good.*

Lucy hip-checks him out of the way. "No! I did. He strung the curtains on the rod, but I did all the drilling. Don't try to steal my spotlight."

Cooper grins down at Lucy. "I think you're using the phrase *all the drilling* a little too liberally."

"I was the one who held the drilly thing and pushed the button to make it spin."

"The *drill*. It's just called a drill. And I'm the one who put the drywall anchors in, lined up the screw, and held it in place so you could push the button."

Lucy sticks her tongue out at Cooper, and he narrows his eyes on her mouth, and I'm honestly scared of what's happening between them right now. It doesn't feel like animosity, I'll tell you that much. Jessie gives me a look that says she's worried too. Jessie swiftly interrupts their weird eye chemistry by hugging Lucy and spilling out all of her gratitude. Their tears are flowing like waterfalls, and that's when I exchange a look with Cooper that says, *Take your wife and get out.*

He chuckles and goes over to Lucy, wrapping his arm around her and steering her out of the room while she's still talking to Jessie. "Okay, and the diapers are in the bottom drawer!" she says over her shoulder as Cooper pushes her from the room like she's a helicopter mom dropping off her oldest baby at college for the first time.

"Later, man," he says before they both disappear into the hallway.

And then it's just me and Jessie. Alone. Finally.

She holds my gaze, and her smile grows slowly, a tilt to it that makes my stomach coil up. "You didn't have to do any of this, you know."

"I know."

"It's too much."

"It's not enough."

She bites her bottom lip and looks around the room again. "I can't stop feeling scared of all this." She says *all this* but gestures between us, and I know she means our new relationship.

I start closing the gap between me and her. "That's okay. I'm not asking you to not be scared, because I'm confident you have nothing to be scared of—and I'm excited to prove that to you."

I run my hand from her shoulder down her arm to intertwine my fingers with hers. Her lashes are cast down, studying where our hands meet. "You're awfully cocky."

I grin. "That's nothing you didn't already know."

Her eyes pop up to me, green and sparkling. "I kinda like it."

Lifting an eyebrow, I step as close as possible to her. "Yeah?"

"Yeah."

I lean down and brush my lips over hers, never finding purchase, just taunting and teasing. "How much?"

Her eyes flutter shut and her lips part. "A little."

I hum and nip at her bottom lip. "How much?"

She grins but keeps her eyes closed. "Some."

"Not good enough," I say, gathering her up in my arms and bending down to lay hot kisses up her neck.

"A lot."

"Better," I mumble against her jawline, and now she feels like a heavy limp noodle in my arms. "How much?" I ask one more time.

Jessie doesn't answer me with words this time.

CHAPTER 38

Jessie

Bliss. Utter bliss. These past two weeks with Drew have felt like a dream, one you absolutely never want to wake up from. Fantasy boyfriends, step aside and hold Drew's beer. He's too good to be true. Yes, we bicker and fight. Yes, he has crazy cowlicks in the morning and bad breath like everyone else in the world. And yeah . . . he occasionally Dutch-ovens me under the covers. But somehow, all of those things just add to why I love him.

We both go to work during the day (I can't bring myself to stop working yet), and I literally miss him all day. He's started doing this thing where he takes a picture of my butt (clothed, get your head out of the gutter) when I don't know it and texts it to me randomly to make me laugh. Yesterday, in the middle of the day, he texted me a close-up picture of my backside in jeans standing in front of the stove with a heart drawn around it. He always adds "I miss you" below the photo, and the first couple of times I replied, "I miss you too." But then he'd send, "I was talking to your butt." So now I know better than to reply that way anymore.

Now we're on the couch, he's rubbing my feet while we watch

TV, and everything just feels too right. He's shirtless in his lounge pants with freshly showered damp hair, and I keep sneaking a peek out of the corner of my eye, waiting for him to go *poof*. There's this sense of foreboding that says, *Things are too good, Jessie. It's time for something bad to happen. He's going to get tired of you.*

"I see you staring at me," he says, not taking his eyes off the TV. "Is this a good *Take me to bed* stare or a *You have pasta sauce on your face* stare?"

"Neither."

He shifts his dark-blue eyes to me and runs his hand over my swollen ankles. *Seriously, little baby, get out of me already.* "So it's a freak-out stare then?"

"Maybe . . ." I bite the corner of my lip, feeling guilty for still doubting him even when he's given me no reason. It's hard to shake the feeling of loss, though, when I've experienced so much of it.

Drew looks down at my feet and smiles. He raises my leg to kiss my foot (true love) and then leans over, raises my shirt up so my belly is exposed, and rests his head on it lightly. "You hear that, baby? She's still got the odds stacked against me." He rubs my belly like it will grant him a wish. "It's so fun proving her wrong every day."

I grin at Drew and shake my head.

He kisses the side of my belly and looks up at me. "I love you. Do you want anything from the kitchen?" And just like that he moves on, standing up to go get us glasses of water. Not because he doesn't value me or my feelings, but because Drew isn't one for fluffy words. Instead, he shows me day in and day out that he loves me and is committed to us.

While Drew is in the kitchen, my phone rings, and I note on the caller ID that it's my contractor, Rod.

"Hello?"

"Jessie! I've got good news for you. Your house is almost fin-ished, and I think we should be wrapping everything up in the next day or two. I'd say you'll be set to move in on Friday."

Friday? As in three days from now Friday? No! It was supposed to drag on for a few more weeks. At this rate, it means I'll be able to move back in before the baby comes. Do I want that? Does Drew want that? It would give us both a semblance of a normal dating relationship that way. He wouldn't have to listen to my newborn crying overnight or deal with stinky diapers in his trash can. Is it wrong that thinking of leaving makes me want to cry? This was never supposed to be a permanent residence for me, and yet, Drew and I were never supposed to start dating either.

Rod and I talk for another minute and finalize all the details. When I hang up, all I can do is stare at the TV blankly. What's the right decision here?

Drew finds me this way when he comes back in the room, and his eyebrows furrow. "Who was on the phone?"

"My contractor."

Drew freezes. "More bad news?"

I laugh, but there's no humor in it. "No. My house is done. Well, nearly. It'll be ready for me to move back in in a few days . . ." I pause briefly before adding, "If I want to."

Drew's eyes narrow, and he leans against the doorframe of the kitchen, looking way too sexy for any regular human. Thor, sure. Superman, totally. Man birthed by human woman, no.

"Do you want to move back home?"

Yeah, right, buddy. Nice try. "Do *you* want me to move back home?"

He grins, pushes off the doorframe, and walks toward me where I'm still lying on the couch. "It's pretty insane to have a girl-friend officially move in after only two weeks of dating." Maybe those words would have made me nervous if the playful glint wasn't present in his eyes.

Instead, I let him pull me up off the couch and allow my smile to tilt. "Completely insane. Add in the fact that I'm about to have a newborn and it's enough to have you committed somewhere."

Drew wraps his hand around mine and pulls me toward his master bathroom. He picks up his toothbrush, hands me mine (because at some point during the last two weeks it started living in his bathroom), and then squirts toothpaste on both of them. Shoulder to shoulder we stand, brushing our teeth, taking turns spitting and then rinsing. Drew is the first one to speak again, and it makes me jump because I had honestly zoned out staring at his abs.

"You know . . . I've been thinking . . ."

"Oh yeah?" I ask, all innocence.

He leans his hip against the bathroom counter and folds his arms, and now it's hard to pay attention again. "It's going to be a huge hassle to move all your stuff again."

"*Huge,*" I say with over-the-top enthusiasm. This conversation we are having is all for show. In case our friends and family have us secretly mic'ed and they play the tapes back later, they will be able to see that we really did talk about it.

He shrugs with half of his face hitched up in a *Who cares?* sort of look. "And honestly, with you being so close to your due date, it probably wouldn't be very smart for you to go back to living alone."

I nod aggressively, like no pregnant woman has ever lived alone before.

"And I have all this space. I mean . . . it's a waste if no one else is occupying the other rooms."

"And the eggs . . ." I say, pointing a lazy finger in the air like *Don't forget about the eggs!* He squints. He's not following my train of thought. "You'll have to throw out the eggs you don't use in a carton because it's wayyyy too many for one person. This way, you won't be wasting eggs."

His eyes widen and he nods in newfound understanding. "Right! You're so right. Gosh, you know . . ." Drew takes my hand again and pulls me toward his bed so we can both climb in like we've done every night for the past two weeks. "The more I think about it, the more I feel like you *have* to stay here. It just doesn't make sense for you to move right now."

I love, love, love the way Drew looks propped up against the headboard with his dark-gray sheets pooling at his waist. I especially love when he holds out his arm for me to curl up next to him. I do, and I fit perfectly—even with my massive belly. And it *is* massive now. The days of *Are you sure you're even pregnant?* are behind me. No one tells me they think I should eat a second hamburger anymore. It's actually really insulting.

"I think you're right. And later on down the line, once the baby is here, I can always move back home."

Drew's body stiffens, and I feel his biceps flex. "You can?"

I look up at him with a grin and stage-whisper. "I'm just saying it for the mics."

His brow immediately clears, and he nods like *Thank goodness*—but then when he thinks on that statement longer, he asks, "Wait, what mics?"

"Never mind. Don't worry about it. All jokes aside, Drew, are you serious? You really know what you're about to get yourself into, right? I'm going to have a baby in a few weeks."

His face falls and he looks stunned. "A baby?! I thought you had a puppy in there this whole time."

I scrunch up my face and try to tickle him, but he knows me so well now that my hand never even gets close to his side.

"Jessie, I've stopped trying to rationalize our relationship because it doesn't work. There's nothing rational about us, but I do know that I love you, and I already love this baby, and I want you here all the time. I want to help you with nighttime diaper changes and hold the baby so you can take a bath." *Sold! Say no more!* "I want to be there for all the little milestones. I just . . . I can't explain it, I just trust us. In some crazy way, it feels like we've always been together."

"I feel that way too. I'm trying so hard not to trust you, believe me—"

"Gee, thanks."

"—but I can't help it. And when my contractor said my house was done, all I could think was how disappointed I was."

"I contemplated sabotaging the rest of the build just so you'd have to stay."

Drew cuts off the light and we both sink down under the sheets. I run my finger lazily over the raised skin of his tattoo and try to convince myself I'm making a mistake. I try to think of all the worst-case scenarios and ways Drew could really screw me over—but nothing. Nada. My heart won't grab on to any of them, because like he said, somehow I know we're meant to be together. Even when my fears sink in, there's a louder voice that says, *This is where you belong, Jessie.*

CHAPTER 39

Drew

ONE WEEK LATER

"Jessie, are you sure about this? Say the word and I'll cancel," I tell her as I throw my bag in the back of Cooper's truck.

She watches me with a calculated grin, looking fine in her short shorts and tank top hugging every gorgeous curve. I don't want to leave her, especially not to go to a stupid bachelor party. Who cares if he asked me to be a groomsman in the wedding? I shouldn't have to go to the party, right?

"Yeah, right! I'm not letting you become that guy who bails out on everything now that you're in a relationship. And I'm definitely not letting you use me as an excuse to avoid camping."

I grin, agreeing that I mostly want to stay because I've become annoying and clingy and need to spend every free minute I have with my hands on Jessie, but a smaller part of me also wants to cancel because I'm not a camper. Neither is Cooper—we're not exactly the most guy-guys out there and have been dreading this trip for weeks. I mean, we both like to hike, wakeboard, and do other things that will make me sound manly and rugged if it's absolutely necessary to bring up, but given the choice between sleeping on my memory foam bed beside my hot girlfriend or on the ground next to a bunch of dudes, I'm picking the bed.

Jessie steps closer with a soft smile and plants her hands on my chest. "It's only one night."

"What if you go into labor? I'll be four hours away—not exactly a quick hop back." I already know that technically the odds are slim that she will go into labor in the next twenty-four hours while I'm away. Jessie visited her ob-gyn yesterday and confirmed she wasn't dilating. She's still a week out from her due date, but I can't help worrying a little.

"Okay, well, we both know I won't go into labor, but even if I do, four hours will be plenty of time for you to get back to me. Lucy's labor was what, like, eighteen hours?"

Lucy yells from somewhere behind me. "Twenty!"

"See! Twenty. You'll even have time to stop and pick me up a sub on your way back."

"You can't eat once you're in labor."

"*What!*" Jessie's eyes bug out of her head. "Are you kidding me?!"

I chuckle and shake my head. "No. How did you not know this?"

"Better question, how am I supposed to not die while sweating and laboring all those hours without eating a sub!"

Lucy scrunches her nose. "I think you might be underestimating the labor process a bit."

"What does that even mean?" Jessie looks adorably concerned. I've been trying to rein in all my baby-delivery knowledge the past few weeks because I know I can hit level ten on the person-who-has-too-much-information-and-doesn't-know-what-to-do-with-all-of-it scale, but now I'm wondering if I shouldn't have held back so much.

Cooper comes out of the house with two travel mugs full of

coffee. Because he's practically my husband, I bet he has even added the perfect amount of my favorite creamer.

"It means eating is going to be the furthest thing from your mind."

Jessie's face looks panic-stricken. "So is it too late to cancel?"

"The camping trip? No." I'm already pulling my phone out of my pocket. "I can just—"

She stills me with a firm hand on my arm, wide crazy eyes staring up at me. "No! The birth! I changed my mind. I don't want to do it anymore. Or maybe you can just whip me up a C-section real quick? Oooh, yeah, that's a fun idea! You can do it for me. It'll be a good bonding experience."

I smile and pull Jessie into my chest. "You're going to do great, Oscar. And I'll be there the whole time, but preferably not with a scalpel in my hand." I whisper over Jessie's head, asking my sister to take Jessie for a sub sandwich tonight. "Just . . . if you start having any pains at all, call me. I'll come straight home."

"Okay, I will."

"Promise?"

"Promise."

Cooper and Lucy say goodbye on one side of the truck and Jessie and I do so on the other. I'm sure we look like teenagers after school, leaned up against the truck, making out with our girl-friends. The neighbors hate us, no doubt. Somewhere a twelve-year-old boy is pressed against the glass and his mom is about to yank him away by the ear.

Once we are on the road, I fidget with anything and everything. The radio. My coffee lid, unscrewing and screwing it back on again. Cooper didn't like it when the lid came off, giving me a death glare that warned I better not spill a single drop on his seats.

When I check my phone for the fifth time, he asks, "You okay?"

I look out the window, feeling like I'm leaving my world behind. When did this happen? How did I become this guy so quickly? The one who's so in love he wants to ditch the rest of his life in favor of spending time with his woman? "Yeah. I think. I don't know. I'm a little worried to be leaving Jessie this close to her due date."

"Say the word and I'll turn around."

I smirk over at Cooper. "You're supposed to be telling me there's nothing to worry about."

"Yeah, but I'm dreading this stupid camping party, so I'm totally in favor of leaning into your fears."

I shake my head as I check my phone for the sixth time. Stupid. She won't need me this soon after leaving. I need to chill.

"Seriously though, she's going to be fine. She's staying with Lucy and Levi, and you know Lucy will be obsessive in her care of Jessie."

True. That does make me feel better. I let out a deep breath and turn on the radio. It'll be fine. I'll be back tomorrow night, ready to be by her side as soon as Jessie goes into labor.

CHAPTER 40

Jessie

"Okay. I've got the popcorn, I've got the candy, Levi is asleep, and now we are ready to binge on—" Lucy breaks off when she looks at me. "What's that?" She points to my face.

I clear my pinched expression. "Hmm? Nothing."

Lucy cocks her head to the side. "It looked like you were in pain . . ."

"Did it? How strange. Oh, you know what? I farted. You probably just saw me when I was letting it out."

"JESSIE ALEXANDRIA BARNES—"

I gawk up at her. "Is that what you think my middle name is?!"

Lucy puts her hands on her hips and stares down at me over the pile of junk food on the coffee table. I'm on the floor sitting cross-legged against the couch because this is the only way I've been able to get comfortable the last few hours. "I don't care what your middle name is right now—"

"Jane."

"You tell me right now . . . wait, Jane? Are you serious? Your full name is Jessica Jane? What was your mom thinking? It's like the female version of Jesse James."

I shrug. It's always stumped me too.

She shakes her head, resurfacing from her mental detour. "Jessie, are you having contractions?"

I squint one eye and make a thinking face. "No. I'm fine. Let's start the movie."

Lucy shakes her head with an *uh-uh* sound and goes to grab her phone. "No. Nope. I'm not falling for it. I've seen these movies and the best friend gets tricked *every single time*. I'm calling Drew."

A humorless laugh falls out of my mouth. "Go ahead! But I've been trying for the last four hours, and I haven't been able to get ahold of him since the pain started."

Phone in hand and pressed to her ear, Lucy slowly turns to face me. Her voice is dangerous when she speaks. "Are you telling me you've been in labor for the last four hours and you didn't tell me?!"

"I didn't want to worry you if it was just a false alarm. They were super irregular at first . . ."

"AND NOW THEY'RE NOT?!"

"SHHHHHH. You're going to wake up Levi!" And any astronauts currently on the moon.

"Tell me, Jessie."

I sigh deeply, knowing the second I tell her the number, Lucy is going to bolt from the room for my go bag. She knows exactly where it is because she's been adding little things to it all night. At first it was a cute overnight bag I got off Etsy. It had a pair of PJs, an outfit for the baby, and a toothbrush. Now, after Lucy has gotten her motherly paws on it, it's stuffed so full of random baby crap that she upgraded my bag to a full-on suitcase. I'm going to have to wheel it into the hospital like I'm headed to summer camp because it's so damn heavy.

"They're coming every five minutes now."

Lucy's eyes double in size and then, yep, she's gone. Her feet thunder down the hall and then she comes back with my go bag (go suitcase) clutched in her hand, a pillow stuffed under her other arm, keys in hand. She zooms up beside me and starts trying to hoist me up off the floor, but I don't budge an inch.

"*Ugh.* Come on, Jessie!! *We. Need. To. Go.*" She's really using all her strength to try to lift me by the armpits. Poor thing can't move me. "Geez, woman. Have you been eating nothing but marshmallows and chocolate for every meal?"

I shoot her daggers. No, vipers. "Real nice, making fun of the pregnant woman's weight while she's in labor!"

She softens and pets my hair. "I'm sorry. I love you, you beautiful goddess."

"Better," I say, folding my arms. "Besides, you forgot your son! Were you just going to drive off without him?"

She gawks like *OMG I would never!* "No. I was just going to . . . get you in the car first and *then* go get him."

"Mm-hmm. Well, it doesn't matter because I'm not leaving."

"You're not?"

"I'm not."

Lucy sighs dramatically and sinks down to sit, throwing her hand over her eyes like she's swooning on a nineteenth-century fainting couch. "You're going to be as difficult as possible tonight, aren't you?"

"I resent that."

I'm not being difficult. I'm just not going to the hospital without Drew. The plan was, I would go into labor and Drew would carry my bags to the car, and then together we would head for the hospital, where he would hold my hand for the entirety of my birthing experience. Drew not answering his cellphone and being four hours away was *not* a part of the plan. It wasn't. So I'm sticking to the plan.

"Drew will be back tomorrow afternoon. I'll wait until then to have the baby." I'm staring at the blank TV like a Zen master.

Lucy cracks up at this. "You'll *wait*?! Oh my gosh, you're looney! You've completely lost it!"

I narrow my eyes at her. "I don't like you too much tonight."

Lucy slides down on the floor beside me and takes my hand just as another contraction hits me. It's so strong and painful I can't believe this isn't even the worst of it. How am I going to do this? *Oh, Jesus, take the wheel!*

Once I've thoroughly crushed Lucy's hand, she gives me sympathetic eyes that make me start crying. She says, "You can't wait, Jessie. I swear this baby will come out with or without your approval. Now come on, we gotta get you to the hospital. I'll keep trying Drew and Cooper on the way."

"WHERE IS HE?! I'M GOING TO KILL HIM," I yell to Lucy in the hospital room during a contraction. I know, I know, never say anything in the midst of a contraction, but it's like your brain short-circuits and you have no control over anything you say. I have a lot to apologize to Lucy for later. And the triage nurse. And the random lady in the elevator.

"I'm sorry, Jessie, I don't know! I've been trying every two minutes. Just focus on your breathing and hold on to hope."

I've been *holding on to hope* for two whole hours since checking in. It's after midnight now and I've been trying Drew since five o'clock yesterday evening, and we still haven't heard back from him. All I can reason is that he lost service while camping. Or he got eaten by a bear. Oh gosh, now I'm imagining Drew being eaten by a bear and I'm sobbing. *I want him here!*

"Shhhhh, it's okay," Lucy says, rubbing her hand in circles on my back. "Even if he doesn't make it in time, everything is going to be okay. I'm here and I'm not going anywhere."

I squeeze her hand to silently thank her.

Lucy tries to distract me with every means possible: celebrity gossip, back rubs, stories I care absolutely nothing about from her stupid childhood (I'm just a little grumpy), and even a song and dance that is so ridiculous the nurse actually asks her to stop. Nothing works. All I can think of is my pain and my sadness that Drew is not here for this. I don't even know why I want him here so badly. It's not like he had anything to do with creating this baby. But somewhere over the past few months, Drew has completely stolen my heart and poured his love into me in such a way that I *feel* like this is his child too. Somehow I just know we are going to be together for the long haul, so I want him here for the birth.

The hours pass in agony and I don't think Drew is going to make it. Around five in the morning, after about twelve hours of natural labor, my phone rings and Lucy answers. "He—"

"HOW DILATED IS SHE?!" Drew yells, so loudly Lucy squeals and drops the phone.

"PICK IT UP!" I scream.

Through the speaker, I hear Drew also yelling, "LUCY! ANSWER ME, DAMMIT!"

"OKAY! EVERYONE JUST SHUSH!" Lucy yells back. She tugs on the end of her shirt like she's regaining her bearings and raises the phone, putting it on speaker.

"Where the hell are you, Drew?" I say, tears running down my cheeks.

"I'm so sorry, baby. I'm on my way! Our phones lost service, and one of the guys severely burned himself trying to start a campfire while he was drunk, so I had to drive him to the nearest hospital, which was seriously in the middle of nowhere and—never mind, I'll tell you the full story later. All you need to know is I just walked out of the hospital and my phone buzzed with forty-two voicemails and eighty texts, and I ran to the truck. Cooper is staying there with our friend and will drive him back in his car tomorrow."

Of course. Of course this would happen! But even hearing his voice settles me a little. "How far away are you?"

There's a small pause, and I imagine him grimacing. "Four hours. Less if I speed."

I shut my eyes and let out a heavy breath. "You're not going to make it, Drew. I'm eight centimeters dilated."

"Don't give up hope yet! I had a patient last week spend three hours going from nine to ten centimeters and then push for another hour! It could happen."

"Are you *hoping* for that?!" I screech.

His low chuckle soothes me even through the phone. "No. I just . . . I love you, Jess. I want to be there. I'm so sorry I haven't been there with you this whole time."

I wipe my eyes, annoyed that the motion tugs the IV line tight. Lucy reaches out and holds my hand tenderly, and I decide it's time to focus on the good. I have my best friend holding my hand and the man I love on the phone with me. I can do this.

"I love you too, Drew."

Drew stays on the line with me the whole rest of my labor. Yes, as he predicted, it takes forever, but he still doesn't make it in time for me to start pushing. Lucy stays with me and supports me the entire time, though, and Drew coaches me through the phone (much to my actual ob-gyn's dismay). My poor doctor has to endure endless questions and obtrusive suggestions from Drew, telling her not to rush me, to not let me bear down too hard, and a whole slew of other comments. She flipped off my phone when she thought I wasn't looking, but I totally saw it, and it made my whole year. Drew is a bossy a-hole sometimes, and I absolutely love him for it. Especially when he's protecting me.

Finally, after nearly an hour of pushing (*You willed this into existence, Drew, and I hate you for it*), he tells me he's in the parking garage and to hang on. But I can't. I can't hang on, and I give one final excruciating push and then the feeling of sweet relief washes over me, quickly followed by the faint cries of my baby.

"Jessie, baby, you did it!" Drew says, sounding emotional on the other end of the line, and also like he might be running. He's out of breath and I think I heard him yell *Move it* at someone.

I'm smiling in pure disbelief that I did it. It's over, and I have a child. I crane my neck to see where my doctor is cradling my baby. "Congratulations, Jessie. You have a baby—"

"WAIT!" I yell before she gets the word out. "Don't say it out loud. I want to be the one to tell Drew."

Not even two minutes later, the door to the delivery room flies open and Drew stands there in workout shorts and a hoodie, hair sticking up all over the place like his hand has been gripping it for hours, eyes red and bloodshot. He's sweating, confirming my suspicion that he ran all the way from the parking garage. His eyes immediately fall to me, and he sighs with audible relief. He doesn't move for a few seconds, just stares, like he's making every effort to memorize this moment, etching it into his mind for the rest of his life.

Finally, his eyes drop to the baby lying facedown on my chest, and I smile. "It's a girl," I whisper through a fresh round of tears. He sputters an emotion-filled laugh as a tear leaks out of the corner of his eye too.

He swats it away and finally steps into the room, going over to squeeze Lucy's shoulder and thank her for being here for me, and then he comes to my bedside and leans over. I should probably care about him seeing whatever it is the doctor is still doing down south, but I don't. I don't care about anything anymore other than this baby in my arms and this man leaning in close to kiss my lips.

"You did it. You're incredible," he whispers reverently, with a smile that soaks my heart in joy.

I watch closely, hardly believing I have him here to experience this with me. Two months ago, I thought I'd be alone in this moment. But instead, I have a man I love and a best friend at my side.

His eyes drop to my baby girl squirming against my chest, and he rubs his hand over her sweet little back. "Well? Who do we have here?" he asks, and the final pieces of my heart left intact burst like confetti at the word *we*.

"Jane Alexandria Barnes," I say, tossing a brief smile and wink to Lucy, who inadvertently helped me name my baby girl.

Drew's smile widens and his eyes pool with tears again. He bites his bottom lip and runs his knuckles ever so delicately against her little spine. "Well then," he says, sniffling adorably. "Welcome to the world, Jane. I already love you, sweet girl."

The rest of our stay in the hospital is a blur of sleepless nights, snuggles, visits from family and friends, and lots and lots of doting from Drew. He never leaves my side, taking the whole week off to stay with me and Jane. One of my favorite sights in all the world is waking up from a nap to the sight of Drew shirtless and rocking my baby girl against his tattooed shoulder while the sun spills over them through the window. He sings to her constantly—usually made-up songs about how precious she is or how hot her mama is—and there's a certainty in his love for us, a finality I don't have to question. Because somehow, it's as if Drew and I were always meant to be. When Drew loves, he loves fiercely. He's not going anywhere, and if there is one thing I'm certain of, it's that Drew Marshall would move heaven and earth for me and my daughter, and I would do the same for him.

But I will *never* tell him where I hid the Frosty mug.

Drew

I t's been eight weeks since Jessie brought Jane into the world, eight weeks since my universe turned on its end in the best way imaginable. Don't get me wrong, I'm exhausted. It's nothing compared to how exhausted Jessie is since she's the one having to wake up what feels like every hour to feed Jane, but we're happy, that deliriously tired happy that comes with building a new family. And a family we definitely are. Jessie and I might not have had a conventional start or middle, but in the end, we are a family.

After we left the hospital, Jessie officially moved in with me, and now it's not my house, it's our house. I'm sure some people think we are insane, but we can't get up the energy to care. Possibly because we're too tired? What does it matter what other people think when we are so happy together?

Jessie's house hasn't gone to waste, though. After meeting his new great-granddaughter, Jessie's grandaddy decided it was time to part with his old home. He packed everything up, sold his house in record time, and bought Jessie's from her. It's all come together seamlessly, and I can't help but think it's because it was always meant to be. He didn't sell the plaid couch, though—that fantastic piece of furniture is sitting smack-dab in the middle of Jessie's trendy living room.

Shortly after giving birth, Jessie texted her ex and told him he had a baby girl. He texted back asking for a picture and a name, and although she wanted to just text him a picture of her middle finger, she did send one of Jane. He actually came to visit once a few weeks ago. It wasn't anything groundbreaking, and sadly, I don't foresee him being in Jane's life much, but Jessie did open the door in case he wants to be around in the future.

It's okay, because Jane already has a man in her life who loves her and will spoil her rotten for the rest of her days. Which brings me to now.

Currently, Jessie is asleep, rolled over to face Jane, who is asleep in the bassinet beside the bed. The sun is up and warm, spilling through the window and casting a bronze glow over Jessie's mostly bare shoulder, only covered by the thin strap of her nursing tank top. I was going to wait for her to wake up naturally, but I can't wait any longer.

"Jessie," I say, running the back of my knuckle gently down her arm. "Jess, wake up." I kiss her neck softly.

She makes the sweetest *hmm* noise as she stirs and rolls over to face me, eyes still closed, a soft smile on her full pink lips. I trace my finger across her Cupid's bow, making her smile widen.

"Wake up," I say gently. "I have something to ask you."

She takes in a deep breath and finally her eyes crack open. They blink a few times before they land on the open ring box lying between us on the mattress. I smile as I watch her eyes immediately shut tight and then fly back open like she's making sure what she's seeing is real. Suddenly, she shoots up in bed, clutching the sheets to her chest and whipping her head around to stare at me expectantly.

"Is that what I think it is?!"

I grin and sit up, set the ring box in her lap, and then lean in close to kiss her shoulder before looking into her glittering green eyes. "Jessie, it's no secret that I love you with everything I am. I never saw you coming, but you and Jane are the best thing that's ever happened to me, and I never, *ever* want to let you go. We did everything backward and out of order, but I wouldn't change it for the world." I raise her hand and kiss her knuckles. "Marry me, Jess. Live with me and let me love you for the rest of our lives."

Her hand has been covering her mouth for half of this speech, and the moment I finish talking, she starts nodding emphatically.

"Yes?" I ask with a hopeful smile.

More nods, then her hand drops away and I can see her beautiful smile. "Yes! Of course, yes!" Jessie tackles me back onto the bed and starts lavishing ridiculous kisses all over my face, each one punctuated by the word *yes* over and over.

I laugh and wrap my arms around her, flipping over so I'm pinning her in. I reach back for the box and remove the ring. I look down at Jessie, blond hair fanning out around her face, soft smile on her lips, camisole askew and showing off her smooth, gorgeous skin, and I memorize every detail before I slip the ring onto her finger.

I lean down and slowly kiss her lips, leisurely lavishing her with affection and trying to savor *her*.

Later, standing in the kitchen, Jessie looks down at her ring, and I see a mischievous smile settle in the corner of her mouth. She lets out a strangled laugh.

"What is it?" I ask, frowning at the sight of her laughing at the diamond ring I spent hours deciding on.

Her shoulders are shaking. "I was just thinking about the ring you gave me for the first proposal!" She pauses to fully laugh now.

"Your colleagues are all going to think I made you buy me a better ring!"

When Jessie and I started dating, we decided I wouldn't correct her prank or tell my colleagues the truth. After my grand gesture proposal at the gala, word of my engagement spread fast around the hospital, and thankfully, no one has come on to me anymore at work. Neither Jessie nor I minded the title either. It feels good that it's official between us now too.

My smile falls, and I narrow my eyes dangerously on her. "I forgot about that tiny damn ring. You know, I don't think I ever properly paid you back for that little prank." I set my coffee cup down gently on the counter, and Jessie stops laughing.

She starts backing out of the kitchen, and I slowly turn my eyes up to her and smirk.

"Oh no," she whispers before whipping around and hightailing it out of the kitchen.

It's no use, though. I'm faster than her and overtake her easily in the hallway. I grab her around the waist and haul her up to me. She laughs and kicks and quietly squeals, all while I carry her to the couch and deposit her on the cushions so I can tickle her relentlessly until our tickle war turns into something entirely different.

I am, without a doubt, the luckiest man alive.

Drew

Let me tell you something: forty-eight-hour shifts at the hospital, delivering babies, and performing emergency C-sections really hit different when you have two kids at home who never sleep. I understand the baby's lack of sleep. Graham is only four months old, so he's excused. But Jane . . . she's three years old now. *Three.* I'm beginning to wonder if that child doesn't even need sleep. She's a new, terrifying super-breed of human that runs on the sleep-deprived tears of her parents. And it's not fair that she's so adorable. I immediately forgive her all of her sleepless transgressions the minute I look at her little round face and bouncing curls.

Basically, nothing makes sense anymore. I'm sleep-deprived and mad at my kids for never sleeping, and yet I'm hightailing it up my driveway because I'm eager to spend time with those very same children who are bound to wake me up a hundred times tonight.

And Jessie . . . my wife. A man shouldn't miss a woman as much as I miss her when I'm gone for two days at the hospital. But I do. I'm dying for her. Deprived of her smiles and playfulness. Her achingly beautiful curves and the sweet peace she drenches my life in. Jessie has been a miracle, and I can't wait to get inside and relax with her after a hard weekend.

Except, when I open my front door, I can't find my home. It's been replaced with a horrifying glitter explosion of a winter wonderland. My eyes immediately land on my wife, frozen in the middle of the living room holding one of our Christmas decoration tubs, and my sister also frozen, kneeling in front of a Christmas tree, mid-ornament hang.

We three stare at one another and blink.

"Stay very still, Luce," Jessie stage-whispers. "I don't think he's seen us yet."

I close my eyes and breathe, counting to ten. Did I say Jessie fills my life with peace? That must be my delirious sleep deprivation talking. I meant chaos. Marriage to Jessie is one long string of shenanigans. And it doesn't help things that my sister is her best friend. The two of them get into more trouble together than a pair of burglars.

"Jessie," I say slowly, opening my eyes to glare at my guilty-faced wife. "What in the hell has happened to my living room?"

She sets down her plastic tub and slowly walks toward me. Her blond hair is piled on her head, and black leggings are hugging her sexy body. Jessie has gotten curvier with each child, and damn, am I a lucky man.

"Hi, honey. You're home!" She wraps her arms around my neck. I do not reciprocate the hug. Or the sparkly smile.

"Jessie . . ."

"Okay, don't yell or you'll wake the kids. I *just* got them down for naps, and they haven't napped at the same time in days."

I frown. "When have I ever yelled?"

"Well, you look like a man who's about to start." She's playing with the back of my hair. It's a tactical move. Seduction. She's trying to butter me up with physical promises for later, but I'm not biting. I'm strong. I can withstand this.

"Do you want to go back to our room with me and change out of these scrubs while I tell you all about it?" She's dropped her voice down to a sultry tone.

My sister snickers beside the Christmas tree.

"No, I do not," I tell Jessie sternly. "I want to know what all this is, and I want you to tell me it has nothing to do with a scheme of any kind."

She scrunches her nose and sucks in a breath through her teeth. "Really wish I could, but . . ."

"It's definitely a scheme!" Lucy says gleefully. She's wearing a sweater covered in jingle bells.

I drop my gaze to Jessie. "Woman. I am running on zero sleep. I am hungry. I am grumpy. I am in no mood for games. Please tell me what all of this is about."

"It's a good thing I bought you the Jack Frost sweater to wear tonight," she says playfully, but then she looks at my glare and backtracks. "Okay, fine! I'm sorry! Lucy and I—"

"Oh, no! There's no Lucy and I!" my sister interrupts, standing back from the tree to put her hands on her hips. "I had nothing to do with this plan other than agreeing to come help you set up after you told me about it." That's usually the way it goes with these two.

Jessie air kicks Lucy. "You're a terrible best friend. I hope Santa brings me a new one this year." She turns back to me. "Okay, well, you remember that sweet lady, Ms. Dorothea, who Grandaddy met on his walk around the neighborhood the other day?"

I nod slowly, already not liking where this is going.

Jessie can tell, so she takes my hand and drags me with her toward the kitchen. "Well, I could tell by the way that Grandaddy talked about her that he really liked her, but he's been out of the game for too long now and isn't sure how to approach seeing her again."

"Did he say this to you?" I ask suspiciously.

"Well . . . not in so many words."

"So no."

"Technically not, but *trust me,* he likes her. And so anyway. As luck would have it, I randomly ran into her this morning at the post office, and the two of us got to talking. Turns out, she's new to the area and pretty lonely." Jessie pours me a cup of coffee and puts it in my hand. When I just stare at it, she mimes how to drink it in case I've forgotten. I roll my eyes and take a sip.

"I think I can see where this is going, and I don't approve."

"You never approve; that's why I don't tell you my plans until they're already in motion." She takes the cup from my hand, satisfied that I've gotten a small dose of caffeine, and then wraps her arms around me and slides her hands up the back of my shirt. I want to groan at how good her hands feel against my skin, but I refrain because I don't want her to think she's won. "So anyway, I had the best idea ever on how to get her and my Grandaddy to meet again. They just need a friendly group gathering to be invited to—and so I invited her to our annual Christmas in July party happening tonight."

"We've never had a Christmas in July party."

"Right. But every annual party has to have a first one. We simply don't plan on telling Dorothea that this is the first. Or that I came up with the idea this morning while talking to her at the post office when I saw that Santa Claus mailers were half off." She slides her hands a little lower down my back. "Please play along. Please. I want to see my Grandaddy happy."

I grunt.

She grins and slides her hands over my butt and squeezes, widening her eyes playfully. "Wow, buns of steel! Have you been adding more weights at the gym?" Another series of quick, firm squeezes. "I'm getting so hot. Take me now, Dr. Marshall."

Don't smile, Drew. Don't do it.

I smile. And then I shake my head, giving in to wrap my arms around my ridiculous, kooky, scheming, sexy, wonderful wife. "It won't work, you know. You can't set people up like in the movies."

"I think I dispelled that theory," Lucy says, stepping into the kitchen just long enough to pour herself a cup of coffee too. She glances between me and Jessie with a smirk. "Jessie . . . why do you think I worked so hard to make sure you were never too comfortable at our place while your house was getting fixed? And Drew, I practically threw Jessie into your path every chance I got." She rolls her eyes. "It's embarrassing you never realized you were set up."

And without a backward glance, she walks out of the kitchen, leaving a stunned Jessie and me in her wake.

"What . . ." I blink down at her.

"Did your sister successfully dupe us? The King and Queen of Dupes?"

I let out a fake groan. "Don't ever tell her that, or she'll be unbearable from now on. She'll expect diamonds for her birthday every year, and on our anniversary posts she'll always comment how glad she is that she set us up."

"You're so right."

I lean down and whisper against her full lips, "I'm always right."

I feel her grin rather than see it. "Except for when I am. Which is all the time."

My lips press into hers, and for a minute I forget how tired I am or that my sister is in the other room or that I'm apparently throwing a Christmas party in a few hours. Even after almost three years of marriage, kissing this woman still affects me like it's our first. One press of her lips, and she's swirling through my veins, slamming into my heart, and commandeering my focus. I put up a fight because it's fun, but I would do literally anything for her, and she knows it.

"Has Lucy told Cooper yet?" I say after reluctantly peeling my lips from hers. "He'll agree that this is a terrible idea."

Except, the front door opens and Cooper steps inside wearing a festive sweater of prancing reindeer and holding a sheet cake. There's a Santa hat on his head too. "I picked up the North Pole cake from the baker; Levi is with your mom making the cookies they'll bring over later, and I brought our snowman inflatables from home. What else am I forgetting?"

"Your dignity," I tell him before taking another sip of my coffee.

He smirks at me but addresses his wife. "Luce, you hired a real-life Grinch to attend the party. Such a nice addition."

"You can't seriously be okay with their scheme?" I ask him.

Cooper walks through the living room and into the kitchen to set down the cake while Jessie leaves my side to go help Lucy with the tree. "Not only am I okay with it, I encourage it." His eyes twinkle with another layer of mischief.

"I'm afraid to ask why."

He taps my chest and the little pompom on the end of his Santa hat bobs. "Since I'm in the Christmas spirit and feeling benevolent, I won't make you ask. It's because when Lucy helps out with romantic schemes, it puts her in a very romantic mood too. And since it's fake Christmas, I got her a present and left it on our bed at home. It's a red—"

I grimace and shove his shoulder. "In what world do you think I want to hear what sort of sexy present you got my sister? I don't care if you're married; my gut reaction is still to rip your arm out of its socket."

He laughs, enjoying pissing me off way too much. "The other reason is, I don't feel like sleeping on the couch. And I'm smart enough to know when to fight something and when to look on the bright side that I get to eat cake and cookies all night."

I'd probably have a more charitable approach to this spontaneous party too if I weren't running on fumes. Better start guzzling this coffee. "I have to give them credit though. This definitely goes down as one of the most creative schemes for getting two people together. And I want to see her grandaddy happy too."

Cooper smiles wide and then pulls something from his back pocket. "It's good you feel that way, because I got you a matching hat." He slaps the tacky red thing on my head and the pompom hits me in the eyeball. God, I'm too tired for this. My self-pep talk from a moment ago fades as I rub my eyeball, trying to get it to stop burning.

I'm seconds away from hallucination and consider telling Jessie that I hope they have fun, but I can't help out. I know she'll be okay with it if I explain how truly tired I am, but just as I'm about to rip off the hat and break the bad news to her, I hear her laugh filter through the room.

It's her laugh that makes me weak. Her laugh that I know accompanies the most beautiful smile I've ever seen. Her laugh that tells me she's truly happy and enjoying this to the fullest. I'm addicted to that laugh, and hearing it reminds me that there's nowhere I'd rather be than at her side tonight—tired or not.

I look over my shoulder at my wife, who is buzzing around the living room, pulling decorations from bins and placing them on various shelves and then hitting her best friend in the head with a Santa Claus pillow. No way would I miss out on this with her.

"JESS!" I yell from my spot in the kitchen. "Where do you want me to hang the mistletoe?"

Jessie

"I can't believe that worked," Drew says the moment the door shuts behind our last guest. Drew's mom took Jane and Graham for us for the night, so we are kidless right now and there's no better feeling for tired parents than the one that comes with knowing you get to sleep past 6:30 in the morning.

"I'm offended at how little faith you had in me. Of course it worked." I take Drew's hand and pull him with me toward our bedroom.

"But they didn't just talk. They exchanged numbers! They're going out for dinner on Friday night," he says in something close to awe.

I shrug like *no big deal*. "And your point?"

He chuckles behind me. "I will never doubt you again."

"Thank you. I want that in a written format, which I will then take and have notarized."

I pull Drew past our bed and right into our bathroom. "Hey," I say with a note of seriousness when I turn to face him. I put my hands on his chest and look into his tired eyes. Even with dark circles underneath them, his blue eyes are still startlingly beautiful. "Thank you for tonight. I know it was hard on you and you sacrificed for me." I kiss him softly on the lips. "It meant the world."

He breathes in slowly through his nose—filling his lungs with my words like they're the fuel his body runs on. "You're my world. When you're happy, that's all I need."

I rise up and press my lips to his one more time, humming my appreciation before I peel away again. "It's a beautiful sentiment. But alas, you are human and do need sleep. And I'm going to make sure you get so much sleep you're going to wake up feeling like Ethan Hunt in *Mission Impossible I.* Unstoppable and full of unrealistic expectations that no more shenanigans will ever befall you."

He laughs gently as I peel his Jack Frost sweater from his gorgeous body. "This doesn't feel like sleep," he says with a wry twist of his mouth.

I turn on the shower so it can begin heating while I turn back to him and unbutton his pants. They fall to the floor with a thud, and his eyebrows lift.

"You'll sleep better after you shower," I tell him with a meaningful smirk of my own. A smirk that makes much more sense to him after I've joined him in the shower. It's completely sacrificial, this shower interlude. One hundred percent because I want to properly wear him out so he'll sleep like a rock. That's it. And if it happens to wear me out in the process so I sleep like a rock right beside him, well, that's just an added bonus.

After we've thoroughly showered, we both crawl into bed and Drew pulls me up close to him under our fluffy comforter. He kisses my head and I kiss his chest.

"I love you, Jessica."

"Love you right back, Andrew. Forever and ever and ever."

ACKNOWLEDGMENTS

Well, dear readers, this is the last of my republished romcoms, and I am a puddle of feelings! Thank you for walking with me on this journey (or just starting with me if this is the first book of mine you've picked up). It's because of you and your love for my stories that they were given a second home with my publisher! So, first and foremost, thank you to *you*!

And second, thank you to my wonderful agent, Kim Lionetti, for believing in me and my stories and getting them where they need to go.

And a big bear hug + thank-you to my publishing team at Dell! You all are incredible, and I'm as thankful as ever for you! We did it. Big sigh of joy and relief.

1

Bree

Balancing two cups of burning-hot coffee and a box of donuts while trying to unlock a front door is not easy. But because I'm the best friend a person could ever ask for—which I will remind Nathan of as soon as I make it inside his apartment—I manage it.

I hiss when I turn the lock and a splash of coffee darts out onto my wrist through the little hole in the lid. I have fair skin, so there's a one million percent chance it's going to leave an angry red mark.

The moment I step inside Nathan's apartment (which really should not be called an apartment because it's the size of five large apartments smooshed together), the familiar clean and crisp scent of him knocks into me like a bus. I know this smell so well I think I could follow it like a bloodhound if he ever goes missing.

Using the heel of my tennis shoe, I slam the front door shut with enough gusto to warn Nathan that I'm on the premises. *ATTENTION ALL SEXY QUARTERBACKS! COVER YOUR GOODS! A GREEDY-EYED WOMAN IS IN THE HOUSE!*

A high-pitched yelp sounds from the kitchen, and I immediately frown. Peeking around the corner, I find a woman wearing a light-pink shorts-and-camisole sleep set pressed into the far corner of the wraparound white marble kitchen counter. She's clutching a butcher knife to her chest. We're separated by a massive island, but from the way her eyes are bugging out, you'd think I was holding matching cutlery against the jugular vein in her neck.

"DON'T COME ANY CLOSER!" she screeches, and I immediately roll my eyes, because *why* does she have to be so screechy? She sounds like a clothespin is pinching the bridge of her nose and she has recently inhaled a whole balloon full of helium.

I would raise my hands in the air so I don't get knifed to death, but I'm sort of loaded down with breakfast goods—goods for me and Nathan, *not* Miss Screechy. This isn't my first rodeo with one of Nathan's girlfriends, though, so I do what I always do and smile at Kelsey. And yeah, I know her name, because even though she pretends not to remember me every time we meet, she's been dating Nathan for a few months now and we have met several times. I have no idea how he spends time with this woman. She seems so opposite of the type of person I would pick for him—they all do.

"Kelsey! It's me, Bree. Remember?" *Nathan's best friend since high school. The woman who was here before you and will be here well after you. REMEMBER ME?!*

She releases a big puff of air and lets her shoulders sag in relief. "Oh my gosh, Bree! You scared me to death. I thought you were some stalker girl who broke in somehow." She sets the knife down, raises one of her perfectly manicured eyebrows, and mumbles not so quietly, "But then again . . . you sort of are."

I narrow my eyes at her with a tight smile. "Nathan up yet?"

It's 6:30 on a Tuesday morning, so I know for a fact he's already awake. Any girlfriend of Nathan's knows if she wants to see him at all that day, she has to wake up just as early as he does. Which is why Satin-PJ-Kelsey is standing in the kitchen looking pissed off. No one appreciates the morning quite like Nathan. Well, except for me—I love it too. But we're sort of weirdos.

She turns her head slowly to me, hate burning in her delicate baby blues. "Yes. He's in the shower."

Before our run?

Kelsey looks at me like it grieves her deeply to have to expound. "I accidentally bumped into him when I came into the kitchen a few minutes ago. He had his protein shake in his hand and . . ." She makes an annoyed gesture, letting it finish the story for her: *I dumped Nathan's shake down the front of him.* I think it's killing her to admit she did something human, so I take pity on her and turn away to set the donut box down on the ridiculously large center island.

Nathan's kitchen is fantastic. It's designed in monochromatic tones of cream, black, and brass, and an expansive window wall overlooks the ocean. It's my favorite place in the world to cook, and exactly the opposite of my dumpy little garbage bin five blocks down the road. But that dumpy little garbage bin is affordable and close to my ballet studio, so all in all, I can't complain.

"I'm sure it wasn't a big deal. Nathan never gets upset about things like that," I say to Kelsey, waving my white flag one last time.

She takes out her samurai sword and slices it to shreds. "I already know that."

Alrighty then.

I take my first sip of coffee and let it warm me under Kelsey's frigid stare. Nothing to do but wait for Nathan to surface so we can get going with our Tuesday tradition. It dates all the way back to our junior year of high school. I was a sort of self-designated loner in those days, not because I didn't love people or socializing but because I lived and breathed ballet. My mom used to encourage me to skip dance occasionally to go to a party and be with my friends. *These days of getting to just be a kid and have fun won't last forever. Ballet isn't everything. It's important to build a life outside of it too,* she said to me on more than one occasion. And of course, like most dutiful teenagers . . . I didn't listen.

Between dancing and my after-school job working in a restaurant, I didn't really have friends. But then *he* happened. I wanted to increase my endurance, so I started running at our school's track before school, and the only day I could make this happen schedule-wise was on Tuesdays. I showed up one morning and was shocked to see another student already running. Not just any student, but the captain of the football team. Mr. Hottie McHotterson. (Nathan didn't have an awkward phase. He looked like a twenty-five-year-old at sixteen. So unfair.)

Jocks were supposed to be rude. Chauvinistic. Full of themselves. *Not Nathan.* He saw me in my scuffed-up sneakers, curly hair piled on my head in the grossest bun anyone has ever seen, and he stopped running. He came over and introduced himself with his huge trademark smile and asked if I wanted to run with him. We talked the entire time, instant best friends with so much in common, despite our different upbringings.

Yeah, you guessed it—he comes from a wealthy family. His dad is the CEO of a tech company and has never shown much interest in Nathan unless he's showing him off on the golf course in front of his work friends, and his mom pretty much just hung around and badgered him to make it to the top and bring her into the limelight with him. They always had money, but what they didn't have until Nathan made it big was social standing. In case you can't tell, I'm not a huge fan of his parents.

So anyway, thus began our Tuesday tradition. And the exact moment I fell for Nathan? I can pinpoint it down to the second.

We were on our final lap of that very first run together when his hand caught mine. He tugged me to a stop, then bent down in front of me and tied my shoe. He could have just told me it was untied, but no—Nathan's not like that. It doesn't matter who you are or how famous he is; if your shoe is untied, he's going to tie it for you. I've never met anyone else like that. I was so gone for him from day one.

We were both so determined to achieve success, despite how young we were. He always knew he'd end up in the NFL, and I knew I was headed to Juilliard and then to dance in a company after. One of those dreams became a reality, and one did not. Unfortunately, we lost touch during college (*fine,* I made us lose touch), but I serendipitously moved to L.A. after graduating when a friend told me about another friend who was looking to hire an assistant instructor at her dance studio just as Nathan signed with the L.A. Sharks and moved to town as well.

We bumped into each other at a coffee shop, he asked if I wanted to go for a jog on Tuesday for old times' sake, and the rest is history. Our friendship picked right back up as if no time had passed at all, and unfortunately, my heart still pined for him the same as it had back then.

The funny thing is, Nathan was never projected to reach the heights in his career that he has. Nope, Nathan Donelson was drafted in the seventh round, and he effectively warmed the bench as a backup quarterback for two whole years. He never got discouraged, though. He worked harder, trained harder, and made sure he was ready if his time came to take the field, because that's how Nathan approaches everything in life: with nothing but one hundred percent effort.

And then one day, it all paid off for him.

The previous starting quarterback, Daren, broke his femur on the field during a game and they had to put Nathan in. I can still close my eyes and see that moment. A stretcher carrying Daren off the field. The offensive coach running down the sidelines to Nathan. Nathan shooting up off the bench and listening to the coach's instructions. And then . . . just before he put his helmet on and entered the game for what would go down in history as his career-making start, Nathan looked up in the stands for me. (He didn't have a private box at that point.) I stood up, we made eye contact, and Nathan looked like he was going to hurl. I did the one thing I knew would help him relax: contorted my face like a ding-dong and stuck my tongue out the side of my mouth.

His face exploded in a smile, and then he led the team to play the best game of their season. Nathan stepped in as the starting quarterback for the rest of the year and carried the Sharks to the Super Bowl, where they took home a win. Those months were a whirlwind for him. Actually, they were for both of us, because that was the year I went from just being an instructor at a dance studio to *owning* the studio.

Today, I'm here for a run with Nathan, and since he didn't play his best last night, I know we'll be running extra hard today. His team still won the game (and they are officially in the playoffs, *yay*), but he threw two interceptions, and since Nathan is a perfectionist when it comes to . . . well, anything, I know he'll be stomping around here like a bear with an empty honey pot.

Kelsey's shrill voice yanks me out of my nostalgia. "Yeah, so don't take this the wrong way . . . but what are you doing here?" By *Don't take this the wrong way,* she means, *Don't take this as anything nice because I fully intend for it to come out extra witchy.* I wish she'd act like this when Nathan is around. When he's watching, she's sweet as pie.

I give her my most sunny smile, refusing to let her steal my joy so early in the morning. "What does it look like I'm doing here?"

"Being a creepy stalker who's secretly in love with my boyfriend and breaks into his apartment to bring him breakfast."

See, here's the problem. She says the words *my boyfriend* like they should be trump cards. Like she just tossed them on the table and I'm supposed to gasp and close my hands over my mouth in shock. *My heavens! She won!*

Little does she know, her card is the equivalent of a lonesome five of clubs. Girlfriends come and go in Nathan's life like fad diets. Me, on the other hand—I was here *long* before two-faced Kelsey, and I'll be here long after, because I am Nathan's best friend. I'm the one who's been through it all with him, and he's been through it all with me: high school gangly phase (me, not him), college football signing day, the car accident that changed my entire future, every stomach bug of the past six years, the day I took ownership of the dance studio, and when the confetti was falling on him after his team won the Super Bowl.

But *most* important, I'm the only person in the entire world who knows how he got the two-inch scar right below his navel. I'll give you a hint: it's embarrassing and has to do with an at-home waxing kit. I'll give you another hint: I dared him to do it.

"Yep!" I say with an overly bright smile. "Sounds about right. Stalker who's secretly in love with Nathan. That's totally me."

Her eyes widen because she thought she'd really zing me with that one. *Can't burn me with the truth, Kels!* Well, except for the stalker part.

I turn away from Kelsey and wait for Nathan. There was a time in my life when I tried to befriend Nathan's girlfriends. Not anymore. None of them likes me. No matter what I do to earn their affection, they are predisposed to hate me. And I get it, I really do. They think I'm a major threat. But that's where the story gets sad.

I'm not.

They all get to have Nathan in a way I never will.

"You know," she says, trying to grab my attention again, "you could just go ahead and save yourself the embarrassment and leave. Because when Nathan comes out here, I fully intend to ask him to make you leave. I've been patient so far, but the way you act toward him is super weird. You hang around him like a clingy piece of toilet paper."

I try not to look too patronizing when I give her an over-the-top *Okay, honey* turned-down smile and nod. Because here's what I forgot to mention before: I'm not a threat to these women . . . until they make him choose. Then I'm more threatening than a glitter bomb. I might not get to sleep in Nathan's bed, but I do have his loyalty—and to Nathan, there's nothing more important than that.

Kelsey scoffs and folds her arms. We're deeply engaged in a battle of frightening expressions when Nathan's voice rumbles from the room behind me.

"Mmmm, do I smell coffee and donuts? That must mean Bree Cheese is here."

I flash Kelsey a not-so-subtle grin. A *winner's* grin.

ABOUT THE AUTHOR

SARAH ADAMS is the author of *The Rule Book, Practice Makes Perfect, When in Rome,* and *The Cheat Sheet.* Born and raised in Nashville, Tennessee, she loves her family and warm days. Sarah has dreamed of being a writer since she was a girl but finally wrote her first novel when her daughters were napping and she no longer had any excuses to put it off. Sarah is a coffee addict, a British history nerd, a mom of two daughters, married to her best friend, and an indecisive introvert. Her hope is to write stories that make readers laugh, maybe even cry—but always leave them happier than when they started reading.

authorsarahadams.com
Instagram: @authorsarahadams

ABOUT THE TYPE

This book was set in Hoefler Text, a typeface designed in 1991 by Jonathan Hoefler (b. 1970). One of the earlier typefaces created at the beginning of the digital age specifically for use on computers, it was among the first to offer features previously found only in the finest typography, such as dedicated old-style figures and small caps. Thus it offers modern style based on the classic tradition.